PRANK WARS

A novel

Stephanie Fowers

Also by Stephanie Fowers

Meet Your Match

Rules of Engagement

A novel

Triad Media and Entertainment
SLC, UT

Stephanie Fowers

© 2011 Stephanie Fowers

This is a work of fiction. The characters, names, places, incidents and dialogue are products of the author's imagination and are not to be construed as real.

No part of this book may be reproduced in any form whatsoever without prior written permission of the publisher except in the case of brief passages embodied in critical reviews and articles.

ISBN: 978-0615587097

Published by Triad Media and Entertainment, Salt Lake City, UT
Triad.film.productions@gmail.com

LIBRARY OF CONGRESS CATALOGING-IN-PUBLICATION DATA

    2012930391
    .1. Fiction. 2 Romance. 3. General

Cover art by Kristi Linton
Cover Design by Jacqueline Fowers
Typeset by Heather Justesen

DEDICATION

To my family, who laughs at dreams but can't resist helping me reach them.

To my friends, who see past me to see me.

To my hopes, who will never rule my life but still make life fun.

To God, who gave me all of them.

AN EXCERPT FROM MADELEINE'S WAR JOURNAL:

Day 114
0134 hours

"People are getting hurt. I'm not talking broken hearts or Jell-O packets in the shower heads; I'm talking real scary stuff. Things like this happen in New York, Chicago, Ogden even, but here in Provo? Something strange is going on here...and it's not just the students.

No one is what they seem. The player? A terrorist. The heart-breaker? A no good spy. My neighbor? They've taken her. The jerk? A pretty decent guy. My roommate? An utter sneak—but then again I always knew that.

Grades? Dates? Pranks? They're nothing to the danger that stares us in the face. You've got to believe me. If I could go back before everything—before the world went terribly wrong—would I change what I've done or have these meaningless pranks made me better able to fight this?"

—Madeleine's War Journal Entry (Wednesday, June 6th)

3 Months Earlier...

MADELEINE'S FIRST WAR JOURNAL

CHAPTER ONE

Day 47
1345 hours

"War rules my life, though strangely I find myself attracted to it."

—Madeleine's War Journal Entry (Friday, April 1st).

"Hey, Madeleine! Your name's Madeleine Doggett, right?"
He knew very well what my name was.

I swiveled in my seat and scowled, seeing Byron...or *Lord Byron* as I called him when he was really bugging me. It made him angry and that was my target. Normally, I would pretend I didn't hear him, but he was looking straight at me with those devilish blue eyes.

"What do you want?" I hissed. Our chemistry teacher lectured in the front, completely oblivious to the talking and fluttering of papers common to a class of four hundred.

"You dropped this."

He scooted forward until we were almost nose to nose and held up a note. My hand lifted, but he grinned, keeping the note out of my reach. *"From your secret admirer,"* he read it to me. *"I couldn't help notice how gorgeous you are. We really need to go out sometime."* He glanced up at me with a knowing look. "Did you give this to me?"

My face got red...until I remembered what today was. April Fool's Day. Apparently Byron really got into the season. I recovered with a snicker, earning a few glares my direction for disturbing the class.

"Nope, sorry," I whispered. "Maybe the note wasn't meant for you. Give it here. It's probably for me."

"Oh, really? I must've written it then."

I turned even redder. So, that's how Byron got all the girls. Not that he meant me to go for his game, he just liked to hijack my emotions and see me squirm. The guy had been a constant thorn in my side since he moved into my ward, and now he had the nerve to be in my chemistry class. I blew my dark hair out of my eyes and faced him squarely. "Did you also blow up a picture of yourself and send it to all the girls in our apartment complex?" His eyes took on a challenging glint, and I smiled disarmingly. "I saw you autographed it for us too, *Lord Byron*. How sweet. Now we can all have a part of you."

Byron matched my smile, his expression cool. That meant he already knew I was the culprit behind that little prank. "You realize you're over your head, right?"

I ignored the threat. He might have the face of an angel, but he had the heart of a devil. I knew how to handle his kind. Ripping paper from my binder, I wrote in my *girliest* handwriting: *"To my secret admirer, maybe you should pay attention in class and stop harassing the ladies."* I dropped the note behind me. "Oops." It fluttered to the ground.

A minute later, a new note dropped into my lap. *"I would never deprive the ladies of my attention—especially when they are in need of my social help."*

"At least they don't need psychiatric help." I threw that one behind me.

A tap on my shoulder signaled me to reach back and Byron folded my fingers over his latest retort, his hand resting too long over mine. I jerked away, refusing to give into his psychological warfare. Unfolding it, I read: *"Maybe we should stop all this fighting and learn to love each other?"*

I wrote *April Fools* on it and sent it back. It earned a laugh from him and my lips curved up unwillingly. If I wasn't careful I'd end up liking Lord Byron as much as his laugh. I forced my lips back down. He was much too smooth and practiced. I needed a guy more...*not breathing*. I still hadn't recovered from my last relationship.

"Hey, did you give this to me?" I glanced behind me, expecting Byron again. Instead another guy beside him met my eyes quizzically. It was toenail guy. He left a pile of toenails on the floor every week in class and had to be the sole reason BYU discouraged flip flops. He handed me a folded up piece of paper, unable to meet my eyes.

I opened up the note and figured out why. *"You're pretty cute,"* it said. *"Here's my number."* And there was my number in black and white.

My gaze shot to Byron as he edged wickedly away from the civilian caught in our crossfire. He was as slick as *James Bond* and twice as rude. "Thank me later," he mouthed. It was like he didn't know what I had been through this last semester. My eyes narrowed at him. I had the dark eyes of a Russian spy, which I fancied made me sinister enough to break an enemy with a glance, but Byron seemed unruffled by it.

"Finals are in two weeks," the teacher droned on with an emotionless voice. "You are allowed one 3 by 5 index card in the testing center." I stared up at our teacher. He looked as bored as we were. Would he never dismiss class? I had a bad case of jumpy leg this time. After a dozen parting remarks, the teacher released us and I scrambled out of my seat with only minutes to execute my perfect evacuation.

Taking a deep breath, I turned to Lord Byron's latest victim, not knowing how to explain the phone number disaster, but toenail guy was gone. No one stood between me and the devil. "Byron!" I tried to find him in the crowd of mingling students. "You can't just..." I stepped back.

Byron was already halfway across the room. He pressed his palm against the wall, leaning over one of the many TAs from our chemistry class. I couldn't tell if she was pretty because I could only see her from the back, but Byron sure acted like she was. Her hair was long and two shades blacker than mine. To top it off, she seemed way more delicate and fragile than me. Byron dripped with charm—something I had never experienced personally from him, but had witnessed plenty of times at ward prayer with his other doomed victims. The girl twisted her Gucci flats shyly against the gray carpet and wrote her number down for him. Typical. Just typical.

I backed away from them both, feeling a strange surge of disappointment. How did Byron always show me up? And without even trying? I didn't want all guys to be this way—a big fat illusion. I flung my backpack over my shoulder and retreated to the back door of our lecture hall. I had my own reasons for taking the back way out of chemistry, and it had nothing to do with Byron. No, my reasons were recorded in *Journal Entry Number One. V-Day.* That was the day my heart broke in two. I had refused to let it rule me since.

Cameron's class was across the hall. It had been our tradition in the beginning of the semester to meet right after class for lunch. As soon as my hands left the door in chemistry, they had found Cameron's. I thought it was love. We had been that cute annoying couple no one wanted to be around. Was it only last spring when I had met him? All the girls had loved him. I should have guessed I'd eventually have my turn with him. In the fall, not only were we dating, but we had our own language. He'd surprise me with kisses, whisper sweet nothings. Cameron must've been caught up in the romance of it too because he asked me to marry him over Christmas break. That was farther than any of the others got. My mom hugged me over and over, and declared it was about time, but Cameron and I didn't make it past V-Day. I had to hand it to him; it was a creative way to get out of buying flowers. I just wished he had bought me a ring so I could've thrown it in his face. Now I just avoided him like he was a Mary Kay saleswoman.

I stepped out of the back exit of the Benson building, letting the door slam behind me. That's when my heart did that weird plummet thing it did every time I saw Cameron. It was weird how I could always pick him out of a crowd of students. He lounged against a tree ten feet away, wearing the vest I picked out for him five months earlier. He played with the ring on a beautiful blonde's finger. His signature leather bracelet slid up his sinewy arm, and he looked smitten.

PRANK WARS

My eyes ran to this new girl. She wasn't Kim. Kim was a beautiful brunette who had been hanging on Cameron for the last few months. A nice girl, who should have been too nice to let him cheat on me. Still, they were officially going out, so why was Cameron flirting with someone else? Number one rule, he cheats with you, he'll cheat *on* you. Cameron chose that same moment to glance my direction. Almost simultaneously, he turned away and stepped up the flirting. The blonde took full advantage of it. Her giggles echoed past me.

Note to my war journal; today is not my day with men.

I tried to remember what all these girls saw in Cameron. I mean really, his mouth was too big, his red hair too slick. Okay, his eyes weren't bad. In fact, they were mesmerizing, but other than that...well, he was really tall and definitely made a girl feel feminine standing next to him. He was funny and clever and listened to everything I had to say...and then one day, his interest faded.

I tried to plot my way past enemy territory down the hill to my apartments, except this time the blonde flipped her hair and led Cameron my way. That's when I did what any sane person would do; I walked slow motion through the thickest part of the crowd to avoid him. It was a perfect spring afternoon for it. The flowers were blossoming and love should've been in the air. It should have been.

"Cameron?" Kim materialized from the crowd and clutched her books close, staring from her boyfriend to the girl he was flirting with. I felt like I was in a rerun, and it was me staring at Cameron with Kim.

"Got to go," Cameron mouthed to the blonde. He squeezed her hand and headed for his stunned girlfriend. He towered over Kim. She sniffed, trying to flounce past him down the hill, her long brown hair swinging against her back.

He reluctantly joined her. Kim's voice rose and I cringed, knowing I was about to witness a lot of tears and accusations. Why did I have to be here for it, besides the fact that lunch was down the hill and I was super hungry? I hid behind a gaggle of girls heading the same direction. "Where were you last night?" Kim asked.

Cameron sighed, his expression turning serious. "I was at the hospital. My grandfather's sick. He had a stroke, Kim."

"Oh." She was silent for a moment, digesting his pity story. Now she looked like the insensitive one. Of course, I knew it was a lie. Cameron's grandfather always got sick when he couldn't think of a better excuse. "It's just that…" Kim fought for words. "Why haven't I seen you lately? Every time I want to hang out, you have homework…or work…or you're tired."

"I'm really busy, Kim. This is the hardest semester of my life. I thought you understood that?"

"Yeah…I do." She rubbed at her watering eyes. "But you still hang out with your friends. It's like you don't want to be with me?"

Cameron looked down at his big hands and sniffed. "It's just…I'm not ready for a serious relationship right now."

I choked back a retort. Where had I heard that before?—oh yeah, in his break-up speech with me, almost word for word. I walked even slower. There was no way I wanted to get caught in the middle of this, but if I bailed now I'd starve for the rest of the day.

Cameron took Kim's small hand in his, every movement gentle. "I hate this. You know I want to be with you."

Kim turned to him, showing me a shocked profile. "Then why are you doing this?"

"I don't feel right about us. I fought it, but I can't see it working. There are some things I need to do with my life right now and marriage isn't one of them."

"But…but…I'm not ready to get married either!" She tried to reassure him, but it wouldn't do any good. Now any threat of marriage—real or otherwise would send him running. "You're the most amazing guy I know, everything about you is what I want."

He licked his lips. "Okay, now you're making me uncomfortable."

She let go of his hand and looked contrite—he managed to look like a lost puppy. "Sorry," she took a steadying breath. "Are…are you okay?"

PRANK WARS

He nodded, his head bent sadly. I felt the anger rise up in me. He was working her like the inexperienced violin she was. "I just don't know if I can ever get married, but if I were to marry anyone, it would've been you."

Liar! Unless in his alternate reality, he wanted to be a polygamist because he said the same thing to me. Even a perfect girl couldn't hold onto a guy these days. It should've made me feel better about all the times I got dumped, but it didn't.

"Would you like me to walk you home?" he asked her.

She sniffed and wiped a hand across her eyes. "No."

Cameron stepped awkwardly back and I ducked behind a group of girls, trying to blend in. He brushed past me, retreating for the gardens—slowly at first, but then faster as if incredibly relieved. He'd better hurry if he wanted to catch up with that blonde.

Kim headed blindly for our apartments. I considered skipping my lunch break, but before I could do it, she glanced back and spied me. "Madeleine?" I managed a smile back at her, trying to pretend like I didn't hear the whole exchange—until she started crying. "I thought he cared about me!"

Oh! I jumped from the protective ranks of the girls hiding me and gave her a hug, patting her back. It felt unnatural because I had no idea how to make anyone feel better, but if anyone could empathize with breaking up with Cameron, it was me. "What's going on?" Somehow I got out the words.

"He doesn't want me. But...I...I came between you two. I deserve it. I just thought...I thought we were meant to be. I'm sorry that I hurt you."

"No," I soothed. He played her like he played me and now he was finding someone else to play. And I would've married such a man?

Kim sniffed and pulled away, hugging her books closer to her. My hand found her arm. I doubted she knew where she was going or who she was talking to or what she was saying, so I guided her to our apartments. "He's confused," she said. "He's hurting right now. He's not ready for a serious relationship."

"He's hurting?" I frowned. He didn't hurt. "Did he *say* he wasn't going to date anyone ever again?"

Kim nodded sadly, not getting what I was saying at all. "He can't…because…because he just isn't ready. He might not *ever* be ready. He'll be alone for the rest of his life and he won't have children or grandchildren or anybody!" The tears streamed freely down her face. She was no longer crying for herself, but for Cameron. He had her right where he wanted her.

I patted her back more firmly this time, trying hard to think. "Yeah, yeah, that poor *dear* thing," but I didn't mean it. "He *never* told you that he wouldn't date anymore though, did he?"

Kim looked confused. "No…not exactly?"

"So, even if he isn't ready to grow up to be a man like he says he isn't…when he's tired of living the life of a monk then he'll go break some other girl's heart? Is that what I'm getting from this?" I tried to stay calm.

"Oh no!" Kim's eyes were bright as she defended the man who had just ripped her in two. "He would never do that!"

We made it across the street and were almost to the steps of our apartment complex when I turned to her. It was time she knew the truth about Cameron. It was the only way she could move on, but before I could open my mouth, a red streak jumped out at us from the railing. "Madeleine! Guess what? Cameron broke up with Kim!"

Kim jumped back about ten feet, but I took it as a matter of course. It was only Victoria. She had red hair that flared out like a flame over her shoulders and a slight build that made it easy to hide from the enemy. We called her Tory for short. It made her sound like the soldier she was. Unlike the other poor girls in our ward, we didn't make fools of ourselves in the dating scene. *Anymore*. That didn't stop us from making a fool of ourselves elsewhere…however.

I shrugged at Kim. "News travels fast around here, I guess."

CHAPTER TWO

Day 47
1410 hours

"The Battle of the Sexes. It's not for crying little girls. We've learned that the hard way. Don't think we haven't had our deserters, our POWs, our casualties, but no one can break or the worst will happen...the guys could win."

—Madeleine's War Journal Entry (Friday, April 1st).

"Oh." Tory tucked her hair behind her ear when she saw Kim. "Didn't see you. Sorry."

Kim just shrugged through her tears and I hugged her again. I wasn't sure how to put her back together, especially since it had grown so hard to feel anything myself. "Are you going to be okay?" I asked her.

Sniffing, she nodded. "Yeah...if Cameron... well, maybe he'll date again...when...when he feels ready...he might." She took a steadying breath and I recognized that noble look in her eyes. I had it for about two days before I found out the truth. "And I want him to...to move on, and take chances with his heart."

I shook my head. Yeah, I couldn't take it anymore. How come I had to be the one who told the girls that chick flicks didn't exist? But it was for the best. "Wow. I can't believe he got you to buy that pathetic line? *When*—and I'm not saying *if*—I'm saying *when* he proves he's a liar, he will *still* have your support? He's good."

"Oh, c'mon, Madeleine."

"You don't think Madeleine's right?" Tory's freckles stood out on her flushed face. In a different, more peaceful world, she'd be a heartbreaker. Now she looked like a punk in her red Power Ranger's shirt, long black Chuck Taylor boots, and gray jeans.

"I just wasn't everything he needed." Kim's voice broke.

"Kim." I wasn't sure how to explain this to a person who thought everyone was as nice as she was. "He's a kid in a candy store. He uses girls for a high and throws them out when he hits the low." She stared back at me with big innocent eyes that didn't blink. "Think about all his exes and all the things he said about them?" I said. "He's going to say the same things about you—only personalized. His new girl is an ocean while you're some measly little river! Remember that sweet, romantic country song? Now you're on the other end. You're the ex who just wasn't good enough because he got bored!"

She gulped, her face white. I'm sure she remembered everything he had said about me.

I shrugged. "Hey, it could be worse. At least you're not a filthy old puddle like I am. I give Cameron two days tops before you won't even cross his mind. And if you do, you're that annoying little bug that eats away at his conscience and reminds him what a creep he is." She gasped, and I tried not to let her pain stop me from telling her the truth. Only cold reality would save her from endless nights of crying for a guy who didn't deserve her tears. "He's tired of you—not because of some tragic flaw or event in his past that keeps him from truly loving you. No—because he's a loser."

"But...but he broke up with me," Kim's voice was desperate and for a moment I felt bad. I just wished I could find her a good guy and fast, but she had to learn to be strong on her own. "How could he blame me?" she said.

I lifted a shoulder. "He'll find something against you. You trapped him. You talked too much. You wore your hair funny. You were too nice, too boring, too loud. You were too eager to please, your forehead's sweaty. Pretty good reasons, don't you think?"

PRANK WARS

"No." She followed me into my apartment. Tory took up the rear. We ran up the stairs until we reached my apartment on the top floor.

"Agreed," I said. "So, let's give him a really good reason to dislike you, shall we?" My mischievous streak was taking over. "I mean, the guy needs a reason, something to ease his conscience. Let's make this break-up easy on him, poor thing."

Kim's lips twisted at the completely ludicrous suggestion. "And what reason could we possibly give him, Madeleine?"

I slammed our front door decisively, making both Kim and Tory jump. "Tell him it was a *wager*."

"A what?" Kim asked.

I gave her an impish smile and headed for my room, passing our worn green striped couches on my way into the hall. Kim and Tory followed me like I was the Pied Piper. "Tell him that you never wanted to date him in the first place, but the only reason you did was because we made a bet that he would fall for you like some kind of fool. Tell him that we were laughing behind his back the entire time." Kim gasped. "It'll be good for him," I reassured her with a pat on the shoulder. "Like shock therapy. He'll think twice before he tangles with us girls again."

Kim looked confused and Tory and I broke into mischievous laughs. It was contagious and soon, Kim was laughing uncertainly along with us. She still wore a puzzled expression, but at least we cheered her up. "Oh, c'mon, that's crazy." She flopped on my bed, pulling a throw pillow to her stomach. "I could just imagine. I wish…" She giggled again. "Oh, you are too funny. You girls!"

"Funny?" I stopped laughing. "No, I'm dead serious. Do it." I sat down at the plotting tables—uh, I'll explain those later—and opened up my laptop at my desk to pull up Facebook. We all knew that Cameron received Facebook notifications religiously on his phone. I pulled up his account and wrote on his wall. "I'm so sorry to hear about your grandfather. I hope he feels better soon."

"What are you doing?" Kim asked. Tory smiled cruelly. She knew exactly what I was doing.

"One," I counted, "two...three." Kim watched me like I was crazy, but as soon as I counted thirty seconds, I refreshed Cameron's page and miraculously my comment had been erased. "Hmm? Why doesn't Cameron want his friends and family to see that his grandfather's under the weather? Could it be that...?"

"...he's not?" Tory finished for me. Kim's tears had magically dried up. She glanced over at Tory, who lifted a brow. "Tell him it was a wager." She flopped next to Kim on the bed. Now there was a devil on each of Kim's shoulders—no angel in sight.

After a moment of gauging our expressions to see if we were serious, Kim decided we weren't and threw her head back. Strangely enough, she was giggling. Her long chestnut hair bounced with her. "Oh, you girls! Thanks for making me feel better. You're right. I can't believe I didn't see it, but...but dumping me was the biggest favor Cameron has ever done for me. If...if...he was playing with me from the beginning then I'm sorry he ever asked me out in the first place." She slid off the bed, looking strong. "He's not worth crying about. I'm not some measly river...or a filthy puddle—in your case Madeleine!"

She left my room with a girl-power spring to her step. Obviously she didn't take us as seriously as we took ourselves. She hesitated at the door. Her expression changed when she looked at me. "You know, I always thought you were the meanest girl in the ward, Madeleine, but you're just a fake, aren't you? You *do* have a heart."

Was that a compliment? I wasn't sure, but at least Kim's tears were gone. They'd be back once Kim started remembering the good things about him. We had to make sure that didn't happen. I waited for the door to close behind her. "We'll spread the rumor tonight."

Tory nodded, expecting nothing less. "Very good, captain." She was enjoying this. I couldn't expect her to take any of this seriously. She had never experienced a player firsthand. She never dated—*ever*. I supposed it was better than a broken heart. "It's a double-break-up-weekend too," she told me in shocked tones. "AmyLee's boyfriend broke up with her this morning!"

PRANK WARS

"Is that an April Fool's joke?"

"Nope."

That meant the fifth break-up in our apartment complex this week. This one wasn't too much of a surprise. AmyLee's latest boyfriend was a snake. His hand was on AmyLee's, but he couldn't keep his eyes off the other girls in the room. Every time his eyes rested on me, I treated him to the evil eye—it was my latest scar from this battle of the sexes. "Why did he break it off?"

"We'll find out, I'm sure," Tory said.

AmyLee was a drama queen. She wouldn't rest until we knew every sordid detail, especially since our apartment was quickly turning into group therapy for the heartbroken. Everyone knew where my sympathies lay; they were never with the male. "He probably wasn't ready for a relationship either," I drawled. "It's growing into quite an epidemic." I pulled my pen from my dark hair. It fell past my shoulders in a messy tangle and I ignored it, rolling the pen between my fingers. "We live among the most scared men in the world, my friend."

I wasn't sure if it was a college thing, a twenty-something thing or even just a guy thing, but where were the manly men? The gentlemen? The men of honor? All over if my mom could be believed. The problem was that if they were manly, they were players. If they were gentlemen, they were scared. And if they were men of honor? They weren't interested in me. And if they were all three? *They were taken.* Seriously, did we all have to fight for Captain Moroni in the next life? I didn't know one girl who hadn't called dibs on him. It was a cat-fight in the making.

"You think these guys are scared?" Tory asked. "Or just playing?"

I shrugged, trying not to think of *him*...and then *him*...and oh yeah, most especially *him*. Yep, Cameron was the straw that broke me. It was humiliating that it had taken so many breakups to know it was stupid to believe *I* could ever have a healthy relationship.

The door opened and my roommate's head poked into the room. Tory and I jumped guiltily when we saw Lizzie's face. She always wore celestial white. Today she wore matching pearls in her ears. They made a great contrast against her dark skin. I tried not to look like I was stirring up trouble. "Hey Lizzie."

Lizzie nodded with the dignified air of an Ethiopian princess. Well, not really Ethiopian—her dad was from Nigeria and her mom was from Washington, but she looked exotic enough. "You're not holding another of those war meetings again, are you?" she reproached. I tried not to look guilty, but to be honest, I wasn't sure how. I knew that Lizzie did. That's why I had offered her the position as my second-in-command in this war, but she refused to take the honor. "Don't you have to get to class?" she asked.

"I'm skipping it," I decided on the spot. It was a business class anyway. My business major was one of the many casualties of my break-up with Cameron. There was no way I wanted to pick out happy brides' wedding cakes when I wouldn't have one of my own. Two weeks ago, I nixed wedding coordinator and switched to General Studies, which meant I had only one year left of BYU before I was out. I was too old to be here anyway. I started school late, switched my major too many times. And now I was twenty-six. Already, I felt like a spinster.

"Enough is enough," Lizzie said. "You've got to stop these *Break-up Anonymous Meetings*! First Johanna, then Emily…and now Kim? You're not helping them!"

"What are you talking—?" It was best to plead stupid, but before I could, in stormed AmyLee in tight leggings and boots. I was glad her wrath wasn't directed at me, but at a supposedly stronger man. She was yet another girl in our apartment complex in need of a battle plan against her ex. I ignored Lizzie's accusing look and indicated a chair. "Sit down, AmyLee."

"I'd rather stand."

Lizzie leaned on the door frame. "Your methods are unhealthy, Madeleine."

"Look, Lizzie," I whispered loudly. "There's only *one* way to get over a man, see him for what he really is. Just consider this my little service project for the Relief Society."

PRANK WARS

"Can you believe that jerk?" AmyLee interrupted us with a shout. I turned to our latest dumpee. "He just *wants* to be *friends*."

"And what's wrong with that?" a chipper voice called from the hallway. We groaned. It was another one of my roommates, a roommate that never seemed to be burned by men. If anyone did the burning, it was Kali. She danced, yes, danced into the room.

"What's wrong with that?" AmyLee repeated in a growl, directing all of her rage against the hapless Kali. "Did *she* just ask me what was wrong with that?"

We all cringed a little bit, but Kali stood her ground proudly in her gladiator sandals. Think unrepentant China doll with dimples, lots of blonde curly hair, elegant cat eyes, a little rude, but with the best intentions in the world. When a guy wants to be friends with Kali, it means he wants to date her. But when a guy wants to *just be friends* with a girl like *us* say, well, we know we're getting the runaround. I stepped protectively in front of the blonde and smiled calmly at AmyLee, redirecting her anger to the correct party. "Tell me what *he* did to you."

AmyLee laughed without humor. "Can we forget for a moment that I didn't even know Brad was alive until two months ago? Then he started hounding me, asking me out, complimenting me, and making me feel— oh, crazy I know— like I was the most special girl in the world to him. And now, just when I get attached, really really attached, he wants to run?"

I snickered; it was getting too predictable. AmyLee's face got even redder at my unnatural reaction, and I shrugged. "He wants to play games, does he? Let's play a game then. It's called turn him up sweet and dump him on his face. I want cookies made, girls. Tender little notes. Steak." They straightened, seeing I was serious.

Tory's nose wrinkled. "But who can do that?"

"I don't know. You're the Relief Society, figure it out!" I kicked off my black and white plaid flats and paced the green shag carpet in my bare feet. Prank wars were my element, *not* pretending to have everything in common with a guy just to get a boyfriend. "First, we'll make sure every girl in his acquaintance gives him the cold shoulder until he's begging for a date. Then we sic our flirtiest, most beautiful gal pals on him, the ones without an ounce of human decency." I glanced behind me at Kali. She was scratching the red polish off her nails. "Do you cook?" I asked her.

She grimaced, still managing to look gorgeous through that nasty little look. "Are you joking?"

"I can cook," AmyLee managed to hiss through her anger.

"Good. By the time we're through with him, he'll want a normal girl so bad that he'll take another go at you…and when he does, simply remind him that you *just want to be friends*."

Her lips puckered. "But what if I don't?"

"Don't worry. *He does*, but this time you're the one who will be dumping him on his head. Do yourself a favor and get him where it hurts this time, will you?"

"His heart?"

"No, AmyLee, his ego." I crossed my arms, full of all sorts of good deeds this morning. I was eager for more. Maybe Kim was right. Maybe I wasn't the meanest girl in the ward. It didn't feel like it though. "Make sure it happens," I told Tory.

AmyLee sighed, but she left much calmer than she had entered. Usually the angry girls got over their men better than the broken-hearted ones did.

As soon as she was gone, Lizzie pinned me down with her brown eyes. "Madeleine!" Her voice was stern as usual, and I didn't take it as seriously as I should—also a usual occurrence. "This really isn't the best way to handle this, you know."

I brushed my hair out of my face and managed an innocent smile. "I know."

"So, why are you doing this?" Tormenting men got my mind off them? It made me feel less like a victim? There was no wrath like a scorned woman? Habit? I wasn't sure really.

PRANK WARS

"Hey, where's my Jell-O?" I heard the staccato sound of spiked heels on the kitchen floor and we all hunched over guiltily. Only one person made my heart quicken in fear. Sandra must be home. "Who took it?" The cabinet door slammed shut. "You know better than to mess with me. I will have your heads!"

Uh oh. The Jell-O might've ended up in the guys' toilets or maybe their shower heads. I wasn't actually sure. We listened to Sandra's heels catch on the gross shag carpet in the hall outside as she came for us. I had no idea why a classy dame like her even stooped to walk on such a floor, let alone rent it. It was anybody's guess why she had signed the lease this last winter semester.

"Lizzie!" Before Sandra could say, *move it*, Lizzie stepped aside, allowing Sandra to glare into my crowded room. Our roommate was a steely-eyed brunette, cold and gorgeous. She was way too classy for a college student and looked like she should be wrapped in a mink, not wearing skinny jeans. Everything Sandra wore was designer from her snakeskin heels to her baby doll shirt and Chanel bag. Her gaze went past a smirking Kali, a fiery-eyed Tory, and then straight for me. "What's going on here?"

"Therapy." I steeled my eyes to match hers. "Would you like some?"

She snorted. "I guess it makes sense. Shrinks are usually more messed up than their patients."

"Are yours?"

"Look," she hissed. "I'm not in the mood for this. I want my Jell-O back. All of it. And if you stashed it somewhere nasty, you'd better replace it fast!" She jabbed her finger at me. "And don't touch my stuff again. Got it?" She stared at my impassive face and pulled away before I could deny her accusations. Lizzie moved out of her way to give her the grand exit she deserved.

"You could get *him* back, you know," I told Sandra's elegant back. It stiffened—just as I knew it would. Yes, Sandra in all her coolness was just another casualty who fell for some smooth guy's act. Or shall we say,

Lord Byron's smooth act. And since Lord Byron recently gave me the smack down, I figured I owed him another one.

Sandra turned to face me and I met her eyes evenly. "And I'm not talking getting him back so you can date him again." I ignored Lizzie's warning look. "No, get him back so that no one *ever* wants to date him again."

Sandra's chin lifted, but only slightly. "Who could you possibly be referring to?"

"The one who made you the bitter woman you are."

Sandra gasped at that. "I'm not bitter because of *him*."

"Really? Then *who* was it?"

"That, dear, is none of your business!"

"We live with your bitterness. That makes it our business…unless you want to start acting like a normal human being again, of course."

"And what do you consider a normal human being?" She snaked her head back and forth at me. "Someone who holds guy intervention meetings for the clinically insane who just happen to lose their boyfriends? I swear most girls I know pull pranks on guys to get a date, but you? You do it because you hate men. Don't you?"

"Don't you?"

"I was asking *you*."

I smiled. At last we had some common ground. Byron recently made the mistake of setting his sights on my gorgeous roommate. The only thing he could possibly see in Sandra was her beautiful face. And though we didn't see much of her, we definitely saw more than that—she was a killjoy. Byron had dropped her on her head almost as soon as they started going out, which certainly didn't help matters at home. Now it was my duty to reach out to her.

"I know what you're going through," I said. "When I went through my last break-up, I cried every day and night—in class, at church, at work, in the car, when I saw babies, when he looked at other girls the way he used to look at me, when I heard the things he said about me. I blamed myself. I thought I wasn't good enough somehow. Too obnoxious, too hard to deal with, too stupid." Sandra's eyes were glazing over and I cut to the chase. "You wanna know the worst part? When he pretended I didn't exist. We could be alone in the same room together and he wouldn't even bother to talk to me."

"Why are you telling me this?"

I paced the room as was my usual habit. "Because one morning, I woke up and thought, 'Madeleine! What *are* you doing? Look at yourself. Your eyes are red. You're miserable, and you're crying so much you're dehydrated, and it's all for *nothing*! He *isn't* crying for you. He doesn't even miss you. He's lost interest. He's not wondering why the relationship failed. He doesn't care and he won't ever care. Your tears will not bring back the man he used to be because he *never* was that man, so quit being a baby about it,' and I did. So now I'm happy."

"You sound real happy."

"I'm free."

Sandra just stared at me blankly and I took a deep breath. I didn't expect her to understand. Some girls lived off the adoration of males and didn't know that life could be habitable without it. "Okay." The more casual I made this, the more chance she would talk. "Tell me your story, Sandra."

Sandra hesitated, her eyes on mine. As always, she was a little intimidating, but to be fair, I've been accused of that too. Her iPhone went off and she heaved a sigh, echoed by all of us in the room. We'd get no information out of her now.

Sandra glanced down at her latest text. "Get off my case, Madeleine." Her fingers flew over the touchscreen while she told me off. Begrudgingly, I admired her texting skills. She was the queen of multi-tasking. "I don't have a story, Mad, so drop it."

I leaned on a table to watch her with steady eyes. "You still like him, don't you?" Sandra froze angrily at the accusation. Before she could snap at me again, her iPhone beeped impatiently. She was getting bombarded with texts. Sandra pulled her cell to her ear and shot me a parting glare. "Mind your own business, brat."

My eyebrows lifted. *Brat?* That was uncalled for. Sandra couldn't be that much older than me. She could even be younger. I had no idea.

"You will not believe what my roommate—" We heard Sandra's voice fade down the hall.

As soon as she was out of earshot, I snapped at Kali. "Quick. Give me the ward directory." Kali's lip curled up eagerly and she ran to fetch it from the coveted spot from the microwave in the kitchen.

"Poor Byron." Tory grinned mischievously. "We'll help Sandra whether she likes it or not."

CHAPTER THREE

Day 47
1452 hours

"War. It starts out so simple: just a bit of betrayal, a bit of pain, a bit of vengeance. And that's when I find myself doing things I never thought I'd do."

—Madeleine's War Journal Entry (Friday, April 1st, moments later).

Kali rounded the corner to my room and threw the directory into my hands. Her bracelets jingled. I flipped to Lord Byron's page. Whoever worked on the ward directory clearly had a crush on Byron, but then again what girl in the 73rd ward didn't? His picture was bigger than any of his roommates' and he had about three different quotes under his name as opposed to the single quote most of us were allowed.

He posed like some sort of GQ model with dark hair and blue eyes. Yeah, the ward directory girl put his picture in color too—normally not a problem, except everyone else was in black and white. The special treatment was justified in the *name* of teasing. He pretended to be disturbed by the attention, but I knew he reveled in it.

"Just look at him!" Kali whispered in her baby doll awe. "He's beautiful. Byron's the reason polygamy was invented."

"Nice," I said in my most sarcastic voice. Kali sighed dreamily, even though I shot her a disapproving look.

Tory peered through her red hair to see. "Yeah, he's hot," she admitted.

"No, no." Lizzie shook her head vigorously. "He's evil. There's a difference."

I smiled at her. Despite our disagreements, we were still on the same side. "Beautiful boys generally are," I said. Lizzie nodded in agreement. "I think that it's time to play a little April Fool's joke." Lizzie's head snapped up, suddenly realizing that our afternoon of intervention wasn't over. "Don't worry," I reassured her. "It'll be worth it. Where's my cell phone?"

"Are you crazy?" Lizzie blocked me from my cell phone. It sat on my bed. "C'mon Mad!" She held her hands out. "Would you just for a moment think things through?"

I tilted my head, pretending to think then nodded, snapping at Tory. "Cell phone."

Tory dove over the bed, slipping easily past Lizzie. She was used to slithering in and out of tight spots when things got dangerous. "Don't worry," she tried to reassure Lizzie. "He won't know it's us. We'll block the call."

"That's not what I'm worried about!"

Tory slapped the cell phone into my hand. The cover was pink camo. I stared down at it. The phone had ruined my life more than once, but there was a time for love and a time for not, and a time for using the phone when love was not in the cards. I eased to the floor. With the exception of Lizzie, we sat in a tight circle around the directory.

"Do it, Madeleine," Kali gushed with rosy cheeks. "He's really cute."

My jaw clenched at her usual failure to see the big picture. "Cute has nothing to do with this." It was possibly the four-hundredth-and-fifty-second time of giving her this lecture.

"Doesn't it?" Tory watched me steadily. She was calm in the face of danger and always throwing unwanted rhetorical questions at me. "Trust me. You can hang up anytime." I tickled the pink camo cover on my cell phone. Byron deserved what he got. He was cocky, arrogant, and now he was moving onto every girl we loved and cared about. Never mind that he thought it was his duty to insult me at every turn. Today's April Fool's joke wasn't the worst of it. "Or don't you remember?" Tory asked. "He called you *desperate* last Sunday." Tory had on her half-smile. It completed her mischievous redheaded look. Anyone who was friends with her knew what it meant. Byron had called me out and she was going to egg me on every step of the way.

"Give me his number," I said.

"Madeleine!" Lizzie tried to convince me with a steady look in her chocolate brown eyes. "Mad! Mad!" By this time, I was beyond reason. I tried to concentrate on her calm voice. "You don't have to do this."

Oh yes. Yes, I did. Even now, Byron had the upper hand and needed to be taken down. I dialed his number and pressed send before I got second thoughts. I waited while I listened to the phone ring. It was a scarier sound than the silence before a battle.

"Hello?"

I gulped, recognizing the arrogant voice, though it didn't sound so arrogant right now, almost human. I steeled myself against its charming tones. "Guess who?" I forced myself to sound sugary *and* happy. It wasn't hard if I imagined the voices of the girls clamoring for his attention at ward prayer.

Lizzie took a steadying breath.

"Um, I have no idea who this is." Byron gave a light laugh that most girls would find oddly attractive. "Why don't you just tell me?"

"How about I just give you a hint?" I told him sweetly. Tory nodded at me in approval.

Byron hesitated a moment and I stood up. It was absolutely impossible to sit still while my arch-nemesis was just breaths away from me on the other line. "Okay, let's play," he conceded, *"Give me a hint."*

My heart flipped at the first surrender. One more mistake like this and he would be ours. I paced the room, not caring who I stepped on, which was Kali. I stumbled over her and she gave a little squeal. I motioned wildly at her. "Alright, alright, first hint." I carefully maneuvered around Kali. She squirmed like a lost puppy. "I'm the one who sits behind you in chemistry." Sort of true, except not. He usually sat somewhere in the back, not like I was paying attention, of course.

"Yeah?"

"And I sing *la la la la* behind your head."

"*What?*" he seemed surprised. "*When?*"

I forced out a stupid giggle. "Only when I'm happy. When the professor is giving out assignments. I love chemistry! I mean—not chemistry—but the word, *chemistry!*" I shrieked happily. I was sure that would kill his ears. Lizzie's lips clenched even tighter together. "What?" I mouthed to her. Her disapproval always made me uneasy.

"*Um, nope, not getting it.*" Byron was starting to sound a little testy. Just as planned.

"Okay, next hint. You *smiled* at me. Remember that?" I stared at my mirror, forcing my face to go dreamy, so my voice would follow. The look didn't fit my dark looks at all and I twisted my lips. Despite Byron's goads, I wasn't completely lacking in girlish charms. I wore a lot of black, sure, but I've been told that my lips are very kissable—not that I've been doing much of that lately. "And uh…in class when our eyes met…" I tried to make the words work on my tongue, but only managed to sound like a gooey Glinda the Good Witch, "it made my heart go pitter patter." I gave another girly giggle.

"*Really?*" Now his voice seemed tense. Good. "*I have no idea who you are.*" It came out flat.

"It's Suzy Q!" I announced with a laugh. "Suzy Q Miller!" I gave another squeal as if he would be just as delighted with the announcement. "Well, it's really just Suzy. That's why you didn't guess it. Everyone calls me Suzy Q for short. My best friend Sandra does. You know Sandra, right?" He wasn't saying anything, and so I easily filled up the silence with silly girly talk. "Well, I guess you might know her, she's your girlfriend, after all. Well, I mean *not now*, I guess." I laughed. "Awkward. But uh, you and I never dated before…so you could date me, right?"

PRANK WARS

"I could?"

I blew out, trying to keep from exploding with laughter. Tory hid her face in a pillow. I saw her body jerking with silent mirth. Kali just looked dreamy. She bounced happily on my bed. I noticed the dignified Lizzie had deserted me. I had disappointed her. My heart lurched briefly at the thought, but there was no turning back. "Yeah, um, so you can take me out to dinner and then to a movie. I really don't care what we do as long as *you* pay for it."

That was the clincher. He would wipe the floor with me for sure, but then I would laugh in his face for buying my stupid story. It was all so perfect. *"Wow, that sounds like a night to remember,"* he drawled. *"I didn't realize how easy it would be to please a girl like you."*

"Yeah, I figure the more dates I go on, the faster I get married, right?"

He burst out laughing. *"Sure."*

I frowned. Byron laughed at my joke? How did he know it was a joke? I took a steadying breath. This was a more treacherous mission than I thought. I was always a sucker for a man with a sense of humor. I couldn't let things get out of hand. "So, uh, how about it, hot stuff?"

He paused for a second and I readied for a fight. *"Okay,"* he said.

Okay? My forehead wrinkled. Did he just say okay? He'd go out with this monster I had just created of myself? What was wrong with him? No guy liked clingy girls. No guy liked high-maintenance girls. No guy liked girls who made *la la la la* noises behind him in class, especially a player like this. He couldn't possibly be serious? I muted my cell. "He said, okay."

"What?" Kali fell off my bed and slid to the ground in surprise. Her blonde hair splayed out behind her. I stared at her just as Tory pulled away from her pillow in stunned silence.

Lizzie poked her head through the door, clearly eavesdropping the whole time. "That's because he's *nice*," she lectured me, "unlike some people."

Nice? Could he actually be nice? No! This man was not nice, not without something to gain from it. He was the biggest noncommittal player I knew, and I couldn't believe that he was getting the best of me. I'd force him show me his true colors. Tonight was the big intramural championship dodge ball game between us and the 104th ward. There was plenty of trash-talking and lots of tempers involved. There was no way he'd miss it. "How about tonight at 5:00?" I asked.

"*Oh sorry. Can't. I'm playing a dodge ball game.*"

I smiled. Now we were getting somewhere. "5:15?"

"*No...*"

I didn't even give him time to explain. "5:30? 5:45?"

He burst out laughing. "*No, I can't.*"

"Oh, that's too bad," I simpered, expecting a set-down. "Are you sure?"

He was quiet for a moment. Every instinct told me not to trust his supposed defeat. "*Why don't you come and be my cheerleader,*" he shot back. What? Shallow guys didn't invite girls sight unseen to their precious games. What if I was ugly? He'd never chance it. "*Maybe we can do something* after *the game?*" he said. "*Yeah, we can take a walk through the trails on campus. Then we can get to know each other a little...better.*"

My eyes widened. Was he really that big of a player or was he playing with me? Did he know what was going on? Or did he think I was someone else? "Uh..." I was thinking hard.

"*I know,*" he suggested. "*How about we do something right now?*"

"Right now?" I tried to keep the panic from my voice and reminded myself that he couldn't reach through the phone and steal me.

"*Yeah. Where are you?*"

This was getting serious. "I...I am just...busy with..." I tried to think of the most disgusting thing possible to a noncommittal guy like him, "my marriage prep homework. Gotta get an A. Whoo!"

"*You wanna put your marriage prep to work right now, Suzy Q?*"

"What? What are you talking about?"

"*Why don't you come over and we'll study it together? Maybe a little chemistry too? You're in my class, right? Yeah, I remember you. Dark hair, right?*"

PRANK WARS

Yeah—no! This was not going the way I expected. He was supposed to freak out because a weird girl was calling to ask him out and then I would let him stew over it for the rest of the day until I called him and bragged how he fell for my April Fools' joke. Why was he actually going for it? And how did he know I had dark hair?

Maybe there was an information leak? There was no way that my number was in his phone. Did we have spies in the ranks? I glanced over at our blonde little Kali. Her cell phone was nowhere in sight. Tory was stunned; her freckles looked a little more pronounced than usual. Lizzie's hands were on her slender hips, a smirk on her dark face. But she was the last person who'd turn against me. How did Byron know? Did he recognize my voice? Impossible. I meant nothing to him. I gulped. "Sure, sure, fine. Sandra's with me. She won't mind tagging along. I'm sure she'll be happy to hear about your sudden interest in chemistry."

"*How about you just come by yourself?*" his voice sounded lazy and just a little dangerous. "*I think we need some alone time together.*"

He was calling my bluff. Now I *knew* he wasn't being nice. I smiled wickedly, getting back into the game. "It would be rude to leave my best friend behind."

"*Then I'll meet you. How about in five minutes?*"

"You don't have my address," I stalled, trying to think of all the addresses of the most annoying girls I knew or maybe of an insane asylum. I gave up. "Or maybe you just don't know what today is?"

"*Monday.*"

"April Fool's day."

He was silent on the other end. It was just enough to make me sweat. "*Oh, so you mean you called me up so you could make me believe that a girl would actually be interested enough to ask me out just so you could tell me it was all some cruel joke?*"

That sounded terrible. "No, not really. I..." explaining made it sound lame because all of a sudden when he repeated it back to me, it did sound lame, plus everyone was staring at me. I was supposed to look strong and somewhat clever.

"How charming of you," he added.

I gave a weak laugh. I couldn't let him turn this on me. "As if you have any problem with girls asking you out!"

Tory straightened nervously. I wasn't supposed to compliment the enemy, even if it was backhanded. I felt my face go red for a lot of reasons. Maybe Byron would think this was funny and it would all be okay. I mean, we just wanted him to sweat, not…not—I don't know—*to have feelings.* I forced my voice into more teasing tones. "Just admit I got you, Lord Byron."

"Only one person calls me Lord Byron, Suzy Q." Before I could hang up in sheer panic, the doorbell rang. *"Hey, let's not fight,"* he said softly. *"In fact, I left a little present on your doorstep just for you…to celebrate the holiday, of course."* My heart made a skydive out of my chest. "Hope you like it, cuz."

Cuz? Was that short for cousin or something?

He hung up, leaving me in stunned silence. I turned to the other girls and we listened to Sandra's heels catch on the carpet on her way to the door. Nothing would stop her from finding this latest humiliation. The front door creaked open. It was followed by a shrill shriek. I thought I had executed the plan flawlessly, but apparently Lord Byron had been onto me almost from the beginning, but when? He had set a perfect diversion by acting the part of the nice guy. That was usually when guys got the best of me.

Sandra stormed into our room, her long fingernails digging into a bunch of crumpled flowers. "Why would someone pick my tulips, huh? I just bought these!" She flung them at me. "I can only assume it has to do with your stupid pranks, Madeleine!"

I picked them off the floor. "I'm sure it doesn't." I said it out of habit.

"There's a note." Lizzie pointed out.

Sandra flung the note at me and she slammed my bedroom door shut behind her. I turned the note over. It was written on the back of some chemistry notes from yesterday's class. Underneath, Lord Byron had colored in a dark black spot like we were pirates in *Treasure Island*. He had declared war. He had officially declared war! I wasn't sure if I was ready for that kind of commitment until I read the note: *"In your dreams, Mad Dog."*

Kali was the first to find her voice. "Mad Dog?" She glanced over at me. I could almost see the rusty batteries working in her brain. "Madeleine Doggett! That's you!" She giggled. "He's so very clever, isn't he?" I cringed at the compliment. "Mad Dog. I'm going to call you Mad Dog from now on! It's perfect."

Tory murmured an excuse and left for her own apartment downstairs. Her red hair shot behind her like a flame. She disliked losing a battle as much as I did.

Lizzie sighed. "I hope you're not planning some sort of counterattack, Mad Dog." It disturbed me how easily my new nickname rolled off her tongue.

"Are you kidding?" I crumpled the paper in my hand. "Lord Byron is no match for me. He won't last a day."

CHAPTER FOUR

Day 103
2232 hours

"The night was crisp, deceptively peaceful. My squadron sat on the green shag carpet in their wary positions next to an open window. We listened to the rain tapping softly into the cold ground as we waited for a counterattack from Lord Byron's men. These scribbles might be my last. But I must tell my story though pen cannot describe the horrors of this last semester."

—Madeleine's War Journal Entry (Saturday, May 26th).

I was supposed to be a regular college student, you know, the kind who eats peanut-butter sandwiches and Ramen noodles, and occasionally goes on a date? Now I cared for one thing only: survival. Okay, maybe just keeping my cool, but still this war was bigger than me now. Had it only been two months since that ill-fated prank call to Byron? Red dye frosted our fingers from pranks gone bad. We never got out of our parking spaces because the guys purposely blocked us in. Anything remotely valuable had gone missing, but nothing could stop me now.

If I could keep Byron busy with meaningless pranks, it meant fewer broken hearts. The only problem was that Byron was a master at delegating. He never had to lift a finger, just coldly executed orders to his men, leaving him freer than we were now. Even worse, I was buried in

PRANK WARS

homework. As much as I hated to admit it, Byron managed to turn every male in the 73rd ward against me. Well, I might've done some of that to myself since I gave dating advice to most of their ex-girlfriends, but still Byron was the mastermind.

A knock sounded on the frontlines, and I stared at our front door with eyes that had seen too much: lobsters in the bathtub, garlic powder in our toothpaste, cow eyeballs served on plates. And now I was caught in my Lucille Ball pajama bottoms. I put down my physics homework and took a steadying breath. "Would somebody open that?"

Lizzie lounged on our ugly green-striped couches. She glanced up from her homework. Her hair brushed against the pages of her Shakespeare book. I coveted her hair in a bad way. It was long and wavy and twisted into a million braids. She looked bored. "Are you sure you want to do that, Mad Dog?"

I grimaced at the nickname. "What? It could be a visitor. Are we just going to let *her* stand outside in the cold? Fine. If that's what you want. You're the Relief Society President. You know best."

Lizzie stared at me. Was it possible for her to make someone wait? Crickets chirped inside the house. They were left over from the great cricket sting last week. With a fed-up sigh, Lizzie pushed off the couch. "And who broke your legs?" She trudged to the front door in her bright blue pajamas.

"The peephole doesn't work," I warned her. She gave me a weird look, and I shrugged. "The guys put it in backwards. They can look through it from the outside and see us, so we—"

Lizzie gave a fed up sigh and jerked the door open. An ugly yellow stuffed animal sat on our porch. I peered closer. It was an ugly duckling, in fact, the *ugliest* duckling I had ever seen. No, it wasn't some sad commentary on us. None of Byron's pranks were that clever. Lizzie didn't look surprised. "Huh? We've been hit again."

"What do we do, Captain?" Kali ran out from the back wearing a shirt with a peace sign. Her blonde hair was in pigtails. I gave her an exasperated look. She had picked up the *captain* thing from Tory.

35

I pushed off paper debris from my lap and rushed to the porch. The enemy was nowhere in sight, but they were definitely out there. I gave the ugliest duckling a wide berth. Who knew where they got it. Possibly D.I. I'm sure it was covered in fleas—just another way to get back at us.

Lizzie fumbled with one of her white canvas flats and put it on, limping forward, a war vet with her share of battle wounds. Her left shoes had all been stolen by Lord Byron's spies just yesterday. "There's a message with that stuffed *thing*." She threw it in my hands.

"*What do you and leftover mashed potatoes from Thanksgiving have in common?*" I read. "*The same thing you have in common with a deer playing on the highway.*" That didn't even make sense, which made the enemy's coup even more triumphant. I raked my hands through my black hair. It had a streak of premature white in it—compliments of Lord Byron…and possibly genetic, but whatever. The phone rang and we jumped. I fumbled with it. "Yes?"

"We have an emergency in the third infantry division, requesting immediate backup. We're stuck in our apartment." I recognized Tory's gruff voice. She sounded frantic. "Get us out!"

"We've got a code red downstairs," I told Kali. "Move."

Lizzie rolled her eyes, but she followed us out anyway. Kali tripped over a forgotten plate of old mashed potatoes left on our porch, which was where all of the guys' rotten food usually ended up. She gasped, but this time in pure hatred. "Ooh, gross," she squealed, kicking the potatoes off her Sketchers. "I just bought these!"

Too late, I understood the note. *What did we have in common with mashed potatoes from Thanksgiving?* Indeed. It was gooey and moldy and had to be months old, but nothing could deter us from this rescue operation. We ran downstairs to force open Tory's front door—except she didn't have a door anymore. We stepped back in shock when we saw the wall of cinder blocks covering it.

"Clear it out!" Tory shouted behind the wall.

I grimaced when I saw the flash from behind. Kali was our little blonde paparazza. She snapped another picture. I'm sure I looked great with my ratty hair. Besides the loss of her Sketchers, Kali never took anything seriously. "I look like Medusa," I warned. "Take another picture and I'll break your camera with my face."

She giggled and another flash burst from her camera.

"Hurry up!" Tory shouted out from the other side of the cinder block wall. No doubt she was eager to get revenge on whoever did this. At least she still had some fighting spirit left. It was more than I had. After the obligatory pictures, we went to work, hauling away the cinder blocks.

Correction, some of us got to work. Lizzie just leaned against the blocks, giving me one of those fed-up looks again. She tied all of her braids into one long side braid. "When is this going to stop?" she asked.

I heaved a cinder block to the ground and tirelessly tugged at another. "Why don't you ask the guys?"

"You're going to leave it up to them?" she asked. I worked even faster, hoping to avoid the now familiar conversation. "You know you could be the bigger person and end this first," she suggested.

"And let them win? Please."

"Are you even getting any homework done?"

I froze her with a look. Well, I tried to freeze her with a look. She just lifted a brow at me. "I don't sleep very much," I admitted, "and I don't need that much sleep, so…"

"They're winning."

I grimaced, desperate to free Tory from her apartment so that I could get someone with some fighting spirit on my side. Already I could see Tory's agitated red hair bobbing over the cinder block wall; it was in a looped bun on top of her head like 'Cindy Lu Who' from the *Grinch*. After taking down another cinder block, I saw her narrowed hazel eyes through the cracks. It startled me and I fell back. Kali slammed a cinder block on her own fingers and screeched out in agony.

"Hurry up!" Tory ordered behind the wall. "Just wait until I get my hands on them. Ooh!"

Kali sucked on her fingers. Lizzie let out another sigh. "They're long gone now," Lizzie said. "You'll never catch them."

"Then why don't you help us? You're the only one, who..." With my eyes on Kali, I lowered my voice. "Lizzie, you're more capable than any of my...ur..." Lizzie's steady eyes were on me, so I modified my speech from soldier talk to girl talk. "I can't do this alone. If you want this to be over then help me. I mean, really really help me."

She tugged on her thick hair, and I knew that meant she was thinking. "Only if you promise to end this, and I mean *really really* end this."

"What do you think I'm trying to do?" She smiled sarcastically back at me, and I stopped hauling cinder blocks much to Tory's dismay. "You actually think I enjoy this?"

"Well, you know you're flirting, right?"

My mouth fell open. She said that to annoy me, didn't she? "Take that back," I said. "This whole thing...is not...don't get the wrong idea. I'm *no* flirt."

She smiled even wider, only now I wasn't sure if she was teasing me. "It's okay to flirt—especially if you mean something by it."

How could she? My dearest, wisest friend, accuse me of actually liking someone like Byron? I saw how players like Lord Byron went through women, a different one every weekend all in the name of "hanging out." And those same women pretended not to care, even though they really did. And the guys were getting away with it. Well, I wouldn't let them—not anymore. Not that I was making much of a difference right now. It just felt better than doing nothing. "Look." My hands landed over another cinder block. "If I want to flirt, I'll flirt...as soon as I find a man worthy of it, but this, sweet Lizzie," I set the cinder block down heavily, "does not fall under the same category as flirting."

She nodded with mock grimness. "Yes, things couldn't be more serious."

"I'll give you a lesson on flirting in more peaceful times, but for now—"

"We stop the bad guys, right?" Again, I detected Lizzie's sarcasm, but I decided to ignore it as long as it came with her cooperation.

PRANK WARS

We were down to the last half of the cinder block wall when Tory scrambled up and over the side like a bat from all that was unholy—well, she sported a Batgirl shirt anyway. "What are you waiting for?" she shrieked. The rest of the cinder blocks toppled under her running legs. Her face was red with fury and she flew down the stairs, taking two at a time. By the looks of things, she looked mad enough to fill the guys' bathtub with an entire school of goldfish—maybe their sinks too.

Kali giggled and scampered happily after her. I jerked my thumb after Kali. "Now, *that* girl is flirting." Already Tory and Kali had reached the lawn below and were sprinting as fast as their short legs could carry them to the guys' apartments. I had no idea what they were planning on doing once they got there. "Now Tory, if you notice the stiff set to her shoulders, is *not* flirting. She's in it for the blood. She's also classified as clinically insane, so…"

Lizzie cracked up at that. "And you?" she asked. "Why are you doing this?"

I noticed the trail of mashed potatoes that Kali had left on the stairs. "I'm in it for the food." I leaned over the balcony, cupping my hands over my mouth like a megaphone. "Hey girls, wait! A little strategy is in order here, don't you think? Girls? Hey!"

But Tory wouldn't listen. She had turned into a little dot in the distance. Kali was a bigger dot in the distance, seeing as she couldn't quite keep up with Tory's fury. Kali's pajama bottoms were a burnt orange blur. She was laughing something. I could hear her high-pitched voice from here. They were both goners.

I sighed. Lizzie and I took the stairs at a more sedate pace. Lizzie was right. The tide this war was taking a ridiculous turn. There had to be a better way to get our message across. "We need a new strategy," I said.

Lizzie thought for a moment. "Do you know anyone with a fog machine?"

"Redundant," I said. The guys put one outside our window to make us think our food was burning. It worked, but on the wrong person.

Sandra freaked out. I still couldn't figure out why she hadn't moved yet, and to an apartment that cost twice as much as ours. At least then she'd be happy.

"Well, maybe if we used the fog machine to stage a ghost?"

I laughed outright. The boys weren't *that* stupid. "What we need, Lizzie, is something of theirs they can't bear to live without, something we can bargain with."

"What? Like their hearts?"

I laughed. "No, like a Care bear. Maybe that Tenderheart bear they have as their apartment mascot. And then we'll take pictures with it all over campus…"

But Lizzie wasn't listening. She had stopped on the last stair that led up to our apartment at the top of the complex. I almost bowled her over as two guys walked out of our front door. They were strangers. The one closest to me dressed in a red button-down shirt and retro jeans like he was ready for a night out in the town. My eyes narrowed in suspicion. They had been in our apartment instead. I stepped in front of the guys, blocking their escape. "What do you think you're doing?" I said in a dangerous voice.

I was standing too close to red shirt guy, so close that I could smell his cologne. Was it Hollister? My nose wrinkled. I couldn't let him know that I liked how he smelled or that I thought he was actually attractive. I took a careful step back. He had blond choppy hair and he gave me a considering look with hazel, heavily hooded eyes. It just figured that Byron would send this guy. Any girl in her right mind would let this guy cause all sorts of mischief in her apartment, but I wasn't any girl—or in my right mind. Besides the cologne, the blond smelled of bad boy smoothness mixed with boy-next-door charm—and yes, I'm aware I can't really smell that. He gave me a disarming smile, his gaze trailing to my Lucille Ball pajama bottoms. "Hey."

I crossed my arms. "Poor things. Are you lost? We can show you your way out."

PRANK WARS

The other guy next to him chuckled, though his eyes darted uncomfortably around. This guy was oilier, and thankfully had less charisma. A lot less. And he was a giant. His Dune t-shirt was tucked into high-waisted pleated jeans were a little too short to meet his socks. He stared a little too hard at Lizzie and me, taking in our flushed faces. "Uh, we were just visiting," he said in a voice that was much too quick.

"Sure, right." Visiting? That didn't happen. The oily guy watched me with a knowing look like I was flirting with him. Apparently everyone thought that. I turned to Lizzie, not bothering to keep my voice down. "They're spies."

The beautiful blond laughed appreciatively. "I'm sorry," he said. "What's your name again?" That was the last thing I wanted—for him to know I was Mad Dog, the target he was sent to terrorize.

"I didn't say." I kept my tone nice and formal. "Now tell me who sent you?"

He grinned, most likely to distract me. "Tell me your name and I'll tell you who sent me." He put his hands in the pockets of his worn jeans and leaned back to wait.

I bit my lip. "Madeleine. Now talk."

He hesitated for a mere second. "Eric."

"Yeah, right," I muttered. He bit his lip to keep from laughing and opted to nod instead. He wasn't going to break, so I turned to the oily one instead. "Hey Dune guy? Got a name?"

The guy with the Dune shirt looked a little ill at ease and glanced over at the blond, who just shrugged at him. He turned back to us and gave us a sick smile, which meant he was trying to be charming. "What will you give me if I tell you?"

The flirt thing wasn't working for me. It never did. "Cut the chase. Do you work for Lord Byron or not?"

"Lord Byron?" The two tested the name out like they were trying to wrap their brains around it. They were either amazing actors…or…or…

"Mad Do—uh, Madeleine," Lizzie corrected, trying to get my attention. "I think they might *not* be…uh…spies," she finished in a whisper. They were clearly listening, and they looked amused in a hardened way. The one without a name even seemed a little dangerous. "I've never really seen them before," she whispered.

"Which is exactly why Byron sent them," I explained. "They're probably from one of his classes." At her doubting look, I decided to prove it. "Okay, Eric and *Dune guy*, what did you steal from our apartment, huh? Come clean. It's easiest this way."

Both of them burst out laughing. "Your apartment?" They pointed to our place. "You live there?" I nodded, waiting for the confession. Eric cleared his throat, trying to look solemn. "We didn't do anything. We wouldn't dream of it."

"You sure about that?"

Eric lifted his hands in surrender. His leather watch band slid down his wrist and he took a step closer to me. "Would you like to search me?"

"Certainly not." I stepped back and almost toppled down the stairs. Eric threw his arms around me and dragged me back up, saving me from certain death. My head landed into his muscular shoulder. Yep. Hollister.

He set me back on my feet, pushing me against the railing. "Careful there, tough stuff."

I was sure my face was bright red. No guy had had his arms around me since Cameron. I avoided looking at Lizzie. "Thanks." It killed me to say it. Eric nodded, holding my gaze. There was something in those hazel eyes, well, besides the flecks of gold that a girl could get lost in—um, whatever it was, it completely played with my head. "Look, you…Eric…whatever…you're up to," I managed to get out, "we're not going to let you get away with it."

"Like what?" the oily guy asked with a snicker. "A bomb?"

It was the kind of sick joke I'd expect from one of Lord Byron's men. I straightened. "I don't know, maybe like a fish left in the vents to rot?" Their eyebrows went up, and Eric grinned "Whatever it is, we'll figure it out." My threat lacked its usual oomph, probably because Eric still had my hands.

PRANK WARS

"I'm looking forward to it." He squeezed them and let me go with a wink. Somehow the move worked for him. It made me want to run in a bad way. I rooted myself against the railing, trying not to imagine what Lizzie was thinking. My hands still held his warmth. Eric must've sensed I was nervous because he smiled reassuringly. "We're legit. I work in the chemistry lab at the school. You should come up sometime and I'll test your frequency waves or something."

My what? What was that? Some sort of chemistry pick up line or the ultimate revenge for asking Byron out on a fake date? It was hilarious in a way, since despite the threat, I wanted to go. "You ask all the girls to come to your lab?"

"Nope, just the ones who accuse me of being a spy." He laughed and so did Lizzie.

I shot her a look of betrayal. There was something strange going on. I felt it in my gut. I just had to make sure. "So, Eric, how do you know Lord...uh, Byron?"

"Doesn't everybody?" Ah ha, he just implicated himself—except no, his voice was teasing. The oily guy without a name elbowed Eric in the side. Eric gave him a swift jab back in the ribs that stopped him from...doing what? They were up to something. It was time to get out of here.

"Just tell Byron 'nice try' for me, okay?" My hand landed on our doorknob.

Eric headed down the stairs with a laugh. "And you can tell your friend I don't do anybody's dirty work." The metal stairs squeaked behind him and he glanced back at me to meet my eyes. "I've got enough of my own."

Ooh, clever, he almost got my respect with that...almost. That was until I flung open the doors to see what remained of my living room. The couch cushions were gone. Gone! One moment I was in my apartment, the next moment my eyes were scanning the darkness outside for those double-crossing sneaks. Where did Eric go? I could only hear crickets. How did those guys disappear so fast? "I know you're out there!" My voice echoed in the darkness. "Come out! You're not afraid of a bunch of girls, are you?"

I listened for a snicker, a snapping leaf, anything to give away their location, but they were too sly for that. I peered out into the black night, and saw two silhouettes. They came out from the darkness and flew at me. I stumbled back as they came into color. Tory ran into me. Kali giggled behind her. She wrapped her arms around the both of us in a big bear hug. Tory and I had to fight to get away so we didn't fall.

"So the guys, they were, like, running," Kali shouted loudly into my ear. I squinted at the sound. Tory was still catching her breath behind her, and I could see her eyes roll at Kali's every word. "And we were, like, we can't catch them—'cause they're guys and all and they're fast, ya know! And then Tory was, like, going really fast and she almost caught one. And he had our cushions! Can you believe it?"

"I know," I growled.

Tory straightened. Her 'who' bun flopped over her head. She glanced over at the apartment next door to ours. There was some sort of notice stuck in the door jamb that I had missed because of Eric's visit. "Hey, what's this?" I asked. Before Lizzie could stop me, I ripped the paper away from our neighbor's door. "Is it an eviction notice?"

"In Provo?" Lizzie settled into the camping chair on the balcony, hiding in Sandra's potted garden of flowers. "I don't think so."

"Maybe it was meant to evict the ghosts," Tory said, "because nobody lives there!" She tried to take the note from me, but I was taller. I kept it easily from her.

Kali gave a little squeal of delight. "Hey guys, don't! Don't talk about ghosts! You're freaking me out. Stop!"

I unfolded the notice. I thought I had seen a girl go into the apartment next door once. When did she leave? Lizzie shook her head slowly. "There used to be a time when we knew our neighbors." She swatted at the mosquitoes that gathered by our porch light. "Remember that? When we did things like normal people?"

I held the paper up to our porch light. *"We know where you live,"* I read then laughed. "Apparently not. Amateurs! The guys put this on the wrong door. They're getting sloppy!" Before I could read the rest, I glanced over at Lizzie's pained expression. "Byron sends his worst men and he loses the war. You're only as strong as your weakest man, remember that." Kali smiled airily at me. I tried to ignore that as I read quickly through the threatening note: *"We want what belongs to us. Don't cross us or we're coming after you."*

What had we stolen from Byron lately that would spawn such a note? Shower heads? Light bulbs? A remote control? It could be anything really. Well, the guys could kiss it all goodbye until they returned our couch cushions, and even then it was iffy. It was getting late and I was too tired for negotiations. Lizzie shoved our door open. Kali followed her inside. I crumpled the threatening letter in my hand, trying to distract myself from Eric's cologne. I smelled like him now.

Sandra met me head on at the door. Her gorgeous eyes narrowed dangerously at me. She tapped the heels of her bronze toe-peaks against the cheap linoleum in the entryway. "We're missing something essential from our living room."

I edged past her through the door, which was difficult, since she had only given me an inch between her and the door frame. Tory wriggled through on her other side. "I'll get the cushions back," I promised.

"When?" Sandra snarled. "I had visitors and they couldn't even sit down."

"Wait a second, rewind." I met Lizzie's eyes. They danced with sudden realization. "Did you just say *you* had visitors?"

Sandra looked guarded. She was one of those girls who thought we were out to get her men, but I *wasn't* one of those girls. At least I thought I wasn't. "Yes," she said slowly. "At least one of us isn't a social recluse."

Ouch, except it really didn't hurt. "Was one of your visitors blond with hazel eyes?" *And incredibly attractive?*

"Oh no. What did you do to them?"

I flinched and Lizzie giggled. "Psycho," she mouthed at me. I turned away from her to take a steadying breath. So our little spies were innocent for once? But that made no sense. Eric had flirted with me, hadn't he? Maybe I just thought he had.

Sandra interrupted my inner dialogue, "Tell me who took the cushions!"

"Ask your crazy ex-boyfriend," I muttered. It was a low blow, but I was tired.

Sandra's hands went to the hips of her high-waist skinny jeans; just another sign that designers had no conscience. "What does he have to do with this?"

"Everyone knows he's missing a few crayons in the crayon box."

Sandra's bracelets crashed together when she threw her hands up. "I'm going to get those cushions myself."

"If we knew where they were, they'd be back already." At her belligerent look, I tried to defend myself. "Hey, you don't see *us* complaining about this."

"That's because you don't care!" She accentuated every syllable with an angry, crisp voice. "I'm not getting through to *any* of you, am I?" She sighed loudly and clicked her red nails together. "We need to call another roommate meeting." We all froze. The dreaded roommate meeting. No matter what time of night it was, it was an excuse for Sandra to sit us down and tell us we were crazy.

Tory tapped me on the arm and bobbed her head. "Permission to take my leave, Captain." Without waiting for my reply, she turned tail and deserted us. It was a trick I wished I could get away with.

CHAPTER FIVE

Day 104
1401 hours

"How long would our lives consist of pretending we were normal people in a normal world? We were two great commanders. Byron was cold, hard, calculating, waiting for me to break. And I knew there was no way that was going to happen."

—Madeleine's War Journal Entry (Sunday, May 27th).

"Hey, look at you! You're so big coming to nursery. Hey, no baby, don't cry."

I walked into the nursery room, seeing Byron awkwardly comforting the bishop's sobbing two-year-old daughter. His dark hair was cut James Bond style—well, current James Bond style—the tousled hair that looks like the guy just crawled out of bed style. Byron had tossed the jacket to his pinstriped suit to the side, and his sleeves were rolled up. "Hey, Carrie, c'mon, you're a big girl now. It's not so bad!"

"Oh, smooth." I headed for the nursery cabinet. "What is that, some sort of break-up line?"

He glanced up at me with blue eyes; they were deceptively innocent and they traveled to my mid-calf boots. I didn't care if he had more fashion sense than me. They were perfect for chasing children. I stomped away. "How delightful. It's my other nursery girl," Byron said under his breath. He caught a tear from Carrie's cheek, but they kept coming. She needed a Kleenex in a bad way. She satisfied herself with the front of Byron's cream colored shirt.

I grimaced, not wishing that on my worst enemy, which ironically, he was. I pulled the kid's favorite nursery doll from the toy cabinet and handed it to her while clicking on the mini CD player to the now hauntingly familiar *Snowman* song. Like magic, she quit sobbing. Pulling out tissues like a doctor doing surgery, I gave them to Byron. Unlike some men, he knew what to do with them. He wiped at her nose. "You'd better get yourself too," I said. "The two of you are twins now." He ineffectually wiped away at his shirt front.

Sundays were always interesting. We had been at this for weeks. New callings made strange bedfellows, though I swear the bishop did this to us on purpose. No, he didn't have the kid just to spite us, but he knew about our feud. Everyone in the ward did. Either he thought this joint calling would solve the world's ills, or this was just for his amusement. Whichever way, he won. Carrie gave me a watery smile and I changed my expression from angry to pleasant. Only in a singles' ward would there only be one kid in nursery. It was worse than solitary confinement and it put both Byron and me out of commission, but neither of us ran away from anything. Carrie toddled over to the wall and began slamming her doll against it.

Byron gingerly deposited the soiled tissues into the wastebasket then pulled out his Chapstick. We glanced up at each other. I had unwittingly pulled mine out at the same time and like swords drawn, we applied the Chapstick to our lips, watching the other with narrowed eyes. "And how is my little Miss Demeanor?" Byron slurred.

I gave him a catty smile in return. "I like your shirt. That's an interesting color. Did you vomit then decide to wear it?"

"Yeah, I think it was your cooking."

"That's funny." I twisted my lips. "I don't remember cooking for you—let alone any man."

"Of course not. No man would come within ten feet of you—unless he was a hit man, of course."

PRANK WARS

Carrie stopped slamming her ragdoll against the wall to stare at us, her jaw slacked. Byron's eyes were on mine, not on the poor citizen caught in the crossfire. His lips curled. He got me good. I wondered how long he had been practicing that one. "Alright, cuz," he said. "We should get along…for the sake of the children."

Sure, he wanted to stop now that he had gotten the best of me. I filled Carrie's tiny cup with water. "Okay," I said. "I gave the lesson last week. It's your turn."

He relaxed against one of the tiny pink plastic chairs. "She's two," he argued.

"And she needs to learn about sunshine and rainbows. I'm just dying to know your take on it, professor." After a moment, he sighed and stretched to his feet. Carrie ran back and forth between us. "Oh, and if you can, try to keep her attention," I reminded him.

"That's where you come in," at my rebellious look, he added, "unless you want me to use you as an object lesson, of course?"

After an inner struggle, I found Carrie's doll on the floor and with some difficulty, I readjusted my pencil skirt and sat down, pretending to play with the doll. She quickly came to claim it and I had her. I set her on the plastic chair and she wriggled down to the ground. I put her back and she collapsed to the floor next to me, her belly heaving up and down in her white fluffy dress. "This is the best we're gonna get," I said.

"Good enough." He got to his knees in front of us. "Okay, open your scriptures to…uh…" he smiled playfully, "Isaiah."

We both just stared up at him. "The lesson's on CTR," I said. "Choose the Right. I don't suppose you know anything about that?"

With difficulty, he kept down his amusement. "More than Carrie's other teacher does." Before I could answer, he plowed to his next point. "Okay, you're supposed to choose the right, not the wrong, class, and sometimes it's hard, and sometimes it's not. Think about it. How often do you want to murder someone—except when playing church basketball, of course?"

I stared up at him. *Oh, murder was always a temptation.* I began to wonder who this lesson was meant for anyway. Carrie still lay there, staring up at the ceiling.

"But you bring a girl into it and all of a sudden…okay, get this, David was a nice guy. Look in Second Kings. He played the drums, so that made him pretty cool, right?" Carrie really didn't notice the false doctrine and neither did Byron for that matter. I had a strange feeling that he was trying to get a reaction from me. I tried not to give him one. "But then this female comes along and they're nothing but trouble. You've got Bathsheba and Jezebel and Potiphar's wife. These women are like knives. You never know when they will turn on you."

I gave him a stern look. "Beware of false teachers."

"Beware of wolves in sheep clothing," he said without missing a beat.

I took a deep breath, thinking hard. "Beware of false pride."

"Beware of covetousness."

What? I tried to regain control of the situation. His eyes danced, knowing that I would pull the worst meaning from that. Did he actually think I was jealous of him, or worse, that I wanted to date him? Never! He was a womanizer. I shifted, feeling antsier than Carrie.

Byron turned to her. "The main thing is to not make any mistakes, okay? You never know when *someone* will use them against you and call you up pretending to be someone else to ask you out." I groaned. Byron's favorite thing to do lately was parroting that terrible phone call that initiated this war so long ago. "It's like this, Carrie," he said. She tugged on her shoe. "This woman I know is purposely trying to drive me—" he paused, watching her kick the shoe away.

"—crazy," I finished impatiently.

Byron glanced at me. "You keep doing that."

"What?"

"You keep finishing my—" he looked down at his fingernails.

"—sentences," I said. "And I wouldn't if you didn't talk so slow."

PRANK WARS

"This girl I know is so prideful," he told the two-year-old. "She could fill the great and spacious building with it." Carrie bobbed her head, her red curls bouncing, not really knowing what she was agreeing to. "And she asked me out first. She was the one who got *my* hopes up."

"Don't believe him," I inserted.

"Why? An attractive sounding girl calls me up and wants to go out? And then she destroys my hopes by saying, 'just kidding?'"

"Excuse me?" I took a deep breath, realizing that I was letting him get to me again. Admittedly, it was the worst thing that I had done for a prank, but there was no way I'd back out now. "You should just forget this girl who called you, Byron. She sounds bossy and weird. She was making *la la la* noises behind you in chemistry. Totally stalker material. How is that even remotely attractive?"

"At least her heart wasn't closed off to men—like other girls I know."

My blood raced at the accusation. "Yeah, but that girl was only after money. She wanted you take her on an expensive date! How high maintenance can she get? And besides, you've done worse things. Look at my hair!"

He leaned back, studying me and I could just imagine what he was seeing, some crazy girl with white in her hair. I tried not to flinch at his penetrating look. "It's cute, but you can't blame that on me. It's called getting on in years."

My eyes narrowed. "You stole my phone and put the wrong names on the numbers. I sent a text about Sandra *to Sandra*."

"Yeah, but have I ever made you think you actually had a chance with me then dashed your hopes cruelly?"

I hesitated. If I said yes, I'd be confessing a crush, if no then he would look like the better person. I tugged my gray skirt over my knees and scooted back to Carrie. "Don't even try to make me feel guilty."

He cocked an eyebrow at me. "It's called choose the right. Our lesson for today."

"Does that also mean no stealing?" I retorted. Carrie tried to escape the lesson, but I held her doll firmly. Byron's lips curled at that and he gave me a single and dangerous nod. "Then I can only assume you took our cushions to clean them?" I asked.

"What cushions?"

Ah, so he was playing that game, was he? "Give them back and then we'll discuss returning the item that belongs to *you*."

"And what would that be exactly?" He found Carrie's treats and peeled open the bag of graham crackers. I had a sneaking suspicion they were for him.

"Why don't you tell me and that way, we'll both know," I said.

"You're the one who took it, so you tell me." He pulled out a graham cracker.

I stole it from him with an ironic smile and gave it to Carrie, who slobbered gratefully over it. "You're the one who gave us the threatening letter," I reminded him. "So you tell me."

"What letter?"

"The one you put on the wrong door. Who did you send on that operation anyway, a complete amateur? You *chose the wrong*. CTW."

His voice turned serious. "Whose door?"

"The door where nobody lives." He still looked blank. "The apartment next to mine?" At his perplexed expression, I pointed to my side as if we were standing outside my place. "To our right? I thought someone lived there, but Lizzie says no. And I have no idea what we have of yours anyway. To be honest, it could be anything."

"Oh, so you have more than one thing of ours, do you?"

I laughed. He wanted everything we took from him? Now he was getting selfish. "Beware of greed, Byron. Consider this our negotiations. You can take it or leave it."

"Beware of secret combinations." But Byron said it without his usual oomph. He seemed to be deep in thought. "Thank you for being the example for our lesson this week, Mad. Can I see that letter?" He said it too quickly.

PRANK WARS

"No. We want those cushions back. I have a roommate who happens to be really mad that we can't sit down in our living room. And I think you know she's the type to do something about it."

He nodded absentmindedly. "I'll find you your cushions if...if you give me that letter." He wasn't making any sense. "Yeah, so...I can frame it." Byron absentmindedly stole a graham cracker off the plastic table.

"That's Carrie's."

"She's not eating it."

I waited for him to put it in his mouth; as soon as he did, I smiled. "Well, she *has* been sucking on it for a while now. I hope she got it nice and soft for you."

Carrie sniffed and wiped at her running nose. Byron gulped the cracker down with some difficulty. "We got a deal, right?"

I watched him suspiciously. He wanted the threat letter? "What about that other thing you wanted?"

Before he could answer, the door opened and AmyLee marched briskly into the nursery, swinging a brown scripture case in her hands. She was armed. Both Byron and I pulled subconsciously back from her. Angry little AmyLee. Her fists tightened on a sign-up sheet she held. She glared at me. The girl still hated me for helping her. She was supposed to get her ex back, and she did...with my interference. No problem. But then instead of dumping the guy like she was supposed to, she dragged her heels and he dumped her for the second time. And guess who she blamed—not the man who made a fool of her for the second time, not herself for disobeying orders, not her mom for bringing her into this cold, uncaring world. No, she blamed me. I guess it made sense.

AmyLee turned from me and shot a broad smile at Byron. It was meant to make me jealous—except why should I care if she got together with my worst enemy? It would be a fitting end for them both. "Why hello, Byron." She waved at the comatose Carrie. The kid was back on the ground, watching the ceiling with dreamy eyes. "You're such a cutie pie! How old are you now, honey, huh?"

Carrie pulled her wet fingers from her mouth to hold them up. According to her, she was five…and after we had taught her to CTR even. "Um, five fingers mean two in kid numbers," I informed AmyLee.

AmyLee put her nose up like I hadn't said anything.

Byron slanted a devilish look at me. "And just how old are you, pumpkin?" he asked me. I shook my head. He wouldn't get that information out of me without torturing me first. "Do you have that many fingers?" he asked.

I threw Carrie's ragdoll at him and it bounced off his shoulder. That brought AmyLee's rage down on me. "Did you really?" Without waiting for my reply, she turned to Byron. He was rubbing his arm. "Is this how nursery usually goes?"

He sighed deeply. It was entirely for my benefit. My lip curled and I tried not to smile, since that's what he was aiming for. "This too shall pass," he said.

AmyLee's face twisted into concern. "Well, I hope this helps." She handed him the scriptures, making a production out of it like she wanted me to care. "You left them in my car, Byron."

Her car, huh? My eyebrow sketched upward. Her turquoise skirt swayed prettily. It was too short so she compensated with black leggings. The ensemble didn't work, so why would the fashion conscious Byron go after her? He didn't even like my boots. Byron turned the scriptures over in one hand like he was palming a basketball. "Thank you for being so honest, AmyLee. Not many people would return such an item."

She giggled too loudly. "Like I'm going to steal your scriptures, funny."

I eyed the brown scripture case. "Well, they do look like an ugly purse."

AmyLee's face scrunched in what was supposed to be a glare. Byron's eyes darted from me to her then he cleared his throat. "You want to steal them, Mad? Go ahead. You need a little religion in your life."

AmyLee barked out a laugh. "You are too funny." She hit Byron on the arm, crumpling up the piece of paper she was holding between them.

PRANK WARS

Whether the women loved him or hated him, the poor boy always got beat-up. "Oh, I almost forgot." She threw the sign-up sheet at him. It almost hit him in the face. He winced. "This is for you. It's this funny thing that the stake came up with…a boyfriend for a week program. Isn't that great?"

No! I ripped it out of Byron's hands. "What unholy…?"

Byron purposely misinterpreted my actions as eagerness. He clapped me on the back, his hand lingering there. "Here's your chance. You can get yourself a temporary boyfriend, Mad Dog. Congratulations!"

I pushed him off. "What were they thinking?"

"Whatever." AmyLee's face pinched with heat. It was the unwritten rule that if I didn't like it, she would. "It's your fault anyway, *Mad Dog*. The stake thinks we need more social interaction. *Somehow* they think that some of us are severely underdeveloped socially. I don't know where they would get that idea. Do you?" Her voice held too much condescension for my taste.

Byron stole the sheet back from me. "Hmmm, so do we get to choose the victim…ur, the…lucky girl that will be our ball and chain for a week?"

AmyLee practically simpered, imagining that Byron was referring to her, but he was just trying to threaten me. I swiped my finger in a cutting motion under my chin as a warning, but I changed it to a scratch when AmyLee glanced over. I didn't want her to know how she could get me back. "No, it's completely random," she said. "We pull names out of a hat. It's going to be so much fun."

Byron pulled a pen out of his pocket. It had a spoon taped to it. One of those things you had in your possession only if you stole it from a bank. Was he really going to do this? I tried to relax. As long as I didn't sign up for it, it was none of my affair. He signed it and passed it onto me. "Knock yourself out."

"Not interested." Before I could pass it off, I noticed that instead of his name, Byron had written mine. I held my hand out for the stolen bank pen. Byron refused to give it to me so I could cross my name out…and write his name in for good measure. "AmyLee," I tried to keep the panic from my voice. "I need your pen, please."

She hid it behind her back. "I don't have one."

"I'll just take the one behind your back, AmyLee. AmyLee? C'mon, just give it to me."

She laughed, swinging her beautiful hair. "It doesn't work. Sorry."

What was I supposed to do—tackle one of them? AmyLee was weaker, but it probably wasn't very socially acceptable. "Oh, well, in that case." I ripped my name off the paper. It was towards the bottom anyway. AmyLee cried out angrily. I handed the sign-up sheet back to her. "Here you go."

She puffed her lips out angrily. "Thanks a lot."

"No, thank-you for the use of your pen."

AmyLee glanced over at Byron, looking for sympathy. She shouldn't have wasted her time. He was incapable of that. "Can you believe her?" she whined.

"No," he finally got out.

"If you need anyone to talk to, Byron…if this gets too hard, just you and her alone with that child, you know you can come to me. I know what you're going through. I really do."

"Hey," I interrupted. "Um, since I ripped Byron's name off that sheet, you can just write it back on there. You know if you really want to help him out and…"

AmyLee slammed the door before I could finish. I could hear her platform booties storming down the tiled floor to Relief Society. For once I was glad I was in nursery. "I guess I was wrong," Byron told Carrie. "Girls aren't like knives at all. They're sweet, demure little creatures." I crumpled the piece of paper with my name on it and threw it in the trash can one-handed. "You know, Madeleine, I've been thinking." My eyes narrowed. He never used my real name. It got my attention, my suspicious attention. "Why can't we just get along?" I listened to the hall outside fill with people. Talking and laughter echoed into our little room. Classes must be out. That was one thing about this new calling. Time sped by faster than it ever had for church. "Oh, don't worry," he said. "Just for two weeks. We'll call it our civil month. And have a big celebration in the end. We'll invite all of our…uh…soldiers. Give 'em a break from the big war."

Considering how everything he did was a trick, it would most likely end up being a civil war instead. Whatever he was planning, he'd turn it on me. I smiled. "Sounds like the makings of the perfect chick flick."

Byron leaned back against a pink chair. "I suppose you consider me the villain?"

I stood up, putting away Carrie's toys. "Not you. That would make you too interesting. You'd probably be the annoying player the heroine hates and then she grows to like because he's hot. I'm sure they break up once the credits finish rolling."

Byron smiled faintly. "You think I'm hot?" I choked. Why wasn't Carrie's mom back from classes yet? I wasn't doing very well in the war of words this week. "You know what's wrong here?" Now Byron was talking to the little girl as if she'd understand what he was saying. I hoped it wouldn't have anything to do with me, but it was a vain hope. "Madeleine's beautiful. She just doesn't know how to work it."

My mouth dropped. "Excuse me?" He glanced back at me as if he were shocked that I had eavesdropped on his conversation. "I…," but I wasn't sure how to respond. "I do too." My cheeks flamed at Byron's sudden laugh. Great. Now I was vain.

Carrie tired of watching us and started pawing through the toys. She threw them through the air like they were fireworks on the Fourth of July. We were both supposed to keep an eye on her, but I felt Byron's eyes on me instead. I finally turned to him and wished I hadn't. He had a serious expression on his face. "Then why don't you work it?" He tilted his head at me. "Does it hurt to feel, Mad? C'mon, you can tell me. What happened to you?"

How dare he throw this psychological warfare at me? "What happened to *you*!" I sputtered back.

"I asked first. Who left you at the altar?"

I went rigid. He thought he was being sarcastic, but he hit it dead on. Next month was the date Cameron and I had set for the temple, June 6th to be exact—in two weeks. "No one you need be concerned with." I was proud of how smooth I sounded.

"Fine, nothing happened to you, but hypothetically speaking, let's say it did? Let's discuss this bubble you have." He made this huge sweeping motion about two feet in front of me. Byron was obsessed with my personal space.

"I'd rather not."

"Okay, we'll just test it." Byron stepped into my bubble. I steeled myself, but forced myself to stay put. I wasn't about to let Byron prove his point. He tapped my arm experimentally like he was some kind of doctor testing my reflexes. "So?" he asked.

"Pretty annoying, but you're not popping my bubble or anyth—" He tapped me on the top of my head, and I laughed. I tried to stop it by wrinkling my nose. This was ridiculous. "Nope. My bubble isn't as bad as you think."

His eyes took on a mischievous glint and he glanced over at Carrie. "Hey Carrie, watch this. I have the force." Byron licked his hand and brought it towards my face.

I scrambled backwards without him having to touch me. "Not cute and not funny," I shouted out.

"What? I wasn't going to do anything. Where's your trust? Do you really hate men that much?"

"What gave you that impression? I just hate *you*." It came out before I could stop it. And of course he leaned closer to me, flashing an infectious grin. I wondered how many women it worked on.

"You aren't hurting me, you know. You're only hurting the Beta Unit."

I snickered. "You are such a nerd and you are so dead. Your place is so dead."

"What's that supposed to mean?"

PRANK WARS

I glanced over at Carrie. "Would anyone like to volunteer their neighbor to pray?   Maybe they can ask for forgiveness—perhaps some protection. They're going to need it when someone trashes their place this week."

Byron had that devilish look. He opened his mouth, but the door opened, saving us all. Carrie brightened when she saw her mother. I brightened too. Her mother had curly blonde hair and a maternal way about her. She held her arms open and Carrie ran into the pink cashmere depths. I stopped myself from following Carrie's example. Where was *my* mother when I needed her? "How was she?" the bishop's wife asked.

"She was really—" Byron stopped, looking at something behind her head.

"—good," I finished without thinking. I avoided Byron's eyes.

Carrie's mom began gathering her things. "Did you have fun, Carrie?" She clucked over her, smoothing down the little girl's hair. "I'm so glad you have such great teachers. I bet you just love them, don't you?"

At her mother's bidding, Carrie waved goodbye. We both waved back like we were the happiest, most untroubled couple in the world. "You know why you finish my sentences?" Byron asked me under his breath.

I tried to ignore him. I really didn't know myself, so how was I supposed to give a satisfactory answer? The door shut behind the mother and daughter and they left us alone together. Byron was still looking at me. I looked everywhere but at him. Finally, I took a deep breath. "Why?" What's your amazing theory?"

"Because maybe," Byron paused for dramatic effect, "we know each other so well that we're actually friends."

I turned slowly to him, shocked. A dimple showed briefly in his cheek before he gathered his pinstriped jacket and walked out of the room.

CHAPTER SIX

Day 104
1604 hours

"In case you read this, all's fair in love and war. The only way to fight fire with fire is to play with fire. It would be the perfect ending to this thing."

—Madeleine's War Journal Entry (Sunday, May 27th).

What was Byron thinking anyway, throwing words like friendship at me? He took playing dirty to a new level. After leaving the nursery room without so much as a backwards glance, I shoved my way through the hordes of student churchgoers. The 73rd ward went to church in the testing center. Many had done it before me and many would after me. It was the least of my concerns. No, I was trying to escape before I saw *him*. And this time, I'm not talking Lord Byron.

The crowd parted just in time to see *him* flirting up a storm with no other than AmyLee, and of course Erika and Johanna and Mickaela. Even Kali! Before I could bolt, I hesitated. My little roommate threw back her blonde hair in a joyous belly laugh.

Everything *he* said was absolutely hilarious…uh, *he* being my ex-fiancé. Cameron even looked hilarious in a mint colored shirt. And yes, I am just being mean, but he started it. What made Cameron think it would be a great idea to move into my ward after the break-up? We had the cheapest housing in Provo, but who does that? It only proved he was a lowdown and mean.

PRANK WARS

Kali hit Cameron, and he playfully hit her back. Then she hit him, and then he hit her. Her peasant skirt fluttered sassily. I sighed, excusing her. There is an unwritten rule for roommates not to flirt with their roommate's significant ex, especially when that roommate was in the same room, but Kali was too in denial to know it referred to her. She wasn't flirting, she was being his *friend*.

Cameron, on the other hand, was an entirely different story. He knew exactly what he was doing to me. His eyes slanted my direction then quickly darted away when he noted I was in the room. His flirtatious teasing got louder. Ever since he broke up with me, he had been adding new girls to his Facebook daily. And these were the kinds that put glamor shots on their profiles. AmyLee tugged Cameron forward by his burnt-orange fat tie, chattering like a chipmunk.

I turned on the heel of my boots, trying to escape—and got caught by President Wilkes. He always tried to make sure I knew how wonderful I was. Probably because he saw how successful Cameron was at the flirting game and how unsuccessful I was. He grabbed my hand to shake it. "How is my favorite girl? You are so great. Do you know that?" Yes, yes, I had heard it already, but I knew the truth and just wanted to escape the room. I nodded, so he wouldn't know I was falling apart. Kali twisted the big turquoise ring on her hand while she listened intently to Cameron. I tried to block them out, but when I couldn't see him, he just made himself louder. So did the girls around him.

I thought I had been a good girlfriend. In fact, I had been nicer than I had ever been in my entire life. Talk about exhausting. And this is how the guy repaid me? He was through with me, so be through with me already. The glass doors were so close, within spitting distance, but I was stuck here by my hand. The stake president shook it meaningfully, peering into my eyes. I hoped he wouldn't find anything too disturbing there. "It's so nice to see you. You seem to be holding up well."

Yes, after the incident. I grimaced. President Wilkes had my back, which normally I could appreciate if I hadn't been stuck in the middle of this flirt fest. If Tory were around, she would create a diversion to help me slip by unnoticed, but I didn't see her agitated red head anywhere. I caught a glimpse of Lizzie. She had kicked off her Mary-Janes and was dutifully cleaning up after the Relief Society in the side room.

"Now I suppose you heard about our program to help you kids start meeting new people?" President Wilkes asked.

I nodded. "Yeah, boyfriend for a week. Sounds a little…uh…interesting."

"Now, don't worry. It's nothing too serious. We just want the guys to take the girls out, show the girls around town, be gentlemen. And if the girls could show them that they're not…all that scary," he laughed, "we could establish some good dating habits in this stake. I would really appreciate your support in this."

I gulped. If I asked, 'in what way,' I'd be signed up for boyfriend-for-a-week before we could unclasp hands. If I just nodded and said, 'Yes, of course,' which was my plan then he'd never know *exactly* how I planned to support this and I'd be home free. "Yes, of course," I said.

President Wilkes let me go. He patted me on the back for good measure. "I sure do appreciate you. Whether you know it or not, you're a leader in this ward. The others really look up to you. You're a good example."

"Thanks." I turned, feeling a little guilty, and resolved to sign up for the next service project…just not this one. Judging by the sounds of laughter, Cameron was to my left. I took the safest route to the door through the crowd of guys who didn't know I existed, past the chattering girls. I waved goodbye to Lizzie who didn't see me and stopped short, not believing who stood in front of the door. Nope. Eric. The beautiful blond from the night before.

I was in a lot of guys' black books lately, but I had *really* made a fool of myself in front of this one. How did I not notice Eric was in my ward? He was beautiful. He wore a sweater vest, looking like a hot Mr. Rogers. He seemed taller than last night, but that was probably because that leering scary Dune guy wasn't around. A quick sweeping glance assured me Dune guy wasn't in our ward too.

PRANK WARS

I tried to retreat, but too late, Eric saw me. I changed directions almost like a dance, heading for him again so he wouldn't guess I was a baby. Eric's face took on a wary expression. I hadn't been the sanest person last night. Braving a smile, I tried to scrape past him through the door. "Hey Eric." I was proud of how casual I sounded. "Uh, sorry about accusing you of stealing." He didn't answer back and I met his eyes. "It's just that it wouldn't be the first time that…our uh friend, Byron sent others to do his dirty work. One time these girls told us they saw something creepy outside." Now I knew I was babbling. "They were just trying to get us to leave our apartment, so—"

"Wait." He was smiling faintly. "So you're saying that these girls like this Byron jerk, so they help him flirt with you?"

My forehead wrinkled at Eric. Fascinating. He was actually very perceptive. Sort of. "Um, no. *He's* not flirting," I corrected. No, that was the one thing I liked about Byron. We understood each other. I stepped outside into the overcast world, and Eric followed me. "I'm not flirting either," I said. "You can catch a man that way, you know."

Eric surprised me by laughing. "You look so dark and mysterious, and then you open your mouth and it's gone."

Was that an insult or…? I decided to give him the benefit of the doubt, since I accused him of being a spy last night. "Thank you."

His eyes danced. "No, it's just that you're very unexpected." I frowned and he grabbed my arm reassuringly. His warmth sent happy shivers through me. "Actually, I think you're perfect. It's like watching a movie."

I wasn't sure how to take that, but I felt I owed him a second chance, a million chances actually, since I had misjudged him—or maybe because I felt some strange attraction to him. It meant I should probably end this conversation before I looked even stupider. "Well, until the next exciting adventure." I pulled away and bounded down the stairs.

"When will that be?"

"You never know." I realized I was moon walking in my attempt not to look like I was running away. "The craziest things happen around here."

He smiled, a real nice guy smile, and it threw me off. "I'll remember that the next time I visit."

"Sandra would like that," I shouted out to him. It was important to put some distance between us. Naming the competition always did that. His eyes didn't leave mine, and I twisted away to break the contact.

"What about you?" he asked suddenly.

My mouth flopped open. Treat a guy like he had the plague and…and…was he actually being nice to me? The glass door next to Eric opened and Cameron piled through with a few women on each arm. No exaggeration. Cameron sidestepped me like I was a pebble on the ground, not even dignifying my presence with a nod. I couldn't help but see the difference. Treat a guy like an all-star and he kicked you to the gutter.

Eric followed my gaze to Cameron. Maybe he *was* a spy. He was certainly observant. Eric's mouth curled up as if guessing my dilemma. If I left him now, I would be trailing Cameron down the hill. I took a step towards Eric, not sure if it was the right decision.

Tory came out of nowhere, a bright spot in a colorful retro dress. "I thought I'd never catch you." She pushed the threatening letter into my hand from the night before. Her face was flushed from running. "No luck, Captain. I did a thorough handwriting analysis. I checked every guy's signature in the ward. No one matched up."

"Every guys'?"

Tory glanced up at Eric's question and her eyes narrowed. I flushed. It was one thing acting like a deranged psychopath, quite another getting caught. Tory teetered on the toes of her orange flats. "No, not *every* guys' handwriting."

"This is Eric," I told her. Tory nodded. The suspicion in her expression didn't change. Before she demanded a handwriting sample…or his fingerprints, I intervened, "Don't worry Tory, he's not our guy."

PRANK WARS

Eric grinned widely now and I cursed myself for coming back to him so he could witness my *movie-like* behavior. My cell phone went off, but instead of the familiar ringtone, *I'm too Sexy* came on. It had to be Byron's doing. A genuine smile curved my lips. Byron was on the other line. Well, it was his roommate's phone. He knew better than to call us with his own. Everyone knew I had *Unmask* on my cell. It was just like *trapcall,* but a million times better. It was essential for prank wars and unblocked any blocked call or private number. Byron was onto me though. Ever since he upgraded to an iPhone, he fastidiously refused to let his number fall into enemy hands. My only hope was stealing his number from some girl's contact list. I flipped open my pink camouflage cell, and answered his call. "What?" I knew exactly what.

"Move your stupid car."

I smiled. "What's the matter? You can't get out? Too bad, Byron. Learn how to un-parallel park."

CHAPTER SEVEN

Day 105
2102 hours

"The debates rage around me as we stand over the plotting tables, ready to launch another attack. I'm not talking about Anbesol on toothbrushes to make your mouth numb and Methylene blue. We were beyond that. Long gone were the days of waking up with fake snakes, cold pop cans, and powdered sugar hidden in our beds, except now we were out of ideas."

—Madeleine's War Journal Entry (Monday, May 28th).

"How about we toilet paper them?" Kali suggested.

"Really? Did you really just say toilet paper them?" I paced, my hands resting on my black yoga pants. This wasn't the usual Monday night activity after FHE, but since the guys' assault on us over the weekend; we were in a state of emergency. "That's so…normal."

Kali munched on a huge bar of chocolate, lounging on a green striped couch. It was the exact duplicate of our own next door, except cleaner.

After Lizzie declared the apartment next door empty, we claimed it as our headquarters. Sandra wanted us out of her hair, and I wanted out of her hair. The only one who had a problem with the new headquarters was…yup, Lizzie. She took a deep breath, staring out the window just waiting for us to get caught. The guys would never suspect where we were hiding if she didn't keep fiddling with the curtain. "I shouldn't have told you that no one lives here," she said. "We could get in trouble for this."

I didn't look at her. "No way. Mike gave us the keys for a reason." Never mind our landlord gave us the ring of keys to the entire apartment complex in case of an emergency, but there were benefits to having a landlord who didn't care what we did. "It's called house-sitting. I know people who get paid for this."

Kali gulped down her chocolate. Why it didn't go straight to her hips was a mystery. She raised her hand. "Oh, oh, I know! Let's frost cupcakes with dirt, so they think they're covered in Oreos."

No. Cotton balls dipped in chocolate, caramel onions, and worms in Jell-O were our usual signature; they'd see through it. "You think this is Relief Society, Kali?" I rolled the batteries from the guys' remote control through my fingers, thinking. We needed an insider's view, and I turned to Tory.

"Okay." She took her hands out of her cargo pockets. "It might sound desperate, but what about…a snowball! I've been saving it in the freezer for months. It's crazy, but it just might work."

I laughed. "What? You want the cops on us?" Everyone knew snowballs were illegal in Provo. I chewed on my tongue, trying to think of something that wouldn't land us in the slammer, even for a few hours. "He doesn't like bad fashion," I said. "What if we fill his dresser with nineties clothes from DI? It's his Achilles heel."

"Really?" Lizzie's flip flops smacked against her heels when she pulled away from the window. "I thought *you* were his Achilles heel."

"If that were true, I would've used that by now." I sighed. We could just avoid all this and give Byron the letter, but the request made no sense. No, he had to have something up his slick sleeves. Why would he exchange the cushions for his own threatening letter? I reread it: *"We know where you live. We want what belongs to us. Don't cross us or we're coming after you."*

But what did Byron want? We already had our decoders on it, well, Tory. I tried to decipher the message myself, but gave up and raked my hand through my hair. "I don't get it." It wasn't often the hostiles had me stumped. "Maybe we should set up some baby monitors?" I spread the map of the guys' apartment complex over the empty living room table. Our new headquarters were a mirror image of our living room next door, only everything was bare. It was like being in another dimension.

"You got a map of the hunk house?" Kali asked. By now she was texting madly, her oversized jewels a blur as her fingers flew over the keys.

"Bunkhouse," I corrected.

"I wouldn't call it that."

"No, you wouldn't." My mind kept wandering back to Byron. He said he wanted to be friends. What did he really mean by that? He mentioned having a party during our civil week. Why? I squinted at the map. "Kali? Do you have a calendar?"

"Nope." She unwrapped another candy bar.

"Tory? Tory?" She had wandered off. I was beginning to crack.

"Wait," Lizzie said. "I have one. She rummaged through her huge monster of a purse and pulled out a mini calendar. I scanned the end of May. There was nothing there. I tried the beginning of June. Besides being the month of birds and bees and love, and my ex wedding date, and all that, why wouldn't he want us to ruin it for him with our prank wars? There was the boyfriend-for-a-week coming up, which he didn't care about. And then…*Battle of the Bands*. That was next week. His band was performing. Still, we'd never stoop to destroying him publicly. Did he just want the extra time to practice? It seemed so trivial. And then this letter? Why would he want it in return for the cushions? "Lizzie," I whispered. "Is there anything unusual about this letter?"

She stretched tiredly. "The paper is normal. The handwriting is foreign. The message is completely cryptic."

"They give us a cryptic message…and they don't want us to figure it out?" I think I was getting somewhere with this. "Well, let's give them a message that's just as confusing as theirs." Kali raised her hand with a jingle of bracelets. We stared at her. She didn't talk, so I called on her, "Yes?"

"How about we deliver the love tree?"

Lizzie sighed. "Well, that would make Sandra happy." The love tree was an ugly, wilted plant haunting our kitchen. We aptly dubbed it the love tree, since it was dying—just like all our love lives.

"That's perfect, Kali," I said. "We'll send them a message they'll never forget. Tomorrow night during ward prayer. Instead of trashing their place, we make their apartment the prettiest thing they have *ever* seen."

Kali giggled. "What? Like a girls' place?"

"They already have our pretty little cushions. Let's just complete the look. Just act casual at ward prayer tomorrow like we're through with this prank war." The bishop had moved ward prayer to Tuesdays, which was a brilliant way to ensure we kept the Sabbath. Ward prayer was good for a great many things, distraction being one of them. And then we'd sneak out after announcements and make Byron's place unrecognizable. I crumpled the paper in my hands solely for the drama of it, plus it made Lizzie's eyes widen, which was also fun. Then I stuck it in my pocket. "Let's make a list of demands, shall we? We'll sign it *unsincerely, uncordially, thankfully, not yours*, the black hole." I laughed at their looks of confusion. "Oh, you didn't know? That's what they call our apartment complex. No one goes in. No one gets taken out."

"And then this ends it?" Lizzie asked hopefully.

I hesitated. The love tree was a terribly stupid campaign, which was why I liked it, but would it really stop Byron? Lizzie was waiting, so I nodded at her. "Yeah, he stops. We stop."

Kali jumped up, interrupting Lizzie's protests. "I know just the stuff to decorate their place with. We need curtains, beautiful curtains...and, and frilly lamps. I hate my lamp. It's perfect. Oh, and anything pink! And doilies! Yeah!"

Lizzie's mouth curled up unwillingly.

"Hey, wait." I held up my hands. "Where are we supposed to get all that stuff this late in the game? Doilies? Do any of us own those?"

"Wait." Lizzie went through her purse and we all gawked at her. She tugged out band aids, tweezers, books, random pieces of string, a glove, and…a doily? Before I knew it, the girls had left the apartment to collect the most beautiful girly things they could find, laughing and chattering on their way.

"Don't forget any ugly stuffed animals you might have!" I called after them. My voice echoed through the empty room. They left the door open behind them and I could see the twilight settling in the soft sky. We were due for some powerful May showers. The clouds hung darkly overhead and for once, I realized just how dark this room could get. Normally, I would turn on the lights, but I was afraid it would alert outsiders to our presence in the abandoned apartment.

I gathered my things from the table. A soft wind pulled at the door and the hinges creaked. I watched the open door swing lazily back and forth. The sound set my nerves on edge and I worked faster, using the light from the outside porch to see my things. It lit the room in an eerie glow. I was beginning to wonder if using the empty apartment as our headquarters was such a good idea when I became aware of a soft scratching coming from the back of the apartment. I stiffened. The hairs on the back of my neck prickled uncomfortably. I wasn't alone in here. A normal person would run. A sane person would run. I mean, the ones who didn't run usually got killed in every movie I had ever seen. I gulped and listened to the scratching get louder. I took a step into the dark hall. "Hello?"

The scratching stopped.

I took a steadying breath. This was ridiculous. It had to be an animal, possibly a rat? I shivered and took a step away from the sound. There was no way I wanted a rat lunging at me from the darkness.

"Help me." It was a whisper, so soft that I almost thought I had imagined it.

PRANK WARS

Wasn't this place empty? Both Tory and Lizzie swore that we had chased our neighbors away, but that didn't stop me from remembering a tiny girl with black hair coming in late one night. Was that during my watch? I had pulled an all-nighter cramming for a test when I heard the sound of a key scraping into the lock next door. Time seemed suspended during this prank war, but was I really *that* out of it? It couldn't have been that long ago. My neighbor was only a memory now. If she hadn't moved from here, what had happened to her? I thought of the threatening note we had found jammed into her door. Maybe it wasn't meant for us. Was it even from Byron?

"Help me." This time it was louder. It was definitely human, at the same time not, like I was hearing some sort of echo from the past.

Stop that. What a completely idiotic notion. "Who is that?" I croaked out.

The scratching started again and I took a deep breath, steeling myself. Whatever it was, I couldn't run like some scared little girl. No way. Not when Lord Byron could catch wind of it. I had always wondered what was going through the minds of potential slasher victims. Whatever possessed them to go investigate? Well, now I knew why. Pride. Plain and simple.

The sound was coming from one of the rooms. If it was our apartment on the other side, the room would've been mine. How ironic. Taking a deep breath, I sternly told myself to open the door. The handle twisted easily under my fingers, and I jerked it open. It was dark inside. I quickly flipped on the light to peer around. There were two mismatched beds. One consisted of a blue flowered mattress stacked on cinder blocks. The other lay flat on the dingy brown carpet. There was no way I was supposed to be here, but still I stepped inside the room.

The scratching had stopped. Yet, it had come from here. I turned a full circle, searching for anything. A forgotten clock that scratched out time, a CD player left on a crackly AM station, an air-conditioner pounding its way on, but there was nothing here that could've made such a noise. By now, it was completely dark outside. I could see the ominous clouds through the metal screen at the window. Everything inside me told me to run. And for once I decided to listen. I turned to escape and ran into the closet door. "Ouch," I hissed in pain. I crumpled to the ground, holding my leg, trying not to look directly at that nasty closet. I'm not quite sure how to describe the horrible thing, but let's just say that the closets in our complex had the creepiest doors ever. They reminded me of the closets found in every scary remake of Japanese horror movies. The flimsy wood could've been made of paper, it was so fragile. I could almost imagine what was behind it—and how easily it could get out. What had the little girl with the black hair left in there for me to find? No one had seen her. For how long had she been missing? What if I opened it…and she was in there?

I scrambled to my feet. That was it. I didn't care if anyone saw me now. I made a dash for the door and froze when I heard it. A long scratch. It trailed from the top of the closet to the bottom, slowly, like a long fingernail dragging painfully on the other side of the door, sounding worse than against a chalkboard. My heart beat rapidly, but instead of running like I told myself, I wrapped my hand over the handle of the closet door. I knew I shouldn't. I knew I *really really* shouldn't, especially when I ripped the door open and saw two eyes staring back at me.

I screamed.

Tory screamed.

I screamed and hit her.

She doubled over laughing.

"How could you!" I shouted, but I was too busy laughing at myself. For some reason, Tory felt it was her duty to keep me on my toes with scary exercises like these. "Oh." I took a shaky breath. "Save it for the enemy, Tory! What were you thinking?"

Tory couldn't answer. She held her stomach, her red hair escaping from her black hoody. No wonder I had a streak of white hair. It was shell shock from all the time spent with these crazies. One thing was for certain: Tory kept my reflexes catlike in times of war. I just wasn't sure how I'd survive it.

CHAPTER EIGHT

Day 106
1856 hours

"I was a true revolutionary. I couldn't live in a place where wrong overcame right and darkness defeated the light. Nothing felt as it should be. And yet, the winds of change hung on the precipice of my life. I could feel it."

—Madeleine's War Journal Entry (Tuesday, May 29th).

Cameron cuddled with his latest fling on the couch near the entryway. Another beautiful blonde with orange skin and indeterminate color of eyes. He gave her a quick squeeze before letting her go. His thick leather wristband slid across her cheek. "Thank you," he told her in a low whisper, "for letting me use you."

She giggled. I frowned. I was caught between the doorway and the hallway on my way to ward prayer. Not only had the bishop changed the meeting to Tuesday nights, but he had also decided to hold it at the Dog House, and it truly was. This was where my ex resided. Normally, I would never trespass these unhallowed halls, except for one sweet thing, revenge.

The winter cold was having a hard time letting us go this spring. Rain mixed with sleet misted the night air outside. I checked the time on my cell phone. Ward prayer started in less than five minutes. Maybe if I gave Cameron and this girl until then, they'd clear out...but why did he do this at the door before ward prayer started? If I didn't know better, I'd think Cameron wanted me to witness his latest conquest.

"Hey cuz, what are you looking at?" Too late, Byron peered over my shoulder, slapping his wet hair back.

I shrugged him away before he could see my ultimate shame of an ex-fiancé. "Nothing."

By now, the usual flock of adoring fans surrounded Cameron. It would make it easier for me to slip by unnoticed. Melanie, a girl with shifty eyes and whose name no one really had to remember, sat next to him on the thick brown couch and mischievously tied the shoelaces of his leather shoes together. He was loving it.

My gut wrenched, and I swiveled away. Byron caught me with firm hands. He was still wet from the rainstorm outside. "Are you crazy? You don't want to miss this. Melanie just messed up Cam's hair. Don't worry though. He got her back," he narrated the scene. "Oh, sick. Now they're..." I hit Byron back. It wasn't one of those flirty hits either. He let out a surprised grunt and let me go. "Wow Mad, how did that guy ever have the guts to break up with you?"

My hands flew to my hips. Who had Byron been talking to? "What makes you think *he* broke up with *me*?"

"Because you're mad at him." Byron pressed his palm into the entryway, surveying the room with a bored look. Leftover rainwater dripped down his face. Despite the soaking, he looked like he could fit into a more romantic era, instead of ward prayer.

I tried to look just as casual as he did. "Well, it's all part of my strategy really. Get the guy to break up with you and you never have to worry about him again. If you break up with *him*, he's always calling and whining, and—" I flinched. Cameron was now wrestling with half the girls on the couch. "Anyway, I'm just happy he's leaving me alone."

"No, you aren't." Byron checked the time on his silver Fossil watch...like...like he didn't just say that.

PRANK WARS

My mouth fell open. This was the worst torture imaginable. I was forced to watch my ex flirt it up with every girl in the ward, and now my worst enemy was rubbing it in my face. "Byron," I finally found my voice, but it was too shaky. "Do you even have a heart? I mean, do you know how it feels to...to..." For once I couldn't make a good argument for myself. I was so flustered. "I'm not stupid, okay? I *was* stupid...before. But...I'm strong now. No one can hurt me anymore—" I wasn't making any sense. To top it off, I heard the catch in my voice. Why was I getting deep with Byron anyway? His eyes didn't leave mine, almost like he was taking me seriously.

"So, how did you get him back?" he asked. "A girl like you would take her proper revenge?"

"No." It hurt to admit. "I cared about him, okay?" I couldn't get anything else out. We were going to get married on June 6th, less than two weeks from now. Even if I gave into my anger and hurt, any further moves against him would mark me the bitter, desperate ex who couldn't move on with her life—though it was very clear that Cameron had moved on with a vengeance. Then he would win. If nothing else, I had my pride. Barely.

Byron studied my face for a moment then his strong fingers slid through mine; it helped that they were still wet from the storm outside. "Just go with it," he said. Before I could object, he tugged me through the crowd of surprised girls. "*Madeleine!*" he called in a loud voice. "Hey beautiful, I was looking everywhere for you." I saw Cameron's head turn at that surprising declaration, but that was all I could see because Byron leaned over my ear, "Let's remind the man what he lost, shall we?" Was it my imagination or was there a slight accent to his words? It sounded slightly British? Maybe?

"Byron," I hissed in a warning. "*He doesn't care* that he lost me." I tried to push him away and he stole that hand too. Now Byron was getting me all wet. It was all I could do not to give away our crazy cover until I saw Cameron's face. It was full of unexplained anger. Was he actually jealous?

AmyLee stood by the door in her oversized short-jacket. Her eyes widened at us and I saw the scene through her eyes. Here I was holding hands with the biggest flirt in my acquaintance, and I just hoped I hadn't given away that I liked it because then my whole cause against men would unravel. Tory stepped into the doghouse, dressed all in black. Her lips formed an O. Of course, my shame wouldn't be complete without Lizzie seeing too. She followed her and covered her smile with a hand. Kali was otherwise occupied. Honestly, I wasn't vain enough to think I was the complete center of attention in our singles' world.

Byron lifted my hand to his lips and brushed my knuckles with a light kiss. It meant absolutely nothing to him—I recognized that devilish look—but no one else would see it like that, particularly President Wilkes. He sat next to the announcement girl, his gaze fixed on us with a slight smile. I couldn't take the false hope in his eyes. Of all our leaders, he cared the most about reclaiming me from my not-so-bright future.

Byron took one look at him and released me faster than he had grabbed me. I stepped back, feeling a little damp—and a little dumped. The night was not going the way I had planned. "Byron!" I gave him a dangerous smile, but with certain eyes on me, that was all I could do. He didn't seem sorry at all. I grabbed his wet shirt and pulled him closer, which I'm sure, only added to our illusion of intimacy. "What's your problem? Are you crazy? Is that it?"

Byron's eyes danced. "Why can't your ex stop looking at you? Do you want me to talk to him?" My gaze followed his to where Cameron sat. For a moment, the girls around him were forgotten. As soon as he saw my eyes, however, he turned back to his women, only he didn't look as into it. Byron shrugged. "Maybe he admires your shirt. What does MAD stand for anyway?"

"Me against dummies."

"Really? I thought it was the nickname I gave you." Byron's leather flip flops collided as he sat down on the light blue carpet. He tugged on the strings dangling from my black knickers. "Sit down," he called

PRANK WARS

loudly. The announcements were starting and I was the only one standing up in a sea of heads.

I flopped down next to Byron just in time to hear AmyLee's lecture. "Okay, listen up!" AmyLee already looked annoyed. She shook the tattered sign-up sheet at us. "Some of you think that boyfriend-for-the-week is just the presidency forcing us to get married or something. But let's be honest. It's just their desperate attempt to get you out of your apartments. Guys, video games are stupid, okay? And girls, Edward and Jacob are *not* real men." Murmuring broke out. "Move your lazy..."

President Wilkes put a loving hand on her back. "Thank-you, AmyLee. I'll take it from here. First of all, brothers and sisters, we'd like to stress how proud we are of *all* of you. Sister Wilkes and I are delighted with your accomplishments. At the same time, we feel inspired to encourage you to fit this program into your schedules. It's a great opportunity to get to know other singles in your stake."

I bit my lip, trying to ignore the stirrings of conscience as he talked about what the program would mean to us, as if we were supposed to be doing something more with our lives...like maybe date. Byron didn't seem to care. "What do you say about my conditions?" he whispered, *sotto voce*. "The letter for the cushions?"

"First things first," I told him. "Did *you* steal our cushions?"

"What makes you think I'd go to the effort?"

I bit down a smile at the familiar. "Okay, then second, do you still disavow all knowledge of that letter?"

"It isn't relevant. Do you want us to give you back the cushions or not?"

"No, we're good." I smiled inanely at him. *We would get them back ourselves.* Byron's eyes narrowed at me. Any outsider would think we were lost in each other's eyes, but I recognized that warlike glint in Byron's. He wasn't happy with my answer. For some reason he wanted that letter, but for now it was in Kali's protective custody.

"Next week, *Battle of the Bands* will be playing at the school." I heard a girl announce in the front. "Our very own Bunk House boys will be competing in it. Byron! Byron!" The unknown girl tried to get his attention. "The name of your band! Tell us the name?"

"*26Down*," a deep masculine voice answered behind us. One of Byron's roommates. I think it was the drummer, yet another man we had to distract from our mission tonight.

"*26Down*?" I asked Byron, hoping to divert him. "Is that your band's minimum age requirement?"

"Guess that means you can join—about five years ago, right?"

No way would I give anything away today, especially my age. We automatically closed our eyes as someone gave a blessing on the refreshments. No amount of blessing would keep Byron safe from me...or make the chocolate fudge cake good for us. I stood up after the chorus of *amens*, seeing Sandra break through the crowd. There was nothing like surrounding myself with former exes to keep Byron properly occupied. "Sandra," I called to her. "Byron wants to tell you something!"

"Really?" There was a slight smile on Byron's lips. "Are you sure you want to do that?" He motioned with his hands. Enter the twins. I found my path effectively blocked by two short Brad Pitts. They stepped on either side of Byron, crossing their arms and breaking into identical smiles—very mischievous ones at that. One had a deeper dimple than the other, but without that give-away; no one could have told them apart. Strangely enough, the twins never seemed to care.

"What's this?" I asked Byron. "Your back-up?"

"My bodyguards." They were almost half his size. What were they going to do?

Sandra sauntered closer. She was fuming. "Byron." Her finger wagged at him at an impossible speed.

"Sandra." One of the twins, the overly-confident one, Adam, I think it was, sauntered over in pristine white Vans to talk to her. It was fascinating to watch...in a sick way. "I wanted to ask you something."

"Oh yeah! What?" she spouted. I wasn't sure how he managed it, but the twin completely changed her course, heading her towards the dessert table. She didn't even eat desserts!

"He's my wing man," Byron explained.

"Wha—? What's a wing man?"

"In social situations, the wing man is the designated guy sent to flirt away the undesirable girl, so that his friend can flirt with the girl of his choice, or in this case, let us finish our negotiations."

"Lame."

"It's a sacrifice all men will make for their mates."

Mates? He made the word sound so Australian. Why did I never notice this accent before? Never mind that the wing man concept would make me rethink all the social experiences of my life, but at least I had a few wing men of my own to throw at him. I gestured Lizzie forward and she swept in. "Hey Byron. How's it going?"

The other twin smiled in that sweet way of his and immediately stole her from me, though in his case, he didn't seem to mind it a bit. He led her away. Byron shrugged at my furious look, and I turned, scanning the room for Kali. If she had been paying attention like she was supposed to, she would be a better decoy than all his monkeys put together. Byron pulled closer to me. "We're not through. Have you considered my white flag?"

Ah yes, that. It had to be a trick. "What is this, Byron? Did the bishop call you to be my friend?"

He tilted his head mockingly. "How did you guess you were our special project, my poor little Miss Havisham?"

"What did you just call me?" Wasn't that some bitter old woman in *Great Expectations*—left at the altar, taught her female followers to hate men? Despite myself, I grinned. It was pretty clever. Suddenly I knew where Byron was going with these peace talks. "Okay Byron, out with it. Which of my friends are you trying to date?"

He tried to shield the look of disbelief on his face. "Oh, that's top secret information."

"Well, you can't date any of them, big boy, so forget buttering me up."

His amusement won over. "You want me for yourself then?"

I matched his sarcasm. "If that's what it takes. Just be warned. I'll take you for everything your worth."

"I would expect nothing less."

"Maybe from a *man*."

"From a *boy*," he smoothly corrected me. "Let's get one thing straight, cuz. I'm a man, and men are different from boys. Boys will hurt you, not men."

I stared at him, confused.

"Hey!" To my relief, Kali shoved her way into the middle of our conversation. The girl was on a mission. She outshone us in all her make-up and jewelry, and she wouldn't stop laughing. She pushed a note into my hands. I opened it. *Tory is ready to strangle you. Move it!* I took a deep breath. With a careful look at Byron, I reached into my pocket and pulled out a crumpled piece of paper. "Give her this," I said in an overly dramatic voice. "It's classified. Make sure no one gets it. No one, Kali."

Kali tried to keep a straight face, but then she broke into another gurgle of laughter. I gave her a warning look and passed her the crumpled paper. She choked on another laugh. The paper fluttered onto the chipped wooden floor, resting next to Byron's flip-flops. Kali's laughter ended abruptly and we met each other's eyes. Mine were accusing. Byron read the girl communication perfectly. We dove for the paper at the same time, but Byron pushed me easily out of the way. He picked the note up, dangling the thing between two fingers. I'm sure he thought it was that threatening letter he wanted so badly. "What's this?" he asked in hushed tones. "A love note?"

Actually it was, and I would *love* to see his reaction when he read it because I made sure it was filled with all sorts of mushy sentiments about him from a supposed secret admirer. But now I had a job to do. I slid away to meet Tory and Lizzie at our designated meeting place in this stormy night. All I needed was five minutes ahead of these boys, and luckily Kali had them well in hand. Flirting was her not-so-secret weapon.

CHAPTER NINE

Day 106
1952 hours

"The cold breeze after the storm contrasted sharply with the danger. I knelt on the porch, the sky still deeply overcast. We had claimed the guys' porch light from operations past, which now forced us to work by the light of our cell phones. No matter. We knew this place well. We knelt, our black stocking caps and gloves blending into the shadows. War. It destroyed everything in its path, claiming everything that it touched. And yet, we found this heady danger addicting like nothing else."

—Madeleine's War Journal Entry (Tuesday, May 29th).

I held my cell phone to my lips. "Tory, are you in position?"

"It's safe to proceed."

I lifted my binoculars, watching Tory to get my bearings. Everyone was in position. Kali was on patrol at the doghouse at ward prayer. Lizzie was with me. She held the old lady perfume in her hand as our only defense. Tory had the most difficult assignment of all—knocking and running—but let's be honest; she was better trained than the rest of us.

With a dignified plop, we threw the dead love tree in place. It was wilted and dying like our love lives. But just dropping off the putrid thing wasn't enough of a message. No, these noncommittal boys needed some wedding invitations, and with a little help from digital wizardry,

Byron found himself married to Kim Kardashian, and the twins had found love with the Olson sisters. We tied the invitations to the love tree.

My eyes didn't leave the door. According to Kali, there was one roommate unaccounted for at ward prayer. Rock. He was the crazy drummer of the group. If he got caught in the crossfire, he'd go absolutely ballistic. The thing about Rock was that he took everything we did as a personal attack, so if he found us, we'd find ourselves talking to his landlord. It was deadly serious business. After much discussion, we decided Rock must be engaged to Lindsey Lohan. It had to be done, but my hand shook on this last invitation, and it clattered to the ground. Lizzie snorted, trying to keep back her laugh.

My lips twisted in response, and I gave her my best mock impression of an angry sergeant. "Get a hold of yourself, soldier," I whispered. We slowly backed away from the scene and hid behind a bush. I picked up my cell. "Fire," I told Tory, and she was off, her red hair flowing behind her. She knocked loudly on the door and turned, finding another bush to hide behind. We waited for an interminably long time, but there was no sound. "We got a green light," I told Lizzie. "Go!" She nodded and we both pulled forward, heading for the door. We tried the doorknob and found it locked. I headed for the window to the side. The pane slid easily under my fingertips. It was unlocked and I opened it all the way.

"Watch for traps," Lizzie warned in a small voice.

My hands were on the sill and I pulled myself up and over, almost kicking Lizzie in the face. She ducked easily. Weeks of experience taught her the usual procedure. I swung my leg over and stared into the room. It was blessedly empty, even the walls were empty. Guys never decorated enough—we were going to change that tonight. Poor things. The swinging bachelor pad needed to be transformed into a cozy suite for newlyweds—as their wedding invitations suggested. I landed on the brown carpet on all fours. The floor creaked under my weight. There was no way to be a proper spy and sneak up on anybody here. I tiptoed to the front door, the floor protesting every step of the way.

PRANK WARS

I let Tory in, and Lizzie brushed past her, carrying a huge laundry bag over her shoulder. She set it down at our feet and it clunked heavily. She silently pulled out the ammunition: a pink afghan, some hideously framed macaroni artwork, surprisingly hardy flowers dried in a forgotten vase, air freshener. Lizzie was our stealth bomber, but at her careful rate, we'd be caught and tortured before she got everything out of the bag. I nudged her aside and dumped the rest of it onto the ground. Lizzie gave a dismayed gasp at the mess.

"Tory," I ordered. "Find the cushions."

Tory went to work, practically sniffing them out like a greyhound. I dragged the lavender and white checkered sheets across the floor and arranged them over the living room window, tying them up with pretty bows. I laid a doily over Rock's elaborate drum set. Lizzie had already fixed the lampshades and arranged cute fluffy throw pillows. She placed dolls and stuffed animals in strategic places until the room resembled something fit for *Malibu Barbie*. Yup, consider it officially trashed.

"Any luck?" I asked Tory. She shook her head. I sighed. "We'll just have to take their cushions until we can work out a deal for ours then," I said.

"What about the back rooms?" she asked. It was forbidden to go back there, Chastity Line and all. I met Lizzie's worried gaze and shook my head at Tory. No time for a fight. There was no telling what or *who* was back there anyway.

My phone buzzed and I glanced down at the text. *The targets are attempting to exit the doghouse*, it read. The impossible was happening. Kali was losing them.

I threw my phone at Tory, knowing my texting skills were too slow. "Quick. Tell Kali to offer them food, good company, anything, just buy us a few more minutes." Tory's fingers flew over the keypad. I ran into the kitchen, throwing ridiculously cute little hand towels over the handles. Tory followed me, texting one-handed.

Lizzie hesitated at the cupboards, staring at the sign hanging over it. "*Do unto others as you would have others...*" I hastily opened the cupboard to distract her, but it was even worse inside. A little heart shaped post-it-note read. *"Be ye Kind," (Ephesians 4: 32).*

"Maybe we shouldn't..." Lizzie began.

"What are you talking about? This is what they want...or else they wouldn't have started this war. Just remember, they stole our couch cushions first."

Lizzie stared at the happy face stickers stuck all over the inside cupboard. "I'm beginning to feel..."

"Don't feel!" This was a set-up, as if the guys couldn't be bothered to physically stop us. "This is completely lazy! They thought these little do-good notes would crush our spirits without them having to lift a finger."

Lizzie tugged at another sign. She read it aloud: *"Please don't! Don't take the cookies (if you're feeling guilty, please flip on the back—there is a nice note)."* She flipped the sign over. *"Help yourself to our cookies, fatty."* She dropped the note as if stung. "What is this—a trap?" she asked.

"They're toying with us."

"Or," Lizzie worked out, "they have a problem with roommates stealing food?"

Tory pushed past her, easily ignoring the messages...either that or she couldn't read. Balancing on the toes of her long black converses, she reached through the cupboards and began ripping the labels off the tuna fish cans. "Tory, no!" I pulled the cans from her hand. "Don't mess with the food. It's the number one rule." Before I could get into it further, my pink camo phone vibrated on the counter where Tory had left it. It was Kali. I answered it. "What's happening?"

"Byron's looking really bored," she whispered anxiously into the phone. *"I think he's gonna make a run for it."*

"Block the door. Anything. We're not finished here." I pried another can from Tory's hands and set it down on the guys' ancient microwave. Without warning, the microwave went off. I screamed and pulled the can off the top. The microwave stopped running, almost like I was a conductor between it and the cell phone. "Whoa! What kind of microwave is this? They're not supposed to just start like that!"

PRANK WARS

"*What?*" It was Kali on the other line. I tried to stay focused. The microwave had gone off for no reason at all...unless it had something to do with my cell phone...except, I tried to remember what we had just talked about in my PHYS 121 class. The microwaves in cell phones worked on completely different frequencies, right? There was no way my phone should've affected a microwave oven. Yet, another student in the class claimed their remote control car moved when their mom turned the blender on. The teacher had said it was frequency interference problems, but this was crazy. I must be holding some brain frying device made by terrorists. It didn't stop me from putting the phone back to my ear. I threw the can back on top of the microwave to see if it would set it off again. Nothing happened. The microwave stayed put. I was crazy, wasn't I? "*Mad?*" It was Kali. I had forgotten she was on the other line.

I licked my dry lips. "Uh, Kali? Is it working? Have you stopped him? Confirm."

"*No, he's going through the door.*"

Immediately I forgot the microwave incident. "Through you? Because that's the only way he should've gotten through the door!" She was silent. "Never mind. Grab his foot or something. Catch him."

"*Are you serious?*" I recognized that rebellious tone.

"Do it!"

I listened to the subsequent screaming in the background—most of it came from Kali. Her phone clunked to the doghouse floor. After a few tense moments, Kali got back on. She was breathless. "*He knows something's up. Abort mission. Abort. He's on his way.*"

"We've got 3.24 minutes until collision," I shouted to the others, hanging up my cell phone. Approximately. We had timed how long it took our fastest soldier to get from the doghouse to the bunkhouse. "Where's our message?"

Tory glanced up at us. "What message?"

"Really?" I cried. "We really forgot the message?" That was the whole point, to deliver a message that was just as confusing as the useless drivel they fed us in a constant basis. I found Byron's laptop and sat down, pulling it to my lap. "What's the password?" I tried to think of the most likely ones. "Tory! Call the boys who live downstairs. Tell them to stand outside their back doors. We'll give them a fresh-baked batch of brownies if they do what we say."

"What?" Lizzie shouted out, but Tory did it without hesitation. She had them on speed dial. No one cared if the boys downstairs were tired of us by now. The bribes should be enough to keep them working for us. Lizzie looked from the battle worn Tory to me sitting calmly on the couch with Byron's laptop. Lizzie freaked out. "What are you doing? We've got to get out of h—"

"Just a sec." I started typing in words. First I tried *Lord Byron*. When that failed, I used his ex-girlfriend's: *Sandra*. Nope. Apparently he wasn't that sentimental. I was desperate: *I don't know*, I wrote. The usual tricks weren't working. "This is ridiculous," I shouted.

"Yeah!" Lizzie was trying to pull me from my seat. "Write the stupid note on a napkin or something!"

Tory carried her cell phone like a walkie talkie, barking out orders to the boys downstairs. She dropped the lilac-spring air freshener and it rolled across the ground. She sneezed and readjusted her phone on her chin, still working out negotiations. Lizzie was more of a wreck. "Hurry! Hurry! How are we supposed to get out of here without them seeing us?"

"What's the magic word?" I asked Byron's computer. "Please?" I typed it in with a couple of random numbers and waited. To my surprise, a bunch of numbers popped up on the screen like some sort of weird code. My head tilted at it.

"What's his major—computers?" Tory asked over my shoulder. She plugged the air freshener into the wall like she was casually finishing up morning chores.

"No, it's…it's…uh, something to do with geology…I think." I quickly changed his screensaver to cute little bunnies.

Lizzie glanced out the window at the parking lot. "They're here. Now what are we supposed to do?"

PRANK WARS

Thirty seconds until collision. "Lock the door," I told Tory. She ran while I wrote a completely stupid and meaningless message into Byron's computer. She locked the door just as the guys landed against it. It crashed loudly. They fumbled with the doorknob. Tory jerked back, throwing down a welcome mat covered in rainbows. She stepped on it to look through the peephole. "They're looking for their keys," she reported.

Lizzie froze next to me. She had never cut things this close before. I was almost done with my message: *"What do you and bunnies have in common?"* I typed. *"Nothing, you're not cute. You're not fluffy and no one wants you around at Easter—not you or your peeps.* Good, nice and confusing.

"What's taking them so long to get in?" Lizzie asked.

"Kali picked their pockets," I muttered. "They don't have their keys." She was the queen of flirtation after all.

I heard fingers running down the same window pane we had used to break inside. Lizzie let out a little shriek. She tugged at my shoulder. "They've got us!"

"As if I'd let us get caught." I grabbed a cushion on my way out of the living room. "Get the other one. Retreat."

Lizzie's eyes bugged out. "What? How?"

"Through the back window in the kitchen," Tory said, cushion in hand. We ran past the fridge and Lizzie followed helplessly. Tory wrestled open the window, still talking through her cell phone to the boys downstairs. "Hands up." She shoved the cushion through. Lizzie gasped just as I stuffed the other one through. I poked my head after it, seeing that the guys and cushions were nowhere in sight. Perfect. The boys downstairs had nestled comfortably back inside with their video games with the added bonus of a few extra couch cushions to rest under their feet. I made a mental note to bribe them with something more than brownies this time. Lizzie's cinnamon rolls maybe?

"Okay, it's our turn," I told Lizzie. "Through the window."

She planted her feet, watching me like I was absolutely crazy. "No way. I'm not doing this!"

"There's another roof to the side. It's safe. We always get out this way."

"Sometimes we get in." Tory informed her with flushed cheeks.

Lizzie shook her head, her long black hair swinging. "I'm sorry. I don't like heights. Just go without me. I'll just get caught, okay?" I met Tory's eyes and our brows furrowed. There was no telling what they would do to her, especially once they saw how beautiful their place looked.

"Go Tory," I instructed. Tory was already out the window. She landed safely on the neighbor's roof to the side of us. Lizzie and I listened to the sound of a window scraping open in the guys' back rooms. They had found their way inside. I tugged Lizzie back into the living room. Her gladiator sandals spanked the back of her heels. The doorknob on the front door turned. I froze. Kali hadn't stolen all of their keys? Of course not. She had other conquests to make—real ones. Byron pulled through the door just moments before we ducked behind Rock's drum set. Byron folded a credit card under his fingers, staring at the transformed living room. He knew how to pick a lock? It wasn't one of those simple ones either. Impressive…but at the same time, disturbing.

One of the twins rushed behind Byron into the kitchen. It was the sweet one, Blake. The other twin came from the back rooms, shaking his head. "What did they do in here?" He didn't sound pleased. It meant we got the better of them this time. It wasn't the fact that we trashed the place; it was the fact that we got in and out, undetected.

"They got our cushions!" the other twin shouted, staring out the window. "Hey, there's that evil redhead!" Tory never allowed herself to be seen. She was using herself as bait to give us a chance to escape. The twins charged outside after her, their arms pumping simultaneously.

Byron was looking at his laptop. It was on the bunny screensaver. "How did she…?" he whispered so softly that I had to strain to hear. But

PRANK WARS

instead of reading the message, he tugged out his iPhone. I saw a bright screensaver over the front. It was a *Ski Utah* one. "Hey, Holly."

Holly must have picked it up mid-ring. Wait a second, Holly? I didn't recognize that name. Byron leaned against the door frame next to his newly furnished kitchen, inches from where we hid. I met Lizzie's eyes, willing her not to make any fast moves. "No, nothing's wrong." He chuckled low in his throat. It sounded ominous, well, okay, if I were being objective, it actually sounded mildly attractive...in an ominous way. "Sorry for checking in so late," he said. Why was he *checking in* with Holly anyway? Unless? Did Byron have a girlfriend? Before I could digest this, he snickered. "Yeah, the usual. It gets pretty hazardous around here." He ran a shaky hand through his already disheveled dark hair. "No, that's the problem. I didn't see her tonight. Something's wrong." There was that accent again. I was having trouble identifying it. He listened to whoever was on his line. "You got my message then? Yeah, well, it got into the wrong hands." He pulled a paper from a pocket and studied it; I recognized it immediately. The threatening note—the s one Kali was supposed to have hidden away. How did he get it?

"I need you to check something for me, will you? Yeah. Tonight if you can." He kneaded his forehead with his fingertips. "Sure. What do you want me to do?" He sounded whipped, but not exactly lovey-dovey. Maybe he was talking to his mom? Wait. He had called her Holly. *Not his mom.* Byron flipped his phone shut and stared over it at the bunnies prancing across his computer screen. A brief smile flickered over his lips. "Unbelievable." He stretched like a dangerous cat and headed into the hall for the back rooms. As soon as he turned the corner, Lizzie and I were out the door. The front step creaked loudly under our shoes. Lizzie slammed the door behind us and I shot her a look of disbelief.

"I'm sorry!" she shouted. "Their air conditioning was on! Their bill's gonna be huge!"

Trust Lizzie to care about those kinds of things. We wove around the dead love tree and dashed into the parking lot. The door scraped open behind us, and I wondered how fast Byron could go when we ran straight into Eric. I stumbled backwards at the impact. "Whoa!" Eric stopped me from falling again. His hands clenched tightly over my arms. "I got you." He grinned at me and gave me a quick hug, shocking me from the tip of my toes to the ends of my hair. His arms were just as warm and strong as I remembered them. He smelled good too, which was lucky because my nose was smashed against him. "You okay?" he asked. *A little embarrassed maybe.*

"Save us!" Lizzie clutched at him. "He's after us!" I wriggled free from Eric, trying to ignore his amused look.

Eric peered over our heads. "You mean that guy?"

Lizzie and I turned. Byron rested one palm against his front door. His lean silhouette looked dark and forbidding. He treated Eric to a fierce glare, almost as if he had completely forgotten about us, but it didn't take long for Byron's gaze to find me. He lifted a brow, not moving from the door. Now that there was someone sane in the picture, there was nothing he could do to us. Those were the rules.

Eric squinted at him. "So, that's the famous Lord Byron?"

I nodded. "You must be new to the ward, Eric."

"You could say that."

"Really? You are?" Lizzie was already recovering from her scare and her politeness had returned. "Where are you living?"

Eric hesitated, digging his hands deep in his pockets and tipping back on his sandals. It was the look of a guy not ready to commit to certain girl visitors. Why? Who was he afraid we'd meet, other girls? He had something to hide and I had somewhere to go. Besides, who knew what sort of trouble Tory had gotten herself into? I turned from Eric and saw a shadow gliding through the alleyway behind the guy's apartments. I backed into Eric and he let out a pained oof.

"Someone's over there," I whispered hoarsely.

He tried to look concerned. "You think it's one of your friends?"

"Oh yeah." I felt stupid. The shadow slipped further back into the alleyway. Only one person I knew would be back there. "I guess it's only Tory."

PRANK WARS

"Who?"

"She likes to spring out at us and scare us, but she's harmless." I grabbed Lizzie's arm. We had to catch up to Tory before she caused further mischief. "Well, it was nice seeing you again, Eric. Hopefully we won't do it again. I mean...hopefully we won't run into you again...uh...hard." I left him and sprinted for the alleyway, but jerked to a stop. Lizzie fell back too.

Eric's fingers were wrapped around my hand. "Hey. Where are you going?"

Why did he care? He was the one who wouldn't tell me where he lived. "Home," I said. "You know, a place where people can actually come and pay their respects?" I hesitated, realizing what that sounded like. "That's not an invitation!"

Judging by his pleased expression, he wasn't taking me seriously at all. "Why? What did I do?"

I jerked away from him. "I don't know. You could try telling us where you live for starters."

"I'm looking into a place right now, so..."

Lizzie directed her huge smile at him. Her face was flushed with adrenaline which made her look even more beautiful, especially since in no way was she dressed in the appropriate prank war attire like I was. I tried not to be jealous. "And we haven't scared you away yet?" she asked with a giggle.

Eric gave an appreciative laugh. His eyes caught mine. "No, no, I kind of like it." There was a wicked glint to his expression, and if he had said it any differently, I would've called him a creep.

"Well, don't move into the bunkhouse," I warned him. "They're trouble." And the last thing I needed was for Eric to join the troop. He was much too charming. Even now, I wasn't sure why he was still talking to us, unless... "Eric, you aren't a wing man, are you? Uh, right now, I mean?"

He went silent, trying to figure out what I was saying. "No, I'm more of a drumstick man."

"Me too." I was glad that he wasn't mixed up in this. Then I realized what I had told him. "I mean, I'm a drumstick girl…uh, not a man."

"Got ya."

I looked behind me. Byron was still watching from the door. I couldn't see him clearly from here, but I knew he wasn't pleased. Strangely, the thought made my stomach turn. The twins tromped up the steps to stand beside him. Tory had evaded them again, except—they had their cushions under their arms. I turned on my heel to stare at them in disbelief. Were they magic or had they sold their souls to the devil?

Tory dashed out from the bush to our side, her face red with fury. How had she escaped the alleyway behind us so fast? That girl had wings on her shoes. One look at her and I knew the boys downstairs were gonna get it—and it wouldn't be Lizzie's cinnamon rolls…or maybe it would, but it would be smeared all over their gamer faces. Those traitors!

CHAPTER TEN

Day 106
2156 hours

"We had been outwitted by those devils again. I tried to think through the arguing voices and accusing shrieks. There were so many questions left unanswered. So many answers left unquestioned."

—Madeleine's War Journal Entry (Tuesday, May 29th).

"There's an information leak," Tory cried. She paced the perimeters of the empty apartment next to ours. "I wouldn't be surprised if they had the place bugged. It was like the twins walked straight downstairs to those gamers like they knew exactly where we stashed the cushions. We have a spy in the ranks!"

Sandra? Kali? She thought the twins were cute, plus she was just in it for the dates, but Kali looked too distraught after her tangle with the boys at ward prayer. Her mouth wasn't full of chocolate…and she wasn't taking any pictures. She moved her hands wildly. "Byron knew what we were doing!" she yelled. "I don't know how he knew. His roommates didn't know. He just sat on the couch, looking at me like I was an idiot."

"You were sitting on the couch?" I asked quickly. "Doing what?"

Kali shrugged. "He let me talk about school like he was my guidance counselor. I just blabbed whatever came to my head. As soon as the twins figured out something was up, my friends and I grabbed them. Byron just let us have our way with them…and…"

"That's how he got that letter," I said, "—probably while you were taking down the twins."

"No, he didn't!" Kali looked shocked—either that or she was a great actress. "Why would he want that anyway?" She searched the pockets of her capris. When she couldn't find the offending item, she held up her hands in defense. "I was working too hard to give up anything. Do you *know* how hard it was to get those keys from them?"

"Yeah? Where are the keys then?"

Kali searched deeper into her pockets and cried out in dismay. "I don't know."

"You gave them back!" Tory accused. Kali denied it. They argued loudly around us. Lizzie sat on the empty couch in silent disgust, which meant I had to bring us back to the real world.

"Okay," I shouted. "That's enough!" Everyone stopped talking and the noise faded like a dying wind. "I don't know how they're doing this, okay. Maybe they're getting their information a different way?"

"Or maybe you're just getting predictable." We all turned as one, staring at Sandra. She had entered the empty apartment as silently as a black ninja and now sat perched on the edge of the couch, her boot clad legs crossed. A soft Indian scarf tied around her pretty little neck. She glanced distastefully around our new headquarters. "What are you doing in here?"

"It's okay. The place is empty," Lizzie explained hurriedly. The last thing she wanted was to get into trouble. "No one's using it."

Sandra glared at all of us, which I'm not sure how she managed. "I just want to know one thing. Did you get the cushions back or not?"

"Not," I answered. "Sorry."

"Why don't you just text him and tell him that I want them back, huh?" We froze. It wasn't that simple. "Or do you *not* know how to text?"

I straightened. Sandra had called me out. Lizzie jumped to her feet, standing between us. "C'mon, save it for the guys."

PRANK WARS

"Or is the real problem," Sandra continued as if Lizzie hadn't said anything, "that Byron hasn't given you his number yet?" Sandra was doing that enunciating thing again, managing to make every word sound annoying. "Now tell me. What missing letter are you talking about?"

"It doesn't matter anymore," I told her coldly. "It's gone."

"That's weird. Why was it so important to him?"

I shrugged. It bugged me that I couldn't figure it out either. "He wanted to cover his tracks. I don't know."

Sandra gathered her purse and pulled out red glimmery lipstick. We watched her apply it to her lips. It was mesmerizing. The girl didn't even need a mirror. "Look, I'm just saying this because I'm worried about your social welfare," she wiped the corner of her lips free of excess lipstick, "maybe mine more. But just back off, okay."

I took a deep breath. This wasn't the first time she told us we were crazy, but now there was something different about it. It was almost a warning. "Or what?" I asked, "Somebody gets hurt?"

Sandra chuckled. She stood up, her light fingers slithering past our cache of weapons on the table: Kool-Aid, lipstick, tuna fish, Jell-O. Her hand rested on the old lady perfume. "When I was a little girl, I played with dolls."

"Oh really?" Kali looked ready to kill her. I should've known Sandra would be a threat to the girliest girl in the room. "I would've thought knives?"

Sandra pouted her overly bright red lips at her. "Honey, the difference between you and me is that I'm not an idiot—oh—and I don't wear tacky fake jewels on my rings." Kali's fingers clenched, revealing a big turquoise ring. Sandra permitted herself a cruel chuckle, and turned on me. "*And* I don't depend on stupid games to catch a man. How about I give you some tips, little ones? Like this perfume." She held up the old lady perfume, not realizing how nasty the stuff was. "Do you even know what this is really meant for?" We all stepped back at the threat. The old lady perfume smelled worse than mosquito repellent. "I promise it's much more effective than what *you* do with it."

Kali couldn't take anymore. She stepped directly into the line of fire and snatched the perfume from Sandra's grasp. Her *fake* rings scraped against the container. "How about you try some of it then?"

Sandra recoiled, suddenly realizing we weren't holding some Jennifer Lopez fragrance. "Why? What is that?"

"Just think of it as a little experiment." Kali cocked her head wickedly. "Let's see how many guys *you* can catch with it."

Sandra tried to give her a stern look. "Get that away from me."

"Kali. Stop." Lizzie was trying to make peace. She held up her hands. "Don't do this." Tory enjoyed the show with a big grin.

"What's the matter, Sandra?" Kali asked. "Will it clash with your Odori Iris fragrance?" This was a pure girly fight. I didn't even recognize that scent.

Sandra tried to shrug her away. "Look, I'm done arguing. You're a child."

"Oh c'mon, baby, I promise. One squirt won't hurt."

As much as I was enjoying this, I knew I had better do something before Lizzie blamed me forever. "Alright, put it down, Kali. We don't want any trouble."

Kali's hand shook on the perfume nozzle, her perfect blonde curls bobbing. "She asked for it."

"Yeah, but don't."

"You don't want to waste your grandmother's perfume, honey," Sandra told her.

That was it. Kali lunged for Sandra, who screamed and ran. Kali was after her with uncharacteristic swiftness. They scurried around the room, shrieking and pushing things out of their way. I shoved between them only to get the old lady perfume sprayed straight into my eyes. I fell back with a grunt. "Ouch!" I couldn't see. My eyes were burning.

"Are you crazy?" I could hear Sandra's loud voice. "That stuff stinks! You almost got me with that!"

"Yeah, so what?" I got to my feet, but I couldn't tell where I was. Tears streamed down my cheeks. "Kali got me in the eyes!" My hands found something hard. The wall.

PRANK WARS

"Don't rub them. Run your eyes under water." I think that was Lizzie. Her hand was on my back and she was helping me into the hall.

"You stupid brat!" Sandra shouted at Kali. "Where did you get that stink anyway—your mom?" I listened to Sandra's ensuing screams. She had only done it to herself. Lizzie's hand left me to stop the fight, and I stumbled into the back where I thought the bathroom was. If it was anything like our apartment, it should be in the far left corner past the bedrooms. I could still hear panicked voices in the distance, but I couldn't concentrate on them. My eyes were stinging. As soon as I found the bathroom, I felt around, not bothering with the lights. After touching everything I could possibly touch in a bathroom, I found the faucet and threw my face into the steady stream of water. The hard part was opening my eyes under it. Nothing felt worse...besides having a baby maybe and I wouldn't know. My eyes were killing me.

The sounds of screaming melted into insults. How long could those two possibly fight? Next, they would get into Sandra's bright red lipstick. I pulled my head out of the water and forced my eyes open only to greet a dark world. This was it. I was completely blind. As soon as I remembered to switch on the lights, I gasped in pain at the brightness, still not able to see.

The sounds of fighting amplified. Lizzie was trying to talk some sense into Kali and Sandra, but they did what I did best and ignored her. I got ready to storm back through the dark hallway, but something made me turn. The door to the back bedroom was slightly ajar. There was a light on inside. The problem was nobody lived here. I felt a stab of warning tingle behind my ears and down my spine. Tory couldn't be hiding in there again, could she? I was an injured woman. Had she no decency?

"Tory. This isn't funny." I pushed the door open and saw a freshly made bed. I made out some floral print—someone was sitting on it. I jerked back, not able to see who it was...a girl, well yeah; it had to be a girl. She was tiny. "Oh no," I whispered. Someone lived here. We were wrong. I held up my hands. "I'm sorry." The girl watched me silently, and without expression. I couldn't tell if she was mad or scared, but the steady stare was freaking me out. I could only see her through my perfume induced fog, but I sensed something was terribly wrong. I had to explain before she called the cops on us or tackled me. I was in no condition to defend myself. "We didn't know." I balanced myself against the wall. "I'm really sorry." Her eyes were unblinking. My heart skipped at an uncomfortable rate. "We thought this place was empty or we never would've…"

"Who are you talking to?"

I turned. Tory, well, I think it was. She had red hair. I gestured helplessly into the bedroom. "Our neighbor."

She was silent for a moment. "There's no one there."

My stomach lurched again. "Really?"

Tory walked boldly into the room, and I followed helplessly after her. I hated not being able to see. "You're talking to a bunch of balloons," she muttered with a little laugh. Stepping closer, I saw the big heart balloons floating over a bed—a little deflated, maybe a week old. Someone lived here. The bedroom was furnished and decorated. Tory picked up some framed pictures. "This has to be the girl who lives here." She shoved one of the pictures into my face, so I could inspect it. "She's in all the pictures." At close proximity, I could see it was the same girl I had seen during my watch, a beautiful girl from the Orient with long black hair. She had a lollipop in her mouth.

"When do you think she's coming home?" Tory asked softly.

It took us both a moment to process the trouble we'd be in. "Run!" We were already out the door. I fell against the wall and stumbled over Tory. She had my arm and we plunged into the living room. I barely made out Sandra and Kali's startled faces. I gathered our things together, hoping against hope that I didn't drop anything as evidence that we had been here. "We've got to go!" I shouted.

"What's the matter?" Lizzie asked.

"Someone lives here!"

"What?" The dismayed voices echoed around the room.

PRANK WARS

"That's crazy!" Kali cried. "There's nothing in here." She opened a dresser drawer below the mirror in the front room and gasped at the pencils and papers inside.

Lizzie ripped open the cabinet doors below the coffee table. "There are games in here...and books!"

"There's stuff in the fridge," Kali cried out from the kitchen. I had no idea how she got over there so fast. I squinted her direction. "Whoever lives here is a neat freak!"

It was just like a horror movie where the quickly gathering evidence revealed who the murderer was after it was too late. Well, I wasn't about to be left behind to meet my doom this time. I rushed out the door and the other girls followed me in a herd of running feet. We ran through a couple on the porch, interrupting what had probably been a touching moment. It was like running through the gauntlet. I stopped short. Lizzie pushed past me, followed by Kali then Tory—a bunch of clowns running out of a toy car.

Sandra was the first to hit the railing outside our apartment door, glaring at Byron. Close up, I could see he was the other half of the couple. "What are you doing here?" she hissed.

"Loitering," he said with a tight smile. Tory, Kali, and Lizzie ran into our apartment. They slammed the door shut as if that would keep out whatever chased them. Before I could make a similar grand exit, Byron turned to me. "What's the matter? You see a ghost?"

"Yeah...yeah, pretty much." I tried to catch my breath. I couldn't really tell who he was with...she had blonde hair. My stomach sunk. Was that his type then?

"What's going on?" he asked.

Sandra threw her hands up and click-clacked away in her cute little high-heeled boots. Our apartment door slammed behind her too. I guess it was pretty hard seeing her ex-boyfriend with another girl. She probably thought I was flirting with him too. If she had tried the same things with Cameron that I tried with Byron...well, Sandra and Cam would deserve each other, but at the same time...seeing Byron with another girl right now kind of hurt, which was really stupid because Byron and I had nothing going on. Wait. Was this about Sandra's feelings or mine?

I pushed against the railing to follow Sandra into our apartment. Before I could, Byron hooked his arm through mine and pulled me back with him. He searched my bloodshot eyes. "You okay?"

Careful. He would make this girl jealous. I turned to this new girl, putting on my polite face. I could make out that she was wearing a raspberry-colored wrap dress with gobs of ruffles. Byron must like his girls high-maintenance. In an instant, I knew who she was. I extended my hand. "You must be Holly." She looked startled, which meant I was right on. I hated meeting Byron's girlfriends, but I tried to get over it by giving Byron a devilish look—the same one he gave me before thoroughly embarrassing me. "It's so nice to finally meet you," I said. "I've heard so much about you."

The girl flushed. "Really?"

I nodded and retreated from them both with what dignity I had intact. Byron called out to me, "Hey!" My hand hesitated over the doorknob. "Thanks for predicting my downfall, military brat." He pulled out an invitation, holding it up with two sleek fingers. It was his upcoming nuptials with Kim Kardashian. "But I'm always on the lookout for trouble."

I glanced meaningfully over at *Holly.* "Marriage is your destiny."

"Would you say my destiny stinks of some weird-smelling perfume?"

I froze. Good tactic. Flirting. And he had me completely flustered. Why was everyone accusing me of ulterior motives lately? "You don't have to worry, Byron. There's no love in this hate relationship." I bit my lip and did the unthinkable. "Besides, I don't practice polygamy."

Byron broke away from his latest girlfriend and threw his foot in my door before I could escape. "What's wrong with you?" he asked under his breath. "Do you think every guy is like your ex? Is that your problem?"

PRANK WARS

I hesitated and looked at him, really looked at him and detected some hurt in those blue eyes of his. I didn't have that kind of power, did I? I always worked so hard to be strong, and that meant lashing out at everything I considered a threat, but what if Byron never was a threat? What if I was wrong? I glanced over at Holly for confirmation, but she seemed distracted by her cell phone.

"Let's talk like real people every once in a while," he said. "Okay? That's what friends do. Think about it." He glanced over at his texting girlfriend. "And why are you calling *her* Holly anyway?"

That wasn't Holly? How many girls was he dating? After a last fleeting glance at his uncharacteristically open expression, I pushed open the door and escaped into my apartment before he could get the better of me again…because he had. My eyes were still stinging, I stunk, and to top it off, Byron had done the impossible—he had pricked my conscience. I leaned against the door, seeing that Kali and Sandra had continued their fight at our new location. This time they were fighting over the ward directory. Tory stood in the middle of the room, looking battle worn. Lizzie nudged me. "Let me get this straight. You know everything that goes on around here and you didn't notice that there was someone living next door to us?"

"Well, you know the old saying," Sandra said in her most sarcastic voice. "You're so busy with the enemy away from home; you don't notice the enemy living under your own roof."

"That is *not* an old saying!" Kali argued.

I collapsed onto our couch, trying to catch my breath. Our neighbor was a stealthy one. If we ever caught up to her, we'd ask her to be on our team…if I wasn't already considering giving up this prank war. Maybe Byron was right. I was taking everything too far. Sure, I had fun while it lasted, but if I had turned into such a social basket case that I assumed every guy was like my ex, maybe it was time to get my head examined.

"She's not in here!" Kali threw the directory aside. "Useless."

Lizzie had our landlord on her cell. "Uh hi, Mike!" She always started phone conversations like she was startled the person on the other line picked up. "Hey, we were just wondering about our neighbor next to us. What? Her name's Thing? Really. Thing?"

"Oh great," Kali looked scared. "Her name's *Thing*. Not only is she lurking in the attic above her closet, her name is *Thing*!" What? Lurking in closets? What had they been talking about while I was gone? "Who would name their kid *Thing* anyway!" Kali shrieked out.

"Thanh," Lizzie quickly corrected us. "Her name's Thanh."

But it was too late. Kali was officially scared. "Where is she then?" she exploded. "Think about it. We haven't seen her since she moved in. She's not in the ward directory. No one knows she exists. She could be a ghost for all we know!"

Sandra sighed heavily and left for the sanctuary of her room...which she shared with Kali. It would be a long night.

"We were just in her apartment," Kali said. "You don't just go into *the* apartment. No one gets out! Now we'll have the curse on us. We're going to die like she did!" Kali was clearly a victim of horror movies. Lizzie rolled her eyes.

"Nobody's dead," I reassured her. "Nobody in the whole world...I promise." I gave Kali a smile, pretending that none of this bothered me, even though thinking about it made me go cold. Sure, it was speculation now, but wait until the lights went out in a few minutes. Then we'd all freak out. We shuffled back into our rooms, brushing teeth, washing faces, getting into ridiculous pajamas. It was all a blur to me—literally. My conscience burned at Byron's words. Sandra was giving us the silent treatment, and even worse, Kali wouldn't stop talking about our brush with death. I tuned her out with my own thoughts.

I couldn't stop thinking about what Byron had said. Had Cameron broken me so much that I was seriously incapable of positive human emotion? If so, I was in trouble. The girl I was now would never be healthy enough for any relationship, let alone a friendship. I had ruined everything with my obsession, but could I even bring myself to care? Byron could be messing with my emotions like Cameron had. And if Byron was being genuine? Well, it didn't matter. Whatever could have been between us was gone now anyway. Already, he was hanging out with nameless girl. Maybe he wasn't playing her this time. He could be sincerely interested in her. That didn't make me feel any better. Why couldn't Byron take this new girl outside *his* door, instead of making me feel guilty and full of regrets? And why was he acting so strange lately anyway?

Lizzie brushed out her long dark hair and tied it into a ponytail at the back of her head. She had had enough of me, but—unfortunately for her—she was the only one I could talk to. "Hey." I pulled my BYU sweats up to my knees and flopped onto my bed, looking at her with bloodshot puppy dog eyes.

She sighed. "What do you want?"

There was so much to ask. "If Thanh lives next door, maybe that letter we found was really meant for her?"

Lizzie's pajamas fluttered over her dark legs as she made her way to her bed. She shook her head. "Thanh's not around enough to be involved in our silly prank war."

I ignored the insult to injury. "I'm not saying that she is. What if that letter on her door had nothing to do with us?"

She stilled for a moment. "Oh c'mon, Mad, you're just as bad as Kali. Look, I'm tired. I have to wake up really early for school tomorrow, okay?" I let her turn off the light and she jumped on her bed. Her mattress squeaked as she readjusted her blankets.

"Because," I continued as if she hadn't shot me down, "it doesn't make sense that Byron would want a letter back that he wrote himself. Do you remember what he said on the phone when we were hiding behind the drums?"

"Goodnight," Lizzie said firmly.

I rolled over on my bed, punching my pillow a couple of times. I closed my poor aching eyes. It was actually a relief. Maybe Lizzie was right. I was just like Kali with an overactive imagination. I yawned, hoping that I wouldn't have weird dreams about all of this. "Goodnight, Lizzie."

"Goodnight." My eyes fluttered open. Lizzie didn't sound like Lizzie.

"Lizzie?" I asked.

"I'm not Lizzie."

I jerked upright just as Lizzie screamed. She reached over and turned on her lamp. Light flooded through the room over a grinning Tory. She sat between our two beds, laughing, her red hair in pigtails. How long had she been hiding under one of our beds? I held my heart. My reflexes would be as sharp as a paper cut once she was through with me…if I survived the shock, of course.

Lizzie pointed to the door. "Out!"

CHAPTER ELEVEN

Day 107
0800 hours

"It was moments before waking. The only distinction between sleep and death...were the light snores coming from our barracks as we ignorantly awaited the cruelties of morning to befall us."

—Madeleine's War Journal Entry (Wednesday, May 30th).

I tripped from my bed and landed on the ground on all fours. The sound of a dozen or so alarm clocks went off all around me.

"Madeleine!" Lizzie shouted. "Turn off your alarm clock!"

"I'm trying!"

I dove under the bed, finding one then two. I clicked them off, but still there were more. I couldn't find them all. Lizzie hopped off her bed beside me, but there was nothing she could do to stop the incessant wailing. It was literally the sound that accompanied our worst nightmares.

It had the evil twins' signatures all over it. Only they would have the nerve to con—must I say it—girls, with no sense of dignity, to sneak behind enemy lines and booby trap our bedrooms with horrid alarm clocks. Now I knew why Byron stood watch outside our front door last night. The deed was probably done while we were busy fighting over perfume at our former headquarters. And he had the audacity to make *me* feel guilty? It was all part of his distraction and I fell for it. I could kick myself.

Our roommates screamed outside in the hallway and Lizzie's head perked up at the latest sounds of war. I tried to ignore the panic welling into my throat. "I'll find the rest of these," Lizzie shouted over the din. Her long legs kicked out from under the bed. "Go find out why they're screaming!"

I wrenched the door open only to be shrieked back by Sandra, "Don't move! They've got the whole place booby-trapped." It seemed that we had had visitors last night. Tiny Dixie cups filled with water were set all over the hallway floor outside our bedrooms. It was a veritable minefield. There was nowhere to step without spilling them all onto the carpet. Sandra was not happy. The sleeves of her red silk pajamas flapped over her hands. "This is ridiculous!"

"I've got to go to school!" Kali whined. *I did too.* Kali tugged on her orange plaid capris, looking mournfully at the bathroom. I raked a hand through my hair and retreated to my room, thinking of our escape options. The back windows? No, too far up.

There was a sudden silence. The last of the alarm clocks had been dismantled. Lizzie set it down on the dresser. "What's going on out there?"

We screamed out a warning, but it was too late. Lizzie stepped into the hall and tripped all over the Dixie cups. She landed face first into them, smashing them flat. "Problem solved," Kali muttered.

I ran to Lizzie's side. Normally Lizzie was extremely calm in tense situations, but now she was absolutely livid. She stood up, water dripping all over her face and down her lavender t-shirt. "Madeleine!" Her finger poked painfully into my shoulder. "You will get those boys back for this. And I mean now!"

Before I could calm her down, I sniffed. The smell of smoke lingered dreadfully in the air. Apparently the boys weren't through with us yet. I hopped over the fallen Dixie cups and ran into the living room, tugging open the front door to see the damage outside. Fog left over from last night's rainstorm obstructed my view. I could barely make out a skeletal silhouette on the lawn. With one leg of my sweats rolled up, I stumbled outside in my bare feet to get close enough to see what they had done. *No, they didn't!* "The love tree!" It was on our lawn burnt to a crisp. A direct assault. They had left a note on our porch, ironically written on the back of the twins' wedding invitations: *There go your dreams...in flames.* My eyes narrowed. Was Byron on something? What was that whole friends' talk? Everything he did was insane: demanding the return of his threatening letter, acting concerned, playing with my emotions. And...and, I couldn't believe he made me feel guilty. I was so stupid.

The clock read a quarter to eight. If I left now, I'd only be fashionably late for physics. I rummaged through my dirty laundry, finding some chocolate brown lounge pants and threw them on, rolling them up to the calf. I recycled my shirt from yesterday.

"Who's going to clean this up!" Sandra's angry voice in the hallway made me hurry. I slung my backpack over my shoulder.

"It's water," Kali snapped back. "It'll dry."

"I'll get it when I get home." Somewhere in my closet I found my brown camo Chucks and slipped them on. I ran outside into the cold and dismal fog, snatching up a hoody on my way out the door. "Don't worry!"

It was all under control. It was all under...who was I kidding? I stopped short when I saw my car in the forlorn parking lot in the back. It was covered completely in diamond murals. That wasn't the guy's artwork. It was actually a deal I got on my car that made me into a driving advertisement. No, the real problem was that my car was propped up on cinder blocks. *Beginner.* The note was tucked under a lone windshield wiper, and I tugged it out before anyone else could see how bad Byron got me this time. I tore it up. How could I let him get away with making me feel guilty? Not just guilty, but broken! How dare he bring up my ex just to use as a stupid distraction?

What else could go wrong? Normally I loved running. Nothing was more liberating or a better way to get out my aggression, but now the way things were, I'd be missing at least half of class if I didn't run. I threw on the other strap of my backpack and ran full sprint into the misty morning, startling a few students on my way.

If I wasn't already struggling with physics, I'd just call it a day and stay home and watch chick flicks with my roommates to recuperate. Chick flicks would be a major regression though. Nobody had a cute-meet followed by a happy ending. Romance was something that had to be worked on with real healthy people. And to tack on my latest worry, I wasn't even sure if I was healthy enough or emotionally ready for love. I used to be…when I was like everybody else. I had goals, dreams, aspirations. That was until I dropped them all and went back to the General Study classes. The only ironic thing was that my new major forced me to take all my hard classes with the men I despised—and worse, my hard classes for spring term were Byron and Cameron's easy ones. So yeah, I could say I was a little bitter.

I rushed up the hill to the Benson Building. It rose from the fog like a monstrous beast. My class was right inside the door. Taking two stairs at a time, I fell against the double doors and scurried inside the room. The eyes of the class zeroed in on me. I was searching specifically for one pair. As soon as I found the owner of those devilish blues, I pounced his way, not bothering to scope out where Cameron sat like I usually did.

Byron looked sleek in his vintage jeans like he had plenty of time to get ready for school—I glared—a luxury he stole from me. I normally sat a few rows behind Byron. Those were the cold war weeks when we pretended the other didn't exist, but this time, I took the open seat next to him and stared him down with my best challenging look. He met it with his self-assured one. I wrenched my notebook and pen from my backpack. "I'm gonna Saran Wrap your car shut," I hissed.

Byron put his finger to his lips, looking meaningfully at the teacher, but his curling lips betrayed him. He didn't care that we were in the middle of a lecture either. "Did you have trouble waking up?"

PRANK WARS

"No...no trouble I can't handle. How about you? Did you have trouble falling asleep last night?"

He shook his head. "Nope. *I* slept with a clear conscience."

"Oh, you have one of those?"

"Don't you? Oh wait, we established last night that you don't." He treated me to a cheesy grin.

"I'll never let you mess with my mind like that again."

"Why? Did you feel guilty?" Lord Byron pushed the sleeves of his V-neck shirt to his elbows, looking like he was ready to do battle without having to break a sweat. "Don't tell me you were going to apologize?"

I'd never admit that now. I swiveled away from him, staring at our physics professor. His bow tie threatened to strangle him as he outlined our assignment for the day. I fanned my sweaty face. It was way too hot in here. My little spontaneous run was catching up with me and I struggled with my hoody to get it off. It was a harder operation than I bargained for. I had absolutely no room and my arms wouldn't come out of my sleeves. "Here, let me get that for you," Byron offered. His hand touched my back and I felt the warmth emanating from him.

My back arched and I did what any girl would do. I leaned back hard, trapping his hand between me and the seat. "Don't you dare help me. I've got it!"

He let out an involuntary laugh, but didn't try to free his hand. "But Madeleine, did you forget? It's supposed to be civil week." Mercifully, he kept his voice to a discreet whisper.

I twisted my lips at the sarcasm and looked straight ahead. "I don't believe in making deals with troublemakers."

"Really?" Byron hesitated a moment, studying my face, as if weighing what was on his mind as too dangerous, but then plunged ahead, "I thought you found trouble as attractive as I do?" He gave me a maddening smile that landed just inches from my mouth. "You were trouble the moment I met you."

I felt myself blushing, probably bright red. He sounded like an evil villain off a spy movie. What was wrong with him anyway? *What was wrong with me?* His trapped arm was still behind me and I realized too late that it looked like we were a cozy couple. This was ridiculous. Byron didn't find me cute or attractive or whatever arsenal of words he used at his disposal. I just couldn't figure out what his objective was yet…until I saw Cameron's eyes on us. As soon as I noticed, Cameron swiveled away. After our little exchange at the Doghouse, Byron couldn't possibly think he was helping me out by making Cameron jealous, could he?

It was worse than being stuck in the middle of a battlefield. Here we sat—my arch-nemesis and my ex fiancé—all in the same Principles of Physics class. There were plenty of physics classes to go around, but once I found out that I shared another class with Byron, I couldn't run like a coward—though it was a temptation after our chemistry class from last semester.

Things just got worse from there. Cameron added our class last second to fulfill the last requirements for his biology major, and I vowed to ignore them all. I struggled with my hoody. Byron didn't bother to hide how funny he thought my dire straits were. Both arms were stuck and by now I had myself a little audience. I yanked away from Byron, releasing his hand. It freed me from my hoody at the same time. I refused to see any analogy about life in that.

Professor Green was still talking about the electromagnetic spectrum. I couldn't pay attention to it at all, something about radio waves and microwaves. And microwaves? Wait, I had a question about that. I raised my newly freed hand without thinking. "Yeah, about that…" I began. Doctor Green stopped teaching to stare at me.

My gaze swept around the class of about 200, including a disdainful Cameron, and suddenly I wished I had asked the teacher *after* class. Byron watched me expectantly and so I had no choice but to take this all the way. "Okay." My voice echoed in the near silent room. "This is weird, but I was holding this can and I was talking on the cell phone at the same time, and then I set the can on the microwave and the microwave went off."

There was a stir in the room, mostly a *this-girl's-an-idiot* stir.

PRANK WARS

"I'm totally serious," I said a bit more loudly. "This happened to me yesterday. And then I moved the can off the microwave and the microwave stopped. Are cell phones and microwaves connected? Like with their waves or something?"

"Maybe there was something wrong with the cord on the microwave oven." The teacher moved to dismiss my question.

"No!" I shouted. The professor looked startled and I took a deep breath. "It's a really old microwave, sure…but maybe it wasn't properly shielded or something? And…it seems like this kind of interference happens all the time with my cell phone and computers."

"Electro smog," the know-it-all kid in the front offered. "The air is polluted with these kinds of frequencies. It has cancer causing microwaves that alter your DNA."

A few ripples of laughter rang out. Byron leaned back with an appreciative grin.

"Her cell phone's gonna fry her brain," someone mumbled behind me.

The girl next to me edged away with comical exaggeration. "Looks like it already has!" There were some snickers at this.

"No, no, no." Professor Green shook his head. "They are not connected at all. And there's no solid proof that cell phones cause cance—"

"Why do you turn off your cell phone when an airplane takes off?" I interjected stubbornly. I wanted my answer and I'd force him to give me a real one. I'd use his brain for my own purposes even if it made me look like a fool.

"That's different." His voice sounded bored. "A cell phone interferes with signals on the same broadband like the radio transmissions needed for a takeoff." He attempted to end the topic.

"Well, my cell phone affects my computer too. Just before it rings, the speakers make weird sounds." I knew something had interfered with that microwave and I wanted to know what.

At least Byron was enjoying this. "You're not going to back down, are you?" he asked me under his breath.

Professor Green gave me a brief condescending smile. Apparently I was the new crazy girl in the class, even crazier than the guy who sat in the front and made everything a conspiracy theory. "Your cell phone can possibly interfere with other radio signals, you're correct, though it's extremely rare, but not with a microwave. They're on different frequencies." He glanced to my side. "Yes." He called on Byron, who had raised his hand.

I groaned inwardly. Now I was in for it. "Can't microwaves interfere with pacemakers too," Byron said. It wasn't really a question.

"It's extremely rare, almost unheard of."

"So if cell phones interfere with pacemakers and so do microwave ovens then there must be some connection between the two, even if it is extremely rare and almost unheard of." He sounded almost sarcastic. "Say they're both on a 2.45 GHz broadband?" I stiffened in surprise. Was Byron taking my side? And how did he know how to talk this way? He was going to be a geologist.

The professor paused to consider. "I've never heard of it happening," he answered flatly.

Byron crossed his arms. "Until now, of course."

"Yes, of course, *she thought* she saw it—but there's more than interference with the signals, the whole microwave oven turned on. There would have to be a power surge." The professor quickly moved on before we interrupted him again.

Byron glanced over at me, shaking his head. "Crazy like Tesla," he breathed.

"Tesla?"

"He's a mad scientist." Great, now Byron was comparing me to mad scientists. I raised my brow at him and he took that as a cue to fill my mind with more nonsense. "He wanted to harness the energy from the air and transmit it from one source to another through waves. No more batteries, no more cords. No more filling up your gas tank. You'd just have one utility bill to pay a month."

"What happened to him?"

PRANK WARS

Byron shrugged. "He died crazy and broke, but he was a genius. If someone had funded his efforts, we'd have had wireless communication almost a century ago...along with wireless energy." And we'd all be dead of some sort of cancerous side effect, I supposed. "What was in the can that you set on the microwave?" Byron asked casually.

"I don't know. There wasn't a label on it." *Tory had pulled it off.*

Byron had a huge smile on his face. "This happened at our place, didn't it?"

Before I could stop myself, I smiled back. "What happened to Tesla's notes when he died?"

He looked surprised that I was still on this. "He had a photographic memory, so most of it died with him."

I stared at Byron, seeing him with new eyes. "You're a nerd," I said with some awe.

He broke into a laugh, and the professor gave us a warning look, but at least we weren't asking him any more questions. "Tesla had a few notes that our government and a few others fought over, most of what he wrote down was taken, never to be seen again."

I leaned back, thinking about what Byron had said. If only a man could talk from the dead. What message would he send us? What if Tesla was right and we could harness a bolt of lightning or change the frequencies in the air? What if it were as easy as pointing it at a microwave oven and turning it on?

"The world is an amazing place," Byron whispered. "If you can imagine it...it can happen."

But only if you had the brains and the will, I decided. There were two different scientists, I realized as I stared at our professor, ones who said *it couldn't be done* and others who asked *what if.* They both knew the rules, but only a few knew how to break them...or tried. I was supposed to be taking notes, but I found myself writing something completely different into my war journal: *Anything is possible. We just have to find out a way to do it. Look at our bodies. If we could get a machine to work similarly...we could be like gods. At least create like one.*

If we weren't tied down by rules—except no! Rules set us free. Like the kite analogy, the string tied it down to make it fly. So, if we could just figure out how to use the rules, we could fly. I wrote this down like they were my last words. My stomach rumbled and I pulled a Twinkie from my backpack to keep my strength up.

"What are you writing?" I jumped. Byron looked over my shoulder at my war journal. "Is that encrypted?" There was laughter behind his words when he tried to study my chicken scratches.

I tried to shame him back. "You know, you shouldn't sit so close. I might get ideas that you like me."

Apparently Byron had no shame because he didn't back off. "What? You afraid I'll break the code? Don't worry. I already know what you're thinking. You're easy to read." I scowled at that and he grinned in response. "Don't take it like that. You're hard to pronounce."

I was impressed. It actually made sense. "Touché," I muttered begrudgingly.

The lights faded and one of the many TAs for our class turned on the PowerPoint presentation about the electromagnetic spectrum. From this distance, I could see she was a small girl with dark hair.

Byron leaned over me. "Hey, did you bring your book?"

"Are you kidding?" I turned from the TA. "That thing weighs a million-and-two tons and I had to run the whole way here."

He sighed and turned to the front. Professor Green pointed out the different wavelength frequencies: gamma rays, x-rays, ultraviolet rays all the way to microwave and radio waves.

"Question." I raised my hand again, thinking about Tesla. "Back to cell phones. Can we transmit energy through the air using frequencies similar to cell phones?"

Our teacher froze at the board. I wondered if I overdid it this time. He took a moment to answer, "That's exactly what cell phones do." It was as if he were explaining this to a child. "They use very specific energy with signals that our appliances can decode, but only the military can transmit tremendously powerful signals. Most low power applications

PRANK WARS

are used only for communications purposes." *Then Tesla was right; transmitting energy could be done.* I smiled. "If we focus any of the energy we are using into a small enough area," he finished, "it can and will do devastating damage."

Now he had done it. My mind went into overload just thinking about what kind of damage it could do. "Cell phone companies can find anyone with a cell phone," I thought aloud. "Just dial a number and the military tracks us. Increase the signal power and they'll kill us." Byron looked surprised. The class started to murmur. There were quite a few laughs. A few diehard students left angrily, the door clicking solidly behind them.

The professor gawked at me. He cleared his throat. "If you want to get paranoid, sure, bad guys can get you…if your cell phone is on. Maybe you all should get the hint and turn your cell phones off." It seemed the professor finally had one over on me. He looked quite smug about it.

The look on Byron's face almost made me stop talking. For once he wasn't laughing. No, he had turned quite serious. I tried to ignore that. "What about the towers next to my apartment?" They were tall ugly things made of white brick marring the sky west of our apartments. Signals could be sent from there. "Are those cell phone towers?"

The professor looked confused for a moment. "Are you talking about the utility towers? Yes, cell phone companies pay them to put their satellite dishes up there."

"What does *provocity* mean?" a girl asked directly behind me. Her voice was high-pitched and nervous. Professor Green looked even blanker than when I had asked him a question. "You know," she desperately tried to clarify before she looked as stupid as me, "that word that's written on those towers?"

The class shifted to look at me, but for once I was innocent. Cameron's eyes were especially condescending. Before I could point out the true identity of our latest scholar, Professor Green answered the question in a long suffering voice. "That would be Provo City, not *provocity*. Any other questions, class, or can we go on?" The girl's seat squeaked as she slunk down into it. It didn't matter if she hid. Everyone was looking at me.

Byron elbowed me. "It's the city we live in, haven't you heard of it, Mad?" he asked way too loud. *He* knew very well that I hadn't asked that. "Hey, but keep bugging the teacher about it," he teased more softly this time. "I'm sure he'll admit it's *provocity* just to get you off his back." He pronounced provocity the same way the girl behind us said it, completely wrong…and with a touch of that accent again.

"Well, it sounds more off with your weird accent," I said. He looked confused, but I wouldn't let him throw me off this time. "Where does it come from? You're not with the KGB, are you?"

He ignored the taunt. "What sort of accent is it? Southern?"

I don't know. It sounded really hot…like he belonged to the *Flight of the Conchords* or something. Yeah, that's how I recognized it. "Did you serve a mission in New Zealand?"

"Nope." He watched the TA. The small girl had left her spot at the computer to pass out our assignments. She wore brightly colored pumps with a Prada buckle. Her long black hair swung behind her. It was just like Byron to check out another girl while sitting next to me. It made me recall the existence of Holly.

"Hey, what were you doing outside my apartment last night?" I asked.

He chuckled, most likely remembering how much I stunk. "Why were you running out of your neighbor's so fast?"

"We found out someone lived there."

He shifted like he wanted to say something, but stayed quiet.

"What?"

His playful nature took over. "Yeah, *someone* does live there. She's—" He hesitated, watching me.

"—hot," I finished for him. I glared and turned away. Forget the ward directory, we should've asked the lady's man who the mystery girl was instead. "So, who is she?"

PRANK WARS

The TA leaned over the girl next to me, counting out the papers for our row. My head tilted when she got closer. Wait. She looked vaguely familiar. Before I could figure it out, Byron leaned heavily over me, cutting off my line of vision and reaching past my startled neighbor. He grabbed the papers from the TA, his broad shoulder knocking into my face. The brunette next to me could have reached it much easier. Why was he bothering being such gentleman? It was completely unnecessary. The papers flicked me across my hair, messing it up even more. I hit Byron back and he smiled mockingly in my face. "Sorry. Didn't mean to touch you."

"Don't worry. I'll wash my hands."

Byron supplied me and the girl next to me our papers, keeping one for himself. My little brunette neighbor didn't mind that her personal space had been trespassed at all. She beamed brightly at him. A faint dimple appeared on Byron's cheek in response as he passed the rest of the papers down the row. I finally guessed his motives. "It's always about the ladies, isn't it, Byron. How can you live with yourself? You player!"

"Thanks?"

No way would I sit with him in physics again. The papers ran out at the end of the row and the hands started to rise. Professor Green turned to his TA, giving her a nod. "Thanh." My head shot up as he indicated the rest of the papers on his desk. "I have more copies over here."

Thanh? I twisted in my seat. Could that be our beautiful Asian neighbor, minus the lollipop? Yes, the TA was definitely her, well, the clearer version of her than the perfume clouded portrait of her from the night before. "Byron." I dug my fingers into his arm and he flinched. "That's her. That's my neighbor!"

He was watching me warily and I considered elbowing him in the ribs to take me seriously, but I resisted. What did he think I was going to do, attack her for having the audacity to live next door to me? I wasn't *that* much of a threat—until I realized what his problem was. "Hey! Was she one of the TAs in our chem 111 class too?"

Byron looked resigned. "No."

He was lying. She was the same girl Byron had been flirting with on April Fool's Day. I bet she had an amazing brain *and* she was beautiful, probably really demure too. I tried not to be jealous. "Did you ask her out?"

This time his smile seemed more genuine. "Nope."

I lifted an eyebrow at him. Now I knew he was lying.

CHAPTER TWELVE

Day 107
0854 hours

"Just when you think you know the enemy...he shows you just how much you don't."

—Madeleine's War Journal Entry (Wednesday, May 30th).

I escaped out the back door of the Benson building. It had rained while we were in class. A thick fog settled over everything. The streetlights above me were on. It was a surreal thing for a spring morning. The bell tower tolled nine o'clock just as my cell phone went off.

"Mad Dog." It was Tory.

"Yeah?"

"Are you coming home?"

"Yeah, why?" She hung up on me and I stared at my cell, trying to figure her out.

"Are you crazy?" Byron jerked my pink camo cell from me. His muscular forearm brushed against mine. "That thing is lethal."

"Yeah, and you've got your own. Go fry your brain with it."

"Don't worry. I have it safely stored away from my heart and organs. Contrary to popular belief, I do want to live a long and healthy life...with kids and stuff."

I wrestled my phone back from him. "People like you shouldn't have kids."

"With people like you?" he asked.

I stopped wrestling with him. "What?"

He grinned. "What?"

I flattened my lips into a firm line. Single life was the only culture where you were making up excuses to part ways before you could say hello. That's how I normally kept things with Lord Byron, but ever since that nursery job, we couldn't stop crossing paths. The bishop had a lot to answer for.

I jerked my phone away from him and we both headed down the lane. The fence was covered in creepers, pyro, and stalkers—a pretty lane of vines with disturbing names. We were very secluded with the fog. My only fear was that Byron would think I walked home with him because I liked him, but I knew better than to fall for him. The rule was to not want anything, especially something like this. Crushes made you act stupid, desperate, and eventually broke your heart. I didn't want any of it. I looked everywhere but at Byron. He broke the silence. "Are you satisfied now that you found your phantom?"

"You knew who she was," I accused.

His gaze shot to mine. Before he could respond, some guy came out of the fog and strode past us. He looked like he was talking to himself, except he was on a Bluetooth. It was the only thing keeping him from looking like a raving lunatic, and he was speaking in a different language. Everyone did here. BYU would be a veritable recruiting bonanza for the CIA, except we were all crazy. I turned back to Byron. "So why don't we ever see Thanh at home?" I asked.

He shrugged. "She's probably a grad student."

"In physics. And stop pretending you don't know. What project is she working on?" He didn't answer and I tried to work it out in my mind. "She's leading a double life of intrigue, working on top secret inventions."

"Yeah, 'cause grad students do that all the time."

I glanced over at him, deciding to make it even more dramatic for his benefit. "And that note you wanted? It...was meant for her."

PRANK WARS

By now his calm exterior seemed a little strained. He downed some tic tacs, his black hair flying back. "Hey, uh…" We had reached a fork in the pathway. He studied my face. "I've got a study group I've got to go to."

So, why was he asking my permission? "You may go then," I waved him away with a casual hand and left him behind in the trail. "I'm sure all the girls in your group will thank me."

"Really?" he called after me, "Did you really just say that?" I stiffened at the familiar incredulous note. "Sometimes I have better things to do than play the field and hang with *hotties*. Sometimes I actually care about school. It's funny, I know."

I stopped short. His attempt at another guilt trip wasn't fooling me. "Is it Holly? Has she changed you then?"

The muscle on his jaw worked overtime. "Yeah, about that? Where did you get Holl…?" he trailed off, remembering. "You were there in my apartment. You heard everything?"

"Of course, and I was thinking—what about that poor flight attendant we all thought you were dating?"

His face got red and he snapped. I actually physically saw him snap, and I jumped back in surprise. "Well, I have two hands," he said sarcastically. "What better use for them. I'll just put a woman on each arm."

"Ooh, I hate…"

He cut me off. "So do I. Players muck up the field." He closed the gap between us, his lips parting to reveal a dangerous smile. I could smell the tic tacs on his breath. "You're not jealous, are you?"

"Yeah, I want to date a flight attendant."

"You should. It's great. And that's the other thing. You should get out more. Do something more than getting your revenge on men. Maybe you could work on your social *provocity* a little."

I gasped, not sure whether to laugh or cry. I loved that he was making *provocity* into a word, but was Lord Byron actually giving me dating advice? "You're right." I walked backwards, trying to put more distance between us. It was my favorite thing to do lately. I tried to match his sarcasm. "You know what the worst thing is? When I get off the phone with my mom and she's always crying. It sometimes makes me think I'm doing something wrong with my life. Poor little ol' me. I think I'll drown my sorrows in ice cream and chocolate!"

He choked on his tic tacs. "Great. Your life *is* a chick flick in the making."

"I don't believe in those, but thanks for the thought. You got me right here." I laid a hand on my heart.

"Impossible. There's nothing there." He was moving away, but it didn't stop us from shouting back and forth between the fog. I could barely see him anymore.

"Wow, you're brilliant," I called. "You've got me all figured out. Forget geology. You should go into psychiatry, Byron. You've missed your calling."

"Get a life."

"Okay, psychiatry is out. Have you tried diplomacy?" I gave him a slow sarcastic clap. "You're truly amazing. No? Okay, espionage. It suits you better. You can't ever give me a straight answer." I was sure he was way out of earshot and I found myself smiling. Fighting with Byron always put me in a good mood. Nothing was funnier than imagining Byron fuming on his way to his study group. Maybe, just maybe he would forget the girls and concentrate on his studies just to spite me. Probably not. The moment I stepped away, I knew he forgot me.

I crossed under a streetlight and it turned off menacingly. Why did those things always have motion detectors that worked against me? The soft pad of sneakers slapped against the cement behind me, and my head perked up at the noise. Whoever it was, they were heading my way. I hoped it wasn't an enraged Byron. The thought made me giggle. Wait, hadn't Tory called to see if I was on my way home? I was due for another scare, and this was just the place for it, dark and forbidding. A twig snapped in front of me and I stopped, staring into the blank fog. I was surrounded by it. Where was she? Behind me or in front of me? Every

PRANK WARS

sense tingled with the danger. There was no way of knowing really. The running feet behind me became more pronounced and I braced myself for the inevitable. But why did I have to wait for her to get me? No! Not this time. If she wanted to scare me, she'd have to fight for it. This time, I'd outrun her.

I picked up my feet and crossed the street into a parking lot. A few drivers circled their cars around me like sharks, thinking I was going for my car. Poor people. I had no parking spot to offer them. Their motors ran gloomily in the eerie light. The fog was so thick I could barely make out their shiny bumpers. I waved them to pass me, and once again they left me in dismal silence.

I lost the direction of Tory's footsteps. For all I knew she could be inches from me, hiding behind a car, in the bushes. Looking every which way, I spotted a poster stapled to an electric pole: *Need help with cleaning checks? We'll clean your apartment for $5.*

Wow, that was a steal. Despite the danger, I tore off one of the numbers...and realized they looked familiar: *Call us. Tory, Madeleine, Kali, Sandra, Lizzie.* I gasped and ripped the fake advertisement from the pole, doing some major damage control. I just hoped I was the first to see that thing or our phones would ring off the hook. Already a few of the numbers had been pulled off. Stupid Byron. Too late I felt the feet pounding the pavement behind me. I braced myself just as the jogger rushed for me, ruffling my hair. *He?* I barely had time to look when I heard the scream. Tory jumped out from behind her tree and the jogger pulled back with a startled grunt. His hand formed into a fist.

"No!" I sprang towards them. "It's only Tory! It's okay!"

The jogger turned to look at me and I fell back in complete embarrassment. Eric? He was in BYU shorts and rumpled J Dawgs T-shirt. Why did he always get caught up in our misadventures? By now Tory's mouth was open, her red hair falling over her face. She made a beautiful mugger in her basketball shorts. I was surprised Eric's heart hadn't melted at the mere sight of her—I mean, after the scare—but he just looked irritated. "Oh, you again!"

"Whoops." Tory actually looked ashamed of herself. She tugged nervously on her *Running is for Criminals* shirt.

"Sorry." I apologized for Tory—she didn't know how to do it herself. "She sometimes comes out of nowhere."

Eric took a deep breath, seeming to count. He turned from me to stretch, leaning heavily on his Nikes, the muscles on his calves flexing. The rubber soles squeaked against the pavement. He kept an eye on Tory like she was a dangerous animal…in a way, she was. "So, what possesses you to jump out at innocent joggers? Huh?"

I shrugged. "We thought you were someone else?" It sounded pretty lame.

Eric broke into a laugh, surprising me. "Remind me to never get on your bad side." Tory looked uncomfortable, her arms stiff at her sides. "Well?" Eric straightened and turned his full attention on me. "You'll have to make it up to me this time, Mad. Maybe dinner? I like Mexican food."

"What?" Even though he was cute, I wasn't giving into his blackmail. I grinned. "You're gonna make Tory go out with you?"

Eric's smile easily reached his hazel eyes. He clearly thought we were a riot. "Wow, it's like you've stepped right out of the pages of a comic book. You're unreal." I reddened in embarrassment and it only made his grin bigger. "Do you ever let go? C'mon, you can tell me. You're the kind of girl who sings really loud in the shower."

"Are you kidding?" I managed a grin at Tory. "I have to be fully aware of my surroundings." Or I'd feel a glass of cold water thrown over the shower curtain.

"Well, if you ever want some real fun, you know where to find me."

"Do you even have a place…?"

He laughed in realization. "Yeah, I'm still working on that. I'll have a housewarming party as soon as I do…though I have the feeling you're not big on parties. Maybe you and I could do something more priv—?"

"No, *we'll* go." I protested. "We love parties." His eyes took on a frustrated glint, and I found myself trying to make up for emphasizing *we*. I don't know why I did it, but there was no turning back now. "I'm sure your party will give me a chance to work on my social *provocity* a little," I used Byron's made-up word.

Eric nodded, never understanding most of what I said anyway. He thrust his hand out to me. "Until our next exciting adventure then." I took his hand. It was strong and firm and felt really nice over mine. He surprised me by pulling me into a huge bear hug. My breath came out with a whoosh of surprise and he rubbed my back for good measure.

I tried not to wriggle free. "I can hardly wait," I muttered into his chest, but I was lying. Not because I didn't like him. I did. Normally, I made the most of everything, just not where guys were concerned because our next meeting would make me look even stupider. He let me go and with a casual salute, jogged away, disappearing into the fog. I put my arm around the forlorn Tory. "You're gonna get arrested one of these days."

She giggled a little bit. "I think he likes you."

"I'm talking about this war, not him." I held up the poster I had confiscated from the pole.

"Oh yeah, that's what I'm trying to say. I've received new *intel*." Tory wiped her sweatband against her sweaty face. "Your mom couldn't get a hold of you, so she called me with the report. She got your engagement pictures in the mail."

I gasped. Fake engagement pictures? Just what my mom needed, false hope. "Byron!" I rushed blindly for home with Tory doggedly matched my stride. He was out to ruin my life.

CHAPTER THIRTEEN

Day 109
1604 hours

"Never underestimate your enemy; never assume he has a heart when he has horns."

—Madeleine's War Journal Entry (Friday, June 1st).

How could he? You left mothers alone! That was the number one rule in pranking...well, I had a lot of number one rules, but that one was definitely at the top.

Tory and I got Byron's apartment door open with an ease born of experience. I was still in my black yoga pants from class, not having time to change. It was our only window of opportunity. We had to wait two whole days to get back at him. Byron was at the gym. The twins were in class. Rock? Well, he might be taking a nap in the back, but nothing stirred him. Gingerly lifting my canvas Chucks, I picked my way through the gauntlet of junk on the floor, a deadly obstacle course for any visitor, let alone cat burglars. "I don't remember ransacking their place," I joked.

Tory laughed, strutting inside. She had changed from her school clothes to a slouchy tee and cropped jeans. She surveyed the damage. There were still remnants of our last visit. The guys hadn't bothered to take down our beautiful curtains. The doilies and stuffed animals were strewn across the room. "Don't they ever clean up around here?" she asked.

"It's kind of cute."

PRANK WARS

Tory gave me a weird look and set our creepy dummy on their couch. It was made up from clothes we found from the DI boxes in the laundry room. It stared back at us with red, cold eyes. The boys would have a mini heart attack when they came home to find the phantom waiting for them. I briefly considered the couch, but it was too heavy to take. Besides, there wasn't enough time. We'd leave it for a different sting. Tory unscrewed the cable from the computer in a vicious counterstrike. She was through playing. "What are you doing?" I asked.

"Just little extras." Tory unscrewed a few light bulbs too, but left them in. The guys would buy new ones before realizing that it was completely unnecessary. They basically owed her their year's supply. I roamed freely through the cramped kitchen. There were a number of possibilities for mischief: a little Anbesol around the top of the milk jugs, fake bugs and flies in their cereal, crumpled newspapers as high as their waists. But it was a covert operation, get in, leave the message, get out. I noticed the black backpack left behind on a chair. It was an ugly thing and I recognized it immediately. It was Byron's, but no way. That was another unwritten rule. Don't mess with school stuff. Almost unwittingly, I found myself picking it up. "No!" Even Tory knew we were getting in too deep. "What do you think you're doing?"

"He declared war," I heard myself saying. "He made us all late for class. He messed with my mom! He deserves it."

She hung back uncertainly. It wasn't often Tory was caught in a moral dilemma.

"Don't worry; it's just a simple extraction." I said. "We'll give it back to him tonight…filled with all sorts of nice things. In fact, we'll leave a ransom note." I picked up a marker from their white board and a piece of pristine white paper from their printer. I began the note in my fanciest flowery handwriting: *We want dates, lots of dates…*

Tory broke into a laugh. "Are you serious?"

"No."

And ice cream on those dates. Lots of chocolate. And maybe…if you could sign up for the boyfriend-for-a-week-program, that would be absolutely delightful too.

"They'll think it's AmyLee," Tory was quick to point out.

"Yep." I turned the paper over and pulled out a white crayon from my pocket. "Now for the real letter." I entitled it: *List of demands*. I brought the crayon to my lips, thinking. Perhaps it was best to keep it close to the letter we found on Thanh's door: *In regards to your backpack: we know where you live, and we want what's ours: the cushions, our peace of mind, our self-respect. Pretty much our lives back. Do it or die.* I put a smiley face on the end, and glanced up at Tory. "See? We can play nice."

Tory's forehead wrinkled. "I don't think they'll be able to read that."

"Not until someone colors over the message with a different color of crayon. It's ingenious, see?" I placed a red crayon under the paper. "Only Byron will get it."

"How?"

"I'll tell him." I threw the backpack over my shoulder. It felt a little heavy...just like the guilt welling up inside me...but as soon as I recognized it, I squelched it. Byron was winning this war because the man had no conscience. It was about time I followed his lead, which meant I'd have no problem taping the *Traitor* and *Disavowed* signs on the gamers' door downstairs. "Let's go."

CHAPTER FOURTEEN

Day 109
1632 hours

"Knocking down doors is much harder than enticing someone to let you in...especially if you're holding flowers."

—Madeleine's War Journal Entry (Friday, June 1st).

Tory and I sneaked inside my apartment moments after infiltrating Byron's apartment. His heavy backpack was flung over my shoulder. Before I could hide it from Lizzie's prying eyes, I saw the scene of carnage before me. The watered-over eyes. The happy smiles. My roommates hugged popcorn and M&Ms close to their hearts. They sat on the floor in a nest of blankets. The cushion-free couch was a little uncomfortable.

"What are they doing?" I asked...though I already knew.

"Watching chick flicks," Tory reported.

"Nobody learns from my mistakes, do they?" It was a terrible thing to do to themselves on a beautiful afternoon—especially with a lonely Friday night looming just hours away. I marched to the laptop, but it was too late. It was already the sappy ending.

My roommates sighed at the touching story on the screen. The man stood helplessly, staring at this woman who was the love of his life, a little unsure of how she'd react to his declaration of love, but sure of his feelings for her. The two were caught in the rain. The camera did a close up on the girl's tears. They glistened. "I loved you all along." His voice broke and he captured her perfect hand in his. Her sad eyes turned joyful. She laughed and he hugged her. He picked her up and swung her around. The rain doused them and they didn't care. The camera lingered on the happy couple then zoomed magically into the sky.

It was done so craftily that even my heart gave a little leap. I closed the laptop with a decided click before the beautiful music from the credits could fill the room. The silence deafened me. Their eyes shot to me. I shrugged. "What? I had to stop it before the guy got tired of her and went for someone else."

Kali uncurled from masses of blankets, dividing the layers from her white jeans. She threw a pillow at me and I easily caught it with my left hand. "What's the matter with you?" she sputtered.

I picked up the DVD cover and shook it at them. "This is just war propaganda designed to weaken you when the enemy strikes."

"Yes, and I love it!" She sighed, folding her knees into her stomach. "I wish I could find a man like that." Lizzie agreed, and I heard the cacophony of sighs. I glanced over at Tory to see her nodding in time with them. I was getting nowhere. Perfect guy. Perfect girl. Perfect love. It didn't exist. To actually believe that there was something more out there, something magical. It made it an even bigger disappointment when the world dumped on you.

I threw the DVD cover back to the table. "These movies are out to steal your money and cheapen your existence. There is nothing like this out there anywhere!"

Lizzie bit her lip. It looked like the movie had caught her in the middle of changing from her school clothes to her work-out clothes; it was that powerful. She had tucked her flutter sleeved blouse into her sweats. "Um, Mad Dog, don't you think that's a little…uh…harsh?"

"What do you prefer? Learning it the hard way or hearing it from me?" I tried to stalk out of the living room, readjusting Byron's backpack over my shoulder. Lizzie's voice stopped me, "Dream killer."

I turned on my heel. Lizzie was calling me out. "What did you call me?"

PRANK WARS

"What happened to your faith anyway?"

"Faith? In what?" I threw my arms out, pointing to the DVD. "Love, romance, whatever you want to call it...it isn't like this. There's nothing to have faith in!"

"Oh yeah?" Kali popped a couple of M&Ms in her mouth and plopped back into her nest of blankets. "My dad loves my mom very much."

Things were so simple for Kali. And to give myself credit, which I did, I thought about what she said. "That's the way *love* used to be," I said, "for some people...maybe."

Lizzie stood up, cleaning the popcorn kernels off the floor as she did so. "You think you're too good for marriage. Is that it?"

"No," I said it cautiously. It was a commandment, wasn't it? Still, marriage was a pretty hard thing to imagine, especially since I couldn't get along with any guy for one day. I had way too many flaws—so did they.

"Well then, if you don't believe in love, then what's stopping you from getting married now?" Lizzie asked in a logical voice. "Even better. You don't even have to wait to love the man. Why don't you just coldly pick out a good guy and marry him?" I froze at the thought. "You can't tell me that there aren't good guys out there...because there are. Go ahead, Mad, you're a God-fearing girl, you know your duty. Go get married."

"There's no guy I want to marry," I snapped.

"Why?"

I faltered before answering. Kali watched me expectantly. Even Tory looked curious. Lizzie was forcing my hand. "Okay, you're right." I should've remembered Lizzie was always right. "That's why this whole thing is a tragedy."

"That I'm right?"

"No." I gave a self-deriding laugh. "I won't marry a man that I don't love. And since I'll never find love, I'll never get married." Maybe that's why I cared so much about this revolution. I'd lose everything if things didn't change. Love. Dreams. Everything. Though to be honest, I think I had lost those anyway.

Lizzie took her bowl of popcorn into the kitchen. "Looks like you're a bigger victim of chick flicks than we are."

"Excuse me?" Byron's backpack bounced against my shoulder. I followed her into the kitchen. Kali picked up her thick blankets and toddled after us. Tory rolled her eyes and leaned against the door. "Why?" I asked. "Just because I think a man won't grab my *perfect* hand? Won't swing me around? Won't say I've always loved you? And if he did, he wouldn't mean it a month later?" I stopped short, seeing the flowers on the table. Three delicate red roses. They were beautiful. "Whose flowers?"

Lizzie threw her bowl into the sink. "They're from your most dedicated admirer."

Byron? My heart fluttered in suspicion. I sat on the counter, keeping my distance from the dying things. "What's wrong with them?"

"And that's your problem. You're suspicious of anything good!" Lizzie was fed up with me. "You tell me, Miss Schadenfreude. What do you think love is then? And before you go off on mutual respect, tell me what you really think."

"It's something..." she had me stumped. I glanced furtively at the roses, expecting them to grow thorns...well, more thorns. Lizzie's steady eyes were on me. Fine, I would tell her what I really thought. "It's something that doesn't exist anymore...not for me anyway."

"So for you, love is so completely out of reach, something so big and so amazing that you think you'll never find it because you've never seen it?" After a moment, I nodded. "You're a worse romantic than Kali." I gasped. Those were fighting words. Lizzie gathered up the dishes from the green carpet. She usually cleaned when she was mad, which was why it was such a temptation to get her angry. This time was an accident. "You'll never be satisfied by a real man," Lizzie accused.

Sandra sashayed out from the back rooms. Her boot cut jeans clung to her leather high heels. As usual she was talking on her iPhone to her

PRANK WARS

latest fling. Lizzie pulled away from the sink. "Specimen one," she said in a low voice. "*She* finds love every day. Explain that. Is it real or is it fake?"

"I don't know." I turned to her. "Sandra?"

Sandra held up one finger, silencing us. Her handkerchief sleeves fell back to her elbows. She was one of those people who demanded politeness to the point of rudeness. "I don't know where you got the idea that we were hiring out for cleaning checks?" I heard her say in clipped tones over the phone.

I bit my lip, looking elsewhere. That's when I noticed the mess in our kitchen. I hopped off the counter and closed the cupboard doors before Sandra noticed and went off on a tirade. Not a moment too soon, Sandra flipped off her cell and opened the recently closed cupboard door. "There's an obnoxious smell in this kitchen!" she complained.

"Is it coming from the vents?" I asked. There was always a possibility of a dead skunk or old pickle juice stashed up there. I went to investigate.

Sandra shook her head, taking her peanut butter out of the cupboard. She studied the contents to make sure it was just as full as before. "Who's been eating my food?" I tried not to look at Kali. Most likely she would be the culprit, but no way would she fess up to it. I stared into the vents instead. Thankfully, there was nothing there. "Quit eating my food or I'll put laxatives in it!" Sandra threatened. I hoped Kali knew she was serious.

"Sandra?" I asked her again.

She got a text. "Just a sec." I was jealous of her dexterity. She texted with one hand while slathering peanut butter over a piece of bread. With a no-nonsense air, she sketched another notch on the peanut butter jar with a Sharpie to mark the new level. No one would eat her food without getting caught. Next time, she'd probably take fingerprints.

"See," Lizzie whispered. Even *she* can find love."

"Real love?" I asked.

"You *are* a romantic."

I winced and made sure I didn't look in the direction of the flowers. Lizzie was out to prove something. Sandra quit texting and turned exasperated eyes on me. "What?"

Just then Kali slid her iPod into the speakers on the counter and began singing off-key to it, not just off-key, but as loud as her voice could warble out the misshapen tune. I tried to shout over the sound. "Yes, um, Sandra? What's your definition of love?" It was a dumb question, and I felt even dumber asking it.

Sandra choked on her sandwich. "You're asking me? Figure it out yourself." She meant to walk out on us, but then hesitated, her face trying to take on a pleasant expression. I could tell it was a difficult process. "Does this have to do with my offer to help you with your love lives?"

"No!" I tried not to reveal my horror at the suggestion. I just needed to show Lizzie how someone else's definition of love was more skewed than my own. "I want to know if love is..." I made something up, "...actually worth the pain."

Sandra glanced speculatively at the roses on the table. She wouldn't if she knew who they were from. "It's always fun when you *think* you're in love." Instead of being pleasantly surprised, I was immediately suspicious of her honest answer. Sandra tapped her long fingernails against the counter. "Even if you don't love the guy, it's better than being home with you..." she uncharacteristically cut the insult off, "with ur, my homework." There was a loud *thunk* above us. It sounded like someone was on the roof. "What's that?" Sandra asked apprehensively.

"Mike's here," Lizzie said in an undertone. "He's fixing the ceiling fan." A cold shiver escaped me. Our landlord was the kindest guy in the world, and he loved to talk about everything. If he caught any of us alone, we could get caught with his blabbing mouth for hours. And I'm not joking. It was the worst psychological torture imaginable.

Kali's singing abruptly cut off. "Did Mike say anything about—?"

"Shhh," I held my finger superstitiously to my lips. "Don't say his name too loud. He'll hear you."

PRANK WARS

Kali lowered her voice. "Did *he* say anything else about...*that girl*?" She hugged her blanket closer to her. She'd be sucking her thumb next.

"Thanh's not a ghost," I told her. "I found out who she is." Tory cast me a betrayed look. "Sorry, I've been meaning to tell you."

"How did you figure out who she was?" Sandra turned to me, seeming unusually interested. I wondered if she was as caught up in the mystery as the rest of us were. It was shockingly human of her.

"She's the TA in my physics class."

"No," they all said at once.

Immediately I was the star with the most information. "She's a grad student. That's why we don't ever see her. She's probably working on some groundbreaking paper or something. We practically live by a famous person...someday." Now I was making it bigger than it was, but nobody cared. Lizzie busily gathered ingredients to make spaghetti. She was not one to be distracted by gossip. "And Byron dated her," I said.

"What?" Even Lizzie was caught by that.

For some reason Sandra hadn't stalked away from us yet. "You didn't tell her we were in her apartment, did you?"

I laughed. Sandra must think I was an idiot. "Of course, I just told her we went through her things and tried on all her clothes. No big deal."

Sandra stiffened then blew out her anger. I watched in dreadful fascination. She was controlling her anger. It was so unlike her. "Uh, sorry, didn't mean to imply that you're stupid."

I was taken aback. Even Lizzie seemed startled at the complete personality overhaul. Was Sandra going through anger management classes or something? Momentarily distracted, Lizzie opened the cupboard door below the counter without taking the usual precautions. Pans and bowls flew out, clattering loudly all over the floor. Kali screamed, trying to preserve her vulnerable toes.

"Booby-trapped again." I would've suspected Tory did it to scare us, except Kali lived with us too and she never put anything away right. We listened to the answering thumps against our floor. The girls downstairs thought we were being too loud and were taking their broomstick to their ceiling again. Kali stomped back, her bare feet making a strange noise against the kitchen floor. It was a sophisticated system of communication. The roses shook dangerously on the table and I steadied them, knowing they'd stink up the place if they crashed to the ground. As soon as the roses were safe, I dragged Byron's backpack to the computer and set it down on the yellowed linoleum.

Too late, I heard Lizzie gasp behind me. "That isn't your backpack."

I hunched over guiltily and glanced at Sandra. Her iPhone was plastered to her ear again. I wasn't supposed to be messing with her ex-boyfriend so much, and I really tried not to, but…he was provoking me. I hated myself for it. "Lizzie, I don't know what you're talking about?" I turned on the computer. "I can't get a new backpack without you freaking out?"

"Not if it already belongs to someone else."

"Don't worry." Tory flopped down on the hard wooden chair next to me. "They'll think it was AmyLee who stole it. We've got it covered."

Lizzie looked appropriately shocked and I flung Tory an annoyed look. "We did AmyLee a favor," I hurriedly explained. "If the guys meet our demands, they'll take her out…on a date, I mean. That's what she wants."

"You don't take school stuff," Lizzie reminded me. I knew that, but Byron broke the rules first.

Sandra swept the kitchen perimeter, still attached to her phone. "What? It's Friday night! You can't just…he's—" She sighed heavily. "How do you expect me to do that?"

"Oh no," I whispered with a meaningful glance at Sandra. "Someone's gonna be home on a Friday night. The horror." Lizzie gave me a warning look.

My computer took a moment to reboot. *"Hello, Mad Dog,"* a little voice chirped inside it. *"Welcome to your computer. What can I do for you today?"*

I almost fell out of my chair. "Who got into my computer?" Nobody knew and I swiveled to look at Tory. She was always trying to hone my skills, but she just looked blank. It could've been anyone really. I took a deep breath, continuing my debate with Lizzie. "Lord Byron crosses the line too. "

Lizzie's face hardened. "He made me late for class."

"He also sent an engagement announcement to my mom. He infiltrated my personal territory."

"Who are you getting married to?" she asked.

"That isn't the point!" Though now I was curious. I logged into my computer and saw the screensaver. Cameron's face floated across the screen along with mine in a cute little collage of typical cheesy engaged couple poses. They made me get married to Cameron? Lizzie caught her breath. These were my old engagement pictures. My mom got *these* in the mail? "What is wrong with him?" I cried, no longer bothering to keep my voice down. "You do *not* mess with people's moms." You did not mess with people's exes either. Sandra glanced blandly over at me, and I tried to keep myself in control, so she wouldn't overhear this. I was too frustrated to think clearly. "Oh," I hissed under my breath, "*Byron* just asked for it…a million times over."

Lizzie was right. I didn't see how life truly was. I wanted my life to be a certain way and it wasn't. I had been pushing at the same stubborn rock forever just to change the way things were…and though nothing was budging, I couldn't leave that rock and find another one. I had already put too much energy and effort into it. What I meant was…I had a point to make; love was dead, and even if no one listened to me, I had to get that across somehow, even if it meant dealing with this kind of scum.

"Don't let this get to you," I heard Lizzie say quietly. "Please."

I could barely hear her voice and I stood up, pacing the kitchen floor around Kali's clogging. "You think I'm the only victim of chick flicks here? What about you? You can't tell me that you've never been hurt by a man. Why haven't you found love, huh?"

"I have. He just didn't love me back."

No words could be more calculated to shock me. "Who?" I growled.

"Actually, it happens all the time. It's just the way the cookie crumbles, ya know?" She smiled what she thought was a comforting smile.

"Who *wouldn't* love you!" I was angry again. I raced to the flowers. I'd uncover the enemy that we were dealing with and make sure my friends were never sad about losing a man again. "Let me see these."

"What are you doing?" Kali asked in some alarm. By some miracle, I had diverted her from her floor stomping. As soon as I got to the table where the flowers rested, I pulled the flowers out of the vase and thrust them next to Kali. She screwed up her nose. "Ooh, those stink!"

"Did I call it or did I call it?" I tugged the note out of the flowers: *"Sorry, you weren't here when I brought these over. Due to your unfortunate absence, I took advantage of your roommates instead. Let's call ourselves even, shall we? Post script: Please return my copy of* Love Whispers in the Rain *when you're through watching it. I need a good laugh."* Byron wasn't at the gym when we stole his backpack, was he? He gave us the chick flick. He messed with my mom. And these roses were soaked in tuna juice. I dragged them across the room, letting them drip heedlessly all over the floor. "This is how fun love is." I chucked the roses into the garbage.

Sandra's face screwed up in horror. She clicked off her phone, cutting off the guy on the other end. "What are you doing?"

Kali peeled the roses out of the garbage and rinsed them. "So what? They're still beautiful. Ouch!" A thorn pricked her. I hated to say I told her so, but I told her so. A loud noise outside the kitchen in the hallway made us turn. Two legs dangled from the trapdoor above the hall. The legs were attached to a pair of dirty sneakers. My roommates' faces twisted into various expressions of horror as the thing descended from the ceiling and came for us.

"Shhh," Kali warned us. "Keep it down…it's Mike." And if he caught us, he wouldn't stop talking.

I watched in horrid anticipation as our landlord crawled out of the

PRANK WARS

crawlspace from our ceiling and dropped to the floor. He was covered in grime and white dust. The fear was almost palpable as everyone turned away from him in one motion, busying themselves with whatever they could find. Even Kali seemed suspiciously preoccupied with the dishes. She wasn't fooling me in the least.

I was the only one who couldn't tear myself away. For some strange reason, I was irrevocably and profoundly attracted to that hole in the ceiling. Even to the extent that I would sacrifice myself and my sanity to find out more about it. I walked towards the hole and held my hands up so I could touch the lip on the ledge. "What's up there?" I found myself asking. I ignored the startled gasps behind me. I had opened the conversation with Mike.

He dusted off the sprinkle of white stuff from his brown hair and gray sweatshirt. "I put Velcro on the edges of the trapdoor." He reached up, snapping the door into place over the crawlspace." It's easier to open, see."

"Uh yeah, I guess if the Nazis ever came for us."

He gave me a nervous look mingled with warning...*as if I'd actually try to explore the place.* "I wouldn't go up there if I were you. It's hot and dirty...and there are spiders."

Doubtful. There were no webs on him. I stared up at the trapdoor and nodded to appease him. "Yeah, sounds dangerous," I lied. "I would *never* go up there."

"You'd better not. I'll tell you one time, there was this..."

His stories were beginning. My cell phone rang and I recognized the ringtone. The Evil Twins. I answered it, knowing that at the least it would keep me safe from my landlord's talkative tongue. "Yes, Byron?"

"I seem to be missing something vitally important."

"Indeed." I tried to keep my voice down with my landlord's eyes on me. "Have you met my demands yet?"

"Yep, boyfriend-for-a-week, coming right up."

I almost dropped the phone. "I don't take kindly to your threats."

"The funny thing is I didn't know you were interested in me? But then when we saw what you wanted…?"

"I'm sorry; you're going to have to look at the small print…on the back. I would never be that desperate."

"Really? That's not what the stake president said."

"Leave him out of this. He has nothing to do with this."

"Now don't worry your pretty little head, Mad. We can just keep this whole boyfriend-for-a-week thing under wraps, but you owe me. I want my backpack delivered to my apartment unharmed. I want the hand-off nice and clean…tonight. No tricks."

"Why you dirty—!" I took a deep breath, remembering the couch cushions. "Tonight it is. Give me what I want, Byron, and no one gets hurt." Before Byron could undermine my resolve again, I hung up. I met my landlord's shocked eyes and cleared my throat. "Sorry. What were you saying?"

"Uh…stay out of the trapdoor?"

Before I could mumble out an answer, I felt Sandra's eyes on me. As soon as I caught her look, she smiled prettily. It was full of sarcasm. "Ooh," she cooed. "Sounds like you've got yourself a hot date."

CHAPTER FIFTEEN

Day 109
2143 hours

"It was Friday night, a night normally reserved for revelry...though I wasn't so lucky. I had the enemy to deal with."

—Madeleine's War Journal Entry (Friday, June 1st).

I slammed the door to my car. Sandra's words still burned in my ears. A date? And then she actually had the nerve to congratulate me. I knew that glint of revenge in her eyes. She knew how much Byron hated me. He'd return the cushions; I'd return his backpack. No one else had to be involved. And after that, I wouldn't either. I wasn't messing with her ex, okay? No matter what she thought.

I stalked around my car in the parking lot behind our apartments and opened the trunk, pulling out my groceries. A shopping trip to Macey's had been the only way to kill some time before meeting him tonight. The sound of my footsteps the only sound in the darkness. The moon was just a faint crescent above me, the clouds dark and ominous with the coming storm.

I'd get what I wanted and then I'd let Byron go. Go clean. It wasn't so hard. I knew exactly how to get Byron back—never talk to him again...because it wasn't nice to mess with my roommate's ex-boyfriend. That's why. I dragged out all of my groceries until I had every last bag. Anything to avoid another trip to my car. The plastic handles dug into my fingers. Sandra wanted those cushions back just as much as we all did. I mean, just one more time with Byron wouldn't hurt and then I'd quit. The crinkle of the plastic was lost in my inner struggle with myself: *I don't feel guilty. I don't feel guilty. I don't feel…*

A faint light illuminated the darkness. It came from the top apartment next to ours. I could see it perfectly from the back of our building. Thanh was home. Even she was staying in on a Friday night. I glanced over at my trunk and realized I didn't have any hands to close the hatch. I tried using my head, but gave up and plopped my groceries down on the hard black pavement. I slammed the trunk shut, and heard an echoing slam above me. A shadow passed the upper window in the back of Thanh's apartment…a taller one followed it. Thanh's Friday night wasn't a complete bust. She had a visitor.

I reached down and looped all the plastic handles through my fingers again. The noises in Thanh's apartment grew louder. I listened to the arguing voices, one female, the other deeper and raspier, definitely male. I heard a crash and straightened. Thanh was throwing her things around. I heaved my groceries into my arms, wondering if I should check on her. It would probably look weird coming from a complete stranger. I heard another crash. Without thinking, I shouted up at the window, "Hey!"

Before I could figure out where I was going with that, the light snuffed out in her apartment and I found myself standing in the pitch blackness, my skin crawling as I regretted my usual recklessness. What had possessed me to shout out like that? Poor Thanh could make a mess if she wanted. She had a life to lead. My groceries grew heavy. My fingers quickly lost feeling, and now I was afraid of meeting Thanh on the stairs. After a self-reproaching roll of my eyes, I two-stepped into the darkness.

The leaves of a bush shook to my left, almost like a sudden wind had overcome it. I stumbled over my feet at the rush of adrenaline. There was no wind here. The coming storm held its breath. I stared at the bush through the darkness. Anyone with less situational awareness wouldn't have noticed a thing, but I knew I wasn't alone out here. Anything could be in these shadows. Anyone. All I had to defend myself was some eggs, tortillas, maybe some toilet paper. Everything a girl needed for a prank war, and they were completely useless in the face of real danger. But why would I have to defend myself anyway? I could just walk away and pretend I didn't see anything, except I did. Something inside me wouldn't let me look away from the bush. For now, it stayed put like any good bush should, but there was something different about it. Something stared back at me from the leaves. It jumped out at me with alarming swiftness.

"Captain!"

I jolted as Tory came out of the darkness. Apparently she had been staking out the premise outside. Not too much of a surprise, except she came out of a bush. "I swept the area." She drew in closer. "Your cushions are in the guy's living room next to the—"

I jumped, seeing the bright light seconds before it enveloped us like a bomb. I dropped my groceries and fell flat to the ground, momentarily blinded. The sound of it pierced my ears. "Whoa." The noise cut out my voice. I squinted through the light, but as soon as it was on us, it was gone. "Tory, did you see that?" I shouted.

"What! I can't see!"

I couldn't either. To top that off, I couldn't hear very well. As soon as my eyes adjusted back to the darkness, I saw Kali tearing around the bend in her Strawberry Shortcake cut-offs. "Oh! No! Way!" she shouted out in her adorable voice once she reached us. "I don't know what the guys did! But that was amazing!"

Lizzie followed, her arms swinging furiously. "Can you believe that!"

"No," I shouted. "No! I can't. It was like a flash bomb. The guys wouldn't have something like that. That's swat team stuff!"

Tory's jaw clenched. "Then what's this!" Lizzie shouted through our deafness. She pushed something at me and it crinkled into my hands. It was another list of demands.

I ran to my car and opened the door to read it under the interior light. *To the apartment known as the black hole: We want a dozen cinnamon rolls, our dishes done, and our place scrubbed clean of any traces of girl stuff. Pronto…or we add more demands.*

"This is blackmail!" Lizzie was properly enraged. "What kind of monster would make a list of demands?"

I met Tory's eyes, ignoring that. "Maybe we should show them the light."

Her lip curled up. "What are you thinking?"

A drop of rain spattered against my nose like a light kiss. I brushed it off, digging through my glove compartment. "I say we introduce them to the old bait and switch game. What do you say?"

"Wait, wait, wait." Lizzie shook my shoulder. "Byron's trying to lead us out of our apartment. Isn't that obvious?"

"We're already out!" I scrambled out of my car. The storm was upon us, and the wind picked at my clothes as I rushed heedlessly through the parking lot to find out what damage Byron had already done to our apartment.

Tory pulled me back. "Your apartment is booby-trapped. We're fine."

"How? What did you do?"

The light from my car shone over Tory's face, making her eyes look demonic through the darkness. "Sandra's there. Remember?"

I snickered. "Oh, excellent. If they can get past her, they have my respect." The rain poured freely down on us as I dove back across the front seat of my car. After a thorough search, I found my flashlight. It was one of those miniature ones. Tory's brow furrowed. It was enough to make me laugh. "It's all part of the plan. C'mon, I'll need all of you for this."

After Lizzie threw my groceries back into my car, we left the parking lot on foot. The rain puddles splashed under our shoes, dampening our surprise attack. "This would be a whole lot easier if we had Byron's cell phone number," Lizzie muttered. She tugged her shirt over her green and white pajama bottoms. Kali skipped to keep up with us. We ducked behind a dumpster, avoiding more giggling civilians that passed us from our ward. Two lovebirds shared a bright red umbrella with polka dots.

I took a deep breath, but not too deep since we were hiding behind a dumpster and it was a little smelly. "Okay, I want Lizzie and Tory to come with me. Kali, take this." I handed her the flashlight. "Set this up in the back of the bunkhouse…just like the guys set up their light. We want them to see that great minds think alike." The flashlight easily fit into Kali's small palm. She looked confused. "We're gonna have our own little firework show from their back window," I explained. "…only this show will be a no show, get it?"

Kali grinned, sheathing the flashlight into the kangaroo pockets of her hoody. She handed me the old lady perfume. "You might need this." She took off with a jaunty little skip.

I took the rest of my team to the front of the apartment complex. We stood under the guy's balcony next to the treacherous gamers' apartment. I splashed my hair from my eyes. "Tory, you stand here with your arms up. Be ready." Tory's lips curled up in approval. She knew where I was going with this. I took Lizzie up the stairs with me. Our shoes scraped against the metal stairs, echoing into the cold unfeeling night. My heart raged against my chest. We had to make this matter. Make or break. I glanced over at my sweet roommate. If anyone could slip past these hordes of evildoers, it would be our stealth bomber. We reached the guys' floor and I inched against the hard brick wall, barely able to see their shadows from the window. I'd have to trust Tory's report that the cushions were there by the—I realized I never asked her *where*. I stayed focused. "Okay Lizzie. Go in and tell the guys there's gonna be a show at their back window. Make sure you herd them *all* into the kitchen, alright?"

Lizzie took a steadying breath and went into the very depths of all that was unholy without even knocking. I listened to the murmur of voices at her entrance. My heart refused to beat more softly. Lizzie whispered something quietly to them. The guys jumped up from their furniture, pushing the couch hard against the wall in their attempts to get into their kitchen fast. In fact, it was faster than I had anticipated.

As soon as they left, I rushed into the living room, keeping to the shadows. I saw the twins at the kitchen window with Lizzie, their Aryan profiles facing the darkness outside. I took a careful step forward. The ground creaked beneath my feet and I lurched to a stop, my eyes on them. They craned their heads outside to see what waited for them out there. Searching the living room on my hands and knees, I found the couch cushions by the light of the flickering TV. Two fat striped cushions. Oh, how I missed them! I gathered them under my armpits, keeping my eyes trained on the twins in the kitchen. One of them leaned against the windowsill. By the looks of his dangerous dimple, I could see it was Twin A. Well, Adam. His brother, Blake was laughing about something. He asked Lizzie a question under his breath, his voice gentle. Lizzie answered softly, nervously slipping her flip flops on and off. Adam grinned and kicked one of them away. Before I could see Lizzie's reaction, I took a deep breath and tried to slip out the door.

"Hey!"

At the shout of discovery, I ran for the door. The cushions were heavy and the twins scrambled loudly after my heels. They were faster, but I had planned for that. I threw the cushions to Tory below and she disappeared with them. The twins tried to scrape past me, but they wouldn't take her without a fight. "Grab a twin," I shouted to Lizzie. I wrapped my arms around Blake's neck and dropped like deadweight. We both went down. Blake tried to push me away, but I held on tightly, knowing he was the nicer of the two and wouldn't play dirty. Adam would've kicked me off by now. Speaking of...from the corner of my eye, I could see Lizzie was having less success with him. Adam easily wriggled away from her and tried to get past me and his brother. I twisted around Blake's back and tripped Adam as he passed. He stumbled to his knees. I stole his black and white running shoe from his left foot, chucking it over the railing. It disappeared into the bushes.

"Are you joking?" Adam found his feet. "Those are Zoom Vomeros. Those are more expensive than your college education!" He went after me. I ducked behind his sweeter brother until someone tugged me from Blake so roughly that I landed hard on my feet. Rock! I had completely forgotten about him. His dark hair was tousled and there were lines on his face as if we had wrenched him from a deep sleep. He looked irritated. I steadied myself. Out of all the boys, he couldn't handle a prank…maybe I could use it against him. "Rock," I tried to sound fragile. "I'm so glad you're here. The twins stole our cushions. Would you please help us get them back?"

He was momentarily confused. I felt his hands loosen over me just enough that I could wriggle away. I tripped to the ground. "Run!" I told Lizzie. "Run!" Blake got to his feet. His shoe was in perfect reach and I stole it from his foot too, chucking it as far as I could over the railing. Rock cried out in anger. I was no longer the innocent girl. They were all after me. What could they do? Catch me? Then what? As soon as I found my feet, I scurried the other direction, taking the stairs two at a time, leading my pursuers away from Tory and the cushions. I rounded the corner of the bunkhouse, hearing the twins' strides behind me; they were uneven with just the one shoe. Kali jumped between us. It really wasn't a sacrifice…I knew she wanted to get caught. Blake picked her up mid-stride and she kicked, her legs a blur of strawberry shortcake pajamas. There was no way Blake could keep up with me with her in his arms. She had ingested about a half a dozen chocolate bars today alone. I applauded her strategy.

Rock had disappeared, too lazy to join the chase. But where was Lord Byron? On a date? Or ransacking our apartment? I sucked in more air, taking quick, shallow breaths. Adam was still behind me. He wouldn't quit. His track pants swished in the darkness. Even with one shoe, it wouldn't be long before he caught up. The point was to distract him from Tory, but I still didn't relish the thought of getting caught, possibly tortured. I wondered how to stop him? A girl? A party? I knew just the place.

I sprinted across the street into Liberty Square's underground parking lot. It was the resident party complex for sophomores and jammed with parked cars. It was Friday night. I wove through the cars and landed on my stomach hard next to a Volkswagen bug. My breathing was too loud. If I wasn't careful, it would give me away.

"Mad!" I could hear Adam's uneven gait on the other side of the Volkswagen, and I held my breath. He was closer than I wanted. "You know we'll just get your cushions back again, don't you?" I squeezed my eyes tight, willing myself not to retort. I breathed out slowly. "You should've just made us some cinnamon rolls then none of this would've happened." I hoped I wouldn't bite my tongue off to keep myself from blowing a fuse at that one. My hand brushed against the old lady perfume. I clutched it. Adam wouldn't take me without a fight.

"Maybe I'll just go after Lizzie. Byron says she cooks better than you anyway."

I threw my hands over my mouth, listening to Adam's voice fade. It meant he was going the wrong direction or he was altering his voice to make it appear that way. The click clack of heels sounded over the pavement and I spotted two high maintenance girls—so high maintenance they could be from King Henry. They headed for their car.

"Hey." Adam said with a cool nod. The girls giggled in response. He had no choice but to pretend that he was going somewhere important.

I peered around the tire, watching him leave the parking lot with only one shoe on. I hoped it wasn't to find Tory…or Lizzie…or whoever really. I took a quick inventory of my wounds. It didn't look good; I had stubbed my toe and my jeans were covered in mud. At least Sandra was watching the home front. She was always so dedicated with her staying-out-of-our-lives capabilities. I caught my breath at a sudden thought. Wait…unless…could Byron get past her defenses? I couldn't believe I had been such an idiot. Of course he could. He was her ex. He was there now. I had unwittingly brought them together. How could I not see that? I picked up my cell phone and dialed, waiting impatiently as it rang. "Tory," I whispered as soon as she picked up. "What's your position?"

"*What's your position?*"

PRANK WARS

My voice caught in my throat. It was Lord Byron. Tory's cell phone had fallen into enemy hands. He had employed the first tactic of war—wiping out lines of communication. It meant only one thing: Tory was POW, possibly being tortured with their most flirtatious methods. "No matter what you do, Tory won't talk."

"*Kali talked.*"

I leaned my head back against the tire. Of course. Kali was our mole. She had infiltrated our ranks with one thought in mind, a date. Byron was smooth, fast talking, eloquent—like the very devil. "*It appears there is only one on your team left unaccounted for,*" he waited for my response, but I didn't reply. "*You.*"

"I'll never join you." It came out more dramatically than I intended it, and I found myself staring up at the two high maintenance girls.

"Excuse me," one of them pointed behind me with manicured nails. "That's my car." And I was leaning against it. I scrambled to my feet, realizing I looked like a homeless woman in my mud spattered clothes. I pulled away from them, tugging down my black shirt where it belonged.

"*Do you really want war, Mad?*" Byron asked on the other line.

Was that a trick question? I ignored the giggling girls behind me, trying to keep focused. Did the guys recover the cushions? I'd force a confession out of Byron. "You'll never get the cushions," I told him.

"*That's alright. I want something else.*"

My heart soared at the victory. At least our mission to recover the cushions had been successful. I made my way to my apartment, the phone still to my ear. I just couldn't imagine what he had done to Tory to get her phone. She wouldn't have gone down easily. Loud classic country music blared in the distance. Inane and twangy. Even if some people liked that stuff, it didn't mean the world shared their same bad taste. Byron was going off on vague threats on the other line, but I couldn't pay attention. The closer I got to my apartment, the louder the music got, and it was giving me a headache.

I froze, unable to keep the horror from my face. I couldn't believe it. My roommates were the ones with the bad taste. The country music was coming from our apartment. Loud and clear.

CHAPTER SIXTEEN

Day 109
2235 hours

"The problem with an archenemy is that he knows everything about me. He knows how to make me scream. He knows how to make me smile. And he'll use them both against me—at the same time."

—Madeleine's War Journal Entry (Friday, June 1st).

I broke into a run and ran up the three flights of stairs, desperate to turn off the noise. The music fairly rocked my apartment. Our neighbors would kill me if I didn't do something soon. I reached the door and turned the knob. It stuck. I took out my keys and wrestled them into the lock. As soon as the knob loosened, I shoved the door open. It stopped short with a sickening clang. The chain was on. No! They didn't. How? I tried the windows, but our place was locked airtight. "Byron!" I shouted into the phone.

"You know what?" he said. "The cool thing about modern technology is that you don't have to shout into it for people to hear you."

"Listen to me. Uh...are any of my roommates with you? I need one of them right now!"

"What's going on?" He knew very well. He was behind it.

"I just need a little something from them." Like maybe an emergency ladder or a top secret gadget to rip open a window.

PRANK WARS

"*I think I have what you're looking for,*" he said in a much too calm voice. "*If you'd like to turn off that wretched noise, that is.*" He clicked off Tory's phone, ending our communication. I screamed out in frustration, hitting the door. How did they do this? Where was Tory anyway? Where were the cushions? No one was doing what they were supposed to be doing.

"Hey! Turn off your music!"

I groaned. The complaints were beginning. No one would call the cops on us though…unless they *weren't* a student. My eyes widened with horror when I saw the light turn on at the house next door. A family lived there. There was no telling what they would do. Fumbling with my cell phone, I started to speed dial all of my roommates for an idea on how to get our place open or at least to stop this noise, but no one picked up: Lizzie, Kali, Sandra. Where were they, especially Sandra? Did she go on a date at the last second? I felt my nose wrinkle at the direction of my thoughts. Was she with Byron?

I kicked the door. Well, I didn't care! There had to be a way to break in. I thought of our landlord. Besides the danger of getting caught by a long lecture, I just didn't have him on speed dial. A neighbor might have his number though. I rushed next door to Thanh's. Her door was already open. She didn't have to know I was the one who shouted up at her from the parking lot earlier. I knocked on the door and it swung open. I gasped and stepped back. The place was a mess. Everything in Thanh's carefully organized cupboards had been pulled out. The stuffing was ripped from the cushions in her couch. Paper and garbage covered the ugly green carpet. This had to be the aftermath of the crashing I had heard, but if Thanh lived in our world, I'd say someone else had ransacked her place.

"Hello?" My voice echoed into her apartment. No one answered. After a moment of stupid waiting, I took a step inside. Muffled country music followed my footsteps inside. At least it wasn't the awful old stuff now. Taylor Swift was singing about finding Romeo. The sound seemed almost haunting in here. What if Thanh was inside…hiding in a paper thin closet? I leaned against a wall, sternly getting a hold of myself. What was wrong me? I couldn't allow some scary remakes of Japanese horror movies stop me from being a good Samaritan. Thanh could be in trouble. I took a steadying breath and felt a presence behind me. I couldn't bring myself to look back. "Thanh?" I asked.

"Nope." The voice was masculine.

I screamed, whipping my head around to defend myself. My fists went up.

"It's okay." Eric stood in the doorway. He had rolled up the sleeves of his blue plaid button-up, the veins standing out on his forearms. Once again, he had caught me in a compromising position. I shouldn't be in here. I realized what it could look like. Still, he was a welcome sight. He held up his hands to show he wasn't a threat, wearing a slight smile. "You know. This is called breaking and entering in some places."

"Not in Provo." Despite my brave words, I had to stop myself from clutching at my heart. I couldn't believe I was inside Thanh's apartment. If I didn't think she was somehow hurt, I wouldn't have trespassed—last time didn't count. I had no idea she was living here.

Eric looked around, taking in the mess with serious eyes. "So what are you doing this time? Sightseeing?"

I shook my head. "I think something's wrong."

"Yeah, me too. Who lives here?"

"Some girl who's really neat, so neat that we didn't even know she lived here last time we...uh, visited. And now look at the place."

He gingerly lifted a scrap of paper with the toe of his Vans, his eyes moved to me. "What should we do?"

"Call the police?" But it was too late. I could already hear the sirens outside. Even the country music couldn't drown them out. The house with the family must've called them. I pulled a hand through my already messy hair. It was a typical end to a typical day. "They're coming for me."

He laughed, but I didn't mind, even though he was laughing *at* me. "I heard the music as soon as I parked my car," he said. "I could only

PRANK WARS

assume it had something to do with *our* next adventure." The blue and red lights cast a glow over his face. It was an attractive one, despite the sinister look. Wait. Sinister? This whole place was sinister. He held his hand out to me. "What do you say Madeleine? Should we turn ourselves in to the coppers?"

I stared at his hand. There was something about Eric that drew me to him. He was so open and affectionate, or maybe it was something else? I didn't think it was bad boy allure because the more I talked to him, the less of a bad boy he seemed. Even at my worst, he was actually pretty nice...in a dangerous way because he was getting through my defenses. "I can help you turn off that noise too," he said. "You want me to break into your apartment for you?"

That was it. My hand was in his. "Can you figure out how to get through a locked window?"

"It depends." He shut Thanh's door behind us. "What will you give me if I do?"

This sounded suspiciously like flirting. I smiled. "I'll stop accusing you of being a spy."

"Tempting. I have something else in mind though."

Before I could ask, I saw the two policemen coming for me. They marched up the stairs. Their hair was buzzed short and both had equally grim sets to their jaws. There was no use flirting myself out of this one, not that I was the girl for that job—I'd need Kali for that. I broke away from Eric to head them off. "Oh, I'm so glad you're here!" It was best to pretend that I was desperate to see them. "My neighbor's place has been ransacked. Thanh's gone missing."

Eric froze. Okay, so I admit that came out pretty crazy, but the police would see the truth of it for themselves. "Missing?" one of them asked. He was a solid guy with a no-nonsense air. His name tag said Officer Oliveira. "What's missing?"

"Thanh. My neighbor! C'mon. Her place is a mess." I ran solidly into Thanh's door. "Ouch." I held my nose. Apparently, the door automatically locked when closed.

"Are you sure?" one of the police officers asked. He held his notebook tightly. His eyes were accusing.

I took my hand from my aching nose. "See for yourself." I tried to direct them to the windows, but too late I noticed the curtains were drawn. "You're going to have to believe me on this one," I said. "We've been inside and it's a mess. Thanh's normally really clean." One of the officers shifted against the railing. I had nothing to convince them with, except my female intuition. "I heard loud crashes earlier."

"Through all this music?" Officer Oliveira asked.

"Before the music. And then...when I came over here, I saw someone trashed the place. And Thanh was gone!"

"You realize we'll have to get a search warrant to check out your claim."

A search warrant? That would take forever. What about poor Thanh? "*I* don't need a warrant. I'll just break in real quick and make sure everything's okay. Just stay out here and make sure no one kills me."

The other police officer's eyes got huge. Before he could deliver a lecture or worse, slap cuffs on me, Byron stepped out of nowhere. I had no idea where he had come from. He looked relaxed like a fine English gentleman out for a stroll...in Nikes. "Good evening. Sergeant. Brady, right?" The officer nodded and straightened out of respect. What a lousy judge of character, especially once I spied Byron slipping keys that looked suspiciously like ours into the pockets of his gray striped khakis. "You don't need a warrant, sir," Byron surprised me by backing me up. "You can check it out if you have reasonable suspicion someone is in danger inside."

After a long look, the officer lowered his notebook. He took his two-way radio from his belt and brought it to his lips. "We have a missing person report," he shouted over the noise from my apartment. He glanced at me. "Do you have a description?"

"Um...she's Japanese?"

"Vietnamese," Byron corrected without a beat.

PRANK WARS

"Vietnamese," the officer said over the receiver. Apparently Byron was a more reliable source. I glared at him just as I saw the little Vietnamese girl in question trudge up the steps behind him. Her face looked unnaturally pale.

"Thanh." Though as I said it, I felt my face drain of color to match hers. There went the rest of my credibility. Thanh's long black hair seemed a little messier than this morning, but other than that she was still alive. Well, as far as any of us knew, but that was just the scary movies talking. Everyone turned to her. Thanh stepped back and I remembered too late she didn't know me. "Uh, we were worried about you," I said. "Your door was open and it looked like someone messed up your place."

She colored slightly. It was an improvement, since she seemed so devoid of color. "Yeah, that was me. I was looking for something..." *Oh.* Now it was my turn to blush. I felt like an idiot. "Am I in trouble?" Thanh asked the two reluctant officers. She sounded tired.

The two were already laughing. "Yeah, your landlord sent us." At her somber look, Officer Oliveira dropped the jokes. "We're real sorry, young lady, for the mix-up. As far as I know you can't get arrested for keeping a messy place. What do you say, Brady?"

"No, but my wife might think differently." They gave into their laughter again.

Thanh bit her lip. Despite her disheveled state, she had incredible fashion sense. Byron would appreciate that. She wore calf-high boots and a plaid dress over her leggings. She was refined and delicate, everything that I constantly proved I wasn't. I glanced over at Eric and then at Byron. Neither of them could take their eyes off her. Byron's were assessing. Eric looked curious. *Men.*

"I'm sorry," Thanh said. "Things are a little hectic right now." She put her slender hand on her door, a book bag and a black backpack slung over her shoulder. She carried more of her books in front of her. "I'm grading tests and working on a thesis. I'll clean everything up as soon as I can, okay?" She faced the group a little nervously. Her big eyes went from me, lingered on Eric, but got even bigger when she saw Byron. "You're here too?" He nodded. I pretended not to care that he had lied to me. These two were way too tight for it to be otherwise. "How was study group?" she asked him.

He cleared his throat. "Good. Thanks. I learned a lot."

She hesitated. "Have you looked over…uh…?" She glanced over at us as if embarrassed to be talking about something as mundane as school. "Have you studied your notes?"

"Almost." Byron nudged me meaningfully with his elbow.

Thanh looked disappointed. "Well, tell me if you have any…questions." She unlocked her door. "Is it okay if I go in?" she asked the police officers. "I have a lot of homework to do."

They nodded at her, their expressions turning gentle—I knew they'd never direct that look at me. "You're fine," the relaxed one reassured her. *That meant I wasn't.* As soon as Thanh closed the door behind her, I knew I was in for it. The men turned on me with various looks of long-suffering. The officer with the notebook wrote furiously on it. The country music grated through the air and they squinted under it. I knew the feeling. My head pounded to the beat. The officers pointed at my apartment. "Are your keys locked inside?"

I glanced over at Byron, wondering what to say. "Uh…I can't find my keys."

"—because they're not *your* keys?" Byron muttered under his breath. My eyes widened. It wasn't the time to grill me about using our manager's keys. I slanted a glance at the officers, but they hadn't overheard. Eric had. He grinned and teetered on his heel, stepping back. I glared at Byron, knowing I couldn't tackle him in front of the police to get my keys back.

"This isn't the first time we've had complaints about things getting too loud around here," the sergeant told me in a stern voice.

"Yeah. Sorry about that," Byron pulled next to me, lending his strength. "We got locked out and I tried to break back in, but just ended up knocking the radio over and it forced the volume up too loud." I studied Byron's innocent face. He made lying look easy. "Right Mad?" he asked. "*You* didn't touch the volume on your radio?"

"I would only listen to country music under torture."

At my words, the music abruptly stopped...as if offended. The air tingled with the silence. I glanced around. Eric was missing. My heart gave an excited leap. He wasn't lying when he said he could break in. I liked that guy, though I knew I shouldn't. He'd get tired of this game soon enough. The two policemen grew noticeably calmer in the silence. Byron squeezed my arm. "You'll have to excuse *us* for acting so...so uh...crazy. I think the noise was getting to Madeleine a little."

"A little?" The sergeant sighed and crossed out whatever he had been writing. He peered at me under stern brows. "We're not giving you a fine this time, little lady." I winced at the endearment, but didn't fight it if it got me out of this. "Consider this your warning. Next time, it'll cost you." That was the biggest threat against any starving college student and they knew it. I nodded wordlessly. After seeming to memorize my face, the sterner of the two turned. His partner followed him down the stairs. As soon as they were far enough away, they started laughing and elbowing each other. Yeah, we were a riot. I leaned the back of my head against the cool bricks of my apartment and closed my eyes.

"Sorry about that," Byron said. He joined me next to my brick wall, and I felt the warmth of his shoulder meet mine. Was he actually apologizing? "You okay?" he asked. I opened my eyes to see him watching me closely. He was being nice, and I felt like I hardly knew him this way, a very dangerous position to be in when fighting a war with him. He reached into his pocket. "I got something for you." I winced, but instead of throwing a frog or a spider, he dropped Tory's cell phone into my palm and closed my fingers over it. His steady hands folded over mine and didn't leave. I waited for him to say something smart, but he studied my face instead. "You haven't seen my lost iPhone *perchance*?" *Perchance* sounded so foreign, especially when he said it with that funny little accent. I shook my head. His lips curled slightly, expecting nothing less. After a moment, he pulled away. "You know, if I don't find it, my mom's gonna think I'm dead, right?"

I smiled inanely at him. "Your girlfriends won't. I sent a text message to them all with a declaration of your love."

"Seriously?"

No. I hadn't even checked the backpack for his phone yet, but a cell phone was just an added complication. I could only have something that time-sensitive in my possession for so long. After I stole his number and maybe changed his ski Utah screensaver to bunnies, I'd give the whole mess of a backpack to him tonight.

"If you did," he accused me in a low voice, "...no woman will have me. You've ruined my future posterity."

"Oh, that wasn't me."

"I suppose *you'll* have to take me then...if no one else will."

A loud clattering interrupted our meaningless bickering. Tory ran up the steps, taking two at a time. Her hair flew behind her, her freckles more pronounced. There was a twinkle in her eyes that I hadn't seen before we left on our mission. I was immediately suspicious. "You aren't dead?" I asked.

"No. We were doing wheelies in the parking lot. It was way fun." Of course it was. She was an adrenaline junkie, but who was she doing wheelies with was the question? And why had she left her post?

"You dropped your cell." I gave it back to her and she casually pocketed it without an explanation. It was very unlike her.

Byron looked from me to Tory. We were both in black. "Adorable," he said dryly. "You match as per usual."

Any goodwill I had for him dissolved. "What's wrong with you anyway?" I asked him pointedly. "What was with that swat team light? And country music? Are you insane?" Because of him, I had to be treated for shell shock.

"What do you expect me to do when you take my things? Serenade you?"

PRANK WARS

I rolled my eyes and pushed away from the wall. Eric was still missing. That was odd. He must still be in my apartment. Why? I left Byron to go check it out. My hands were a little shaky from my encounter with the police, and I was beginning to worry Eric had gotten hurt. The front door was open. I thought Eric had gotten through the window, but the chain was off. I pushed the door open a crack and peered into the darkness inside. It was eerily quiet.

"Hey, guess what?"

I jumped. My head almost collided with Byron's jaw. He was right behind me. He smiled faintly when he saw he scared me. "You can just walk in. You live here."

"Oh really?" I muttered sarcastically. Tory and Byron had my back. I couldn't show them I was a coward. Taking a deep breath, I stepped boldly into my own living room. "Eric?"

Tory brushed past me, making it impossible to be properly scared. She threw off her black stocking cap and hoody and threw them on our couch...on the green striped cushions. They had made it here after all. So when had the operation gone wrong? She landed next to her things, making herself comfortable.

I headed for the hall, my feet catching on the carpet. Where was Eric? Had he just unlocked the door for me, turned off my music, and after his good deeds disappeared like any good phantom should? Because of how stealthily he disappeared, I wouldn't be surprised to find a red rose placed on our messy kitchen counter as a symbol of his presence. But we were on the third floor. There was no way to slip past us. The light from the porch outside shone through the drapes of the open kitchen window.

"This place is freezing." Byron edged past me, flipping on the light. "They were right when they said the woman is the heart of the home." I made a face at him. Something was wrong. I couldn't quite place it. Byron walked past our dead plants and lingered at the dead roses. Despite Kali's ministrations, she couldn't save them. "You've got a graveyard in here." When I didn't answer, he glanced over at me. "So, my stuff?"

I turned from the open window. "Yeah, your favorite DVD," I purposely misinterpreted. "AmyLee borrowed it. I hear she's having some girl party or something with all of her really cute friends. There's going to be a pillow fight, so you'd better go get it before it's too late." Byron wasn't moving, so I tried to brush past him into the hallway. He was too close to where I hid his backpack. I wondered if he could sense it with some hidden secret power.

With one step, he blocked me. "I'm not leaving until I claim what's mine." My breath caught at the threat. Lizzie pushed the door open from outside and it creaked in complaint. She was covered in mud and looked exhausted. She took a shaky step inside. Byron actually looked happy to see her. "Hey Lizzie."

She smiled faintly and collapsed face-first onto the couch. Luckily, there were cushions on it. "Did you give him his backpack yet?" Lizzie's words were almost lost in the cushions.

Not yet. It was hidden safely away where no one could find it—not even the Nazis. Byron was standing right beneath it. He watched Lizzie pityingly and to my relief, moved away from me, sinking down into the couch beside her. He patted her leg. "If I get postcards from my backpack on some exotic vacation, you'll be packing your own bags, Mad Dog." I squirmed in guilt, but fought it, remembering what Byron had done to my mom. Instead of doing something stupid and giving away my best hiding place, I stalked into the back to get my toothbrush. His voice echoed where I stood in the bathroom. "Hello? There's no use hiding behind enemy lines!"

"You were supposed to give us our cushions back!" I shouted back at him. I pulled my toothbrush from its little cup holder and stuck it into my mouth. It clanged against my teeth. I returned to the living room with it dangling from my lips.

Byron looked surprised. No doubt he thought I would bring him back his backpack. After all, he had been so charming. If he left, I could, but as of now, I had to play it cool. He lifted a shoulder. "What can I say? My men mutinied against me."

Very unlikely. I pointed at Lizzie with my toothbrush. "You've put us through a lot these past months. Just look what you did to Lizzie!"

"And Thanh," he said in a much too casual voice. I wasn't tricked by it. Byron wanted information on her. "Why did you tell the cops someone trashed her apartment?"

"It was a mess."

He lifted a brow in response. It was my favorite move and I was annoyed that we shared it. It was like we were becoming the same person. "So is your place," he said wryly. "Did bad guys trash that too?" With a violent toss of my hair, I marched into the back rooms. He shot up from the couch, trailing after me. "I'm sorry. I just want to know what happened out there." I heard him pace the hallway that separated the men from the back. "Who was that guy you were hanging out with anyway?"

I popped my head back into the living room, startling him when my eyes met his just inches from his face. I took the toothbrush out of my mouth. "Jealous?"

"Yeah, I wanna date someone who can break into my apartment."

"Are you talking about Mad Dog?" Lizzie asked.

I made a face at her. Lizzie couldn't resist, could she? The front door swung open and Sandra slipped into the apartment behind Byron. It took a moment to register. Sandra! We had a population problem. She unwound her silky scarf from her neck, looking gorgeous in her baby doll shirt and big flashy jewelry. She stilled when she caught sight of her ex, but her voice sounded smooth and sultry like hot chocolate. "Hey, isn't it guys out yet?"

Byron leaned against the hall entryway that separated him from me. His tanned elbow dug into the door frame. "Nope. I've got five seconds."

I glanced at the clock. He was right. Sandra smiled wickedly and counted down like it was New Year's Eve, "5, 4, 3, 2, 1. Guys out!"

"Give me a second," he sounded annoyed. "So, that guy, who was here...?"

"Guy?" Sandra asked. "Madeleine had a guy in here? She's not hiding a boyfriend from us, is she?"

Byron hesitated then shrugged, taking on a resigned look as if ready for the onslaught of girl talk. But I wasn't about to let Sandra know that I was poaching her territory...again. Eric was her guy friend. Maybe she wanted something more. Byron slanted her a sideways glance. "He can pick locks too," he said. "He slipped into your place and disappeared like David Copperfield. Amazing, huh?"

She frowned and he nodded at her. "What did he look like?" she asked him.

I didn't like this new camaraderie between my two worst enemies. Together they could be an unstoppable force. I tried to throw them both off. "Hot as sin," I said. "Why do you ask?"

Byron and Sandra exchanged knowing looks. I couldn't figure out what was going on between them. They weren't secretly dating, were they? Holly had better not be Sandra's code name. Byron dug his palm against the door frame and pushed off it. He retreated for the front door. "Bad things will happen if you try to keep what's mine, Mad Dog. Just remember one false move and your name and my name ends up on a sign-up sheet...together."

"Oh, no worries," I said. "I'll bring what you want...with flair."

"You have until tomorrow morning. I have to study."

"You have band practice in the morning," I reminded him. I stuck the toothbrush back in my mouth for emphasis.

"Then don't be late." His hand was on the doorknob. "Oh, and Mad?"

"Yes?"

"You probably won't be able to feel your mouth for the next two hours."

I slowly drew my toothbrush out from my lips. Maximum Strength Orajel? Anbesol? Possibly. Already my mouth was getting numb. It was

PRANK WARS

strange that I didn't notice it immediately. Before I could beat Byron down, the door closed behind him. "The guys have been in here," I warned the others. There could be stolen pillows, hard box springs switched with our real mattresses, Vaseline on the pillows. "Sweep the rooms."

"This is so stupid." Sandra escaped into the back, but I couldn't help notice she followed my advice, though very casually. Once she was done sweeping the back for any mischief, she came back out and pulled a towel from the rack in the bathroom.

I held my hand out in warning. "Careful. There could be Kool-Aid on *dat*."

She snorted.

"Umb, you bight want to check de showerheads." To my dismay, my voice was getting muffled. The Anbesol was kicking in, but I kept trying. "...Dere bight be somb jewwybeans...or bouweeun cubes."

Lizzie sat up. "She means there might be jelly beans and bouillon cubes in your showerhead. Just be careful, okay?"

"I cat feel my mouf!" To make things worse, I was drooling. Jerk! There was no way I would pull any heroic acts to get Byron's backpack to him tonight under these conditions, especially not as the drooling fool.

Sandra dramatically swept the towel over her shoulder. "I can't believe that I'm living with such children. I am done with all of you." She slammed the bathroom door behind her.

I met Lizzie's brown eyes. She just rolled them. Tory hopped playfully to our dishwasher. "Are these dishes dirty?"

"Yeah, but there are only about four plates in there," Lizzie slurred tiredly. Tory slammed the dishwasher shut and started it.

"Nmpphh!" I tried to stop her. It would take all the hot water and give Sandra a cold shower. That was torture. "The Gibbebba counthenthon!" I couldn't get it out, but the Geneva Convention *had* made certain rules against torture.

It was a good thing that Tory was so closely in tune with me because she understood. The bad thing was that she wouldn't do anything about it. "That only applies to prisoners of war," she retorted.

We heard Sandra push the shower curtain aside, followed by a high-pitched scream. I didn't blame her. Even I couldn't stand an icy cold shower. The bathroom door wrenched open. "Why! Why can't you just stop?" Sandra shrilled. She wasn't wet at all.

Lizzie sat up in concern. "Are you okay?"

Sandra tossed our phantom dummy onto the floor. The one we left on the guys' couch. It was a bit wet. "A man." It was all she could get out. "A man was in the shower!"

"It's only a dummy," Tory muttered. "And you killed him." More like ripped his head off. Sandra had some good defense moves on her. Too bad she didn't work for us. "Did you get your aggression out?" Tory asked in a dry voice. I gave Tory a warning look. Sandra slammed the door shut to the bathroom again and I just hoped it would be for longer this time. "It was meant for you," Tory said, calmly buttering her toast. Wait, *her* toast? I just realized who was snitching all our food.

CHAPTER SEVENTEEN

Day 110
0942 hours

"There was a time when Saturday mornings were lazy, when we took the time to feel the sun on our faces. Now, the world was dark and joyless, except what we provided from our own idle hands."

—Madeleine's War Journal Entry (Saturday, June 2nd).

"Hey you!"

A youngish-looking guy stopped to rest from his Saturday morning jog to study my car. It wasn't because it was a diamond advertisement either. It was because he was hearing voices. After a moment of no sound, he started back on the road.

"Where are you going? I'm over here!"

He stopped again and looked around for the disembodied voice. Kali and Tory ducked down under our living room window, giggling at their latest unsanctioned hit. Tory's pink low-tops dug into the couch. She brought her walkie talkie back to her lips. "Get me out of here. I'm stuck. Yeah, you in the black jogging shorts. Do you mind giving me a hand?"

He grumbled and set off at a brisk pace to finish his jog. Kali's face fell. Another guy got away. The other walkie talkie was hidden under my parked car, the power button duct taped on. Ever since Tory scored the walkie talkies, she couldn't resist messing with the minds of poor hapless civilians passing by our apartment complex.

I swept my spoon listlessly around my cereal bowl at the kitchen table, staring despondently down at the twin's list of demands: *We want a dozen cinnamon rolls...* Blah, blah, blah. I turned the note over and picked up a red crayon in the hopes of finding something more interesting behind it. After a few scribbles, I was happy to learn that Byron didn't disappoint me. Words formed under my crayon, revealing his hidden message beneath: *Madeleine Doggett. Not even your eyes— black and beautiful as they are—will perceive the mischief that awaits you. Meet me at your place alone and no one gets hurt. Bring the item.*

I smiled. It would've been helpful if I had gotten this message last night. I traced the words with my fingers. He thought my eyes were beautiful. Did he mean it? He was acting strange lately. He had seemed so concerned about Thanh last night that I had found myself lying awake nagged by suspicion. If I didn't know better, I'd think Byron had found love. So, why should I care?

"Has anyone seen our ring of keys?" Lizzie dragged a five gallon garbage bag of clothes into the living room, wearing the blue terrycloth shorts she usually reserved for pajamas. And no, she wasn't stealing anyone's clothes. It was all part of our stake service project. We were having a clothes swap then giving the rest to DI. She snapped her fingers in front of my face. "Mad! Are you listening? I've looked everywhere. Rebekka got locked out of her apartment."

Sandra snorted behind me. She was making a sandwich for an early lunch and she carefully tried to keep the mayonnaise from dripping onto her designer dress. "Our landlord probably took them back when he found you were using them for evil."

"No," I muttered into my hand. "I think it was Byron."

Both Tory and Kali gasped at the front window. Lizzie looked scandalized, sitting on her bag full of DI clothes. "He had *better* not."

I shrugged. "He had some keys in his pockets that looked pretty familiar."

PRANK WARS

Sandra's eyes narrowed at me. She had been in a bad mood since last night. I didn't see why. Besides Thanh, she might very well be the other woman. Or was it Holly? Or? Who was I kidding? There were too many girls in Byron's life to guess which one was the girlfriend. I could only do so much. Without really thinking about it, I took a black marker and scribbled over Byron's list of demands. *"Return to Sender."* It was brutal and would do the trick. "Tory, do you mind delivering something for me?"

She eagerly pushed away from the living room window when a sound from above us stopped her in her tracks. It was a muffled ringing coming from the sky, well, the ceiling to be more precise. Sandra tilted her head. She left the kitchen to follow the noise into the hall. I busied myself at the table, hoping the ringing would stop. Maybe Sandra wasn't imaginative enough to figure it out. Her footsteps came to an abrupt halt under the trapdoor in the ceiling. She looked up, her chin tilting at a dangerous angle. "What do you have up there, Mad?"

I scooted away from the table, knowing the best hiding spot in the whole world had just been compromised. "Well, that's strange. How did something get up there? I wonder what it is?"

"Get it down," she ordered.

With a smile tugging at my lips, I yanked on the rope attached to the trapdoor. The whole thing unfolded from the Velcro and almost hit me on the head. Lizzie let out a nervous shriek. "I've got it!" I shouted out. "It's okay." I dragged a chair beneath the crawlspace and scooted Byron's black backpack from the darkness of the attic. I shrugged at Sandra's look of disbelief. "What? No way would anyone think of looking up here, even Byron…unless he called his own number…but I have his phone, so…."

Lizzie looked disapproving. "Why haven't you given it back yet?"

"Oh, I was going to, once I could get to it." Since the jig was already up, I unzipped the pocket in front of the black bag to find his iPhone. My hand brushed past some keys and some lip gloss…not Chapstick. Wait? Next, I found a make-up mirror, and some pink pens. This couldn't possibly be Byron's? Unless he had taken up a collection from the girls he dated. I took out a purple wallet and opened it, examining the driver's license of a beautiful, now familiar, Vietnamese girl: *Thanh Phan*.

"This is Thanh's backpack?" I said dumbly.

Lizzie pushed me out of the way to see for herself. Kali could scarcely believe it. "You stole Thanh's backpack?"

"No!" Tory rose to my defense. "*Byron* stole Thanh's backpack. Mad would never."

"Yeah? Why would Byron have Thanh's backpack?" Sandra asked.

"They're probably dating," I said, knowing I had to face it. "How else could they get close enough to switch backpacks? Maybe they went out to lunch and it happened?" The mystery was solved. It was a major blow—not to mention to my detective skills—that I hadn't figured it out by now. I shook my head. "I thought he was going for Holly?"

"Holly?" Sandra asked in her clipped voice. "Who?"

"Oh, just some girl he was talking to." I sighed. Whatever the reason, I now had Thanh's backpack. She was a grad student. There was no way Thanh wouldn't have noticed it missing. That was likely what she had been looking for last night. She had torn her whole place apart then headed to the school to find it. That was the reason she looked so worried when she returned, and I had been completely responsible for it all. Rummaging through her backpack, I found a cute pink phone. Before I knew it, I scrolled through Thanh's contacts. Byron was nowhere in there. Did she have his number memorized then? I went through her missed calls and saw that most of them were blocked. Poor girl was flooded by telemarketers. She needed *Unmask*. Without really thinking, I typed my registration number into her phone. It was the least I could do for taking her backpack.

Sandra bumped my arm. "What are you doing?"

"Nothing." I threw Thanh's cell back into her backpack next to her keys and zipped it up, not liking how wrong this prank had turned. It seemed poor Thanh was the brunt of all of our misdeeds lately. I'd have to do more than install *Unmask* to make up for it. Maybe I'd take it out

PRANK WARS

on her boyfriend. No, that was worse, wasn't it? "I need to return this," I said.

Lizzie gave a firm nod. "Would you like me to go with you?"

And watch the sweetest girl in the world get dragged to jail with me? "No thank you, I'll do this alone." I threw the strap over my shoulder.

"Wait," Sandra's hand was on my arm. She needed to cut her nails; they were digging into me. "What if Thanh wanted Byron to have her backpack? Here." She tried to relieve me of my burden, taking on some weird motherly air she never used before. "I'll take it to Byron and ask him what's going on. Okay?"

I wriggled away from her, fingernails and all. "Don't worry, I'll be fine. I got myself into this. I'll get myself out. It's totally cool." My brave words had absolutely no effect over her. Sandra's blue eyes got even colder and they were fixed on Thanh's backpack. What had gotten into her anyway? She seemed more bothered by this than Lizzie. "I'll be back, okay?" I wasn't sure why it was necessary to reassure Sandra anyway. "If Thanh's not there, I'll take it back to Byron and wash my hands of it. No big deal."

Sandra threw her hands up in the air. "Fine, do what you do." She picked up her iPhone almost simultaneously, taking refuge in her room across the hall. "Pick up already." I heard her say. She gave a sound of disgust and chucked her phone onto her chic black and white comforter. By the sounds of things, her latest boyfriend wasn't about to let her boss him around. She glared at me through the crack of her half-closed door and slammed it. So much for her sudden burst of kindness.

I left Sandra and the comforting arms of my more sincere roommates to make my way to Thanh's messy apartment. One peek through Thanh's window as I passed and I knew she hadn't had time to clean up. I should probably pull a Lizzie and help her out. I knocked on the door and waited. No one came. It wasn't too much of a surprise. I dug the toes of my canvas shoes into the edge of the welcome mat, thinking of a way out of this predicament. How come Byron wouldn't admit that he knew who she was, especially since they were dating? My stomach sank as I imagined her hand in his, but I knew I needed to bury my traitorous feelings; they were getting me nowhere.

Thanh should've contacted Byron to warn him of the little slip-up with their backpacks by now...except she didn't have a phone anymore. That made sense. Still, why didn't she say anything to him last night—unless she was too shy? She had looked a little scared when the police had us surrounded. Add the gawking neighbors, and everything could've slipped her mind. Maybe Byron already told her he had everything under control. It was pretty arrogant of him since he was dealing with me. At the same time, if he had explained to me that I had his girlfriend's backpack, I would've surrendered it immediately. I tried to recall what Thanh had said to him last night, but all I got were images. Fear. Disappointment. Tired eyes. She had seemed so alone. I shifted under the guilt, the backpack burning a fire of shame against my shoulders. I had to get it back to this girl.

I knocked again, but Thanh was not opening her door. What was I going to do? She couldn't do without her backpack for another day; she was a grad student. Thanh's keys were in her backpack. How bad would it be to just unlock her door, shove the bag inside her apartment, and forget all about it? I'd let Byron worry about getting his own stuff back and forget this ever happened. I dug around for the keys, but once I found the heavy ring of them, I had another problem. Thanh had more keys on it than most people owned in a lifetime. They were all different sizes and shapes. I inserted a few keys into the keyhole with no success and immediately lost track of where I was. I took a deep breath and marked the first key on the ring and tried again, praying no one caught me, especially Lizzie. Well, maybe Thanh could be worse. My fingers fumbled with the last key and I turned it, praying for it to work. Nothing happened. I stepped back. Seriously? A million keys and none of them belonged to her apartment?

A quick double take behind me proved no one had seen me from the ward. A few pickup trucks and a trailer full of bedding, electronics and winter clothes had been parked next to the street. They were there for the DI service project. Cameron was at the wheel. A few girls flirted through the window by the front seat. Lizzie tromped over to the truck with her bag of DI clothes. One of the twins reached down from the truck and hauled up her stuff, throwing it onto the already heaping bed. None of them were paying attention to me. So far, so good. Thanh's curtain was still drawn. I made my way to the window and tried to open it. It was locked.

Thanh's phone went off in her bag. I pocketed the keys, scrambling through the junk in her backpack to find her cute little phone. I hoped it was someone who knew her well enough to help me return her stuff. I dragged out the pink studded cell and stared at the caller ID. It wasn't registering a number or a name. It must be a telemarketer. After a moment of stupid waiting, the number shifted into view and I grinned. *Unmask* unblocked the call. No name registered, but it was good enough to cause damage. Thanh could thank me later. I flipped the phone open. "Hello?"

"*You finally decided to answer, did you?*"

It didn't sound like a telemarketer. More like an angry man. "Yeah?" I answered.

"*You made me wait long enough. We had a deal, now give me the keys and I make sure nothing bad happens.*" Some idiot was trying to disguise his voice, but it wasn't too hard to put everything together. Who knew that I had Thanh's backpack and would also try to scare me? Byron. The freak show's band practice must be over. It should've tipped me off when I saw the twins helping with the service project.

I readjusted Thanh's phone against my ear, almost laughing with relief. "No," I retorted. "I want *my* keys, you jerk!" My landlord was going to lecture me for days if we didn't get them back, not to mention Lizzie.

"*It isn't about what you want.*"

Well, didn't Byron sound condescending? I smiled. He was in for it now. "Yeah? You totally went behind my back so you're the one who'd better watch out."

"What is this, a game to you?"

I shook my head slowly. "Oh no, my friend, this is war. You don't get into a war with me, understand? Because I will win!"

He was silent for a moment. *"Who is this?"*

I smiled. "Your worst enemy."

He didn't respond.

"Byron?" I asked. No answer. He had hung up. Byron really messed up this time. I had been trying to get his number forever. Sure, he couldn't have guessed that I had already installed *Unmask* on Thanh's phone, but he had to know it was a service I provided for all my friends. I found the number on caller ID and pushed reply to call him back.

"Hello?"

"You know," I went on as if he didn't just hang up on me, "…if you want something from me, why don't you come and get it? I'll be waiting for you, sweetie." He hung up before I could tell him that I had something else for him too: Thanh's black backpack. I tried to call him back again, but this time he wasn't answering. I threw the cell phone in my pocket. "Coward," I muttered. Tossing the backpack over my shoulder, I barged into my apartment. Kali and Tory looked up guiltily from their walkie talkies.

"Just me," I reassured them. I headed for the trapdoor and stuffed Thanh's backpack into the attic again. As soon as I got some answers, I'd release it into Byron's semi-capable hands to give to Thanh. "Hey, anyone want to go on a visit to the bunkhouse?" Kali perked up, but I refused to look at her. She'd just destroy the integrity of the mission. She already had a date with Blake from last night's fiasco. "Tory," I called behind my shoulder. "Let's go."

Kali pressed down on the walkie talkie to get over her disappointment. "Hey, cool shirt," she cooed through it. "It matches your eyes, hotty."

Blake turned a full circle outside. He stood on the bed of the truck in a pile of vaguely familiar doilies and pink curtains. For once I could tell the twin apart without waiting for the telltale dimple. He jumped down from the truck bed. Kali gasped and ducked down behind the front window, her body convulsing with giggles.

Shaking my head, I grabbed some orange sticks and arranged them hurriedly on a plate. I had been trying to get rid of them for months now. They were horrid little things from my aunt for Christmas and just perfect for Byron. I handed Tory the plate of goodies. We looked like we were on Relief Society business, nothing more. "Kali," I called. "Watch this backpack with your life. I want to do a little investigating before I turn this over to *you know who*."

She nodded absentmindedly.

CHAPTER EIGHTEEN

Day 110
1013 hours

"It's a dreadful day when you can't trust the enemy to do what he's supposed to do."

—Madeleine's War Journal Entry (Saturday morning, June 2nd).

Rock's drums assaulted our ears. Tory and I stood uneasily on their porch, shifting our weight. Byron's roommate was going crazy with them and it sounded like the noise was coming from the back room. There was no possible way anyone inside could hear me knocking. Balancing the orange sticks, I tried it anyway, along with the doorbell. The drums didn't stop and I tried again and again and again, putting my finger over the peephole for good measure.

After no response, Tory took her hands out of the kangaroo pocket of her pink hoody and tried the door herself. The door opened easily, and I shook my head. When would Byron ever learn? Tory stuffed some tissue paper into the doorknob hole in the front door then stuck some duct tape over it. There was no way the guys could lock the door on us now, well, unless they used the chain. I was sure it would only work the first time around and then they'd be onto us after we broke in. I pushed open the door.

"Wait up."

PRANK WARS

Tory and I both turned to see a lone figure walking up behind us. His gray hood was over his head. I squinted. He looked like one of my soldiers in olive green cargo pants rolled up above the ankles. He must be a biker because he had the muscular legs of one. As soon as his lips quirked up, I knew who it was. "Eric?" I tried to stay focused, but a little part of me melted. "What are you doing here?" I shouted over the noise. Even after all my warnings, he couldn't possibly be looking into staying here, could he?

"I'm waiting for…" his words were lost in Rock's killer drum sequence.

"I can't hear you," I said. "Rock is on one!"

"Rock?"

"The drummer."

"Yeah, he's my friend!" he shouted. That wasn't what I asked, but it answered my question anyway. At least Eric was friends with the sanest roommate in the bunch. It wasn't saying much. I stepped over the threshold, searching for any sign of Byron. Eric caught up to me and laid his hand over my arm. I could smell the familiar scent of his Hollister cologne. "So what are *you* doing here?" A little smile played on his lips like he expected me to say something outrageous. He eyed my plate of orange sticks.

Byron rounded the corner of the hall and almost ran into us. "Whoa." He stopped himself in time, looking shocked. Apparently I had caught him by surprise. Byron was still in his striped shirt from work, the top button was undone and the sleeves rolled up. It was untucked over his mesh basketball shorts. The guy had some hairy legs. Seeing my discomfiture, Byron looked roguishly into my eyes. "Well, how about that? I almost got a hug."

I turned red, trying to ignore Eric's knowing look. It looked like the orange sticks were for Byron and I tried to pretend that I didn't care that my honor was at stake. "In your dreams," I told Byron, mostly for Eric's benefit.

Byron was unruffled. "No, it really almost happened."

To my outrage, Tory agreed from the kitchen. "Yup." She said it absentmindedly, which only meant she was pilfering the silver.

"Knock it off, Tory," I called to her. "We're under a white flag. Remember?"

Byron leaned against the wall, crossing his arms across his chest. He seemed to dismiss Tory, keeping an eye on Eric like he was the dangerous criminal instead. "Sit down. Our place is yours."

"I'm sure some of it is." I passed our *friendship plant* on the way to the couch. The leaves were turning green and no longer drooped in its normally sad way. The crab meat we put in as fertilizer was helping, though it certainly wasn't helping the smell. I faced Byron and his eyes met mine. "I'm here under a flag of truce, Byron."

"It's a pleasure to see you too," he drawled in a truly villainous way.

"Don't be sarcastic. I know what you're up to." I watched him closely, but besides a slight flicker of his eyes, he gave nothing away. He was hiding it well, whatever it was. "You know why I'm here too," I said.

"You made me food?"

"You know I don't cook...ever."

That stopped the conversation dead in its tracks. "S—say what?" Byron stuttered. Even Eric stopped smiling. You would think I had committed some unpardonable sin.

"I...I'm not a great cook." And it was completely off the subject. "I've got something more important to discuss."

"Ah yes, the orange sticks." Byron spared them a glance.

Eric accepted the plate for him, I could only assume out of politeness. As he sat down with the nasty little things, Byron brushed past him, stealing the whole plate. He tore the first orange stick apart, followed by the rest in front of Eric's stunned face. Soon they lay in a waste of chocolate and ripped dried fruit. Byron lifted the mess to his nose and smelled them in front of our shocked eyes—my pretend shocked eyes, Eric's real ones. "Interesting," Byron said in some amazement. "They're clean. Too bad. I love those things."

PRANK WARS

Was he crazy? I made a face. By now Eric was trying to hide his laughter. For once I wasn't the one who looked stupid. "What? You don't think she poisoned them, do you?" he asked.

I straightened. "I told you, Byron, we were visiting under a flag of truce."

Byron seemed amused by the statement. "I seem to remember during the last flag of truce that Rock ate a whole batch of brownies made with Methylene blue and the twins got their fill of Oreos filled with tasty toothpaste filling. Something like that is hard to forget."

Eric looked fascinated. His friend Rock was completely forgotten (a typical guy thing). The drums had stopped and the shower was on. I took a steadying breath. "Are you still missing your iPhone, Byron?"

"A few other things too."

"Your physics book?" Again, he nodded, but slowly. "Well, how about you borrow mine...or maybe Thanh's? Oh wait; you don't know who Thanh is. Our TA. Remember? The one you're dating? You are, right?"

"What are you talking about?"

By now, we had Eric's undivided attention. This was better than a daytime drama. I tried to forget that. "Oh, I don't know," I said. "Maybe I'm just wondering how you called me...if *I* have your phone?"

I got him there, but he covered up his guilt well. "When did I call you?"

"About two minutes ago. Five!"

"I didn't call you," he told me flatly. "But if you want me to, we can pretend I did. Now, give me the items we discussed and we'll call ourselves even."

"Or what? I end up on the next Police Beat? What's your game, Byron? I mean, it's really cute that you and your girlfriend have matching backpacks and all, but you could've told me about that and avoided this whole mess!"

For once, Byron looked confused. "W—what?"

"You and Thanh's coordinated backpacks. Poor Holly will be devastated." He still looked blank. "I have Thanh's backpack, not yours, Byron."

"You do?"

"Unless you own a pink cell phone, well, you don't! And *you* called me on her cell phone anyway, so…you already knew that I had it, so quit pretending!"

Byron was already on his way out the door. "Where is it?"

I blocked his way. I wasn't sure why, but I didn't quite trust him with Thanh's backpack with this reaction. "It's too late, Byron. I gave it back to her already." Byron hesitated in the doorway, watching my face for more lies. "So," I said, "if you want *your* backpack, I suggest you ask her about it on your next date."

Eric pushed away from the couch, jerking out his phone and quite suddenly texting. His eyes were cold. "Kids, it's been fun, but I've got to get to work." My stomach lurched, knowing I was responsible for his sudden exit. It had finally happened. I had chased him away. My blood ran to my face when I realized I had sounded like Byron's jealous girlfriend too.

Byron refused to move from the front door to give Eric an easy escape. Eric came up to his shoulder, and he met Byron's eyes, so the two could do that dangerous measuring-each-other-up guy thing. Why were they doing that anyway? It made me nervous, and I pulled on Byron, catching a sinewy arm to drag him back. Eric's gaze swept past me like he didn't see me and he hurried down the stairs. For once, he wasn't smiling. I pushed my hair out of my eyes, feeling sick. "Thanks a lot, Byron."

"Oh, I'm sorry. Do you want me to bring him back?" Byron seemed only mildly annoyed, but I knew better. "Maybe you should try toning down the flirting a notch. You're painfully obvious."

He knew very well that I was incapable of flirting. Obviously. I had ruined whatever I might've had going on with Eric. I sighed. "It isn't what you think."

PRANK WARS

"Yes, it is, so you'd better be jealous, Byron." Tory rambled from the kitchen; her pink hoody zipped up to her neck. It was apparent she was hiding something. I rolled my eyes. We were under a flag of truce. Could she take nothing seriously?

"Empty your pockets," Byron told Tory in a resigned voice. She smiled innocently and took out a few utensils then tried to push past him. He stood resolutely in front of the door. He gave her a hard look. "All of it." She laughed and unzipped her jacket, dumping the rest of the contents into Byron's hand. They were only spoons. I couldn't believe that she would risk the mission with those. Byron turned to me. "Your turn."

I drew back, insulted. "I'm under a flag of truce. The only thing I have is information."

He smirked and ripped the duct tape from the doorknob hole on his front door and handed it to me. "I believe this is yours, Captain."

I took the piece of tape with all the dignity I could muster. The door slammed shut behind us. The mission had been compromised. I didn't even think to ask him how to contact Thanh, so I could return her backpack. And did Eric seriously hate me now? Maybe it was for the best. My hands felt shaky. I had lost them all in one day. Well, maybe two days. Tory and I headed down the stairs towards the parked trucks. The stake had relocated the charity drive to the guys' apartment complex. The guys had added a punching bag to the pile of overflowing clothes. As soon as we reached the first truck, I let out a quivering breath, unable to bottle up my sudden depression. "Tory!" I whined. "Where did I go wrong?"

"Are you kidding? That was awesome." Tory gave me a mischievous grin and pulled out a huge book from behind her back. She had wedged it under her hoody. I couldn't believe I hadn't noticed her suddenly flat square back. The girl was magic. She waved Byron's PHYS 121 book in front of my face with both hands.

"Tory! You can't steal…" I stopped myself from the lecture. "Wait, but *Thanh* has his book."

"Nope, we have it."

"He told me that he needed his backpack so that he could study physics? He acted like he didn't know that he had Thanh's backpack."

"He lied."

"Why?" Gripping the physics book in my hand, I turned around, ready to confront Byron with it just as Kali ran past me in her bare feet.

She laughed with high-pitched giggles. Tory and I involuntarily brought our hands to our ears. "Run! They're going to catch us!" she shouted.

Lizzie met her on the other side of the apartment complex, out of breath. She leaned against the bunkhouse apartments, her white shirt blending in with the white brick. As soon as she caught sight of me, she stomped my way, looking indignant. "Tell the twins that they *cannot* give our stuff away to charity."

Kali's face was pink with exertion. Her blonde hair wisped around her head like a halo. She ran for one of the charity trucks and grasped the tailgate. Using it as her leverage, she kicked her way over the top and burrowed deep into the donated clothing. "Hide me!"

I obediently piled some clothes over her. Lizzie dove over the top, tackling the pile of clothes like a leaf pile. The two wriggled around the litter looking like playful little puppies, their legs and elbows popping up everywhere. I tried not to roll my eyes, *but I did*. What would the DI workers think when we donated two of our girls to them? I threw one last pillow over Kali's blonde hair just in time. I saw Blake barreling our way. I hoped he wasn't here to haul the trailer away. "Hey girls," I whispered, "...maybe this isn't such a good ide—"

"There you are," Blake said. I swiveled to him. He looked mildly annoyed. "Would you mind telling your roommate that if she doesn't give me back my watch, then I'll be forced to do something she or I *might* regret."

Now I knew what Lizzie was talking about. This prank war was completely out of control. "I'm not your messenger girl, okay, Blake? Grow up and ask Kali out like a real man."

PRANK WARS

He grinned in surprise, his dimples standing out. "You got my name right."

Adam sped around the truck to join his twin. I noticed he held our TV remote in his hands. My eyes bulged. "What are you doing with that?"

"What? It came with your TV. You decorated our place. We're just finishing the job." Adam laughed at my expression and dodged past me, his twin at his heels.

Lizzie poked her head out of the clothes, startling me. "Do you see what I'm saying?" she cried.

Kali's head joined hers, giving them a conjoined twins look. "So, Blake stole our walkie talkie, right? And we ran after him probably about four blocks and they hid behind this dumpster and we scared them on the other side." She started laughing at the memory. "And then we took some of their stuff and they were like, 'get them!' And then we came over here and ran into you, and then you—"

I held up my hands. "I know what I did!" Wait. Who was guarding the backpack? "Is anyone still at home?" I asked.

Kali shrugged, not realizing that everything depended on her answer. "Sandra, maybe."

I leaned my head back. Useless. Sandra proved she wouldn't guard anything of ours if it cost her the least bit of exertion—let alone her life or anything precious like that. She'd leak the whereabouts of the new hiding spot just to get back at me. I took off running. Tory knew what was up. She was at my heels and quickly overtook me. I tried to tell myself the heavy physics book was slowing me down. Tory was soon a speeding little torpedo in the distance. "Find the backpack," I cried to her. She gave me the thumbs up, her red hair flying behind her. I rounded the corner, keeping to the sides of the bunkhouse apartment building, seeing Sandra's BMW ahead of me. The engine was on and it waited at the corner. Sandra must be heading for the library to study. If I could just reach her before she pulled away, she could tell me what happened to Thanh's backpack. I pumped my arms even faster.

I peeled the passenger's side open, grateful that it was unlocked and jumped in. I turned to the driver and dropped Byron's physics book at my feet. Sandra wasn't at the wheel. Eric was. This wasn't her car. Eric watched me in complete surprise. I did it again. I was cursed. "Uh, hi Eric." He was grinning at me again. "Look, this isn't what it looks like. This is totally the case of mistaken car identity."

"What's that?"

I squinched up my nose and tried to translate for myself. "Eric, I did not mean to jump in your car to scare you. I'm not Tory!" He laughed loudly. I brought my eyes to the sky, leaning my head against the seat. "Seriously, things aren't always this crazy around here."

"Are you trying to change that?"

I met his eyes, relieved to see that he was in a better mood than when we were at Byron's. Still, I was tired of making a complete fool of myself. "My life really isn't like a comic book. I dunno. Maybe it's more situational comedy. I just wish *I* thought it was funny."

"Sitcoms never are."

"Thanks, Eric." I took a deep breath, staring out into the parking lot. We were completely hidden from the outside world. This was my first time being alone with Eric, and the funny thing was that I felt completely at ease. Now I just hoped to make up for offending him today. And for jumping into his car. And for a ton of other things really.

"Sorry." We both said at once.

Eric grinned and I let him finish his apology first. "My car is such a mess." He put his arm around me to reach behind his seat. It was a little awkward, so I inched away, pushing against the car door while he rearranged his coat over whatever mess he didn't want me to see in the back. He needn't have bothered. His car really wasn't that bad.

"Don't worry about it," I found myself saying. "I'm sorry too for...pretty much everything. My social provocity is really lacking lately."

After a moment, his arm left me and he smiled at me. "Well, how about we start again?" I felt a rush of relief at his words...and then a little panic. What did he mean? What were we starting? He pushed his emergency brake down, watching me in that amused way of his. "Hey, I need to get back to work in a little bit…"

"Oh sorry, yeah." I didn't even know what he did at work. I knew nothing about him. I was bad at this. "So uh…you work at a lab at the school," I prompted. "What do you do there?"

"We're working on a top-secret experiment right now."

"What is it?"

He laughed. "You just come right out and ask it. Don't you? No torture involved."

"That only comes later." I grinned, settling into the passenger side. He had my full attention. "So top-secret, huh?"

He got comfortable too. I could tell this was a subject he didn't mind talking about. "How old are you?" he asked. I stiffened. It was death to admit you were over a certain age around here. He read my look and grinned. "No, don't tell me. I have ways of knowing. You know those ringtones kids set their cells on in class so their teachers can't hear?"

"No!"

"Well, no one under twenty-six can hear it."

I didn't like the sound of that at all. He seemed oblivious to my discomfort and just patted the steering wheel. "Anyway, if you want to come by my lab to get tested?"

"Can you hear the frequency?"

"Not that one."

I relaxed in relief. "Well, I won't be able to hear it either. I'm kind of on the edge of that number."

The appraising look he gave me made me believe that he didn't care. "I'm getting something to eat, do you want…?"

I took a deep breath, reading the vibes. He was asking me out again, so why was I fighting this anyway? I liked Eric a lot. Why else had I been worried that I pushed him away at Byron's? But we always crossed paths when I was running from something, and bad habits were hard to break. I took a longer look at him. Eric was really cute. He seemed amusing and nice and fun to be around...*just like Cameron*. I was really messed up, wasn't I? Byron was right. I was incapable of liking someone, especially someone I *liked*—as if I ripped out that part of my heart that could feel. I bit my lip, but before I could make any life-altering decisions for this guy, I heard a knock at my window.

I turned, seeing Tory's face in the way. I jumped back. She scratched at the door, forcing me to open it. Kali jumped in front of her, waving her hands wildly. Lizzie was right behind her. "Tomorrow...at *Battle of the Bands!*" Kali cried as soon as I got the door open. "He's worried about something and he's going to meet someone there. I heard him talking!"

I wrinkled my nose. "Who?" Tory took one look at Eric and put a hand on Kali's shoulder. She instantly clammed up. There was no need. "You were just saying something about *Battle of the Bands*," I urged.

"Um, yeah." Tory's face screwed up in thought. "Did you know that there are bands playing at the school at 7:00 tonight?"

Kali *wasn't* going to say that. I glanced over at Eric. Tory didn't want him to overhear, and this was just the excuse I needed. "Maybe another time," I told Eric. "I need to..."

He tipped the bill of his cap in a rakish way. My smile matched his. It was impossible not to like him. "Yeah, next time for sure," he said.

I slid out of his car, feeling a little sheepish, especially since I had jumped into it so brazenly. It was almost like destiny...or bad luck. On closer inspection, his car was the wrong shade to be Sandra's. Eric reached down by the passenger's seat and picked up the physics book I had dropped. His eyes met mine. "Is this yours?"

"It belongs to a friend."

Tory blinked. It was the only thing that betrayed her. Lizzie smiled, not knowing the significance of my statement. Eric handed me Byron's book. "So, how well do you know this *friend*?" he asked.

I gave a noncommittal smile. "Enough to recognize his stuff."

"Enough to know what kind of man he is?"

I nodded slowly.

PRANK WARS

"And you like that type?"

This time my smile was more genuine. "No." I closed the door and fell into step beside Kali and Lizzie. Tory followed at a more sedate pace, falling behind. She watched Eric's BMW drive away, his engine purring like a cat. The guy had it together, so what could he possibly see in me besides entertainment? It was something to think about in more peaceful times, but for now I turned back to Lizzie. "You overheard Byron then?"

She nodded. "He was getting rid of all our girly decorations in the truck, and he was talking to some guy. I didn't recognize his voice."

Kali pulled forward with renewed excitement. "He was talking about Thanh and how something strange was happening with her."

"How do you know he was talking about Thanh?" I asked.

Lizzie gave Kali a piercing look then shrugged at me. "He called her the target."

"That could be anyone." *Maybe even me*...if he was talking battle talk, but if he were talking love then he could possibly be talking about Thanh...or Sandra. The mysterious Holly was out of the game it seemed.

Kali stubbornly stuck to her claim. "No, it really was Thanh."

"He said her name?"

"Well, not quite," Lizzie said after getting an elbow in the side from Kali to second her claim, "—but Byron said she has something for him. Probably the backpack. She's ready to talk. He seemed hopeful."

I crossed my arms. Well, it definitely wasn't *me* then. I would never talk.

"They're missing something and he needs to go in before it's too late," Kali finished excitedly. "She's starting to get cold feet, I think. It's *so* romantic."

I took a deep breath. He was finally going to ask someone out for real. I glanced over at Tory. She had been too quiet. Her face was pale under her red hair. "So, what's the damage?"

"The backpack's missing."

"From the trapdoor?" She nodded slowly. I rearranged Byron's physics book in my arms. Sandra must have told the evil twins where it was. Maybe they made a deal for the remote. Byron had proved a great distraction. Well, Thanh's knight errant stole her backpack for her. She should be happy. Still, none of it made sense. Byron had all the makings of a player, but besides his brief fling with Sandra, I never saw him in action before. I had begun to think Sandra had scarred him. Something more was going on, but I couldn't put my finger on it. "Did he say when he was *going in*?" I asked.

After an encouraging look from Kali, Lizzie set her dainty shoulders to give her reluctant report. "*Battle of the Bands*, but don't mess with the concert tonight, guys! I have to hand out name tags. It's for school credit."

Kali hopped up in excitement. "We definitely *have* to go!" she announced. "Blake's been talking about it all weekend. He told me if I came to see them perform, we could do something fun after." She gave a little whoop. "I think he likes me!"

Something told me there was more to this invite. Maybe that's what Tory sensed too. She knew the ways of the evil twins. Her arms were wrapped stiffly around her stomach. Still, Thanh would be there and I wanted to make sure Byron returned her backpack. After all, she trashed her own place to find it. But if I were being brutally honest with myself, I just wanted to know if there was something else going on between her and Byron. He would never let on if he saw me, which meant this would have to be a covert operation. I nodded. "We'll go. Just not the way they expect."

CHAPTER NINETEEN

Day 110
2014 hours

"Undercover. The enemy has many different faces—some of them much too attractive."

—Madeleine's War Journal Entry (Saturday Night, June 2nd).

"What are your names?"

The twins stood in front of me and I watched them closely, my pen poised. They smiled mischievously at each other, too eager to wreak havoc than to see through my disguise. "Blake," Adam said.

Blake dimpled. "Adam."

I gave Blake a name tag that said *Number one*, and Adam another that said *number two*. They looked surprised and I shrugged at them. Adam tried to switch with Blake to get *number one*. I grinned. Of course the numbers would cause sibling rivalry. Blake finally gave in—he usually did. They walked away in their strangely attractive plaid pants. The brunette next to me sighed. I elbowed her. "Get a hold of yourself, Kali."

Battle of the Bands was progressing nicely. Lizzie had groaned when I announced my intention to hand out name tags with her at the entrance, but after we promised to behave ourselves, she had eventually given in. My eyes shifted to Tory. Her hair was in a short black bob. She wore a tuxedo shift dress and cropped red jacket. It was not her normal look at all. She wrote *Brad Pitt* on a name tag and handed it over to some blond guy. I turned to her. "Is my hair too big?" I asked.

"You're in the land of big hair...so no."

Tonight I was the blonde. It was weird what a different hair color did to my identity, that and changing my style to be more like Sandra's. Horrors of horrors, I had on red heels and a flirty black dress. No one recognized us. Well, they might Lizzie. She looked hot, but her dark skin was a dead giveaway. We set her in the crowd with red hair and a cell phone to keep a lookout at the front of the ballroom. Sandra had pronounced us stupid and deserted us for the dance floor, her white and black zippered heels especially loud against the wooden floor.

"Name," I barked. "Take a name tag or you don't get in." A guy stood in front of me. His eyebrows rose in surprise. *Strong silent type*, I wrote. I slapped the name tag on his chest. He made room for a cute little couple. *Romeo and Juliet*, I wrote down for them. I gave them their name tags. "Be safe tonight." There seemed to be a rush at the tables. *Napoleon*, I wrote for some kid with curly fro like hair.

"Hey," he complained.

Another guy placed his hands squarely on the table in front of me. "How are *you* doing?" he asked meaningfully.

I stared back. Apparently blondes did have more fun. I was getting more hits than ever tonight. I scribbled down what I thought of the guy. *Player*. I gave him his name tag and his mouth made an *O*. "Next," I called.

Kali wrote *Bathsheba and David* for the next couple. *Jezebel* for some high-maintenance girl, *my future stalker* for some guy flirting with her. She had a stack of *single white female* name tags. The guys grabbed these ones like hot cakes. Kali giggled, tap dancing her embellished flats against the ground. For a brunette, she wasn't doing so bad. The next guy in line met her eyes and stole her marker to personalize his own name tag. He wrote *secksi* with an accent over the i. They shared a smile.

Tory wasn't about to be outdone. She sized up the next guy. "What's your phone number?" He looked confused, but he gave it to her anyway.

PRANK WARS

She wrote it down on his name tag and stuck it on his chest. "That should do the trick." The corner of his eyes crinkled up when he saw it, but as soon as he left, some girl laughed and accosted him by putting his number into her cell phone.

"My name is Anne." A girl stood stiffly in front of Tory with a no-nonsense air.

Surprisingly, Tory wrote it down without a fuss. She turned to Anne's boyfriend. "Andy?" she asked.

"What? No!"

Tory gave it to him. Soon a thick crowd of students surrounded us, demanding more name tags. It was a hit. No one wanted their real names anymore. "You got any more *single white female*?" a guy asked me.

"What are you doing?" Lizzie made her way to our table. Her name tag said *Cleo*. It was supposed to be her cover, but apparently everyone had a cover tonight. "This is getting out of control! I don't think one person has their real name on."

"How convenient for them certainly." I handed out another one.

"You don't understand! *I* was put in charge of this!" Some guy patted his friend on the back. As soon as his friend turned, we saw *Celestial* on his back. The magic was spreading. Lizzie buried her head in her hands. "I'm going to get into so much trouble."

"Why? You're *not* doing it."

"I'm supposed to be." She tried to shove me over.

A blond guy used Lizzie as his distraction to slip past. I waved him over politely. "Get your name tag." He ignored me and headed straight for the crowd. I stood up, my chair scraping loudly behind me. Kali and Tory rose to their feet next to me like enraged sirens. "Get your name tag!" we all shouted.

Lizzie looked scandalized. Kali scampered around the table and grabbed the guy's arm, dragging her new hostage to the table by the bicep. As soon as I saw she had Eric, I ducked my head. He had the alternative rocker look with the short-sleeved shirt over the long sleeves. He looked way too good for me to keep my cool look. "Is this absolutely necessary?" he asked with a laugh.

"You can't come in without them," Tory informed him soberly.

"Here's your name tag, *friend*!" Kali wrote it onto his name tag.

"*Friend*?" he read with distaste. "What happened to my real name?"

"Boring." Tory glanced over at me. I pretended to be interested in my marker. "Each to his own, I guess."

Eric grabbed my marker from me and wrote *boy* next to *friend*. "Much better." He stood directly in front of me, meeting my eyes before slipping it on. "By the way," he told me, "you make a great blonde. If you get out on the dance floor, save a dance for me." He winked at my astonished face and disappeared into the crowd.

"He recognized me," I told Tory. And I didn't want him to go, but I didn't tell her that part. Before Tory could respond, Cameron broke through the crowd with a coven of girls. He sported a white Jonas Brothers shirt that said *Team Selena*. Actually, it was just an American Rejects shirt, but a girl could wish. I hid my face with the blonde hair of my wig. If Eric recognized me, my ex-fiancé would for sure.

"Cameron." He impatiently tapped the table next to my fingers. I inched them away and found the marker Eric just discarded. Cameron didn't recognize me. One of the girls next to him inspected her perfect nails. It was disturbing what kind of girls Cameron went for after me. She was definitely cursed with coolness.

I turned to her. "And your name?"

She looked me up and down. After an appropriate insultingly long wait, she said, "Chloe."

Property of Chloe's. I wrote it down and with great daring, slapped Cameron's special name tag onto his broad chest. "Here ya go, boy toy."

He laughed, trying to get a closer look at me. I kept my face averted. He peeled at his name tag. "No, we're not a couple," he defended himself *as if it were a sin to be dating someone*. "It's not like that."

Chloe turned the flirt on and tapped his name tag back down. She met my eyes with a challenging look. "Sure, it's like that." Her fingers trailed to his biceps. "He's my big strong man."

That was it. Chloe earned her name tag. I slipped it to her. *Cameron's fan club*. I gave the girl on Cameron's other side hers too,

PRANK WARS

Wife Number Two. The third girl I gave, *Cameron's Fling.* They stared down at their name tags. "Have fun tonight," I sang.

Cameron refused to be dismissed. He lingered over my table. "Are you always this mean?" Uh oh. I squirmed uneasily. I had made him interested with my cruelty. It was completely ironic since he wasn't interested when I was nice to him.

The MC introduced the next band as they made their way onto the stage. *26Down.* It was Byron's band. Well, not really *Byron's* band. Rock forced him to play the bass once Byron moved into their apartment. As soon as I heard Rock go off on his drums, I gave Cameron a stern look. "This band is awesome."

"Are you kidding? I know those guys. They're idiots."

"You should really go dance." I waved his new girlfriend over to him. "Take him away, Chloe."

He didn't take his eyes off me. "It would take a really hot girl to get me to dance," he said. Before I could kick him under the table, Chloe's hand released Cameron's strong bicep, and she stared at him with shocked eyes. Good. The girl had a self-esteem. "Uh," he stammered. Even he knew he had said the wrong thing. "I mean…*you're* a hot girl too," he told her. "She'd just have to prove that she was really into me. That's all."

"Oh, you want strings attached, do you?" I asked. "Sounds like a commitment." Whenever I said things like that, Cameron usually looked at me like I was stupid, but since he didn't recognize me, he looked intrigued. I knew once he figured out who I was, he'd have an attack of the vapors. I tried to think of a way to escape before that happened.

26Down was already playing on the stage up front. Blake took the microphone, flinging his guitar strap easily over his shoulder. Adam stood to the side with his guitar, wearing his *number one* name tag. "I'm sorry," I told Cameron without an ounce of remorse. "These guys are super hot. I gotta go see them play." I shoved from my seat. Lizzie was more than happy to take my place. She rolled her eyes at Cameron and he stiffened when he recognized her.

"But our shift isn't over yet!" Kali was at my heels.

"We've done enough damage," I said, not slowing down. "We've got work to do."

Tory nodded. "I'll go decorate Cameron's car." She pulled out a backpack full of toilet paper.

"You mean Byron's, right?"

"Nope." Tory left us, looking intense. She just didn't get it. We weren't out for revenge tonight. We didn't even know what we were fighting anymore.

"Oh, hey, wait!" Kali smiled and gave me a name tag, patting it down on my shirt. I glanced down at it. *The Hottest Girl You've Ever Seen.* She laughed. "I want you to have fun tonight, missy!"

She was missing the point. I pushed my way through the crowd. The incognito name tags had a rowdy effect over these people. Everyone danced, doing fake machine guns and hippy style wash-the-car moves. A guy did the robot into the middle of the dance floor. The sound of exaggerated cheers haunted me. Byron was planning on closing in tonight, but on what? A date? Or something else altogether? I had to keep my mind open to every possibility, but first where was Thanh in this mess? *26Down* started their second song. Kali stared admiringly up at Blake. She grabbed my hand and squeezed the life out of it. "Kali!" I complained.

"Sorry." She let me go to fan her face with exaggerated motions, hitting me a few times in the process. "He's just really cute."

He was insane. Blake threw the guitar behind his head and plunked out a complicated tune. He made their bass player look like a slacker. It was Byron, after all. He looked half asleep in the back. His cowboy styled button-up wrinkled over his bicep. His fingers moved automatically over the bass, but he was searching the crowd for something…maybe someone. I tried to follow his gaze and it fell on me. His lip curled up. Impossible. He recognized me. Why had I bothered with this stupid disguise then? Someone elbowed me in the side and I turned in irritation until I saw Eric. "Going for a new look?" he asked.

PRANK WARS

I elbowed him back. "How did you know it was me?"

"I'm sorry. Did I blow your cover? What conspiracy are you uncovering now?" He tipped his head back, taking a nonchalant drink of his pop.

I scanned the crowd for Thanh. "Something's definitely going on."

"Yeah." He nodded, staring at the guy doing the robot. "This place is crazy. What do you say we head somewhere sane?"

That was the last thing I wanted. Well, the sane bit. I needed to find Byron's connection with Thanh. Something wasn't adding up. Why I cared? For starters, Byron had lied to me. "I just have to check something out first," I said.

Eric looked bored. "Let me guess, Byron's trying to take over the school? What's he going to do, turn the Y into a U?" He took another drink; he made it look so good, I stole his cup from him. Eric's bored look evaporated as soon as I downed his pop. He looked intrigued. "Do you always take things that aren't yours?" he shouted over the noise. Before I knew what he was doing, he took my free hand. I went stiff with surprise. "See, now how do *you* like it?" he asked me.

I liked it a lot. I studied his waiting, slightly teasing expression. It was weird, but all I could think of was how close he was to the enemy. Maybe he could help me. "Hey, do you spend a lot of time at Rock's?"

"What? Rocks?"

He couldn't hear me over the music. I leaned over him to shout. "The drummer?"

"Yeah, what about him?"

"Did you see a black backpack at his place?"

Eric's nose wrinkled and his hand slid from mine. "Backpack? What does it look like?"

"Um...black. I'm just wondering if a friend of mine got the right one back, that's all."

He laughed, his eyes not leaving me. "Why don't you just ask your friend?" Eric was so innocent. Before I could answer, a short girl sped past us. Her black hair swung against her back. It was Thanh. She still didn't look happy, which made me think she didn't get her backpack back after all.

I returned Eric his empty cup. "I'll be back." I headed for Thanh, leaving Eric behind in the heavy applause.

The MC stepped to the microphone. "Cool, guys," his voice blared over us. "Give 26Down a big hand. That's right! You're so sick you're sick." He tipped his cowboy hat at us. Only a BYU student would be so bold as to mix country with alternative rock. "While we wait for the next band to set up, we got some sweet prizes. Hey, maybe if we draw some names, we'll figure out a few real names out there, people?" His eyes trailed to a girl below him. "I know your name isn't *call me*. But seriously, I wouldn't mind." A few ripples of laughter. Thanh kept getting away from me. Dressed to kill in a high waist pencil skirt and silk blouse, she looked ready for a secret rendezvous. I had a few guesses who that would be with. Above me, the MC drew a name out of a hat. "Cameron...uh...Cameron Hoogendowzer?"

"Hornberger!" Cameron shouted back from the crowd.

"Whatever your name is, congratulations, guy. Come get your floral perfume." He glanced over at Cameron's disappointed face. "Uh, sorry, dude. Maybe you can give it to your girlfriend." *Wife number two* and *Cameron's Fling* clapped their hands in excitement. I hid a laugh. *Cameron's fan club* was gone. I guessed Chloe had better taste than I thought. Thanh covered the full length of the ballroom faster than I could get through the dancers in this crowd. Once she hit the hallway, there was no telling which direction she'd go. "Prize number two," the MC shouted. "This is a good one. Fifty dollars' worth of tanning at Sunny Salon." The MC pulled out a name. "Cameron...Heizendine."

There was a collective catcall and I was momentarily distracted from Thanh. Someone had padded the box with Cameron's name. My first guess was Tory. Cameron froze on his way back to his girlfriends. The MC laughed. "Hey, you got caught, buddy." He drew out another name. "Cameron again!" Everyone laughed. A few murmured angrily. Yup. Tory. "Okay, we're gonna have to pull out all of Cameron's names from the box before we pick another winner," the MC said. "Meanwhile, how about we have a little *Battle of the Sexes*?"

Everyone cheered and jumped up around me, blocking my sight from the exits. There was no way to tell which way Thanh had gone. She was just too short. I needed higher ground.

"Now is your chance. C'mon, guys, girls. It's open mike night. Anything goes. He's hitting on your best friend, let him have it. She's spending all your money? Well, you won't take it." Even though the MC couldn't possibly see me, I gave him an annoyed look. Why did some guys think women were just after their money? All the money in the world wasn't worth dating a guy we didn't like.

The crowd went wild, especially when the MC handed off the microphone to a guy waiting in the wings. He had a cocky grin and a knit skull cap. He had the makings of a jerk. "Hey, peeps!" he shouted down at us. "You girls whine and complain about not getting married, but let's talk about why it hasn't happened for you sweet little things, shall we?" He had better not go there. "How about the number one thing that will get you dumped. You wanna hear it!" Even the girls were screaming to hear it. Traitors. Somehow they thought they were exempt from these insults. "You are way too desperate, women. Why do you say things like *when will I see you again? Where are things going? We've got to talk.* You girls are way too focused on commitment. Chill out. Get it through your thick skulls; we're just dating, babe. And don't even get me started on return sister missionaries…"

Some of the guys shouted out in appreciation around me. My glare was completely wasted on them. Their attention was on the weasel above us. A few guys gave their girlfriends weak smiles. "Get this," the guy complained above us. "We're paying for the dates. We're paying for the ring. We give you our name and our money and for what? After all the bleach and fake bakes, your looks are gonna fade like a nasty tattoo."

To be fair, I noticed a few guys' mouths hang open at that. "Whoa!" a guy shouted up at him. "Your girlfriend's gonna kill you, dude!"

Laughter spread through the room. The punk on the stage brought the mike to his lips. "You're thinking it. I'm just saying it. In a few years, they'll be just like their moms. Why do you think we run away screaming like little girls when we meet the future in-laws? It's not that we're afraid to commit, we're just afraid to commit to *that*. So, do yourself a favor, girl, and keep the family hidden."

No, he didn't! I turned viciously on him. "Your mom!" I shouted back through the crowd. At the moment, the stage was the highest place I could think of to locate Thanh. I stalked up the steps, taking two at a time.

"Oh," the MC called. "Looks like we've got a contender."

I wrestled the microphone away from the MC before he could say anything else stupid and pointed viciously at the guy with the skull cap. "Congratulations. In less than one minute, you made sure that no girl in this room will *ever* date you."

The girls cheered. The jerk smirked back at me. I wouldn't leave until he cried. "So, Mr. God's gift to women, what makes you think you've got anything to offer the ladies, huh, besides that amazing skull cap you've got to hold your big head in? So far, you've mentioned your bags of seemingly endless gold? Even if you have money, which I seriously doubt, it would never make up for being stuck with you. So, what else do you have to offer the girls besides your dark and hollow soul?" I lifted my brow at the guy.

"Why don't you ask the girls who won't leave me alone?" he answered smoothly.

"That's called Stockholm Syndrome. They need their heads examined so that they'll know they don't need you. Anything you do, we can do *much much* better. Face it, little boy. Girls can make their own money. We can make our own fun. We can do more with our life than get tied up with some nut job like you. The only thing that can entice us is love. Oh, so maybe that's why you're so mad? You're not that loveable, are you?" I made a little moue with my lips. "Did some girl dump you on your head like you deserved?"

PRANK WARS

The guy didn't seem at all upset. Of course not, he still had poor misled girls wrapped around all his fingers. And besides that—I was so gullible—this guy had to be a set-up to get the crowd riled up. Not even Cameron was as bad as this. From the corner of my eye, I saw Thanh disappear into the exit at the far side of the ballroom. I might never find out if her backpack had been returned to her. I stuck the microphone back in its stand. The girls shouted for me to continue, but I couldn't. "Do yourself a favor, girls," I said as a parting shot. The guy with the skull cap would never be moved, but at least I could help them out. "Don't go for a guy like this. Go for a nerd. I've heard tale that he'll love you, never take you for granted, and treat you really well."

"Are you sure about that?" I swiveled at that familiar voice. It was Byron. Another jerk had taken skull cap's place. Byron still wore his bass strapped over his shoulder and looked calm like he was ready to do battle. "Or will he just play video games all day and ignore you?"

"Even better," I retorted. "Then he won't be around. Sounds like the perfect man to me." I was losing Thanh. I backed away.

"At least go for the jerk," Byron said. "Then you'll know what you're getting into. That's what *we all are* to you in the end, right? Jerks?" I rolled my eyes, turning away. "This world will never make you happy, will it, Mad Dog?"

That stopped me short. "Not while you're in it, Byron," I retorted. The crowd made a mock noise of shock. The microphone was somehow back in my hand. "In case you haven't realized, players are a dime a dozen these days. I'm tired of players. I'm ready for a change."

The girls cheered.

"And what exactly is a player?" Byron asked, stopping my grand exit yet again. Was he kidding? He might as well ask a missionary what our church was about. He knew he'd get a soliloquy from me with that.

"Ooooh!" That was Cameron making catcalls in the front. *Great.* Now my honor was at stake.

The microphone tightened in my hand. Byron asked for it. "Definition one: a guy who doesn't think that the girl he's dating is human. He lies, uses, and throws the baggage away. Sound familiar?"

"Girls do that too."

"I have never treated anyone the way guys have treated me."

"Neither have I." He said it with that stupid accent that I was starting to like. "Here's my piece of advice for you, Mad. Get over it. And one other thing; if you think I'm such a jerk then leave me alone."

I stared at him. What? The girls watched breathlessly below us like this was their favorite soap opera. The guys grinned uneasily. I tried to register what Byron was saying with all those eyes on me. Did I even think he was a jerk anymore? Right now I kind of did, but lately? I wasn't sure. Could I like a guy without him turning on me in the end? Tons of songs on the radio talked about love—a whole enterprise dedicated to it and I never really felt what they were talking about. And if I had, it never turned out to be real. Did that mean something was wrong with me? Or was this love thing just a trick and there was something wrong with all of us? "You're right," I told Byron. "I should never open my heart. Happy?"

I tried to retreat, but he wouldn't let me. "Who says? You?" I stiffened. With all those eyes on me, I wasn't about to admit that my only experience with love was to be used and thrown away. "What happened to love suffereth long, is kind, is not puffed up, Madeleine? If you can't open your heart…you're broken."

He just called me broken. I could add that to his long list of insults against me. And in front of the majority of the school? I took a deep breath. "You are wrong. I am so happy." To my horror, my voice broke. It was a terrible way to prove my point.

"You don't sound like it."

My eyes narrowed. Byron was crazy…and I would prove it, gladly, except…my eyes went to the exit where Thanh had disappeared.

"Relationships are messy." I heard Byron say. "None of us are going to get it right."

"No, we're not," I agreed, sliding the microphone back into its holder. "Especially you…and me. You want me to leave you alone? I'll leave you alone,"—*with a vengeance.* I took the stage steps two at a time away from Byron, so he could see for himself how serious I was—I never wanted to see him again! I plunged headlong into the crowd. They made an amused path for me. I felt a few pats on my back and shoulders. Some guys just grinned at me, but no one got in my way. I felt my face flush beat red. I had lost...badly. I wasn't sure where my usual focus in the heat of battle had gone. The next band came on stage and the MC introduced them with a relieved voice.

I took a deep breath, not believing that I had just told Byron off. It felt good and very wrong at the same time, and I tried to push it back to the part of me that couldn't hurt. Tears glistened in my eyes when I remembered Byron's face when I had called him a player. He did not look happy. What had possessed him to come to the aid of men everywhere anyway? I was tired of being on opposing sides. I didn't want to fight him anymore.

I broke out of the ballroom, my footsteps echoing across the empty hall. My conscience wouldn't leave me alone—it lectured me like it was Lizzie, and I tried to wrestle it down, so I could focus on Thanh. It was useless. I couldn't bring myself to care if she got her stuff back or what she might mean to Byron. What did I think I could do for her anyway? I couldn't control everything, or how Byron felt about her...or me—well, I *could* make him hate me. I could call him a jerk in front of the entire school. I groaned. Was it too late to apologize? Sort of. There was no way I wanted to face those people in the ballroom again. Or Byron. I leaned against the wall to the atrium, finding the darkest corner with the bushiest leaves I could find, Byron's words stinging me all over. Obsessed. Unhappy. Broken. I didn't want him to be right, but was he?

I took a deep breath, listening to the music from the ballroom. It sounded distant. Behind the sound, I caught the faint snatches of whispers that formed into words. I wasn't alone in the atrium. I listened to the hushed voices. *"...not here."* I glanced around the corner into the atrium and stiffened when I saw one of the voices belonged to Thanh. I half-expected to find a glass slipper in her place, not the actual girl. Her small frame blended into the shadows.

"Where are they? Do you have them?" *someone* asked her. The lights were dim, and I couldn't get an ID on whoever talked to her. Whoever it was had a stiff set to her shoulders and long hair. I couldn't make out the exact color in the darkness. Thanh's eyes swept carefully around, and I pulled back into the shadows. The last thing I wanted to be caught doing was eavesdropping. "You can give them to me now," the silhouette whispered harshly to Thanh. "I'll make sure they get into the right hands."

Thanh shook her head. "I don't know who to trust." This was a weird conversation. The rest of their words were lost in a murmur. I tried to get closer without being seen. A branch smacked me in the face.

"You'll be hurt. Come back. We'll take care of you."

"I need to talk to him." Thanh said in a louder voice.

"Did you make contact with him? Does he have *them*?"

"I tried to…Tuesday night, but there were some students, and then—please, where is he?"

The girl talking to Thanh shifted. I still couldn't see her face. She seemed a part of the shadows. "Stay here. We'll protect you…he's coming."

"Who?" There was real fear in Thanh's voice.

Too late I heard the footsteps come up behind me, and I reacted to that fear. My heart closing in on my chest. I had nowhere to hide…except the coat closet across the way. Being June, there weren't that many coats in there. A few slickers. I scurried across the hallway and ducked inside just as I saw the legs stalk past. The owner of them hesitated when he passed the closet and turned…to look straight at me. My stomach sank. Of course it was Eric. He had found me in another compromising position. The way things were going, he'd find me in an asylum next. "What are you doing?" he asked.

Thanh's whisper died and I heard a scuttle of feet like mice running away with cheese from a trap. I managed to give Eric a weak shrug. He leaned against the closet, watching me with heavy-lidded eyes. He extended his hand, and I stared at it. "You hiding from your roommate again?" he asked. Compassion laced his voice. "I thought I saw you coming this way."

It was a pretty good excuse and I nodded. "Tory's been really, um..." I crawled out of the closet, dusting off my black dress while I was at it, "I'm trying to figure out, um..." I really had no idea what I had overheard to be honest and I couldn't concentrate on what I was saying.

"I know. I saw." Eric pointed the general direction of the ballroom. He had witnessed my little *Battle of the Sexes* for himself. "Are you okay?"

I heard more footsteps, and knew they belonged to the one Thanh had been frightened would come. I scuttled back into the closet, but not before I grabbed Eric's arm and dragged him down with me. He was stronger than I thought, but he grinned and let me muscle him in. "What are you doing?" his voice was muffled in the closet. He readjusted himself and pushed closer to me. I got a good view of his hazel eyes; they watched me with more emotion than I could read. The band playing in the ballroom had shifted into a slower song—if we weren't stuck in a closet, I'd get lost in it. "Well, it's not every day I'm alone with the hottest girl I've ever seen," Eric said softly. My mouth opened, but nothing came out. "Your name tag," he reminded me.

I looked down at it. "Oh yeah, Kali gave—" The running feet got louder and I stopped talking just as Byron flew past. I felt like an idiot. I stood up and rammed my head against the hangers. "Ow." They swung loudly above me.

Byron hesitated at the threshold of the atrium and turned. "Madeleine?"

Eric laced his fingers through mine in response. I stiffened in surprise. My other hand went to my aching head. It found a lot of blonde hair instead. I couldn't think straight. Byron retraced his steps, coming back for me. "Byron," I managed to get out, "you're not...a jerk."

"Yes, I am." Byron stopped when he saw Eric. His gaze trailed to our hands. "Am I interrupting something?"

Immediately, I felt guilty and didn't know why. I was embarrassed about raging at him so publicly on stage—maybe that was it. Had Thanh been waiting for him this whole time? After seeing Byron, I knew she had been talking about how they mixed up their backpacks, not something more sinister. If that was the case, that made me the villain of this story. Byron still stared at me and I tried not to squirm. Eric's touch burned into mine. It wasn't just the familiar feeling of a male hand over mine; it was having Byron as my audience. *Still.* He, of all people, should know to leave us alone. I nodded quickly at Byron to send him on his way.

Byron leaned next to the coat closet, not taking the hint. "It's quite a view over here, isn't it?"

Was he kidding? There was only the atrium—if we could call it that—with only some sparse trees. Again I nodded. "It's really…really…uh…"

"Romantic," Eric finished for me. His eyes crinkled into almonds—very attractive ones. He thought this was hilarious.

"Look." Byron took a deep breath like he was thinking hard. "I'm sorry. I got carried away. I do that sometimes. It's just that…what were you telling those girls? You really think you're better off without us?"

Eric moved closer to me and smiled sardonically at him. "What do you think?" He gave my hand a significant squeeze and lifted it needlessly for Byron's inspection. Byron stiffened angrily.

It was all I could do not to pull away, but I didn't want to fight anymore. "You're right, Byron," I attempted my apology. "I *should* try—"

"What did you do to your hair?" Byron asked unexpectedly.

I stiffened. He didn't like my hair? What was his problem anyway? Anyone with any sense of decency would go away. Obviously Eric and I were in the middle of declaring our love. Well, we weren't, but we all knew what it looked like. I stepped angrily forward. "Blondes have more fun and I'm having more fun!"

"What's on your name tag?" Byron's eyes hadn't left mine, which meant he had taken me all in the moment he saw me. "The hottest girl I've ever seen?"

"You'd better say it like you believe it, Byron."

He allowed himself a smile. "Well, you're a blonde now, so maybe..."

What? My hand left Eric's and I shoved Byron back hard, my blonde hair swinging around my face. "Hey, not so fast," he complained. "I'm not ready for a relationship yet." I hit him angrily. "Okay." He gave me a devilish grin. "I give under torture! You're hotter as a brunette, okay?"

"That's *not* what I wanted you to say."

"Yeah? But I'm a jerk, remember?"

"I said you weren't! Weren't you listening to me? I'm trying to apologize!" My hands were all over Byron and I froze at his satisfied look. This was what he wanted. For some reason when he saw me with Eric, it made him want to antagonize me. If I had something going on with Eric, *which I didn't*, Byron would try to ruin it. But now I didn't know what to do. Every instinct told me to beat Byron and every instinct cried out against taking Eric's hand. Not that I didn't like the feel of Eric's hand over mine. I did, but I just wasn't sure about my feelings for him. It was like anger was all I had to give anymore. It was too sobering.

By now the band was done playing and the MC called more names from the drawing. At least he wasn't calling for Cameron anymore. I put my recently freed hand to my aching head and turned to Eric, having no idea how to explain myself. Maybe Byron was right. I was broken and I needed to fix myself. I just didn't know how.

Eric was already grinning. He laid a comfortable arm around my shoulders and I tried not to fight him in front of Byron. Maybe it was good to let go of my inhibitions; I had too many. "C'mon, let's get out of here," Eric whispered into my ear. "I want to show you my lab. I would love to know what's going on in that head of yours."

Byron's quick eyes shot to him.

"You could even make yourself a cool ten bucks," Eric told me.

Students were often given incentives for letting grad students experiment on them. It was actually tempting. "Really?"

"What do you do at your lab?" Byron asked him with a probing look.

"Oh, just experiment on poor unsuspecting females. Nothing big."

Byron didn't seem amused at all. He'd normally enjoy the joke, but the two faced each other warily, making me feel like the third wheel. There was something more than me going on. To my relief, the MC called Eric's name for the drawing. It was perfect timing. "They've got your name," I told Eric, cracking a smile for his benefit. "They're onto you."

"I believe congratulations are in order," Byron told him with an equally straight face. "You can finally get your nails done...*Eric*."

Eric suddenly looked dangerous.

"Why, Madeleine?" Sandra came up behind us. I didn't even hear the click clack of her high heels. As always she looked like a model in her slate gray twisty dress and leather leggings. She smiled in her fakest way and I squirmed, trying not to imagine what she saw. "I see you're hanging out with our *best friend*."

Eric or Byron? I knew what it looked like. I was poaching her men again. All of them. Byron nodded at Sandra in greeting. Eric squeezed my arm and stepped away, no longer looking like was going to punch Byron. Now that Sandra was here to protect me from the big bad wolf, he seemed okay with going back to easygoing. "I'll pass you off to better hands then." He gave me a tight hug, pressing me to his chest. "Visit me tomorrow if you can. The offer still stands." He tilted his chin to whisper in my ear, "Maybe then you'll tell me what this is all about?"

I smiled faintly in response; though I had nothing newsworthy for him. After a moment, Eric released me, not going back to the ballroom to collect his fifty-dollar nail coupon. The prize would probably fall to Cameron then.

Sandra licked her lips like a cat. "Looks like love," she said in an insinuating voice.

Byron made a sound of exasperation. "She doesn't need your stamp of approval."

"What's the matter, Byron?" Sandra said. "You wanna hug Madeleine too?"

"Of course...just not goodbye."

I didn't have time to reassure Sandra that Byron was messing with her at my expense because she simply glared at him and gave her glamorous heels leave to storm away. Byron refused to watch her go. Instead he patted a bench for me to sit. "It isn't as cozy as a coat closet, but I need to say something. Please?" He caught my elbows and gently tugged me down beside him on the bench. At his pleading look, I stayed put, uneasily adjusting my skirt around my knees. "I meant what I said, Madeleine. I'm really sorry."

He was actually serious. I felt my stomach clench at the thought. I felt horrible too. "Me too. So, do you—?" I stared into his blue eyes. This time, they weren't full of mischief. They were sincere. He suppressed the usual jaded look for once and allowed me to see what was there—tenderness. I gulped. "Do you really want me to leave you alone?"

"No," he gave a self-deriding laugh. "No, not at all."

"Oh." I was making lots of surprise sounds and it suddenly made me laugh along with him, the two of us acting all sheepish like this. "I can't have you *wanting* to spend time with me, Byron. That'll ruin the fun."

His hand tightened convulsively over mine. In a way it was comforting, but why was he being so nice? I should've been more suspicious, but right now I didn't want to be. It felt too good sitting with him and just being myself—like we had known each other for years. "Why is that?" he asked after a moment. "Are you afraid to just let go?" He looked deeply into my eyes, and I wondered if he could read mine like I could his. "You should really stop thinking so much, Madeleine. Accidentally slap me in the face when you point at something. Knock over my prized trophy collection. Burp more. Step on my toes when we're dancing."

I laughed. I couldn't imagine dancing with Byron, but I think I would really like it. Was he even a good dancer? I studied him. Fighters like him generally were. He could lead me effortlessly across the floor. It could be so fun...and would never last. "And then what?" I smiled to soften the harshness of our reality. "You'd think I was an idiot before long and start rolling your eyes whenever I talked."

I thought it was a joke, but he tilted his head at me. "What guys have you been dating?"

I couldn't leak those kinds of stats to Byron. They were terrible, but then I thought of Eric. He hadn't rolled his eyes at me once. It was like he actually thought I was cool. I didn't get him at all. And there was someone else I didn't get. Byron. Here we were, sworn enemies, sitting side by side on a bench, cozily discussing social problems like we were friends. I shrugged. "I have to be tough now. My dad isn't here polishing his rifle on the porch, you know? It's just that...you try being cold *and* warm at the same time. It's impossible to get anywhere with a guy that way." He studied me a moment before nodding. I took a deep breath, deciding to trust him. "Do you know what June 6th is?"

"Wednesday?"

"It was the day I was going to be Mrs. Cameron Hornberger."

He leaned back and I saw the realization fill his eyes as they lifted to mine. "That's just four days away." I nodded, trying not to give away how much that hurt. "Come here," he said. Byron wrapped his arms around me. The warmth of them sent a comforting happiness through me. He squeezed me, but it wasn't suffocating at all. I felt like I belonged there. I felt a tear escape down my cheek, but it wasn't because I had lost Cameron; I think it felt good that Byron cared. "You know you made a narrow escape, right?" he asked. "You want me to throw a party for you? June 6th, right?"

A smile tugged at the corner of my mouth. "Would you?"

"If you promise to leave the rifle home, Tex. I want you. Only you there." I nodded dumbly. "Stop worrying so much. I'll be the mean one. I'll sit on the porch and glare at anyone who dares talk to you."

He already did that. As soon as I was sure the tears were concealed from his knowing eyes, I pulled from his arms and took a long look at him. "You'll interview all my suitors?"

He took a moment before answering. He opted to play with my fingers instead. After stealing one of my rings, he nodded. "Sure, but I can't promise that any of them will make it past me alive."

PRANK WARS

I laughed. Was he seriously offering his help? But we were born to make each other's lives miserable. What if I could trust Byron? I already knew everything about him. He had charmed almost every girl in our acquaintance just like he was charming me now. He didn't want me...not like that. I really wanted to fall for him right now, but if I allowed that, I'd just be another number. If I was lucky, maybe an ex. But we understood each other a little better than that. He wasn't offering himself to me as my new boyfriend. Just his help. I had to see things as they were, see him as he was.

The question was could I trust him as my friend? It was tempting. I could still enjoy his company. Be with him, let him help me. I could lead a normal life. Maybe see what I had going on with Eric. The only reason I hadn't really gone for him was because I didn't know how to trust. That had to be the reason? But guys knew guys. Byron could actually be a good judge of character. If he were to be my rifle, I could give love a chance without worrying what would happen to me in the end. Byron could tell me if a guy was messing with me or not. He'd know their intentions.

I could imagine how well switching from enemies to allies would work. It made me laugh. I stood up, offering Byron my hand and he let me tug him to his feet. The soft material of his shirt rubbed against my bare arm. He was warm and strong. Maybe that's what I would borrow from him instead. I found myself smiling.

"You know any time you need a guy, I'm here for you." He grinned self-consciously. We both realized how that sounded, but we both knew what he meant—even if I knew it more than he did. "Of course, it would be easier if I had my phone," he said.

I gasped. "I don't have it and you know it!" He grinned at me, and soon my smile matched his. "Thank you," I whispered.

It was an uneasy truce, after our heart-to-heart was over and he finally released my hand. I should've guessed it wouldn't last long. In fact, I should've ceased all further communication with him.

CHAPTER TWENTY

Day 111
1931 hours

"My hands were shaking and I threw them in my pockets. I was about to do the stupidest, scariest, sanest thing that I could think of—go after a boy."

—Madeleine's War Journal Entry (Sunday Night, June 3rd).

I usually made it a rule to never enter the Eyring building. Sure the dinosaurs were great and the fake dollar bill was always tempting, but it was meant for the brains and future millionaires of America. I was neither. However, Eric was here and his invite to spend a quiet Sunday evening with him was a challenge—and I never backed away from a challenge, especially with Byron's *Broken* accusation running through my mind. I couldn't forget the apology either—and his offer of help.

I smoothed down the diagonal stripes of my summer dress, making sure nothing was unzipped or untied or torn, just trying to borrow a bit of Sandra's fashion sense for the evening. I could do this, even if it meant texting Eric for directions and taking a million stairs down a winding hallway to Eric's underground lab. It was eerie down here and I had no idea the place existed until now. My hand poised above Eric's lab door to knock, and my mouth went dry. Nothing seemed so hard.

C'mon, Mad. I mean, you're Mad Dog, the Great War General leading the girls of the 73rd ward to victory. You meet men head on, not

PRANK WARS

run away from them like a beaten dog. But this was so different. I took a deep breath and lifted my hand.

Someone beat me to it. Byron slid beside me, knocking hard on the door. He looked dangerously sleek in a button-up shirt with baby pink stripes. Pink? Only a fierce general could get away with such a color. He certainly hadn't worn it to nursery today. Before I could order him to go away, he turned to me with a devilish grin. "By the way. Thanks for the new paint job."

I had nothing to do with that. Tory decked out Byron's car as if he were getting married with pop cans, streamers, cheese wiz, the works. She must've hit him after she got Cameron. I smiled. "Yeah, congratulations on the civil union by the way."

Byron shrugged, onto something else. "What are you doing here? Trying to make an easy ten bucks? On Sunday? I'm shocked."

"No, I'm taking your advice."

"What?"

I smirked, knowing I had surprised him. I wiped my hands on my dress. They weren't sweaty, but just in case they were I wasn't take any chances. "I'm trying to be a normal person. Now, let me do my thing, okay?"

Before Byron could disappear, the door opened and Eric shot me a smile that melted me. It wavered when he turned to the guy next to me. I shrugged. "I think Byron wants to get tortured too."

"Brave man." Eric said dryly. "What do you think drove him to it?"

"Why don't you ask him yourself?" Byron asked pleasantly. "He's standing right here."

I smothered a laugh with a cough. Eric seemed more formal than usual in his faded blue polo and lab coat. Take away the offended air and he certainly had the cute boy-next-door look down. He ushered us inside the laboratory, his broad shoulders covering the door. We passed the computer on a desk and the stacks of papers he was grading. Fat books littered the shelves. There were two doors that would work as escape exits if anything went wrong. A curtain divided the room into two. A waiting area with comfy seats stood outside the curtain and a TV monitored the room inside. "Wow, what is this place?" I asked.

"We use it for our department's experiments, not just mine. Here, let me make the *new person* a file." Eric shot Byron an annoyed look.

Byron stretched out as if he were attempting to fill the room. It was a tough guy thing. It was too bad because I needed Byron's unbiased opinion on Eric. He'd have to give him a chance first. I turned away from them both, studying the cabinet full of files. "Has Sandra been tested yet?" At the sound of her name, Byron turned from the book shelf with sudden interest. Eric's beautiful almond eyes slanted at him. I realized too late I should've tried harder to push Byron away at the door. I laughed to ease the tension. "You couldn't get Sandra to sit still long enough before she threw something, huh?"

Both boys humored me with a courtesy laugh. Eric eased a seat over to me. It reminded me of a dentist's chair. "Make yourself comfortable." He handed me a clipboard where I could fill out my personal information. Eric chucked the other clipboard at Byron. "Here you go, bad boy. Here's your chance to be a part of something."

Byron caught it easily. "What would that be exactly?"

"The mysteries of God. It's what science is all about. Everything about your body is a miracle, more complex than any machine."

I straightened in my dentist's chair. I never heard Eric talk like this. I liked it. Byron gave Eric back his clipboard after filling out the minimal requirements. "Yeah? So why did you ask Madeleine to come?"

Eric seemed calm, but his knuckles were turning white over his clipboard. They'd turn into fists next. "We're finding the keys to unlock the deepest recesses of our minds. The first step is starting with signals we already know exist. For example, the frequencies that your ear picks up; they're much more sophisticated than any cell phone." Eric fit an ear bud snugly into my ear under Byron's watchful gaze. "Your ears are just one of the receptacles that receive signals," Eric explained. "We aren't aware that most of these frequencies exist." He pushed a button. "Can you hear this?" I shook my head. "How about this?" I shook my head again.

Byron pulled away from us, his curiosity satisfied; maybe it was because Eric wasn't actually torturing me. He wandered the room, picking things up to examine them. He stopped at a black safe, but didn't touch it. It was sealed to the wall.

"How about now?" Eric asked me. "Hear that?" I shook my head. He inched closer. "I like your dress," he whispered. "You look beautiful." I smiled reflexively. Yep, I heard that. Eric grinned to himself and set another frequency. "How about that?"

I kept shaking my head until I heard a tiny buzzing sound. "Hey, I caught that."

"Good." He leaned back. "I was beginning to think you were completely deaf."

"Oh yeah?" Byron asked. "What's the diagnosis, doc?"

Eric refused to look at him. "You have the hearing of a fifty-year-old man with hair in his ears," he broke it to me without an ounce of remorse. I laughed. I had quite a few lawn mowing jobs as a kid and I loved my earphones...*but still*. "Let's just say that if you ever teach, even your middle-aged students will be able to take calls in class without you knowing." My mouth fell open. How depressing.

"What are you doing with this information?" Byron asked. I tried to think of how it could be used besides killing anyone who could hear the frequency, but I was out of ideas. Clearly, as Eric accused, I was stuck in comic book world.

"Now *that* is top secret," Eric said. "So are you going to do this or what, *Lord Byron*?" Eric finally looked at him. Byron laid something inconspicuously back on the table, no expression on his face. Months of experience told me he was hiding something. I tilted my head to see what Byron had abandoned back there. It was a class picture with Thanh.

I jumped off the dentist chair. "Does Thanh work here too?" I scooped up the picture. She stood in a white lab coat with her class. Eric was standing next to her. "Oh look. There you are, Eric."

Eric smiled tightly, but when his eyes rested on me, they were pleasant. He gave Byron an ear bud. "Yeah, Thanh. She's in our ward, right?"

"Yeah, Byron is dating her." I put the picture back down.

Eric turned quickly at this. Byron did too. "Dating?" Byron asked. "Where did you get that?"

"Your backpacks," I reminded him. "You can't hide that from me."

"So when does that mean you're dating?"

Eric jabbed at another button. Byron wasn't concentrating on him. "Yeah, I can hear that," he said. Eric hit another button. Byron nodded. "Yep."

He could hear all of that? I was starting to get jealous. "How old are you, Byron, sixteen?"

"Relax," Eric told me. "I'm going backwards." He picked another button. "Did you get that?" Byron shook his head. "Unless we've got another case like Madeleine's, we've got a 26 to 32 year old here. Is that right?"

"Sure."

Eric gave him a hard look then wrote on his file. He carried it to the other room, leaving me alone with Byron. We only had half a millisecond of awkward silence before Byron predictably broke it. "I like your hair. It's not—" he hesitated.

"Blonde?" I asked.

He cracked a smile. I had finished his sentence again. "Go ahead, Mad."

"With what?"

"I just gave you two compliments. It's your turn."

"No, you didn't. You gave me one compliment and it was a backhanded one."

"Okay, you were great at nursery today and you look good in black *and* I like your boots. Are you going riding?" I gawked at him. "*Now* you owe me three."

"Who says?"

His eyebrow lifted. "And then we can practice our sweet nothings to each other." He leaned in closer to me. "How about it, cuz?"

I laughed then realized what he sounded like. "You did that accent again."

"It's a speech impediment I had as a kid. You making fun of me? So?" he asked me offhandedly. "How well do you know Eric?"

I knew Byron had buttered me up so he could ask me that. "About as well as I know you."

"He's Sandra's *friend*?"

I laughed. "Why do you want to know, Byron?"

"Just concerned. Have you seen them talking?"

Was he jealous? I had no idea why that annoyed me. "Look," I settled back into the dentist chair, "I'm not talking, even under *your* torture."

"That can be arranged. So, you like that guy, huh?"

I glanced over at the door, but Eric was nowhere in sight. "What? Were your spidey senses tingling? Yeah, I like him. It's obvious, don't you think?"

"Yeah, well, that makes sense because he's a total June 6th."

"Excuse me?"

"A jerk."

My ex-wedding date meant a jerk now? I tried to shush him before he said something stupid—well, at least something loud. He lifted an elegant shoulder. "Who cares if he overhears? The guy can't wait to get you alone so he can teach you a little social provocity. He's just dying to run his fingers through your luxurious black hair." He quite suddenly reached out to touch my hair himself, "...and white."

I yanked back. What was all that talk about being nice? Byron was behind my shock of white hair in the first place. "You're the jerk! Is this about Sandra? Are you afraid he likes her? Well, who cares if he does? You're a player. You know the rules. You played her, now move on!"

He leaned back, satisfied. "See, that wasn't so hard, was it? They're dating. So the question is what are *you* doing here?"

I felt like a fish with the way my mouth was gaping. "I...they just know each other. I met him after I came back from some prank you pulled. He was leaving my apartment with some huge giant. Look, they're not dating. I wouldn't poach like that."

"What night was that?"

Eric came out from the back, bringing us permission slips. I couldn't tear my gaze away from Byron. How did he do that? He got it *all* out of me, absolutely everything he wanted to know. I had to give him props—he was the master interrogator. All he had to do was push my angry button and I talked, but why did he want to know? Now it was my turn to get it out of him. I was a girl; after all, I had my ways.

"Sign here," Eric told me. He held the pen out to me and I accepted it before he let it go. Our hands brushed. Eric smiled. His eyes were in it and I couldn't look away. He didn't seem like a June 6th to me. Still, I'd take Byron's accusation into consideration—even if I didn't want to. Eric's easy manner was mesmerizing enough to blind me.

Byron nudged me aside, completely ruining the moment. "Where's my ten?"

Eric sighed heavily and relinquished the pen to dig into his pocket for his cash. His gaze left mine and he looked frazzled. Poor Eric. Maybe I could make it up to him somehow...like maybe a date. If Eric asked, I knew I'd say yes. Byron was biased anyway. I glanced over at him, and with a jolt of surprise, realized how much Byron disliked Eric. He was watching him with a narrow look. Byron was keeping his promise to me, wasn't he? He was my watch dog. I wasn't sure if I wanted that anymore. I think I trusted Eric. I could handle things now. That was what being normal was all about. Taking chances. Taking care of myself. I could do it. I just had to figure out how to call Byron off the hunt.

CHAPTER TWENTY-ONE

Day 112
2054 hours

"I've been called a lot of things in my lifetime, but a liar isn't one of them. Although maybe that'll change...because what I'm about to write I wouldn't believe if I hadn't written it myself."

—Madeleine's War Journal Entry (Monday night, June 4th).

It was the usual Monday night after FHE. Kali and Lizzie lay on the fort they built, passed out in the living room. Kali wriggled her toes in her tie-dyed socks, the only sign she was alive. Dry peanut butter sandwich wedges and school books lay scattered between them. It was the most peaceful I had seen them in a long time. Ever since Kali declared her love for Blake, she had redoubled her efforts in an even lengthier and dirtier battle with his apartment. Strangely, I found this prank war escaping from me. The black hole—as we were now dubbed—embarked on unauthorized missions without me, and the twins were an unstoppable force in return. It seemed that none of these self-proclaimed soldiers needed me...or Byron anymore.

It was time to hang up my combat boots and try out what I had going with Eric, except I couldn't get Byron out of my mind. I stared up at the starry ceiling; it was covered in glitter. The crickets chirped softly in our apartment. What made Byron decide to be so strict on his *one* promise to me? It was flattering in a way, but so stupid. He was worse than a guard dog; he would never follow my orders. And yet? Maybe he had reason to be wary. I had to see things unclouded. Logical. I gulped. What would it be like to be free to feel instead?

I rested my chin into my hand, staring out the window into the storm. It was darker, blowing occasional gusts of rain into the mysterious night. Anything could happen out there. A soft wind whispered against the window. I stared at the leaves dancing under the streetlights. It was one of those haunting nights where—except for the ghosts of lingering memories—I felt so alone. What had happened to me anyway? As a kid, I never envisioned listening to the snores of exhausted *soldiers* and waiting for my enemy's next move, an enemy that I wasn't sure was mine. I just wanted to feel real again—not just to have love, but to be capable of giving it. Now I couldn't be sure what I felt...or who I felt it for. It meant I had to clean up my life. Start afresh. My sigh got lost in the howling wind. The storm had picked up and through it, I heard a tapping against the front door. My senses, heightened by these past months, tingled with the danger.

The door. I glanced over and fell back with a start. It had cracked open. I sat up on the couch, watching it creak slowly more so, leaving an even bigger gap between the wall and the black world outside. It was either the wind or a very dramatic terrorist—or—I held my breath. We were in the middle of a prank war. No one had locked it. What were Kali and Lizzie thinking? I took a shaky step, willing myself to go to the door, knowing I had to slam it shut on whatever force driving it open. But on what? If I opened the door and saw eyes staring back at me? No, I wouldn't look. Just shut it. I couldn't get my mind off thoughts of ghosts and masked intruders. I forced one foot to follow the other and placed my hand on the hard wood of the door. I should slam it shut, I opened it instead.

Tory screamed out at me, jumping from the darkness. I screamed with her and my hand went to my head then my heart. "What are you doing?" I shouted. "You are one scary girl! Do you know that?"

PRANK WARS

She nodded. "Just keeping you up your training, captain." She brushed past me into the apartment, looking like she was ready for bed in her black sweat capris. I read her green t-shirt: *Mean people are mean.* You could say that again. The rain from outside pelted me from outside and I pushed the door shut on it, shaking my head. Tory went to the window and peered out. "There's Thanh," she said.

I joined Tory at the window, seeing the dainty black-haired girl. The rain pelted over her, soaking her. Her small feet clad in striped Prada heels splashed through the quickly forming puddles. Her matching umbrella seemed purely decoration. Oh, poor Thanh. She came back from the school this time of night? It was the sad lot of a grad student. Tory pulled away from the window, fixing her damp red hair at our mirror at the end of the hall. "The guys are going to strike tonight," she reported.

"Yeah? So what?"

She glanced back, looking confused. "What did you say?"

"Let them. This war isn't exactly…uh—" I saw her face turn wary. "It isn't going anywhere," I finished lamely.

"What did *he* do to you?" Tory asked. "Byron's messing with your head, isn't he?"

"Oh please, Byron? It's not Byron."

"Oh yeah? He took your fighting spirit. You can't let him do that to us. When did he turn from public enemy number one to a person of interest, huh?"

"Tory! I don't want to ruin your fun. It's just…it wasn't Byron anyway. Maybe Eric. I don't know."

"Eric? That's even worse." Tory paced the room. She reminded me of myself two weeks ago and she was making me dizzy. "Are you crazy? He's not your type."

Now I was surprised. "You don't even know him."

"I don't need to. There's nothing there. You need someone low maintenance, someone more your match like Byr—, uh…" Now it was her turn to look sheepish. "He's totally wrong for you, okay?"

"Yeah, because everyone's wrong for me, but that's not the point." I glanced back out the window at poor Thanh struggling with her bags and trying to balance her umbrella. She was getting hopelessly wet. "Healthy relationships aren't supposed to be love/hate," I argued. "They're not hopelessly stimulating from finish to end. Not the ones you can trust anyway. Love just happens between two normal people. What's attraction anyway, but a trick of the moment? I mean, you have to be attracted sure, but love takes time and work. Pure emotion can't be trusted."

"Well, that's boring." Tory crossed her arms.

Tory's pep talk wasn't helping anything. I had a problem. First step was admitting it. Second step was doing something about it. I had to date. I had to step down as their leader. "Tory, I think I've led you astray…" I watched Thanh come closer to the apartment. Bright headlights came the other direction. They slowed as they neared her. "We can't cut out guys completely. It isn't going to help us." The car stopped next to Thanh. It was a silver sedan. It was all I could make out in the rain. Thanh kept walking. The car kept up with her. That was weird.

"Well, we can cut out the stupid guys," Tory said. "I don't know why you—?"

I stopped listening. Someone got out of the car and followed Thanh from behind. I couldn't see any of this very clearly. The rain was getting worse, but I think Thanh didn't like it. She broke into a run. I plastered against the fog of the window, trying to see better. Whoever was behind her caught up to her and grabbed her by the arm. She screamed, trying to get away. "Did you see that?" I shouted at Tory. I ran for the door. "Let her go!" I reached the porch and ripped past Sandra's potted plants into the pouring rain.

Before my very eyes, Thanh was tugged into the car. I ran down the steps, trying to get to her in time. The car sped away, water spraying out behind its wheels, leaving me behind. The rain soaked me in a matter of seconds. I ran after the car before realizing there was no way I could catch it. I didn't even have a license plate number. This was crazy! Did I really just see an abduction?

I ran back for the apartment and got a paintball bullet in the leg. I gave a frustrated shriek. Tory was right. The guys planned an attack. This wasn't Byron though. It wasn't his usual signature; it lacked imagination. I zigzagged around the hostile fire, recognizing a few gamers from below Byron's apartment. They were all in black and they were armed. Where were they when Thanh got taken? "You idiots!" I shouted. "Do any of you have a cell phone?" I got hit in the back for my efforts. I ran back up the stairs, shrieking for Tory.

Tory was already outside, Kali behind her. "Don't worry!" Kali shouted at me. "We're on it." She rushed past me in her daisy print pajama bottoms, brandishing a potato gun.

"You don't understand!" I shouted.

One of the twins grabbed Tory. It was hard to tell which one, since his face was covered with a black hoody and contrasted dramatically with his blond hair escaping out the sides. Adam? I was positive once I noticed his precious Zoom Vomero shoes. The rain ran past their faces. Tory gave out a little shriek, trying to beat him away. Kali gave one too, but it was because she wanted to be taken. Blake looked more than happy to do the job. Lizzie came out of the apartment, rubbing her tired eyes. Her hair was curly and free from its usual confines. She stood on the porch, careful not to get wet. "Lizzie!" I was out of breath when I reached her. "Thanh got kidnapped. I mean for real! She got kidnapped. Where's your cell phone?"

Lizzie looked confused and I ran past her into the apartment, searching for my own cell phone. I found it in my mess of a room and dialed 911 with shaky fingers. For as much as it was engraved in my mind, it was possibly the only time I had ever dialed it. I got an operator. "My neighbor's been kidnapped!" I shouted into the phone.

The operator seemed incredibly calm after such a stirring announcement. I gave our address and tried to describe what had happened. "I didn't get a license number, but the guy just took her." I was babbling, trying to figure out how we could ever find her.

"What direction were they headed?"

Uh, I tried to think of the direction. My thoughts weren't coming in straight. I pointed and tried to mentally think where I was. East. The mountains were east. "East!" I shouted. The lady gave a distraught noise. I think I hurt her ears. "East," I said in a softer voice. "Then they turned south." I heard the sirens before I saw the red and blue lights flash against the walls from the living room window. "You're here!" I said in relief. I wasn't sure what any of us could do now, but we had to try. Her life could be in danger.

As soon as the police were on the scene, the activity halted on our front lawn. The guys from the bunkhouse took off with their weapons. Some of the girls chased after them. I watched Sergeant Brady and Officer Oliveira get out of their car, surrounded by the remnants of battle: silly string, water balloon fragments, a huge paintball mess quickly getting washed away by the storm. I ran down the steps, my zebra-striped pajamas slapping over my ankles. The water trickled down my face. My hair drenched.

The officers didn't have their usual condescending look—until they saw me. "What's going on?" the sergeant asked. He didn't have his notebook this time. He was almost as wet as I was.

"You remember Thanh, right? The girl who's place was really messy. Okay, someone just pulled her into their car."

"She got in their car?"

"They took her," I explained in frustration. "She didn't want to go."

"Was this part of your game?"

"What?" I recognized the condescending expressions all too well. "No, this is totally different. She's not even involved in this…uh game. I hardly even know her. We have to find her!"

One of the officers moved to the stairs to find some shelter from the rain. The wind tugged at us. I was freezing. "Where was she when they took her?"

"Just by the curb to the side over there!" I pointed out into the street.

"Where were you when this happened?"

"In my apartment."

"The third floor? And you saw her kidnapped in this storm?"

"Yes!" I couldn't believe they were doing this. They just saw me as the crazy girl who got locked out of her apartment with an overactive imagination. We were wasting valuable time and it was all my fault.

"And she didn't want to go?" Oliveira prompted.

"Look, do you want me to find her myself!" I threw my arms around myself, trying to keep warm. I shivered uncontrollably. "It happened just like I said."

"What did the car look like?"

"It was dark, I don't know. It was a sedan…a silver one. I don't know what make." Even I was frustrated with my answer.

"So, we're looking for a silver sedan?"

"Yeah! I'm sorry that's all the information I have. I didn't see it very clearly, okay? Hypnotize me to get the make of the car out me. I don't know. But she was taken. Don't you get it! She's gone."

Tory peeled out of the shadows, looking sheepish. "No, I'm back!"

The officers relaxed. "Is that her?"

"No!" I wanted to scream, but I forced my voice to be calm. "That's Tory. Thanh's a girl from Vietnam with long hair and a big black backpack. Don't you remember her?"

"What's happening?"

The cops glanced up and visibly relaxed when they recognized Byron. His dark hair was wet and he was out of breath. He wore black jogging shorts like he had been running. It was terrible weather for it. He pulled the black hood from his face. Water drizzled down his face.

"We're investigating a kidnapping claim. Are you a witness?"

"No."

"Wait," I said. "Byron's dating her. He has her number. Call her! See if she answers."

Byron looked confused. "Who?"

"Thanh."

It wasn't the time for Byron to look annoyed at the dating accusation, but he did anyway. "What happened to Thanh?" he asked.

"This girl saw her taken away in a silver sedan," the cop filled him in. "You have her number, young man?"

Byron nodded, looking grim. "It's in my iPhone." He tried to find it, but with a jolt I remembered why he couldn't. His iPhone was lost. Byron gave up as soon as he remembered too. "I've got the number memorized." He recited her number to the officer. So, Byron wasn't dating her, was he? Liar. No guy would have a random number memorized.

Sergeant Brady dialed the number. He waited, but with no results. Maybe now he would believe me. "She's not answering," he reported to his partner.

Byron glanced over at me and then at the officers. He seemed to come to a decision. "Uh hey, I think I know a friend who might be with her. Could I use your phone?" Without hesitation, Sergeant Brady gave him his cell phone. Byron gave me a tight smile when he saw my eyes on him. Not only did he know her number, but he knew the number of someone who *might* be with her? Their relationship was turning from casual to serious in a matter of seconds. "Hey, this is Byron." He readjusted the phone against his ear once he got an answer. "Um, the police are here and they're pretty concerned about Thanh." He waited a minute. "Yeah, they want to talk to her and they'd better or...yeah. She's with you, right? Hold on. I'm giving them the phone."

Byron handed Sergeant Brady his phone. "Thanh?" Brady asked after a moment. "Am I talking to Thanh? Oh, good."

I froze. That meant she was alright. I still couldn't deny what I had seen. "Where is she?" I asked.

The officer ignored me. "This is Sergeant Brady. We've got a concerned neighbor who thinks you might be in trouble. Are you in a place where you can talk? Are you alright?" He waited for a moment.

PRANK WARS

"Your neighbor claims that you were taken by force by a passing vehicle." I bit my lip. It seemed ridiculous now, especially if she was with a trusted friend, but still Brady drilled her. "You can answer in the affirmative if this is true." He listened for a moment then turned to me, his expression unreadable "She's okay," he told me.

Was she? But someone took her—except she was safe now. But what if she wasn't? What if the friend we called had taken her? I knew it was ridiculous, but still these nagging doubts rushed through me. My hands curled into fists and I blew into them to keep them warm. "Are you sure?" I argued, but it was more with myself. I wanted to believe that she was okay, but my eyes had seen something else. "What if that isn't her?" I asked. "That could be any random girl pretending to be her. Get her social security number! See if it matches!"

Tory bobbed her head next to me in agreement; the water flew with her hair.

Sergeant Brady took a steadying breath. I knew I was driving him crazy. "One more time, Thanh, and I apologize for the inconvenience; we'd like to confirm this is you. Give me your full name."

"Social security number," I urged.

He shook his head at me, listening to the other line. Apparently she had a pretty long name, longer than any social security number I had ever heard. Still, it wasn't enough for me. How were we to know that this was her or that she wasn't being held by force? Maybe I had seen a lot of movies, but I wanted to see her and make sure a gun wasn't being held to her back. "Where is she?" I asked.

The sergeant was already irritated with me, but still he repeated my question. He passed the message on to me, "She's at her boyfriend's house."

"Oh." I glanced over at Byron. He didn't seem crushed. He looked antsy like he might leave us at any second. Maybe a girl was waiting for him at home. It was past curfew, wasn't it? "Wait," I grasped at straws. "Thanh can't be at her boyfriend's. She's breaking curfew. Tell her to get back here." Even Tory looked at me like I had gone insane, but it would be the perfect proof to make sure Thanh was okay.

Sergeant Brady rolled his eyes. It was more expressive than I expected in a guy his age. "Well, you're late for curfew then, young lady. Come home." He hung up his phone with a decisive snap. "Happy?" he asked me.

I had to be, but it just didn't make sense. I thought my eyes had seen something else. Thanh didn't want to get into that car, but maybe the boyfriend had been joking around with her in the rain or something? Byron wasn't that boyfriend anymore. My spirits lifted and then I frowned. Why would that make me happy at a time like this? "Is there a way to take her in, so you can talk to her?" I couldn't believe I was asking it, but I was. Tory backed away and I should've taken her lead.

The officers stared at me like I was a raving lunatic. Sergeant Brady forced his voice into dulcet tones: "Other than breaking curfew, we don't have anything on her, but we could find something on *you* if that's what you're looking for." He glanced around at the remnants of the battle on the grass. Luckily, it was starting to melt away under the rain. "Curfew breaking is the least of our concerns right now."

"But we don't have to be *in* our apartments. Just out of the guy's apartm…" my voice trailed off at their grim faces. Sergeant Brady meant it. He would slap charges on me if I wasn't careful. No amount of charm could get me out of this one—not that I had any. "Okay, well, are we done here?" I clapped my hands, "or do I have to fill out some paperwork?"

"We're done…for now."

I nodded, and quickly made my escape, belatedly noting Tory had already done so. The little deserter. Before I could move past Byron, he squeezed my arm and tugged me next to him. "Hey," he whispered into my ear, "you did the right thing."

I could just imagine the police beat on this one. Brady and Oliveira returned to their patrol car, their bodies stiff. "Yeah." I was drenched and cold and bitter. Byron actually felt pretty warm. I shivered and he pulled me closer.

He ran his hands down my wet arms, splashing away some of the rainwater. It warmed me instantly. He cracked a smile. "Just because someone has a love life, there's no reason for us to get jealous, right?"

I almost laughed at that one. "Yeah. Thanks."

After a moment, he let me go, taking his warmth with him. He jogged away in the rain, his Nikes sloshing against the wet grass. Byron didn't have a love life? I gave myself a mental shake. That was a strange thing to get out of this night. I dripped past Thanh's window. Her curtains were open slightly. The mess in her apartment cast looming shadows across the checkered linoleum inside. A black backpack sat on the kitchen floor. The zipper closed. Thanh had her backpack. I *was* a raving lunatic.

I tugged on my door and let myself in, dripping over the blankets that made up the fort in our living room. Kali and Lizzie looked cozy with their towel covered heads pressed together, their skin bright and rosy from the storm. They stopped talking as soon as I entered. It meant they were talking about me. Most great leaders were betrayed by their most loyal supporters in the end. I should've expected it. I hesitated in the entryway. "What?" I asked. They looked blank. "Why don't you just lecture me and get it over with, Lizzie?"

"Do you want me to?" Lizzie said with the predictable lecture to her voice. "Kali was just talking about…" Kali gave her a warning look to stop her from saying it.

"…a boy," I finished for Lizzie. And they couldn't tell me? Was this what my life had come to? Riddled with paranoia? It hurt that I couldn't be trusted with normal girl talk anymore. Boys weren't to be trusted. I saw a kidnapping when there was none. Thanh's messy house was a ransacking. That threatening note on Thanh's door was a…was a…wait? Was it really meant for us or for Thanh? I wished that I could look at it again, but Byron had stolen it. Why did he do that?

I heard a phone go off in my room. It didn't sound like my ringtone. Lizzie sighed. "It's been going off all night."

I flung open my door and shuffled past my opened physics book on my desk. The ringing wasn't coming from that mess. I moved to the laundry hamper and followed the sound through my dirty clothes. I scraped my jeans out from the bottom and found a cell phone in the pocket along with some keys. The cell was cute and pink with diamond studs just like I remembered it. Thanh's. Oh no. No wonder she couldn't answer her cell.

It stopped ringing as soon as I had it in my hand. Those were the jeans I had been wearing when I tried to return Thanh her backpack on Saturday. The keys didn't work in her door and I had thrown them in my pocket. Her cell phone followed the keys after I got that threatening call from Byron that day. I winced, knowing I was in for it. My room was a thief's den. I checked the caller ID and saw the number unblock again. I could just press the call back button like I did last time and fess up to the dirty deed. I pressed it against my wet cheek, took a deep breath, and called the person back.

A guy answered. *"So there you are."*

"Oh, I'm not Thanh."

"I know."

I readjusted the phone against my ear. It was so small that it was threatening to slip away. "Look, are you with her? I need to talk to her?"

"I want something from you first."

He wasn't making any sense, though it was beginning to sound like the same guy I talked to on this phone before. I stared at the number. It was the same one. "Byron?" I accused. What was he doing? The idiot was trying to get Thanh's phone back for her. He was a man of his word I was coming to find out.

A soft knock sounded at my door and Tory barged into my room with drenched hair. The bells above the door rang merrily. I set them up there to make sure Tory couldn't sneak in without my knowledge—

PRANK WARS

apparently they worked. "Just a sec," I told her. I went back to my conversation with Byron. "What do you want?"

"S*omething in that backpack is missing. And I think you know what it is.*"

I laughed. "Yeah, *this* cell phone for starters." He was silent on the other line and I knew an apology was in order. "Look, I'm sorry. I saw you returned Thanh's backpack to her. I'm glad she got it back."

"What?"

"Yeah, I saw it on her kitchen floor tonight." I laughed in realization. "Unless it was yours? You got yours back, right Byron? Oh, I've got your physics book too. Sorry about that."

"*Don't make me come for you.*" He was starting to sound testy.

"Or what are you gonna do? Call the police on me? I guess that would work. They already hate me." I flopped on my bed, enjoying the conversation. If there was one thing I loved, it was teasing Byron.

"*I'll do worse.*"

I laughed again. "Okay, come and get me, tough guy. I'll be waiting for you. If that's your backpack at your girlfriend's apartment, you might want to pick that up too. Seriously man, don't you ever study?"

He clicked off his phone and I giggled. Tory's eyes widened and I covered my mouth. Did that sound just come from me? Like I said, I was seriously going crazy.

"Who were you talking to?" she asked suspiciously.

"Byron."

"How? I thought you stole his phone."

"For the last time, I did *not* steal his ph—!" My eyes widened and I dropped the pink cell phone to the floor. "Holy cow!" Yes, that was an understatement. Byron had lost his iPhone. Who did I just talk to?

MADELEINE'S LAST WAR JOURNAL

CHAPTER ONE

Day 112
2217 hours

"Who is my enemy? To be honest, I have no idea. They don't know who I am either, so in a way that gives me the advantage."

—Madeleine's War Journal Entry (Monday night, June 4th).

"Something weird is happening." I tugged some dry clothes onto my wet body, and stuffed my war journal into the back pocket of my red sweats. The rain from outside had turned into a torrent, raging against our little red brick apartment. I picked up Thanh's cell phone from the floor, staring at it. Whoever had been on the phone was angry.

I turned to Tory. I only had a hunch, a very crazy hunch. I replayed the whole phone conversation through my mind. I had asked to talk to Thanh, but the guy said he wanted something from me first. Did that mean whoever called really had Thanh, assuming he wasn't her boyfriend? I saw her taken, didn't I? The police had talked to her on the phone, but there was no way to know it was Thanh. Even if it had been, was she somewhere she could talk openly? She had been taken! I knew it. Before I could get the police to listen to me, I needed cold hard evidence—or at least someone chasing me. I could arrange that.

This guy said he was missing something. He didn't seem interested in Thanh's cell phone. I glanced over at the keys I had taken from her backpack. Maybe those? They didn't open Thanh's door; they opened something else...obviously; they were keys. My thoughts kept circling to the backpack. Whatever this guy wanted could be resting on Thanh's messy kitchen floor. I brushed past a wet Tory; her *mean* shirt clung to her, her red hair curling. "Don't let anyone in. Lock the apartment up and I mean it."

These were orders that Tory understood. She nodded. "What about Sandra? She isn't in yet?"

I tilted my head at her. "Of course, she's the exception. You can let her in." I thought that was obvious, but maybe to a soldier used to strict orders it wasn't. "As much as I hate the thought, Byron might have something to do with this."

"Just as you were beginning to like him," she said under her breath.

"What?"

She gave me a playful grin. I wrestled with the idea of telling Tory everything, but there was no time. Mystery man was onto me. I might as well have begged him to break back into Thanh's place to steal her backpack and help himself to whatever else he wanted. The only thing I didn't spill was her bank account number. If there was something vital in that backpack, we'd have nothing to bargain with to get Thanh back. She'd be lost forever.

I rushed out into the hall, thinking hard. There was no way to get into Thanh's unless I broke a window. I didn't know how to use bobby pins or credit cards like Byron did to pick the lock. Our ring of keys to the apartments was missing. It was way too late to call Eric—Mr. Magic fingers himself—no way inside Thanh's at all...unless?

I looked up and saw our trapdoor to the crawl space. We had a trapdoor, so would Thanh. The crawlspace over the ceiling would take me to her place. I took a steadying breath. This guy was practically a Nazi anyway...if my landlord ever cared to question me. I tugged on the string. The trapdoor ripped away from the Velcro. I felt warm air rush down on me. "Get me a chair," I ordered Tory.

PRANK WARS

Before I knew it, I was stomping against the floral seat, but I couldn't get up into the ceiling. Tory put some books under my feet until I was tall enough to poke my head through the trapdoor. I stared into the blackness. If this was a scary movie, this would be the moment something would fly at me from the shadows. Even Tory held back. I propped my elbows on either side of the crawlspace. "Get me a flashlight."

"What are you doing?"

I flinched. Lizzie! She wouldn't let me go without a fight. Kali made squealing noises beneath me, her towel falling off her head. "I have to get to Thanh's," I explained. "Something big is going on, bigger than all of us."

"You're gonna hurt yourself!" I nodded and kicked my legs to force myself up. "There could be spiders!" she warned. I hesitated. This was bigger than spiders. I kept going. "What if the ceiling caves in?"

"Lizzie! I'll keep to the rafters. I've been in an attic before."

"At least protect yourself from the insulation!" I heard her scurry from her room and back. She threw a long sleeved hoody up at me and some gloves. "Put those on."

Was she mental? I was burning up, but at her insistence, I wrestled on the extra clothing. It was worth it if it kept spiders away from me. The black hoody was tight over the bulging pocket that held my war journal. I grimaced at that. When had I packed that along? It was too late to dump it now. Tory clambered up the chair onto the books, shining the flashlight through the crawlspace. I winced through the beam of light, expecting to see a metallic layer of spider webs. Everything inside this deep hole was covered in insulation, though surprisingly clean of bugs.

Grateful for the gloves, I pushed into the darkness, keeping to the rafters as promised, sliding hand over hand and keeping low like a Russian dancer. I passed something loud and whirring like a fan beneath me. I think it was the bathroom. I gave it some space. The kitchen probably was on the other side. How far was Thanh's apartment? Tory's flashlight faded, and I barely caught sight of the depression ahead. It was covered in torn insulation. I brushed it free and found another trapdoor. I wasn't sure how to open it, so I pushed. Nothing happened. I extended my leg in front of me and kicked it with the heel of my converses. It flew open. Darkness gaped below me. I turned to Tory. Her head was a silhouette behind the shaft of light. "I got it!" I said. "Close the trapdoor on that side and get rid of any evidence I was up here."

"Don't come back this way!" Lizzie warned. "Just use the door like a real person, okay!"

I nodded. After a moment of staring down into the dark abyss of Thanh's apartment, I dropped to the messy ground, landing on my hands and feet. My eyes adjusting to the shadowy hall and overturned tables in the living room. I tore the gloves off, feeling the piles of rough paper under my fingers and stood up. This was real illegal trespassing. "Hello?" I hoped Thanh would answer back, but no one was here.

Standing on my tiptoes, I closed the trapdoor and kicked through the papers. The sound of them crunching beneath my converses broke the unnatural silence on the way to her kitchen. I tugged the fridge door open on a whim. Nothing there, except some moldy food. I kept it open, but it wasn't enough light to keep my legs from colliding squarely with the table, which woke up the computer. It added a blue eerie glow to the kitchen. I squinted through the blue light, seeing Thanh's email was open. A full page of unopened messages sat in her inbox. A few in Vietnamese. I clicked on one of the more recent messages.

"Thanh, this is your boss. Lydia gave me your email. why haven't you called me back?" —Maybe because I had Thanh's cell phone. I felt terrible. I returned to her inbox, marking the message unread. If anything, it made me realize I had missed some vital clues. I should've checked Thanh's cell phone before this. It made a square lump in my side pocket. I tugged it out and went to the messages, setting it on speaker phone. The first one was from her boss again. She hadn't come to work in days.

I placed her cell phone on the table and searched for the backpack. It still lay on the floor next to the table. My hand hovered over it. If I

PRANK WARS

took it, the guy with the threats would know I was onto him and come after me. Was I prepared for that? No. I landed on my knees, listening to Thanh's boss go off on the next message about how this was so unlike her.

I had to work fast. Keeping one ear trained on the front door, I unzipped the front pocket and found Byron's school ID. *Byron Schipaanboord.* No wallet. If so, he might've tried harder to get this back. The backpack was officially his, but I wasn't sure if the switch was an accident anymore. The next message was in Vietnamese. The tone was motherly, worried. Someone's daughter was missing. It only made me work harder. I opened the middle pocket and found some physics notes and a test graded by Thanh. I read the comments on the bottom: *Byron, we really need to talk—Your TA.* He got a perfect score, the jerk, so why would he have to talk to the TA—unless Thanh thought he cheated? Or was it something else? A break-up? Right now I leaned towards something more serious. Without another thought, I folded the physics test into a neat little square and stuffed it in my back pocket.

"Thanh." I recognized the voice in the next message and it sent a jolt through me. It belonged to the same guy I had talked to earlier. *"You know who this is. I'm tired of waiting."* Same clipped voice. Same threats. Same hang up style. No, it didn't sound like Byron. After suffering a few more messages like this, Thanh's inbox was empty. Not sure how much time I had, I searched the side pockets in the backpack. My fingers brushed Byron's missing iPhone. I recognized the screensaver immediately. It covered the front of his sleek touchscreen iPhone with a shot of him skiing. It would look better if the jump had been off a bunny slope. I tucked it into my pocket, not wanting anything important to fall into enemy hands, but what was the guy really looking for? I heard a key sliding into the front door.

"Tory?" It came out a squeak and I stopped myself from saying more. What if it was Thanh? If it wasn't, I couldn't take my chances. I pushed the fridge door shut. It shuttered out the light, leaving me with the eerie glow from the computer. I tried not to imagine Thanh's surprise once she flipped on the lights and found her snoopy neighbor sitting in the middle of her kitchen floor—or worse, my surprise when I saw it wasn't Thanh.

The front door creaked open and I army crawled my way to the cupboard door below the sink. The whole set up in the kitchen was just like ours; I knew it by touch. I opened the cupboard below the sink, hearing the footsteps in the hall. They came for me. I squeezed inside, folding my body next to some stinky garbage. The door wouldn't close behind me. I was in the way. I had no time to wrestle with it. The kitchen lights flipped on, sending shafts of brightness through the cracks of the cupboard door. I closed my eyes, putting my head down.

"Yeah, I'm in." I didn't recognize the voice. It seemed muffled and out of breath, but I could tell it was male. I opened my eyes to face whoever it was, seeing only two feet clad in Nikes and some muscular calves. "Yeah, find out what she knows." His voice jarred the silence. The intruder was either talking to himself or he had a cell phone. I opted for the latter. "I almost had it Tuesday night. A bunch of kids got in the way. One of them walked right into it. Scared her good." He gave an impatient growl. "Yeah, it works. It messed with the cell phones, didn't it? It'll do the job. We just have to get to it."

He leaned over the backpack and I peered forward, trying to see his face. My makeshift lookout was terrible. I could only see hands. He lowered an android phone to dig through the backpack. After a moment, he raised it up, narrating, "Still looking. What does it look like?" He wrestled with the backpack, getting more agitated and less understandable. "I think that…yeah, yeah. You know what?" Now he sounded angry. "She's been here." I held my breath. Had the computer screen tipped him off? My knee hanging out from the cupboard? "No!" he shouted. "I'll get it. *I said I'll get it!* You'll have it by tomorrow night, okay? We won't need her anymore after that."

I didn't like the sound of that. I forced my breath out, keeping myself perfectly still. The intruder stood up to pace the kitchen. "Give me the meeting place. Hold on. Not yet! I need something to write on."

PRANK WARS

He attempted a laugh. "I can't believe the little neat freak didn't clean up after us." He jerked a notebook off the ground. My war journal! I must have dropped it when I ran into the computer. He opened it to a blank page and scrawled something over it. "Midnight. Yeah, I'll have it by then." He listened for a moment. "Or she's dead," he growled. He heatedly ripped off the paper, throwing my war journal back onto the ugly green carpet.

My eyes narrowed where it fell. The guy drifted into the back room, still searching. Maybe for me. I tried to pretend it was just like old times and I was on another mission against the guys—except getting caught then didn't mean death. I crawled out of my hiding spot. My blood pumped loudly against my ears, deafening me. I scooped up my war journal and rushed for the front door. I heard a crash behind me and stumbled, whipping my head around. No one was there. Curses echoed through Thanh's hallway steps away—an unfamiliar sound at BYU—but they weren't aimed at me. The intruder had run into something; he had no idea I was here. I could close the door inconspicuously behind me…and maybe get a rope and lock him in. The guys did it to us all the time, just tie the rope from the knob to the railing on the balcony, and we'd nab him.

I scrambled onto the balcony and ducked past Thanh's window, trying to shove open my door, but it was locked. I knocked furiously, no longer attempting to be quiet; I kept my eyes trained on the apartment next door. My fingers battled with my emotions to keep working. My whole body threatened to freeze up. Tory's head popped out from our kitchen window. She smiled. "Sorry, no one can get in."

"Are you crazy? Open this door!"

She disappeared from the window and I turned back to the apartment. It was too late to lock him in, but if I could see whoever came out, I'd know who I was dealing with. I just had to stay hidden. I searched furiously for a hiding spot. Sandra's potted flowers weren't big enough. There was nowhere to hide. I felt the back of my neck turn cold. Thanh's door was opening. I stood in full view. My stomach felt like it deserted my body. "Open up!" I whisper shouted through the door. I scratched at it, trying to keep quiet.

"It's open." I heard from the inside.

The doorknob turned mercifully under my hands and I shoved my way into the living room. Tory jumped out at me and I fell against our door, shouting out in fright. "The window," I ordered mid-scream. "We have to see who it is." I scrambled to the window and saw the back of a head, a hoody pulled up over a face before it disappeared into the darkness. Thanh's black backpack was flung over his shoulder, and he carried a ring of keys. He was tall…well, that narrowed it down, a tall guy with a mean disposition.

I thought of calling the police…and telling them what? I broke into Thanh's place and overheard a guy talking on the phone, but I wasn't sure what he was talking about? They already thought I was insane. "Did you see who went in?" I asked Tory. She looked blank. Why hadn't I given her orders to watch the door? "He's got keys to her apartment! They're our keys!" I realized. "Our missing keys!" I thought Byron had stolen them.

"So? What if this guy is dating Thanh?" Lizzie leaned against the wall, kneading at her wet hair. "And he was just picking some stuff up for her?"

It was like no one believed me anymore. "He has *our* whole ring of keys," I explained. "Whoever he is, he can get into *our* apartment now."

"I think he already did," Tory said, "if he's the same one who took the keys."

True.

"What's going on?" Kali came out from the back with a toothbrush stuck in her mouth. She looked tired. It was way past midnight, which meant we were already in Tuesday. We had school in a few hours.

I took a deep breath. "We're in big trouble. If they don't get what they want, I think someone's gonna get murdered tomorrow at midnight. Actually, I think it might be me—now that I think about it." That pretty much stunned them all. Tory collapsed slowly onto the couch. I think she was the only one who believed me. "Do you have any food?" she asked.

I jerked in indignation and marched into the back, coming out of my room with Thanh's keys. I slammed them on our end table. "They want these...at least what they can open. That's why they kidnapped Thanh."

"What? That girl?" Kali's eyes got big and she moved her toothbrush aimlessly in her mouth. She still thought of Thanh as the spirit that haunted the apartment next door.

Lizzie clasped her fingers, trying to appear calm. "Are you sure about this?"

I shrugged, knowing it would be next to impossible to convince them. "They thought Thanh had these keys—I think that's why they took her, but when I stole Byron's backpack, I accidentally stole Thanh's backpack instead. Don't ask me why they even switched backpacks in the first place. He might be involved in all this. I don't know."

"But how did *you* get the keys?" Lizzie asked. As always she was being sensible.

"I put them in my pocket. Her cell phone too."

Lizzie looked shocked, and I just ignored it. I had other things to worry about like being hunted down, tortured and eventually murdered. "We need to figure out who Thanh really is," I said. "What does she have that someone big and bad wants? Second, where do these keys fit? Third, what does Byron have to do with this?"

"Maybe he's a spy," Tory said. She shrugged at my look. Kali giggled.

Lizzie held up a finger. "Let me get this straight? You're accusing Byron of being a spy...a real spy? Like an operative for a foreign agency or something?"

"Uh, well, that was Tory actually, but he *could* be hiding something. I don't know what."

Lizzie laughed. She sounded a little nervous, but to me it was sounding more and more plausible. Maybe Byron wasn't a spy in the full sense of the word, though it was eerie how well he fit the James Bond mold, complete with an over-abundance of women. He dressed really well too. And what was with never doing his homework and still getting all A's? I sighed. None of that was good evidence. It just seemed lately that something wasn't right. "He's Sandra's ex," Lizzie argued. "Don't you think that's mixing pleasure with work?"

"It's his cover?" I gave a ragged laugh, not really knowing what I was saying. Still, my gut nagged at me like I was missing something. I'd hate for him to be caught up in this intrigue with Thanh; he'd be just as much a victim as she was. "Look, I don't have it figured out yet. He's got an accent too. Don't you think that's suspicious?"

"This is BYU. A lot of people have accents."

"They don't pretend *not* to have accents—every guy knows that's a chick magnet! Besides, everybody has a link in the Mormon world. Someone went on your same mission or someone knows you from your ward back home or someone knows someone who knows you. Where are Byron's connections? He's got none. I've checked."

"You've checked?"

I had the grace to blush. "Yeah…I took things a little too far before and so…"

"We could stalk him on Facebook," Kali suggested.

"I did that," I told her flatly. "This is real now. Are you going to help me figure out what's going on here or not?" Lizzie looked nervous. Kali just laughed some more. I didn't have to look for Tory's reaction. I knew she'd have my back. If I could present it as a game, I'd have Kali. As for Lizzie? I could appeal to her common sense, but I wasn't sure that would happen with this story. "Okay, pretend we're just going up against the guys on a simple op." I paced the room to calm myself down. "Our first goal would be to get Thanh back, right?" They nodded—some more enthusiastically than others. "Let's look at our assets. The police won't be any help; Brady and Oliveira won't listen to us."

Lizzie crossed her arms. "So you get some evidence to back you up."

I let out a relieved breath. Once Lizzie suspended her disbelief, she was invaluable. "How much evidence do you have?" she asked in a logical voice.

"Some guy broke into Thanh's," Tory suggested.

I shook my head. "The cops will blame it on the prank war." I scrounged through my pocket, digging out the TA note to Byron. Thanh's cell phone. Gummy worms. How did those get in there? Keys. Byron's iPhone. I went through his texts; finding terse messages from H—. *"Where are you?" "Call me when you get this." "Pick up your phone." "Acknowledge." "Is everything alright?"* Wait, they were all from H—? Was that Holly? Byron had named her H— on his phone. How unromantic.

"Well then," Lizzie said. "If we can't prove something's going on, then we just make the bad guys prove it for us."

I nodded, feeling the same energy as before. We were in plotting mode again, except it had a different charge. Things were scarier. Thanh's life was in danger. I had no idea who she was, but she was a neighbor, a daughter, a friend. She was important to the people who left those worried messages behind. "Those guys want something in this pile." I shoved the mess left over from my pockets to my roommates—minus the gummy worms. Those had found their way into Tory's mouth. "We just have to figure out what they want."

"How?" Lizzie asked.

"We set a trap," I decided. I picked up Thanh's pink phone from the pile. "Let's invite them to play with us."

"Is that wise?" Lizzie's eyes were dark and scared.

"Don't worry. I know what I'm doing."

"And if you're dealing with Byron?"

I snorted. "Are you kidding? I said he was *involved*, not the mastermind. No, this other guy's an amateur. He leaves traces of himself everywhere." I opened my war journal and found where the paper had been ripped out. "Pencil." I held my hand out to Tory. She thrust a pencil into my hand and I colored over the blank paper on my war journal. It picked up the address the guy had written on the sheet above it. The meeting place was off Bulldog Avenue. "Girls, we've got ourselves an address." I typed it into my cell phone and Denny's popped up on my GPS. "They're meeting at Denny's tomorrow at midnight. That's how long we have,"—before someone was murdered...or the bad guys got what they wanted. Both were bad. I took a steadying breath and found recent calls on Thanh's phone. As soon as I found the number behind the threatening calls, the danger tingled under my fingertips. It felt as bad as calling a boy. I squeezed my eyes shut and pushed redial.

Lizzie jumped forward to stop me. Her eyes were big with fear. Not bad for someone who didn't believe me. "You're calling him?"

I nodded. Once I heard the familiar voice answer his phone, I steeled myself, pulling from my years of prank war experience. "Hello again," I said. "Guess what? I know who you are." The guy was silent on the other end, not falling for my trick to identify himself. "It looks like I have something you want."

"It would appear that way." He sounded amused.

Amused? It wasn't any kind of clue, so I tried again. "How about we help each other. You give me what I want and I'll make a little arrangement?"

"Are you really in that position?"

My gaze dropped to the pile of evidence on the table and I took a gamble. "I have the keys." He didn't argue, but waited for me to continue. "You *do* want the keys?"

"I'm listening."

I gave my collection of friends a thumb's up. Apparently we *were* in the position to bargain. "What are you willing to give me for them?"

"Let's decide that when we meet."

I wanted to make the deal for Thanh, but I wasn't sure that I wanted to give away my cover of obliviousness yet, not before I put my puzzle pieces together. And there was no way I was meeting up with this guy either. I threw a cocky note into my voice. "We'll meet tomorrow evening for the trade-off...*Byron*." I listened to the guy's heavy breathing on the other end, hoping to throw him off with the wrong name. "You'll never get the keys back without me, so you'd better do what I say. I'll tell you where to meet...and I want you to bring Thanh or you won't get them back." Lizzie's eyes never seemed so huge before and I knew I had to make this good. "Yeah, I want to meet your girlfriend. You can't hide that you're dating her anymore. Is she with you now?"

"Yeah."

"Well, congratulations on a new relationship. I want to talk to her."

"No."

I sighed. He was making this hard. "You'd better bring her tomorrow, *Byron*...or no deal."

"When?"

"Expect a call." This time I got to hang up abruptly. Three pairs of eyes met mine. I sat heavily down on our ugly couch, my legs feeling weak. "I didn't get much. He wasn't talking."

"At least you set the bait." Lizzie said, forever optimistic.

I sighed, shifting through the keys trying to figure out why they were so important. "And what is the bait?"

"Who cares? It's not you," Tory muttered, "...for now."

I nodded, feeling my nerves quiver at the danger. I'd be safe until my fake meeting tomorrow. The guy on the other line thought I'd dance right into his hands and he wouldn't have to do a thing. Another phone went off in my room. It didn't take a genius to guess it was Byron's. I dove off the couch and went after it. My roommates followed. I scooped it up with one hand.

"Pull back, Byron. We're on target. We have the girl." It was the same guy I had talked to on Thanh's cell phone. My heart went hollow at the familiar voice. I listened for more information, but he wasn't giving me any and there was no use pretending to be Byron—I couldn't fake his faint accent anyway. I felt sick. My worst fears had been confirmed. *"Hello?"* the guy asked.

I hung up on him. Byron's iPhone the only thing real in my world. I concentrated on it. It felt hard and big in my palm. I hadn't really believed it until now. One phone call had stolen my trust. My reality. My friend. He wasn't just involved...he was in on this. Eventually I became aware of my roommates' worried faces. "Hey, guess what?" I couldn't control the pain invading my voice. "You know that guy who wants the keys? He just called Byron to tell him they have the girl—me. They're working together." Kali's eyes got huge. Lizzie's face changed to disbelief. I wanted to be like that, but the betrayal filled me with rage. I had trusted him, told him my dating woes, gave him permission to weed out the June sixes! That jerk! I ran a shaky hand through my hair, trying to breathe normally. "And Byron said *I* had no social *provocity*! Me?" I shouted. "Well, he's right. I didn't see him coming at all. He wasn't going to be my watchdog. He was watching me to make sure I wasn't onto him!" I charged through the room, not caring where I went. "Tory!" My hands flailed. It all fit together. "He knew the number of the friend Thanh was staying with!"

Tory shrugged. "Yeah...and the cops talked to her."

"Did they really? The guy I talked to says *he* has her. Byron always knows what's going on. Whenever something suspicious happens, he's just a step away. And now that guy tells him he has me. Like I'm some sort of tool. Oh, Byron is not getting away with this." I realized I still had Byron's iPhone. I dialed it.

Kali was fascinated. "What are you doing now?"

"Calling myself. I need his number. Tomorrow, nice and early, I'm giving his iPhone back to him...with flair."

Lizzie flopped down on our big wing-backed chair, her long hair dancing around her shoulders. She closed her weary eyes. For once, I was more worried than she was. At least she didn't have the burden of believing a thing I said.

CHAPTER TWO

Day 113
0612 hours

"Every moment built up to this point; every skill I've acquired, every pain-filled memory leads me here. Finally, I know what I am made for."

—Madeleine's War Journal Entry (Tuesday June 5th).

I found myself shoving the doors open to the gym early the next morning—earlier than was humanly decent—wearing my best cover yet. I was a high-maintenance girl with a pink workout top and matching leggings. Lizzie altered my face with a heavy make-over. And since guys could never separate make-up from the face, Byron would never know it was me...at least not at first glance. Just to make sure of that, I adopted the movie star in hiding look with Sandra's *Audrey Hepburn* sunglasses.

The smell of sweat and fatigue was overwhelming. To be honest, I was more of a *Smith Fieldhouse* girl, but apparently this was the only place where Byron could get away from me. His daily work-out was at seven am. The information cost Kali dearly. She had promised her whole weekend away for it; she wasn't too heartbroken since it was with Blake.

Pulling out my cash to get a day pass, I leaned against the counter and swept the area with a nonchalant glance. The gym was filled with serious-minded individuals concentrating on their workouts. Nobody looked at anybody, which made me the odd one out. I thought these places were pick-up joints? I tried to decide where Byron would torture himself first. Weights, treadmill, an aerobics class—they had a sign-up sheet to learn Zumba. I cracked a bitter smile, but of course, it was just a foolish dream…unless he had an ulterior motive with a hot instructor. Yeah, he was back to the player category as far as I was concerned. Throwing my gym bag over my shoulder, I wandered through the muscle-bound men. The TVs blared above me. What was Byron's connection with Thanh? TA? Study partner? Boyfriend? Kidnapper?

    Just as I was beginning to think Blake was a no-good liar and gave us false information, I spied Byron next to the treadmills wearing his ARMY t-shirt. He hadn't started his work-out yet. His hoody was still on and he was deep in conversation with a youngish looking guy with an indeterminate hair color and the usual workout clothes. Definitely someone who could get lost in a crowd.

    I tried not to feel anything when I looked at Byron, but I couldn't swallow my anger. What was he doing anyway? I wanted him to be the guy I quarreled with, not some shady character who kidnapped poor grad students. Watching him now, he looked tired, but not on the lamb. Either he was innocent of all charges or he was good at what he did. I mentally slapped myself. Seriously? Byron was never innocent. I couldn't fool myself anymore, even if I desperately wanted him to be what his lies made him out to be. It all seemed ironic now.

    I popped in my earplugs, pretending to listen to music as I unrolled a mat from the corner of the room. I sat down on it and listened to Byron talk to nondescript guy, performing a few sit-ups while I was at it. Sure, it wasn't the most comfortable cover, but I'd do anything to get my guy—especially one who tore out my heart. I listened closely. So far, Byron was shooting the breeze, but it wasn't about girls. It was about the weather. That was a major tip-off that something wasn't right. After what felt like a million sit-ups, they started talking freely just like I knew they would. "You've been AWOL the last few days?" his friend said.

Byron gave a frustrated sound. "Yeah, about that. My phone's gone missing. That's not the only thing. *Where is she?*"

"Don't worry about it. Everything's under control." Was it really? I could only assume they were talking about Thanh, but what if they were talking about real college things like crushes? With no names, it was hard to tell.

Byron dug his hands into the pockets of his hoody, keeping his expression cool. "I assume you have a plan?"

The guy turned from me and mumbled under his breath, "...find it for us." I managed to make out the last part. Byron looked surprised. The other guy swigged down his water. "After that, I give you permission to follow like a lost little puppy. Just make it quick."

"Is it the real thing?"

"Don't worry about it. We're one step ahead." The guy handed Byron something small and compact. "Don't lose this one. I need you to—"

Someone turned the radio on next to me. Are you kidding? I squinted, trying to hear Byron and this guy's conversation over the noise, but it was useless. Squinting had nothing to do with hearing. Byron gave an easy laugh that broke through the loud music. "I could use a floater like her. She's got imagination."

"Keep her busy."

"How?" The radio buzzed every time I came up from a curl. I was in the way of the reception. "She's so incredibly hot." I wrinkled my nose. Byron had shifted topics mid-sentence. "I just don't know if I could tie myself to one girl though. I'm such a player. I can't help what I am." My eyes narrowed behind my shades. The conversation had taken a ridiculous turn. Byron hadn't moved, but that didn't mean he didn't know I was here. "I just wish Mad Dog would marry me."

They were onto me. I rolled onto my stomach and walked away from the mat, trying to figure out how to complete the next part of my mission with my cover blown. I still had a drop to make.

I lingered at the front desk, waiting for Byron at the exit. He had to leave sometime. I filled out a whole stack of comment cards at the desk before I got nervous. There wasn't a back entrance to this place? Before I could desert my post to check, I spotted my target. Byron threw a towel over his shoulder, his hair wet from a shower. I let out a breath, but before I could try anything, he passed me and laughed. "Nice shades." I scowled after him. He passed me then hesitated at the exit, placing his hand on the door. I didn't move. He glanced back at me. After treating me to an expressive roll of his eyes, he came back, walking backwards in his Nikes until his shoulder touched mine. He leaned an elbow against the counter. "What are you doing?"

"Can't a girl get a work-out without getting harassed?"

"Is that a rhetorical question? It's a gym." Byron plucked the comment card from my hand, purposely invading my personal space, but I didn't fight him. I studied his face instead. His mischievous eyes held mine a little too long, but other than that, I couldn't believe how good he was at his cover. After looking confused at my lack of spirit, he read the card I had filled out: *"I can honestly say that I'm the person I am today because of these simple workers nay, these astounding workers."* I pulled his iPhone from my pocket, my eyes darting over him to make sure he didn't notice my sleight of hand. He kept reading, *"If this isn't service with a smile then I know not what is."* Byron broke into a laugh and glanced up at me. I hid his iPhone behind me. "You wrote an essay." His hand found mine with the pen. "Let me play." In a trice, he had my pen.

I clutched his iPhone tighter with my other hand. Before he could get two words down on his comment card, I noticed his duffel bag and got an idea. "Nice bag. What do you have in it—a body?" Before he could fight me, I slid my fingers under the handles and lifted the bag, pretending to weigh it. It actually was a little heavy. "Byron, is it really necessary to bring everything you own to the gym?"

He didn't even look distracted. My fingers weren't fast enough when he wouldn't take his eyes off me. Couldn't he blink or something? I pretended to stumble over the weight and he reached out to steady me. I saw my in, slipping his iPhone into the kangaroo pocket of his hoody.

PRANK WARS

My other hand clutched his forearm harder than I intended and I felt his muscles flexing under my hand.

"No, I've got it." Byron retrieved his gym bag. He tilted his head as if he wanted to say something. I waited. His chest rose in and out, and for a moment our eyes locked, his blue eyes penetrating my dark ones. He covered the moment with an easy laugh. "You should leave this stuff to the professionals, cuz."

And that was it. I had lost him forever. I blinked back my frustrated tears. "I can handle more than you think," I retorted.

Byron nodded. "Good." Before he could quite make his exit, he glanced back at me. "Hey, Mad. Check your pocket. I think I left something for you in there."

I rummaged through my pockets to pull out a note written on the back of the comment card: *Call me.*

Byron put two fingers to his mouth and blew me a kiss before he left me and my slackly hanging jaw. Always two steps ahead like some nerdy chess player. Yes, I was cross! How did he know I was returning his phone? I pushed through the same door he had, and wasn't surprised to see he had promptly disappeared. My arms fell limply to my sides. He couldn't know what I was doing. There was no way. I found my car slathered in diamond advertisements and collapsed into the driver's seat. I leaned my head against the wheel and started my car.

Country music filled the inside.

I shot up in my seat. The station was set on country. My fingers ran over the set stations and I found them all set on random channels. I'd never willingly torture myself with this music. "Byron!"

The message was clear. He could get into my car. He could get into my house. He could get into my pockets. He could do anything he wanted to me. Any sane person would be scared to death, but I was annoyed. I pulled viciously out of the parking lot. He just saw me as an annoying pest he could toy with and throw away. Maybe the fact that he underestimated me would work in my favor. It always did.

CHAPTER THREE

Day 113
1842 hours

"I can feel the scent of fear, hear the exchanged glances, see the whispered words. You see me watching my laundry, but let's be honest, I'm watching you."

—Madeleine's War Journal Entry (Tuesday, June 5th).

"The bird has flown the coop," Lizzie told me on the other line. *"I'm the only one on Tweedledee and Tweedledummer."*

"You're joking?" Our makeshift surveillance had been like this all day. My roommates were supposed to be holed up in the apartment with the twins. Kali couldn't just abandon Lizzie to them. "What's her 20?"

"Don't know."

Kali had the difficult task of stopping Byron from going anywhere after his last class. I still had some more investigating to do. "Do we know where the bird has flown?"

"Nope." Lizzie laughed on the other line, having no idea how serious this was. Tory was busy taking a test. It was like no one really believed we were dealing with anything scary like murderers or kidnappers or terrorists.

"Is she still in radio contact?"

"She's not answering her phone. But don't worry. The targets are in position. We're playing the 'what-is-my-weakness?' game. We'll have Byron's location in no time."

PRANK WARS

I froze. "Please tell me you are in the bathroom and the twins didn't hear you say that!"

"Oops. I guess I forgot to secure the line."

I sighed. "Text me all vital information at 1900 hours."

"What?"

"Seven o'clock. That's in fifteen minutes." I hung up the phone.

"You know the school provides free counseling." Sandra pulled her clothes out of the dryer. Big sunglasses covered half her face. The straps of her red suede heels spiraled around her ankle, coordinating perfectly with her skinny jeans. It seemed days since I last set eyes on her. Ever since *Battle of the Bands*, she had been completely AWOL. It usually meant there was someone new in her life.

I sat on the washing machine, trying to decide how to approach this. I dug my camo converses against the metal. "Let's talk about boys." Yeah, I just went out and said it. Sandra looked taken aback. "Tell me about when you dated Byron, Sandra."

She pulled her clothes out of the dryer faster. "What is there to know?"

I knew this was going to be difficult from the start. I just shrugged, knowing I was about to do the unthinkable—fake an interest in Byron. "I was just wondering. Where did you meet him?"

"He's in our ward."

"But you were dating him before either of you moved in."

Sandra gave me an angry glare. "We're done dating. It's over. If you want to date him then be my guest. I doubt he's interested."

"Excuse me?"

"To use your own words, *my dear*, you don't prank people you want to date. If a guy's interested, he'll just ask you out. Get over it."

She didn't just call me *dear*, did she? I took a deep breath and tried to stay focused. Why should I care if that lowlife wasn't interested in me anyway? It was about figuring out where he came from. I ignored the sting and plunged ahead. "I'm just conducting a routine background check. I have a good friend who's interested in him."

"A good friend?" She didn't seem to believe me.

I answered her with a cocky grin.

She stopped messing with her clothes long enough to glare at me. "He's a decent guy, okay? When we broke up, it wasn't like he went around dissing me or trying to flirt with every girl who moved to get my attention—not like your guy, so I'm sorry, but he's way out of your league."

My eyes narrowed. "Well, good then," I sputtered. "But how much did he tell you about himself? Does he have any family around? Did you hang out with his friends?"

She took an exasperated breath. "We weren't dating for years, honey."

I winced at yet another term of endearment. I nervously rolled up my brown lounge pants to the calf. "Where's he from then?"

"Nowhere sinister and evil if that's what you're concerned about."

I supposed that meant that she was onto me. "Why the accent then?"

"Wow, you really have the cross-examination thing down."

And she really had the closed-mouth thing down. What was her problem? I'd have to start torturing her soon. I hopped off the washer. "How come you can't answer any of my questions?"

"How come you're asking them?"

"You know nothing about him, do you? You just dated him because you thought he was hot."

"What's wrong with that?"

Now she was making me mad. If this were the real world, Sandra had played him good. "Didn't you care about him at all?"

She nodded, folding a shirt army regulation style and patting it neatly into her laundry basket. "He liked *me*."

I stiffened. *That's it?* "What's his favorite food?"

"Chinese."

"What does he like to do?"

"Nothing. Are we through?"

PRANK WARS

"Seriously? Pretty much you're telling me you have no idea who he is. You met him randomly and without knowing anything about him, you went steady then broke up for absolutely no reason and now you hate him?"

She refused to dignify anything with a response. If Byron really was what I suspected, she'd be the perfect cover. All he had to do was pay attention to Sandra, stroke her ego then *bam*; he had a reputation and a history. No one would question who he was. Sandra threw the last of her clean clothes in a basket and dragged them out the door of the laundry room on her hip. "What's going on, Madeleine? Lizzie said you were up to something...like you were way over your head." It was meant as a slam.

I smiled. "I'm *never* over my head."

After a moment of waiting and not getting anything more from me, Sandra jerked angrily away. "We'll see about that." She stalked out of the laundry room, the door swinging after her.

I scooped my cell phone from my pocket. It was time to call in my best weapon. She had better be on radio contact.

Kali answered in a cheerful voice. *"Hey, guess who I followed?"*

"Please say Lord Byron."

"Yep, the evil general himself." Finally, some luck. The girl was making more progress than any of us on her first real stakeout. *"Blake was like, he's going out, and I was like, so where's he going? And he was like, I don't know, we're guys, we don't care what our roommates do, okay? But I knew that was a lie 'cause Adam gave Blake a look, like I can't read a look. And I was, like, I'm gonna run to the store and get some girl stuff. Lizzie, stay here. I'll be right back, and Blake wanted to come with me, so cool, huh?"*

I stiffened. "Is Blake in the car with you?"

"Do you think I'm an idiot?"

Right now she was the best ally I had. "No!" I said quickly.

"Well," she sounded slightly mollified. *"Good. So now I'm just following Byron's car to see where he goes."*

"Do we know who he's meeting?"

"That's a negative, Mad Dog."

I winced at the name. "Do we have a 20 yet?"

"English, Mad."

"Do you know where he's headed?'

"Negative, but I'm on it. Um, yeah, about that. I'm driving your car right now."

I stifled a groan. Kali was trying to shadow Byron's car in broad daylight with the most noticeable car in existence, especially to him. I hung up and tried to get a firm grip on myself. It was time to use a little psychological warfare. I'd get Byron to talk. Believe me, I'd make him sorry he ever laid eyes on me—I just had to remind myself it was all part of the plan. I found his number. Byron answered it on the first ring. *"Hi. Is Mad there?"*

"Don't play with me. Why do you have my number on your phone?"

"Usual protocol." I heard the wind behind him as he spoke. He was outside. *"What's going on?"*

"Do I always need an excuse to call? But now that you mention it, you *do* know that MormonVille is a small place, right?"

The sound of wind broke off and was replaced by murmuring and the clinking of glasses and silverware in the background. He had just walked into a building. It probably was a restaurant. Had I interrupted him on a date? I felt absolutely no remorse. *"What are you getting at?"* he asked after a moment.

"No one knows who you are. No former mission companions, no former ward members, no former roommates. No friends. No family. Your current roommates and *one* ex seem to know next to nothing about you."

He was silent for a moment. I think I caught him by surprise. *"You've been checking up on me. I suppose I should be flattered."*

"Don't be. Have you seen Thanh lately?"

"No." It came out flat.

PRANK WARS

"She came back last night and we got to talking. And she had some pretty interesting things to say. Why didn't you tell me what was going on?"

"*You never asked.*" He didn't miss a beat. "*So tell me, how is she recovering from her curfew breaking?*" I knew he didn't believe a thing I said by the tone of his voice.

"*Do you have reservations?*" I heard a female voice ask in the background. It sounded like a hostess.

He fumbled with his iPhone. "*Just a sec,*" he told us both.

I listened carefully. "*Would you like to be seated?*" the same female voice said. "*Follow me.*"

Was this a date or something else? If I listened long enough, I would know. I just had to keep him on the phone. "Thanh asked for that note we found on her door," I continued. "You remember the one. I believe you wrote it…and then you wanted it back again? Thanh's not sure why you wanted it so badly. You mind telling me?"

"*I never told you that I wrote that note.*"

"Yeah, but that was in front of the children. Face it, Byron. You're like a soggy brown banana; the only use for you now is to get cooked."

That forced a laugh out of him. "*Really? What's that supposed to mean?*"

I grinned. No idea. It felt like old times—before he was an evil hit man with kidnapping tendencies. My heart sank at that.

"*Here you are.*" I heard the hostess say. I waited for whoever Byron was with to say something. Maybe I could get an ID on the voice.

"*Wait a second,*" he told me. "*I've got a call.*" He took the other line and with a click I was treated to soft elevator music. If it was meant to get rid of me, he had another thing coming. Most likely, he did it so he could talk freely to whoever was there, so why didn't he hang up on me altogether? He came back a few minutes later. "*Hey, how about we meet up later tonight?*"

I froze. Was that a date—or? "I'm busy. I have something that belongs to Thanh and I need to return it to her."

"What's that?"

I got a call from Kali on the other line, and smiled viciously. Revenge was sweet. "Just a sec, Byron. I have to get this." I clicked over, hoping my music was just as annoying as his.

"I'm stuck," she said.

"Really? How bad?"

"Pretty bad. There's this guy and we sorta dated a couple of months ago and we, like, never officially broke up 'cause we never officially went out, ya know? And I told him I'd call him back, but I haven't. And he tried to call me and I didn't pick up and he texted me tons and now he's here, so..."

I leaned my head back in exasperation. "Where's Byron?"

"Brick Oven. He got out of his car and went in. There was no one with him and he didn't take the phone off his ear the whole time. Maybe he's meeting someone inside. Look, I'm parked outside. There's seriously no way I can get out with that guy hanging around."

I sighed. Normally, a decoy like this was Lord Byron's handiwork, but even this was too brilliant for him. This was just pure dumb luck. "Just go into the restaurant and if this guy sees you, just act stupid. It's not that hard."

"I'm not stupid, Mad, okay? Thanks a lot!" She hung up on me. She seemed pretty sensitive about that lately.

I clicked off on her line and gradually became aware of the restaurant sounds on the other line again, but there was no talking. It was either a really boring date or Byron knew I was back. "You there?" I asked him.

"Yeah. Hey, I think I might see Thanh later on tonight. Why don't you just let me deliver whatever it is you want to give her?"

"Deliver what?" I asked.

"Whatever it is that belongs to her."

"No, don't go to all that trouble. You're on a date." He didn't deny or confirm. We were going nowhere, and yet, I got the germ of an idea. "Maybe I can drop her stuff off at her lab?"

PRANK WARS

It seemed like he was holding his breath. *"You could."*

"I could just leave what she wants under the doormat." He was silent. It was like setting a trap for a particularly clumsy and stupid bear...a dangerous bear. "By the way, what's your favorite food?" I asked.

"Pizza." Not Chinese, huh? Sandra knew nothing about him. *"Why?"*

"No reason." I saw a shadow streak past the glass window on the dryer. With every ounce of control I had, I kept myself from recoiling. Whatever the reflection was, the actual thing was behind me. I felt my back arch at the danger. Maybe it was Tory, but what if it wasn't? Whoever had been in Thanh's apartment knew who I was. He had been in my apartment and took that backpack and now he was mad. What if he couldn't wait until tonight to take me out? I watched the figure through the glass. It streaked towards me. I screamed and jerked around. Eric jumped back, almost dropping his laundry.

"Eric!" I stood up. "I thought you were Tory. Sorry! I'm so sorry!"

He smiled, wearily setting his laundry down by his Nikes. He looked like one of my soldiers in his green cargo pants. "You really don't like her, do you?"

"Of course I like her."

"Mad! What's going on?" Byron asked. I remembered belatedly that he was on the line.

"I'm sorry. It's just Eric. Gotta go."

"Madeleine, wait."

"Hey, tell Thanh where I'm putting that stuff she's missing, okay?" I hung up on him. Byron would be officially out of the way when he searched for the keys under the doormat. As if I would ever leave them out in the open. He wasn't dealing with nursery kids anymore.

"Hey." Eric began throwing his clothes into the washer. "You're not talking about the same Thanh I work with, are you?"

And that's when he had my full attention. Now I knew the reason behind Eric and my surreptitious meeting. It was destiny. He was the only way I could help Thanh. I stepped in front of him, blocking him from going anywhere. "Your lab? You work in the same lab. You do experiments in your lab. All of you."

"Uh, yeah."

Maybe that's where the keys belonged, to *something* in there. "You lock up your experiments?"

He watched me like I was crazy, but his lip curled up. At least he was enjoying this. "Yeah, we don't want anyone getting into our stuff. Some of us are working on some pretty intense stuff."

Thanh's keys fit somewhere in there. She was a grad student, wasn't she? She was working on experiments. Could that be what these people wanted? Whatever these keys opened could be what these bad guys were looking for. If I could get to it first, I'd have something to negotiate with to get Thanh back. "Take me to your lab," I said.

"Why?"

"Top secret."

"Oh no." Eric backed away, but his dancing eyes betrayed him. I could tell I still amused him—at least that. "Don't get me involved in this."

"Please!" I tried to think of a good way to get him to do it. Feminine wiles were beyond me. Before I started begging, my phone vibrated and I got a text from Kali. I could use a few flirting tips from her. Unfortunately I couldn't text fast enough to ask. I scanned through her message: *"I've got Byron in sight. He's on a date with Sandra."*

I almost dropped the phone. Sandra had been defensive about him. Still none of this made sense. It didn't fit his cover at all....unless he was regular old Byron on a regular old date. My heart fell. No. If that was true, *player Byron* was better than the alternative. It just didn't feel better. Sandra didn't like him for real. He didn't really like her. Why was I feeling this jealousy? I mean, I couldn't have planned it better if I had ordered Sandra on the assignment myself...if he even needed to be distracted.

I slanted a look at Eric, knowing I had to figure this out. "This isn't part of a prank war. I've been missing my purse since I went up to your lab. I think it's still there."

PRANK WARS

Eric smirked at me. For some reason, he didn't seem to believe me, but after a moment, he nodded. "Just as soon as I put my laundry in." He gave a cheerful laugh. "Don't try anything funny, Madeleine."

What was that supposed to mean?

CHAPTER FOUR

Day 113
1932 hours

"What I see is not what you see."

—Madeleine's War Journal Entry (Tuesday, June 5th).

Tory, of all people who should believe this wasn't some stupid prank war anymore, was still in the testing center. I texted her and told her to get over here. She probably wouldn't get it until it was too late. *Curse chemistry.* I texted Lizzie to hurry with the twins, Kali to bring my car back, Sandra to keep Byron busy. *Oh yeah, I'm onto you, Sandra.* Pretty much I was going solo on this mission—well, besides Eric's company, and he had no idea what danger we were in. I slung my backpack over my shoulder, wondering how to keep it that way. The squeaks of our shoes against the marble staircase broke the silence on our way through the Eyring building, past the dinosaurs, the vortex cannon, the wave-a-tron.

The setting sun of this frustrating day filled the windows with orange and pink light, but was extinguished the farther down we went to Eric's underground lab. I avoided his eyes as I worked out my strategy. Searching the lab like I was looking for my purse could only take me so far, especially when I started testing out the keys on everything I could find. Far too soon, we reached the lab. Instead of opening it, Eric rounded on me. "Are you really missing your purse?" His voice echoed through the empty hall.

PRANK WARS

I could lie or— "Why else would I force you to come all this way?"

"I was hoping it was an excuse to get me alone."

I tried not to shake my head so violently. In a different world where I liked to exercise and I was a lot better at flirting that might be possible. Eric was very attractive. His smile was infectious, and his strong hand was over mine. Wait. It was. He turned my hand over in his. His hazel eyes probed mine and I couldn't look away. He leaned closer and I could smell his familiar scent; it drew me in. He rubbed his thumb over my fingers. "Do you have a problem with this?" I wasn't sure. "You're fascinating," he said. "Do you know that? What are you doing tonight?"

I was getting killed. I tried to pull away without hurting his feelings. "I'm not doing anything if I can't find my purse."

"Don't worry." He smiled with perfect teeth. "I'll pay."

For what? I laughed nervously. "We'll talk who pays after we get this door open." I was proud of my noncommittal answer, but I think it only encouraged him. His arm rested on the door behind me, his blue sleeve tightened over his bicep. He seemed very big all of a sudden. I twisted the knob behind me, but it was locked. I felt claustrophobic. "Don't you have the keys?" I asked. "We should go inside."

"That might give us a little more privacy."

Wait. No! The femme fatale act just wasn't working for me. "Look, I really don't have time right now. If you could just get this door open ..."

"Oh, I think I'm missing my keys," he said in a lazy voice. "You don't happen to have an extra set, do you?" Well, I had the ones that belonged to Thanh, but that hardly counted. I studied his amused face. He had no intention of letting me in, did he? Was this his idea of cute? Well, it was annoying.

"Ah lovely. I see you're in good hands." I recognized that low sarcastic tone—and the faint accent. I peered over Eric's arm. Byron was breathing hard like he had run a far distance to get here. He didn't look like a spy, just a regular college student in white tee and jeans, so why was my pulse reacting this way? He was supposed to be with Sandra. He was probably really dangerous. Not probably—he *was*, so he needed to stop affecting me like this. "Having some trouble?" he asked. Now that he had us in sight, Byron slowed, coming towards us like the most relaxed guy in the world.

After one glance at Eric's dark expression, I kinda wished Byron would hurry. "Yeah, my purse is in the lab. Eric was going to let me in, but he *forgot* his keys."

"Hmm." Byron leaned over the both of us, which made things a little crowded. "Do you mind?"

Much to my relief, Eric jerked away from me. Super arch-villain or not, Byron was my knight in shining armor. I tried not to show how glad I was to see him. He would probably kill me along with Eric once he got what he wanted—though looking at his familiar face, I couldn't bring myself to believe it.

Eric glared at Byron, not happy with the third wheel. I couldn't explain myself, so I avoided talking. Byron studied the number lock to the side of us. Before I could suggest some possible number combinations to break the code, he ripped the number pad open and found a key behind it. My eyes almost jolted out of their sockets. "How did you know that was there?" I asked.

"Janitorial job. These things are all over the place."

Yeah, right! I didn't question him though. Byron was getting me inside and away from Eric and for now that was all I cared about. He unlocked the door and let us in. Strangely enough, Eric wasn't making a fuss. I saw the confusion on his face. He wasn't the only one. Byron was helping me, so what was the catch? We wandered inside Eric's lab while I tried to figure out where and how to start. The room was stifling hot. Eric planted his feet firmly in the doorway. "Do you see your purse, Madeleine?"

Byron turned to me with a knowing look. "This is about Thanh, isn't it?"

I shrugged. Of course it was. "Why the interest, Byron? You wouldn't happen to know where she is?"

PRANK WARS

"Not really." He didn't bother to bring up my lies about seeing her earlier. "She didn't show up to our study group today. That's not like her."

"When did you have a study group?" I had been tracking him all day. There had been no pit stop at the school.

"Early."

"What time?" I checked under a stack of papers and opened the filing cabinet. Byron hesitated then smiled. Now he knew I was onto him. I stuck my ear next to the wall, listening. "You're dating Sandra again, I see."

"Yeah, about that." He leaned his fist against the desk. "Should I be concerned? Kali is stuck in your car right now. She hasn't left it for a while."

Eric's fingers dug into the door handle. "What's going on?"

"Byron's an idiot," I explained.

Byron didn't look insulted. "Never listen to Mad, she's a consummate liar." I brushed past him, trying to find what I was looking for. I landed on the ground, searching under the desk. Byron didn't bother to help. He glanced over at Eric. "Where's *your* research?"

"Top secret," Eric reminded him with an arrogant lift of his shoulders.

Byron smirked. I popped away from the desk, trying to imagine what those bad guys wanted. What did Thanh have that they didn't? I lifted up a *Book of Mormon* from the shelf. No, nice thought though.

Byron passed me and tapped me on the forehead. "Hurry up. We're on a tight schedule." I scowled in response.

"Are you sure it's in here?" Eric complained.

I waved at my flushed face. "It's getting hot," I muttered.

Byron laughed. "Would you like me to leave?"

"Yeah," I said, "...and get a fan while you're at it! Why don't you help me instead of just standing around?"

"Help you find what?"

"Her purse," Eric answered in a hard voice.

I wandered back to the desk. "Maybe your lab partners thought the purse belonged to Thanh," I mumbled out an excuse for such a thorough search, "—and they put it in *here*." I opened the drawers, but there was nothing that looked like it needed to be opened with a key. No fake bottoms or backs to the drawers either.

"Are you sure about this?" Eric asked.

Even though I was terrified of him moments before, I was beginning to feel sorry for him. Watching me run around his lab like a rat had to make him nervous. "Oh, it's in here," I said. "That's what Thanh said."

"Before she was taken." Byron was clearly enjoying this.

"Taken?" Eric seemed surprised. "What?"

I glared at Byron. My hands rested on the safe sealed to the wall. It was the same one Byron had discovered the last time we were here. Now it held new meaning. I searched for the lock. "That's an amazing hiding place for a purse," Byron said with a caustic grin.

"Actually, Thanh asked me to pick something up for her while I was here, and I'm just..." My fingers wrapped around a wire coming from the box.

"What? No!" Eric tried to stop me. "You'll set off an alarm."

"That's very unlikely."

An alarm went off above us. Loud and whining. It echoed through the hall. Eric stepped back, anger making his arms stiff. "Wow," Byron muttered, "what were the odds of that?"

I wrestled with my backpack, pulling out Thanh's keys. This had to be what we were looking for. I fumbled through the ring, picking out the most elaborate key. It was one of those electromagnetic keys, so no amount of picking would ever get it open. I found the lock and shoved it in. The alarm cut off and the door to the safe swung open. Byron whistled.

Eric watched me with a new respect. "How did you know that would work?"

PRANK WARS

"Um, Thanh told me to use the keys to get her stuff for her," I re-explained. No one seemed to be listening. They were studying what was in the safe. It looked like a control box of sorts, lots of buttons, and gauges that I'd never be able to figure out. I knew so little about it that I felt like a caveman, but it would save Thanh. The drop-off was tonight and now I had something to bargain with…unless Byron tried to wrestle the box from me. I wasn't sure how to get it past him.

"What's that?" Eric asked.

"Don't know. Don't care." I reached for it.

"No, no, no," Eric warned. "What are you doing? You don't even know what that is."

Byron watched him carefully. "Do you?"

Eric didn't answer. That meant he didn't. He would be safe from Byron for now. I took a deep breath. Whatever this thing was, I'd have to take a chance to get it out of here. "Thanh trusts me with it, so…"

Eric narrowed a look at me. "Are you sure?"

"When have I ever lied to you?" *Plenty of times.* It was just a rhetorical question really. I carefully pulled out the control box. It was pretty light, considering. If my backpack could handle my physics and Shakespeare books together, it could handle this. I wrapped my gym clothes around it as padding and gently placed it into my backpack, zipping it shut. I closed the safe, hoping no one would discover what I had done until Thanh was home. I took a deep breath, and stood up. Byron didn't move from my path. If he wanted to play the concerned card, I'd make him play it, especially since Eric was here and could stop him from stealing it from me. "It's evidence," I whispered to him. "Now we can call the cops."

"I barely believe you," he said under his breath. "You need more evidence before taking…"

I stared at him. He believed me? Well, if he was behind all this, he should, but if he wasn't? I was touched. Eric cleared his throat. "You can't leave until I clear this. I'm sorry, Madeleine." Eric slid Thanh's backpack off my shoulder.

It was all I could do not to rip it from him and make my escape, but Byron's presence put the odds against me. I had been so close. "Clear it?" I asked Eric.

"With Thanh."

I exchanged glances with Byron. He didn't seem worried. "Let him make the call. It's better this way."

I abandoned Byron to follow Eric into the other room, but I couldn't get between him and the backpack. Aggression emanated from him. I had never seen Eric this way—then again; I had never pushed him this hard either. Eric ripped Thanh's number off the wall and set the backpack on a hard-backed chair a little too hard. There didn't seem to be any other way out of this room besides the door we'd come through. I couldn't think how to outsmart Eric either. Pleading wouldn't do any good. Eric's cold eyes told me that. As for the truth, who would believe it? Eric dialed Thanh's number and I cringed, realizing her cell phone was in my backpack. The pocket was about to go off. I waited a moment, but it didn't ring. The thing had finally died. It was my last shred of luck.

"Madeleine?" Byron called me from the other room.

I poked my head past the door. Byron leaned against the desk, not looking concerned at all. It was all a game to him. He waved me over. I deserted Eric in the back, feeling strangely relieved as I distanced myself from his righteous indignation. "What's your problem?" Byron whispered. "It's just like any other prank. What would you normally do to get what you want?"

"I'm not playing this game, Byron."

"I'm looking at your options right now and I don't think you have a choice. Now let's work together and get this thing out of here." I tried to wrap my brain around working together. If Byron was behind this, he could very well be the key to getting Thanh back. "I'll do the intercept. You be the distraction, Madeleine." He looked intently into my eyes. "You have to trust me."

If I didn't cooperate, I'd never get Thanh back. I could form a temporary alliance and figure out a way to *distract* Byron later. I held my breath, studying the room. He wanted a distraction. But how? I studied the room, my gaze latching onto the safe. Byron met my eyes, seeming to read my mind. He put his hand up to stall me, ticking the seconds off on his fingers. Then he nodded.

I tugged on the wire that wrapped around the safe and the alarm went off again. Eric barreled out of the room and I held up my keys. "Don't worry. I'm on it!" I put the key into the lock and the alarm stopped. Byron disappeared into the back room. Immediately, I stepped in front of Eric, blocking him. "Did you get a hold of Thanh?"

Eric shook his head just as Byron emerged from the back with my backpack on his broad shoulder. He widened his eyes at me and tilted his chin at Eric, and I got the hint, stumbling into Eric's arms. Eric caught me just like any gentleman should, though his arms were a little rougher. I tripped him, making us both fall flat to the ground. "Madeleine!" Eric tried to wriggle away from me.

Byron stuffed something into the safe. "Madeleine, you can't take it. If Thanh wants it, she can get it herself." He slammed it shut as if returning the control box. I knew better. It was the old bait and switch.

Before Eric could react, two security guards poked their heads into the doorway. They looked way too young to be protecting the world from us. Their hair was in disarray and their uniforms drowned them. Their eyes widened when they saw the pile of Eric and me on the floor. "What's going on?"

"Uh." Eric was still trying to get up, but my leg kept tangling through his. Byron had me in an instant. He dragged me to my feet, sliding my backpack over my shoulder in one expert motion. I barely even noticed it, except for his warm hand and the sudden heavy weight. The control box was safely inside. Byron let Eric find his own way to his shaky feet. As soon as Eric did, his eyes rushed suspiciously to us. The security guards looked on expectantly.

"Hold on," Eric snapped at them. He went into the back room then came out, this time with a smirk. I didn't get it. His eyes ran over me with a knowing look. My face got red. That had better not have anything to do with our little entanglement. Whatever this new smug attitude was about, I didn't want anything to do with him anymore. Maybe I didn't have a heart—or maybe? Maybe my heart felt taken. My eyes avoided Byron's.

Eric handed the security guards the badge he picked up from the back. "Thanks officers, I work here. Sorry for all the commotion. I think we've got it figured out now."

The security guards nodded and retreated. "We were just leaving too," Byron said. Before I could react, he had my elbow and led me out with the men in black.

Eric stretched out across the door frame, his smoldering eyes running from Byron to linger on me. They burned into me as if luring me back. "You're leaving already?"

Without thinking, I shoved closer to my worst enemy. Byron's jaw tightened grimly, and I felt my pulse rush at the danger. I shouldn't seek solace in his arms, but one look at Eric's stony face made me trust Byron just a few seconds longer. I hurried down the hall with my newfound protector, not knowing if I was walking into more danger.

I heard Eric close the door to the lab behind us. It was as easy as pulling a fast one on the twins, and I should've known something was up.

CHAPTER FIVE

Day 113
2115 hours

"Something strange is happening in Provo, and the only other person who suspects is Lord Byron, my worst enemy. And I will never join sides with him, even if everyone else thinks I'm crazy."

—Madeleine's War Journal Entry (Tuesday, June 5th).

"Thanks for giving my phone back. Now my mum won't think I'm dead." Byron threw his iPhone on the dashboard of his black Suburban, still playing the normal college student. "Look at all those messages."

I hesitated outside Byron's car in the school parking lot, which was pretty awkward, considering he was already inside and staring at me expectantly to get in. Our eyes locked. After a moment, he patted the bench seat next to him. Through my tingling senses, I realized the Suburban didn't hold the usual bucket seats in the front. It was the perfect date mobile for a player. And for Byron? I wasn't sure, but I could find out exactly who he was...if I had the guts. Did I have other options? I had nothing to go to the police with. Thanh was in danger. It seemed easier facing Byron and appealing to his better nature than bargaining with the nasties he worked with to get her back. By now Byron was fiddling with the radio as if he didn't have any murderous thoughts on his mind. Maybe he didn't? Maybe he did.

I stared resolutely at his iPhone, knowing I had a move to make. "I don't think all those messages are from your parents." I forced my voice to sound light. "You have quite a few girls' numbers in your address book, you know."

He cocked a brow, but kept working on the channels. "They're just friends."

"That's not what their texts said." I took a deep breath and grasped the end of the bench to pull myself inside his black Suburban. I clutched the door handle and tugged. The door slammed resoundingly. I was really going through with this. Byron started the car as if taking me to my apartment. My fingers crept to his iPhone. As soon as I had it, I forced myself to read the long list of names aloud. "Who's Annabelle? And Angelina? And Bambie? And Trixie?"

"Who?"

I'm a horrible text messager, especially on a touchscreen, so let's just say that punching those names into his iPhone was a huge feat for me. They all had Tory's cell phone number. I pressed down on one of the numbers and called her. "What?" I asked to distract him from what I was doing. "You don't recognize those names?"

He shook his head, keeping his eyes on the road.

As soon as Tory picked up, I turned the speakerphone on. She would keep quiet when she saw it was from Byron's phone, who—by the way—didn't notice my sleight of hand. "You player," I told him, pretending that I wasn't turning his iPhone the direction of our voices.

He grinned. "Where did you get my phone anyway?"

I took another steadying breath, trying to see him for what he really was for the upteenth time since I found out the truth. Was he a man who hurt people to get what he wanted? "I found it in Thanh's apartment," I said.

Byron's grin turned into a clenched jaw. "How did you get in there?"

"Hey." The leather seats squeaked when I shifted. "You should be grateful. I risked my life to get your phone back for you."

PRANK WARS

His eyes wouldn't leave mine. I never thought I liked the bad boy, but here I was with the enemy. I was painfully aware of everything about him: that we were alone in his dark car, that he was bigger than me, that he was possibly dangerous—but not in the way Eric was dangerous. I didn't sense that in him. I sighed when I realized what I was doing. I was blind, wasn't I? I didn't want to admit it, but—Byron made my boring life interesting; he was fun to tease...and—I liked him. It made me do stupid things like get into his car. "So, what's going on?" he asked.

My hand clutched the straps of my backpack. "I don't know." And that's when I decided to recklessly lay all my cards on the table. "Just that you're a dirty spy."

"You demoted me? I thought I was the general." He knew I wasn't talking about the prank war. I could tell by the careful way he watched me.

"Let's not pretend anymore, Byron," I said.

It was raining again and Byron put his wipers on. A pair of pantyhose stopped it from wiping the windshield effectively. It was a beautiful trick, but it didn't make for very clean glass. He glanced over at me.

"Sorry," I said. "Old habits die hard."

He unrolled his window and tugged the pantyhose off the blade. "So, what's with this Eric guy? Is he the new general in your life?"

I blew out in exasperation. "This isn't the time, okay?" He stared at me, forcing a shrug out of me. "I'm sorry I made you my watchdog, not like you had any intention of helping me out in the first place. Admit it!"

Byron ignored that. "*You* admit it. He's a June sixth freak."

Were we seriously still on this? I had other things to worry about—like saving the world. "Seriously Byron, none of this matters. I'm through with guys right now. We have other things to talk about."

"Oh, I get it. You'll curse God and die. I like it. Nice and dramatic."

"What? No, I'm not." How dare this *spy* lecture me...although he was starting to confuse me. What cold-hearted asset talked this way? I tried to bring myself back to the interrogation. "Okay, let's talk about what you want."

"Suzy Q Miller," he said with that stubborn look. "I want her. She was so sweet and bubbly when she asked me out on April fools."

That forced a laugh out of me. "And clingy and bossy. Why did you tell her yes anyway? She was terrible!" He didn't answer, which made me suspicious. "When did you figure out it was me?"

"The moment you said hello."

"Oh." I rested my head on my hand. "So, you're only a little bit crazy."

"There's nothing crazy about going after what you want. You should know."

My eyes flicked up to him. What was he saying? We drove into the parking lot. He had taken me back to our apartments! Byron stopped his car, turning his full attention to me. It was one of those moments when I normally bailed out of the car. I took a deep breath. "Byron?"

In the darkness outside, a shadow moved behind his head. It had hands. My stomach clenched and I ducked below the seat before I figured out it was AmyLee. Her ponytail bounced as she walked past the windshield. Byron knocked his elbow against the steering wheel, laughing. "What? You're not afraid to be seen with me?"

My heart wouldn't go back to normal. I felt like an idiot. "Sorry...just thought...I saw someone."

"Yeah, good idea. We'll just pretend we're friends if anyone asks."

I glared up at him. How could he joke at a time like this? "Is that what you do with Sandra? What other roommates are you dating without my knowledge?"

His lips tightened at the insult. "All of them."

"Oh, I'm sure you're so innocent. You were just plotting with Sandra to take over the ward...or was it the world?"

"Like you and Eric?"

"Yes, like me and Eric." If he had something going on with Sandra, I would definitely pretend to have something going on with Eric.

"Hey." He bit his lip to keep from laughing, which only made me angrier. "Sandra and I aren't dating. Now it's your turn to tell me the truth." He leaned against the seat, peering down at me crouched below the bench. "Don't worry. AmyLee is long gone and I won't tell her a thing."

I got back into my seat, feeling my face go red. How did he get to me like that? "Eric and I aren't dating."

"See, that wasn't so hard."

My eyebrows went up. If we were playing the truth game, I had a few more moves to make. "Tell me what's happening, Byron. Who are you really?"

He hesitated and crossed his arms. "Byron Schipaanboord. Geology student. Nursery teacher extraordinaire."

"Liar. You cross your arms across your chest when you think you've outsmarted me...like now. You haven't by the way." He looked surprised. "I know everything about you, Byron—even how you bluff."

"I doubt that."

"You can't stand spiders. You listen to girl music. And...and when you're feeling out of place, you lean against things."

He laughed like he thought that was funny, but he was still conscious enough to uncross his arms. He leaned towards me, messing with my bubble. "Like this?"

Besides a catch in my breath, I refused to react. He was only trying to distract me...at least I thought he was. "Th—that's why you play the knight errant," I said, flicking his chest for emphasis, proud of how much control I had over my fingers—well, they were my fingers after all. I lifted my chin, looking directly into his eyes. "I don't know what you'd do if you felt a girl didn't need you. You look at me when you think I'm not watching. The only time you really seem like you're having fun is..."—I stopped—*when he was with me.*

His blue eyes darkened and I realized too late that I had gotten so into my tirade that I had moved far closer to him than I intended...or had I intended this? My hand was still on his chest. He looked at my lips. Only a breath away from a kiss. "Well, then I guess you know who I am," he said softly.

I held my breath. I was supposed to find out if he worked for some evil terrorist, not get close to him. But what would it be like to trust Lord Byron just this once? He laid his hand over my own and I could feel his heart quicken under our fingertips. I think I would like it. Wait? Was that the right answer? "Why don't you tell me who you are," he said. "I talk. You—" he hesitated.

Talk. I bit my lip down before I could say it. Another shadow passed by his Suburban and I stopped myself from colliding into Byron for protection. It was just AmyLee returning to her car for more groceries. My eyes darted nervously through the window, and I felt myself mumble out an excuse. "Sorry, I...I'm kinda..."

"—alluring and mysterious." His lips curved cryptically up. "Now, it's your turn, Madeleine. Who are you really? Suzy Q Miller? Prank war general extraordinaire? The *hottest girl I've ever seen.* A combination of everything, none of the above? You be honest with me. I get honest with you. That's the deal." *That was blackmail!* I hung back and his eyes filled with regret. He reached out, touching the white streak in my hair. "You're not afraid, are you?"

I stiffened. "*I* have nothing to hide."

His fingers left my hair, leaving behind a lingering sadness where my heart should have been. "When you lie, you don't show your gums. Did you know that?"

Everything was so wrong, but being with him had always felt perfect. He was right here and yet I had already lost him. My eyes watered. He watched me with growing concern. "And...the way you're holding your head right now? You're trying not to cry. Every time I see that...you're not trying to rip my heart out, are you *Mad Dog*?"

I winced. Really? He had just said Mad Dog? My anger wrestled with my sadness, and thanks to my self-preservation, my anger won.

He grinned in approval. "That's better. I'll take the wrinkled nose over the sad eyes any day. My favorite one, Madeleine, is when you try to stop your lips from twitching. That means you want to laugh. You love to laugh, but you've never had a man you could trust enough to be yourself around, so you chase them off. You're a bigger commitment-phobe than any June sixth I know."

My lips moved before I found words. "You are such a jerk."

"Sorry, we're talking about you." Byron reached for my hand, and unwound my fingers from his iPhone. Once he had it in his possession, he clicked it off. Tory was no longer a part of our conversation. He gave a low laugh. "Now that we can talk freely, I want you to know that no matter what you find out about me tonight, the way I feel for you isn't fake. It never was."

"What?" Listening to him, I half knew what his words meant. I think he was admitting that he worked with that cranky guy on Thanh's phone. Did that mean we were officially enemies? I searched his face and knew he wasn't lying; he was bad! *But I liked him*...and if I wasn't mistaken—his fingers trailed to my neck and he pulled me closer to him. Yep, he liked me too. I closed my eyes, all too aware that I was about to kiss Byron. And what about Thanh? My eyes opened. What about Holly? I pulled back and his eyes followed me; for once they were serious. One thought of Sandra jolted me into being sensible. If Byron wasn't a threat to the free nation, he was still a threat to women everywhere and now he thought he could play me too? I straightened. "We have things to discuss," I told him. "I have something you want."

"No," he said firmly, "you don't."

"Really? Really. I can't believe this. So, you're just going to let me take my backpack with me?"

He inclined his head soberly, and I felt my heart drop even lower. He was going to make me meet up with his scary partner instead of working out the negotiations with me. I was used to being on my own, but this felt worse. The man I couldn't get enough of was feeding me to the wolves. "Tell the bad guys hi for me," he said with a dry smile.

I lashed out in anger, my fingers scraping over the door handle. Maybe someday I'd look back and call myself a fool for getting involved in this whole mess. But I couldn't stop myself from doing what I was doing now, and for now that meant getting as far away from Byron as possible. I tugged the strap of my backpack over my shoulder while I still could. The door wouldn't budge. I tugged at it ineffectually, but it must have some stupid child lock on it. I started getting anxious. "Hey!" My voice broke. He wasn't holding me hostage, was he? "Byron!"

He reached over me and unlocked my door. "Be careful out there, cuz."

I pushed the door open. "I'll do what I want."

"I know. Don't hate me when you get my message." The moment my converses touched the pavement, I turned on my heel to stare at him. He could be talking about anything. He nodded at me, seemingly more in control of his emotions than I was, though he *leaned* back against his seat. I suppose I was back to wrinkling my nose I was so angry. We were quite the pair. "Talk to you soon," he said.

My breath caught at the sarcasm in his voice and for once I followed my own get-over-a-man tactic. "You're not the only player around here, ya know. This whole thing…us—whatever this is—was only a wager."

He had the nerve to laugh outright. "Like I haven't heard that one before."

I was pretty sure he hadn't, but I slammed his door for good measure and stalked away.

CHAPTER SIX

Day 113
2154 hours

"Have you ever made a mistake and realized it seconds too late. Those seconds yawned into deep misunderstandings that could never be corrected even if you had a couple million years? Those are some pretty powerful seconds, I'd say."

—Madeleine's War Journal Entry (Tuesday, June 5th).

Eerie silence flooded my apartment. "Hello?" My voice echoed into our dark living room. Everyone had deserted me. I tried the switch in the hall and heard a dull click. The light had burnt out. I picked my way through the darkness, trying to keep a clear head. It was pretty hard, considering Byron had almost kissed me, and due to my lame interrogation skills, I knew less about him than before. Even worse, time was out. Creepy-voice was expecting a call from me to make negotiations. There had to be a way to stall him, forget that I had practically challenged him to come get me.

I tried to hear past my shoes pressing into the ragged carpet. No heavy breathing. No shifting in the darkness. No one was waiting for me. I let out a shaky breath, my head finally clearing as I came up with a plan. I was going to outsmart this guy. He was meeting at Denny's in two hours. I could crash the party, but could I do it without getting killed? I had Thanh's control box as evidence now. What if I produced my evidence to the police and—? I sighed. They would just take it away and take me in. They wouldn't bother investigating the scene at Denny's. Thanh would be lost forever. And the control box was probably more important than everything else put together, which meant I had to plan a way to get Thanh *and* the box. In real life, it didn't seem very simple.

I tried the hall light and couldn't get it to work either. I hesitated under the archway. Two lights out. That was way too much of a coincidence. My feet rooted to the carpet in response. "Hello?" My heart felt unsteady. "Is anybody here?"

The seconds felt agonizing as I listened intently for some sound to give away the presence of an attacker. If some bad guy waited in the darkness, he would've grabbed me by now—I would have. My fingers scraped over the rough plywood of my bedroom door and I pushed it inward, feeling my way to the next light switch. It made a dull click under my fingers. It was either a blackout or Thanh's kidnapper had a taste for suspense. Using the moonlight from the window to make out the shadows of my bedroom furniture, I felt my way through my desk drawer to find my flashlight. A hand flashed out from under the bed and twisted around my ankle.

I screamed and Tory popped up from the bed, her red hair flying over her face. "How was the date?"

"What? Date?" I tried to pull my jumbled thoughts back together. "What are you talking about?"

"Remember? I heard your whole conversation in Byron's car. I was on the stake-out, so spill."

"Why did you turn out all the lights?"

"I didn't." She clicked on a flashlight and put it under her face, highlighting it in a most unflattering way. She wore her *Simon says I'm Hot* tee. "We have a black-out."

"Sounds convenient." I threw the backpack off my shoulder and unzipped it. More than likely the twins were trying to get back at us for something. I wasn't sure what, since I was sadly out of the loop with the latest pranks. I didn't want to think about other reasons for a blackout.

PRANK WARS

Unwinding my gym clothes from the control box, I found a physics book in its place. No...he...didn't. The control box was gone! Byron stole it—maybe while he was putting the moves on me. I knew physics books were heavy, but...that dirty player! Was this his message? "He turned on me!" I shouted out. "He's so...bad! He's the bad guy!"

Tory peered at the physics book, not getting it. "Why? Did he take Thanh?"

"I don't know!" I made a turn around the room, trying to gather my thoughts. It had to be true. Why did he steal her control box? I was going to make a deal for her. He didn't want to give her back?

"I don't believe it." Tory balled her hands into fists. It was an odd thing coming from her. "He's too good for that."

Then what was he doing with the control box? I needed to get to it before it was too late, but I was running out of help. "Where is everybody?"

"Oh, it's terrible. The guys took Kali's baby blanket and they're holding it hostage. And they're making her do all sorts of things to get it back, and AmyLee joined the guys, along with tons of other girls in the ward. Isn't that lame? So Lizzie had an idea and they went..."

"Wait, they're out pranking?" I never felt so betrayed. My life was in danger here.

"Uh, yeah."

I stared out the window, seeing all our hair supplies hanging from the windowsill just out of reach. That was the last straw. It was just another distraction set up by Byron to get my friends out of the way. He didn't have to lift a finger, just rile up the twins and they'd take care of everything. "Rotten pranksters." I tucked the heavy physics book under my armpit and threw Thanh's cell phone into the side pocket of my capris. Tory grinned and followed me out the door. Though missing a few initials from her CTR ring, I knew I could trust her. We had real bad guys to worry about, not silly little boys.

Shouts and screams littered the air in the guy's parking lot, but I headed straight for the middle of the melee, determined to get my army if I had to drag them all out by their pigtails. The rain had stopped only to be replaced by flying toilet paper, silly string, cheese wiz. The Hunkhouse was making their final stand against the Black Hole.

Kali rushed past me, looking like she had come straight from her cycling class. Her hair was scraggly and she had no shoes on. Even stranger, her face was free of all make-up. "It's the guys' fault!" she shrilled. She hid behind me, covering her ears. "Get rid of that noise! It's killing me!"

I glanced over at Tory and she shrugged. Blake peeled out of the shadows dressed all in black. Kali chucked some water balloons over my shoulder. Blake didn't try to dodge them. She missed him every time. Kali shrieked at him, "If you asked us on more dates instead of hanging out all the time, we wouldn't be doing this." She heaved her last water balloon at him and it skidded harmlessly past his feet.

"Unacceptable, Kali," I couldn't stop myself from saying. "Keep your eye on the target!"

Kali rushed around me and fell into Blake's arms, taking my advice quite figuratively. The girls were falling in droves, catching the men of their dreams—I had always assumed nightmares. Byron's tormented roommate Rock stumbled out of his apartment, looking disheveled. When did he start living at his own place? His heavy rock T-shirt was rumpled beyond recognition. And he was after Lizzie. Did he even know she existed? She was laughing and flirting. The strings of her apron trailed after her as she escaped. Her shoes were missing too. I felt like a stranger in my own cause. "Turn off that noise!" Rock shouted.

"Tell that to your roommates," Lizzie retorted. "They're the ones doing it!"

I glanced over at Tory. What noise were they talking about? I couldn't hear a thing. By the look of confusion on her face, she couldn't either. It seemed the only one on my side was as deaf as I was, but at least she didn't care about boys.

Adam blocked our pathway, his track pants swishing. Tory stopped short and their eyes locked. *What? No!* The twin? The cocky one? She couldn't possibly. She had no feelings that I knew of.

PRANK WARS

"Tory," I said in a warning voice. "I need you."

She nodded. "Right captain." She tried to spin away...until Adam held up a poster of Justin Bieber. Her mouth gaped open.

"Does this belong to you?" he asked.

She glanced over at me. "That isn't mine."

"Of course not." I tried to make a hasty exit with my only ally in tow.

Adam opened his big mouth: "Then I guess you won't mind if I dispose of this?"

We heard a ripping sound and Tory circled. Her long red hair flew around her shoulders like a flame. She was after him like thunder on lightning. "Tory, no!" It was just a trick. The ripping sound came from his mouth, but Tory tackled Adam before she realized he hadn't done anything to her precious poster. Adam laughed, holding it out of reach. She beat on his back, the gray pinstripes of her skinny jeans a blur with each wild kick. They joined the throng of fighting couples, leaving me behind in stunned silence. I hadn't seen that one coming at all.

Thanh's cell phone rang and after checking caller ID, I answered it in one fluid motion. "What do you want, Byron?"

"Are you alone?"

Of course. All of my allies had fallen. "You've really outdone yourself this time, Byron. Consider me clapping slowly and sarcastically."

"You got my message then?"

"Of course. Why did you do it?"

"I couldn't let you get in the way, now could I?"

My eyes narrowed. "Where are you?"

"Coming for you."

I turned to see Byron striding through the airborne whipped cream and flour. None of it touched his pristine white tee. Everyone else was covered in it. Most of them clutched at their ears. That's when I figured it out. No one over 26 could hear it, but it irritated everyone younger and sent them into this prank warring frenzy. Byron had stolen one of the frequency signals from Eric's lab and amplified it. He was attacking my soldiers—and my age!

Byron clicked off his phone and grinned crookedly at me. "Looking hawt, Dog."

I could only guess that meant I was covered in flour. "Well, if it isn't the great and clever Lord Byron? You are such a June 6th!" A tortilla hit him in the shoulder, disturbing our clever banter.

I laughed until something big and hairy jumped out at me. It had me by the arms. I shifted to see a gargantuan face leering angrily down into my eyes. Whoever it was looked vaguely familiar, but was covered in black war paint, blending in completely with all the other pranksters around here. It took me a moment to find my scream, but when I did, it startled even me. "Let me go!"

My attacker dragged me painfully away from the group. It didn't feel like a prank. His fingers dug into my arms and when I tried to twist away, he jabbed me hard in the side. I cried out in pain, a part of me realizing that he meant to hurt me. I panicked, knowing this guy had something to do with Thanh, not some flirty skirmish between girls and guys. I kicked him in the knee and he let out a grunt. His fist came at my face. I grimaced just before Byron jerked him back from me. I stumbled over my feet and landed into the ground.

My attacker aimed a clumsy punch Byron's way. He blocked it easily. The guy growled low under his breath and I stiffened when I saw him pull out a gun from his pleated jeans. Before I could shout out a warning, Byron had him by the arm, wrestling him back. I couldn't see who was winning. Byron aimed an elbow in the big guy's face. The guy grimaced in pain and butted his head against Byron's. His head whipped back, but Byron didn't let go. Instead he dealt the guy a vicious uppercut to the kidney. If the attacker got any more good hits in, we'd be in real trouble, especially if I didn't do something fast. I couldn't find a real weapon in the sea of fake ones. Water balloons, flour, toilet paper, whipped cream, cheese wiz, marshmallow cream. Old lady perfume! I grabbed it with trembling fingers.

PRANK WARS

"Mad!" Byron shouted. "Get out of here. Don't muck around." There was that accent again. The guy shoved Byron back, his hand against his chin. Byron was a lithe devil, but this guy was huge. Byron couldn't hold him back for long. "Madeleine!"

I rushed forward with the perfume and sprayed our attacker in the eyes. Both Byron and the guy fell back, their eyes watering. Byron took advantage of the opening and knocked the gun away. The big guy stumbled back, screaming out. Now that the attacker was somewhat incapacitated, I tried to figure out how I knew him. Even under all that paint, I never forgot a face, well, I shouldn't, especially someone clad in such outlandish clothes. He was wearing a *Wile E. Coyote* shirt for Pete's sake! "You're dead," he hissed at Byron—mighty bravely for someone not holding the gun anymore. "You won't live through the night."

Byron's form went dangerously calm. "What's your plan? To kill me with that stench?"

The guy reeked of old lady perfume. Sweat mingled with paint dripped down his chiseled face. "We want the girl."

My stomach tightened when I realized he meant me and not Thanh, but why? I didn't have the control box anymore. Byron cast him a menacing look, but he didn't pull the trigger. I hoped he'd do the normal thing and call the cops. I think we had some pretty good evidence for Brady and Oliveira now. "Tell your superior to keep away from her or he can't hold me responsible for what I'll do." Byron's accent was all over the place like he wasn't trying to hide it anymore. "He has what he wants. Now tell him to get lost."

Holding his head, the big guy glared and limped away with his message. I elbowed Byron. "Why did you let him get away?"

Byron squinted at me with his one good eye; the perfume had grazed him. "What is that awful stuff? It's nasty as..."—he didn't compare it to anything.

I identified his accent. "You have some explaining to do, New Zealand!"

"You said you got my message!" he accused.

"Yeah. You took the control box! Did you give it to whoever that guy works for? What's wrong with you?"

"I didn't give it to him...I *let* him have it. And that wasn't my message anyway." The physics book lay on the ground by the dumpster back where that guy grabbed me. Byron picked it up, black paint smudged all over his fingers. "Here's my message." He handed it to me. "Behind the front cover."

I opened the book. *"Don't worry, I'm with the CIA."* I glanced up at him. No invisible crayon, no lemon water, no blood, no nothing. "That's a really stupid message."

"Yeah, well your war journal wasn't much of a read either."

I hit him with the physics book, not hurting him in the least. "New Zealand's not with the CIA," I told him.

Byron took out a handkerchief and started wrapping his hand. His knuckles were covered in blood. "We're the SIS and we're your allies. The CIA needed my skills to make up a special team, mostly because I came to this school six years ago and know the culture already, plus I'm a physicist, speak passable Vietnamese and I'm fluent in German—that was a bonus from my mission."

No way. That would put him in his late twenties. Maybe early thirties. I always figured I was the older one. For once my age worked for me. "If you're the CIA then why aren't you after the guy who took the control box? Huh?"

"Yeah...because the CIA is a one-man operation? I thought you watched more movies than that?"

I gulped. If I hadn't just seen him fight, I would never have believed him. I didn't want him to be anything else but Byron, though CIA agent was better than believing he was a black-hearted kidnapper. "Who else is on the team?"

"Confidential."

I glanced around at all my friends with a suspicious eye. It could be any of them. They had the perfect cover; they were all idiots. "So what? You're some agent playing the field? Why did you let Thanh get taken then?"

PRANK WARS

"Just as you surmised." He tied off his bandage with a snap. "Thanh made a little someth'nk someth'nk for the government. Grad students do it all the time, but this one got the attention of some undesirables. They called me and the rest of my team on a protective detail to watch her and the *item of interest*. It's too powerful anyway. We're gonna destroy it. It won't see the light of day."

"But *they* have it now!"

He led me behind the dumpster by my elbow, giving us some privacy. "*They* think they have it," he said in an undertone. "We gave them a decoy…a fake. Get it?"

All that for nothing? "But they have Thanh?"

"No, we do. Everything's under control. She's in our protective custody."

Relief washed over me. I wasn't going to die tonight. At the same time, I felt incredibly stupid. "So, who's the bad guy then?"

"We call him the white hawk, our female agent does actually. She thinks he's hot."

"Sandra!"

"Where?" Byron turned, looking for her. "I don't see her."

"Knock it off. I get it now. She moved into the ward at the same time. You still talk after the break-up. I can't believe I didn't see it before." I laughed, partly in shock. "Sandra was way too mean to be real."

"Sorry to disappoint, but that's really how she is, cuz."

His New Zealand accent had the same effect chocolate and cologne had over other girls. He should probably suppress it so I could think clearly. "Why did you help me steal the fake control box, you jerk? That was a lot of work for nothing."

"It had to look real." He tugged on my arm, forcing me to follow him. He was stronger than I thought. "Let's get you somewhere safe."

How did I know he was telling the truth? "Wait, did you plant all the evidence then? The threatening note? The backpack? The keys?"

He laughed. "No." *What about the meeting at Denny's?* "You're just unlucky to the days," I heard him say.

My eyes narrowed at him. His dark hair was disheveled from the attack and he was smudged in black paint, but now that I saw him for what he was, I could see that he was as mischievous as ever. "Where are the bad guys now?"

"It's covered," he said. I dug my heels into the ground. If he didn't know about Denny's, it wasn't covered. "Look." Byron's eyes pleaded with me to keep moving. "I can just throw you over my shoulder and drag you out of here. None of *our friends* would question it."

He was right, and I tried to figure a way out of this. "Okay, assuming I go with you Byron, I have one last request." I smiled, making sure I showed my gums this time. "If we're safe now, I'm dying of hunger. What do you say to Denny's?" I watched to see if Denny's was significant to him.

Byron glanced down at his iPhone. "We have some time to kill, but...how can you possibly want to eat at a time like this?" *Byron didn't know where the drop was.*

My mind shuffled through the stored facts. The cranky guy threatened me so I would steal a decoy for him, and then in the next breath called Byron to say he had Thanh. Something wasn't right. Thanh didn't want to go with whoever stuffed her in that car. And if that had been the cranky guy? He didn't sound like someone I could trust, so why did Byron? I glanced over at him and immediately recognized that closed-off look. I'd never be able to convince him of any of this. No doubt he was already planning on packing me off to some safe house and then it would be too late.

"Yeah." I found myself nodding. "And it's redneck night, so...you need to fit in, so..."

He laughed. "Only in Provo would there be a redneck night."

"Are you saying you've never dressed up in all of your years of service?"

"Only suit and tie just like a good little spy." He was being sarcastic. "I've never gone hick." We only had an hour. I was sure his job was to distract me until after the drop-off. He came to a decision and gave a brisk nod. "Let's go then. You're not going anywhere without me."

I squared my shoulders, knowing I had to play this smart. I couldn't prove anything yet, but I was pretty sure Thanh's life depended on us being there. Byron slowed his long stride to match mine, following me to my diamond advertisement of a car where I had stashed my wigs and whatever else I planned to use as our covers tonight. The only difference was that I thought Tory would be tagging along with me instead.

Byron grimaced at my car. "And that's not conspicuous? I'm driving." Trust him to be rude about it, but as long as he suspected nothing, I'd take it.

CHAPTER SEVEN

Day 113
2334 hours

"Life is but a stage, I am merely an actor. The curtain will fall and in moments, it will all be over."

—Madeleine's War Journal Entry (Tuesday, June 5th).

    The long blonde wig looked a lot stranger on Byron than it would've on Tory, but he looked hot in it anyway, tying it into a ratty ponytail behind him. It wasn't exactly BYU standard, but it *was* redneck night, so no one would notice. I twisted my red wig into two braids to look like Pippi Longstocking. To complete the look, I gave Byron a tattered jean jacket and baseball cap then threw on an oversized slouchy shirt over my black one that said, *"I'm with Stupid."*

    We walked into the restaurant, ignoring the stares of the other rednecks. Well, at least Byron did. Most of Denny's patrons weren't rednecks either. They looked like a bunch of BYU students. To my relief, Byron didn't ask questions.

    "I'm totally twittering this." I heard someone laugh at their table. They stared at us and I tilted my chin up—going out in public looking like a fool was just one of the sacrifices I gave for my country.

    Byron's lip curled up at my discomfiture. He wasn't actually enjoying this, was he? "Don't look now," he told me, "but the paparazzi's here. Pose for the picture, pumpkin." I glanced up just in time to catch someone snap a picture at us from the booth over.

PRANK WARS

The waitress at the front studied my hair. I'm sure it looked great under the florescent lights. And yes, *that* was sarcasm. Her hair was almost as blonde as Byron's wig and teased high with a ponytail bobbing out beneath it all. She melted when she saw her male counterpart. Even when Byron looked like he had crawled from a beat-up pickup truck, I had competition. Byron leaned over the hostess's little podium with a familiar air. "This here's my girl, Ashley Q Miller May."

That was cruel. I returned the favor. "And this here's my sister's *ex*, Joe-Joe Rocky Joe Jr." I said it in the worst Southern drawl I could come up with.

Byron gave me a surprised look, which meant I had outdone him. "How's the grub in this place?" he asked the waitress, quickly adopting my twang. Apparently Midwestern accent wasn't the only thing he could mimic.

"Grub?" the waitress asked in confusion.

He grinned and I wished it was toothless. "Throw some road kill on the grill. We're a'celebratin'. This pretty little thing just..." His brow furrowed and he looked at me, thinking hard. I smiled prettily at him, hoping it would shame him into being nice. It didn't work. "She just won the Little Miss Rodeo Competition," he said. "You should' a seen her in the long john competition. She looked almost as good as my best huntin' dog. Go ahead, Suzy Q...uh...May. Tell her all about that spitting contest you done won."

My eyes narrowed at him. "How about I demonstrate it right *now*?"

The waitress blew a bubble with her gum, not impressed with any of my honors. "Get a booth, right?" Byron said with a wink. "Give us your finest, and dim the florescent lights, will ya? This here's a special night." He was making my skin crawl in a creepy way, except...the dimple in his cheek was standing out and I kind of liked it. That meant we were both messed up. The waitress gestured us to follow her. Byron tugged on my hand. "C'mon, cuz."

"Hey." I pulled away. "That's not short for cousin, is it?"

"Don't worry. We're kissing cousins." *That's what I was afraid of.* The waitress brought us to a shadowy booth. It cut us off from the rest of the world—a good thing if we were trying to hide, a bad thing if we were trying to find someone. I drummed my fingers against the table while the waitress passed us our menus. Byron leaned back on his bench, glancing up at her. "What kind of vittles you got?"

"I'm not sure. What are vittles?" the waitress began. I felt sorry for her. At the same time, she was in my way. I tried to peer past her to see who else was in the restaurant. I wasn't sure how I was going to find the team of kidnappers, besides checking their shoes to see if they matched the ones I saw from under Thanh's sink.

"Grits?" I heard Byron ask.

"What is...?"

"How about some gizzards?"

The waitress looked relieved that she finally understood what he was saying. "Yes. Yes, we've got that." She started writing it down.

"Well, we don't want that." Byron turned back to his menu.

I gave him an evil grin. "As long as we don't have to kill my pet pig for supper, I've got an appetite for most anything."

He met my eyes knowingly. "How about some biscuits and gravy." He read her name tag, "Hilary?" He leaned towards me, taking my hand in his. "I'm going all out for my sweet sugar dumpling. Forget the brats for the night, little girl." He peered up at the waitress as if bragging. "We got a dozen or so out on the farm."

I pulled my hand away. "He's talking about his dogs," I translated.

The waitress stared at me. "Are you wearing a wig?"

"She'll take a cheese sandwich," Byron said. He plucked my menu out of my hand and thrust both our menus at the surprised girl. He was really taking his part as sexist pig to heart. I glared at him. "Make it nice and burnt on both sides." He gave me a sly smile. "Just like your mom's home cooking, darling."

"Your ma!" I said after the waitress was out of earshot. I hoped he got that I was insulting him.

PRANK WARS

"What? This was your idea." Byron switched to his normal bored voice, but he still lounged on his seat like a womanizing hick. His eyes were alert, however, and his gaze swept the room. "I'm just making it more believable."

"Really? Because I thought you were a lot better at your covers than this?"

He hesitated for a second. "That's an insult, right?"

I rolled my eyes. *Apparently not.* "You'd better share your biscuits and gravy with me because I'm not eating a burnt cheese sandwich. I'm the one who's starving, remember?"

He watched me, not listening. "No offense," he said once I was done moving my mouth, "but I like your dark hair better."

I stared at him. "Did you hear what I said?"

"Yeah, but it's not like you're going to eat anyway." I scooted indignantly away from him, which only made him laugh. "Just admit you're up to something. We're not here because you're hungry. I know you better than that."

"You are so suspicious, Byron—just not enough. Okay. What makes you think Thanh is safe?"

His eyes grew weary. "I told you she was."

"What if I proved otherwise?"

"Unbelievable, Madeleine. Is that why you dragged us here?"

If I admitted that, would he drag me back out? Before I could answer, the waitress plopped gravy and biscuits on the table in front of him then gave me my cheese sandwich. It was well-done, but at least it wasn't black. Before I could switch it out for Byron's biscuits and gravy, I remembered I hadn't eaten all day, and took a huge bite. The waitress left and I gave Byron my most innocent look. "See, I'm eating." I spilled some cheese on my *"I'm with Stupid"* shirt.

"Nice touch. All over your Sunday best."

I tried to scrape it off, but it was there to stay the night. I glanced up at Byron, and saw that he was still watching me. I knew I had to buy myself more time. "All those pranks," I asked. "Did you do *any* of them?"

"Only the good ones." He gave me a secretive smile.

The door opened from outside, and the wind along with a loud group of BYU students barged their way into Denny's. *All girls and one guy.* I knew exactly who it was without looking, especially when I heard that loud bellowing laugh. Cameron filled the doorway in all his Abercrombie glory, battered pre-beat jeans and all. The girls danced around him in cut-off jeans and skirts. I tried to slink into my seat to hide. We weren't the only ones going to Denny's as rednecks.

"Don't worry." Byron looked amused. "I don't think he'll recognize you, Pippi." Cameron hadn't with my blonde look. Still the more hideous I looked, the more of a chance I had of blowing my cover. Byron met my eyes. "I'll take him out if he tries anything. You want me to pretend to be your boyfriend?"

After a moment, I nodded. Byron looked surprised and I shrugged to deflate his head. "It's just a cover. You do that all the time, right?" His grin broadened and he eased a little to the side to enjoy the show. The waitress released the booth next to ours to Cameron and his little harem. One of his girls had a giggle on her. They made it hard to properly scope out the restaurant. "You get all sorts of culture here," I muttered under my breath.

Byron finished his biscuits and wiped his lips with his napkin. "You ready to go?"

I planted my feet in my converses, munching slowly on my sandwich. The door opened again and I watched a happy couple walk inside. Nope. Too happy. It was impossible to get a good look at everyone from our booth. "What time is it?" I asked

Byron checked his watch. "June 6th. Your ill-fated anniversary, Miss Havisham. This wasn't exactly the party I had planned for you."

I felt my stomach lurch, but not for the reasons I thought it would two days ago. *They were meeting here at midnight.* I pulled out Thanh's cell phone, seeing he was right. It was midnight. The restaurant bubbled with suspects, and Byron wasn't taking any of this seriously. I rested the cell phone against my cheek, trying to decide what to do. That guy's number was on Thanh's cell. I found a *formerly blocked* call and pressed reply. A phone went off somewhere behind us. I twisted, seeing the back of a blond head, a tanned neck, and broad shoulders. The target sat at a table with another guy, whose head was tilted away from us. They both searched their pockets. The happy little ringtone could've come from either of them, which meant they worked together.

"Gotcha." I closed the phone and the ringing stopped. I met Byron's eyes. "The suspect is here."

"Excuse me. What?"

"One of those guys at that table over there," I disclosed. "I just called him." I leaned over the table to Byron. After a confused look, he met heads with me. "I made a deal with this guy to get Thanh back. Funny thing is why would he do that if he worked *with you*? He stopped bothering me after you released the decoy. He's not a nice guy. He left threatening messages on her phone...all the time."

"Wait." Byron looked confused. "You talked to somebody else besides me?"

"Yes. He said he had Thanh. Why would he lie about that?"

"I'm sure it's a—"

"Set up," I finished for him. "You have to believe me. Your superiors are lying to you." My phone vibrated. The jerk tried to call me back, but I was too smart to leave the ringer on. I texted him back. *"We're onto you...White Hawk."*

I held my message up to Byron with a sly smile and pushed send. Byron was seconds too late before he pulled it from my grasp. "Don't!"

"He has Thanh," I explained.

"I told you *we* did."

"Did you see her with your own eyes?"

"Look, this isn't how we work. I do my job. They do theirs. I'm not involved in every part of the..." He took a steadying breath. "We shouldn't be here. If this is a sting, we're gonna compromise their mission. We need to get out of here."

The blond was on his cell phone and he stood up from the table, looking out the window into the darkness. He had cargo pants and Nikes. I recognized his profile immediately. "Eric."

Byron's hand landed over mine. "Wait! Don't move. He's in on this, alright."

"He works with you?"

Byron ran a hand through his hair—only to find that stupid wig. He didn't remove it, especially now. "No. And we never figured out how you wound up with him in the first place."

"He's Sandra's friend…and your roommate, Rock's?"

Byron shook his head at me. "He was the x factor. Sources told us that we had an information leak, but who it was remained a mystery. That's when we were sent to watch over Thanh. We didn't know his identity until he showed up with you."

"You knew he was dangerous and you let him follow me around. Are you crazy?"

"We had to figure out if you were in on this too."

"What? Me?"

"Oh c'mon! Eric made arrangements to do a physiology experiment at the Eyring building? Really, Mad? It's only engineering over there. The fact that you didn't know that made you suspect." He motioned for the waitress to bring the check.

"—because everybody knows that," I slurred sarcastically. "I'm a General Studies major. Give me a break."

"Look, when the target transferred from the U…"

"Well, why didn't you say that from the beginning? He's a hardened criminal then."

He leveled an annoyed look at me. The waitress set our check down and flounced off. Byron pulled out some cash from his wallet, keeping his voice down. "He was a surprise to us too. He was the one who left the threatening note on Thanh's door. I only started tailing him at *Battle of the Bands*. If it means anything, Mad, I always thought you were clean. Of course, it would've made you more interesting if you weren't."

PRANK WARS

My eyes narrowed. "Excuse me?"

He chuckled low under his breath. "Mad, no, I'm really glad you're on our side."

"Because I'd take you out otherwise."

His expression took on a challenging glint. "That would've been the fun part...but honestly, I've never—" He got silent and I pulled an eyebrow up to get an answer out of him. He let out a breath of surrender. "I've never had more fun with an ally, so it actually would've sucked if you were on the wrong side. Okay?" I smiled. He considered me an ally? He tugged on my hand. "Let's go."

The door opened from the outside and another of my favorite people made her grand entrance. As always Sandra wore her heels, the straps spiraled in zigzags around her ankles. She tore big sunglasses from her face, posing at the door to search out the restaurant, clutching her LV designer bag in a fierce grip. I ducked, more terrified than I had been all night. We were going to blow her cover. "She's going to kill us, isn't she?"

Byron wasn't listening. He had grown stiff. "What's she doing here?"

As soon as Sandra spotted Eric, she gave him a brilliant smile she never reserved for her roommates, only for cute guys...and double crossing criminals at that. Eric pulled out a seat and she made her elegant way to him, sitting across from him with daintily crossed legs. The other guy at Eric's table greeted her, giving me an excellent view of his face. He had nondescript face and hair, could easily get lost in a crowd. It all connected in my head. I recognized him from the gym. "All these assets are working together to catch the guy threatening Thanh?" And I had bumbled into their way over and over again. I was worse than a third wheel.

Byron glanced over, looking irritated, but not at me. "What's Hölle doing here?"

I made a face. "Holly?" *The Holly* that Byron had been calling? That was no name for a guy, which made me even more fascinated. "Good cover."

"No, it's his real name. I work for him. Ian Hölle."

Oh no. Byron was right. They were already taking care of things. I was way over my head. "Okay, let's get out of here," I whispered.

"Sit down…and keep that stupid wig on. None of these people are supposed to be here. Eric has the control box already."

"That's how you did it? You took the *decoy* out of my backpack and left it behind in the lab for Eric to find?"

"If I hadn't caught up with you tonight, you'd be dead. He never would've let you leave with it alive."

Oh. That was a disturbing thought. "And now they're trying to gain his trust?—find the others who work with him?"

"No!" Byron shook his head furiously, but kept his voice down. "Not those two. It's not their job. Sandra and Hölle were supposed to escort Thanh to a safe house."

Hölle swept the room with a long and hard look. Byron took my hand calmly, giving me an intimate smile. "Look at me." His fingers tangled through mine, but I had enough sense to keep up the act. With the worst disguises in history, this would take a lot to make it look real. Despite the danger, my skin reacted to his touch. I took a steadying breath. "Well, I suppose this is keeping you preoccupied," Byron said under his breath. "Thanks to you, that was my job for the day." His eyes watched me tenderly, and for once I wondered if it wasn't all part of the act.

"Going on a date with another woman?" I whispered. "That's how you keep a girl preoccupied?"

He gave me a tense smile. Of course it did. "The date with Sandra also doubled as a debriefing," he said. "They were keeping us both busy while they did their dirty work." He let out a frustrated sound. "No. Don't look back." Apparently Hölle was still acting as look-out. I couldn't see what was happening and the tension was killing me. Byron was kind enough to narrate for me, probably to stop me from turning back and transforming into a pillar of salt. "He's giving her something in a briefcase."

"He's returning the control box. He feels guilty."

PRANK WARS

He snorted at my sarcasm. If Sandra and Hölle were supposed to escort Thanh to safety, that meant they had her somewhere close by—but where? We had absolutely nothing to bargain with to get Thanh back. If they had lied to Byron about why they had Thanh, they had lied about the control box too. "Byron," I said. "The control box wasn't a decoy, was it?"

He shook his head slowly. I felt my heart sink. Now it was in the wrong hands. But what was it for? Would a lot of people die because we got the box for them? Byron's eyes didn't leave Hölle's table. "I need to figure out what they're up to."

"How?"

He shrugged. "You need to leave and tell someone what's going on." He grew silent, thinking hard. "I don't know who to trust at headquarters. Just call the cops, alright?" I tried not to panic. No police officer would take me seriously, especially Brady and Oliveira. Byron squeezed my hand. "Under law, they have to investigate your claim. Tell them it's a domestic abuse problem…"

The waitress wandered over to us, carrying food for another table. "You *are* wearing a wig," she accused. She held a tray with an order of salad without the dressing. That would be Sandra's order.

I fumbled with Thanh's cell phone. "What do you have for dessert?" I asked the waitress. I found the settings on Thanh's phone, setting them on auto-answer. The waitress tried to adjust her tray to give me the menu from the front pocket of her apron. I nodded at Byron. "Hold that tray for her, will you?"

"You can't," she started.

I gave Byron a look and he acted the distraction, reaching for her tray. My fingers joined his on the tray and I slipped Thanh's cell phone under the pile of napkins next to Sandra's plate. "Actually," I said. "I guess I'm not that hungry for dessert."

The waitress popped her gum in surprise. After looking from Byron to me, she left us to give Sandra her order. Byron let out a breath. "What did you just do?"

"Bugging them. Give me your phone." With a questioning look, he dug out his iPhone and handed it to me. I inspected it. The usual Ski-Utah screensaver was gone. It wasn't the one I returned to him at the gym. "Where's your other phone?" I asked.

"The CIA supplied me with this one when the other came up missing. Just one of the perks."

I turned it over in my hand. "Did Hölle give you this?"

"Madeleine!"

"Sorry. What's Thanh's number?" Treating me to an incredulous look, he gave it to me anyway. I punched it in. "Her phone will automatically answer our call," I explained. "Then you can listen to everything they say. It's our usual phone tampering protocol."

"And you don't think Sandra will find Thanh's phone in her food?"

"Are you kidding? That girl doesn't eat." I pressed send, calling Thanh's phone then gave it back to Byron, muting our side of the conversation.

He held it to his ear. After a moment of breathless silence, he grinned. "We could use someone like you on the team."

"Lucky for you I'm available tonight."

With his free hand, he pulled out his other iPhone with the Ski Utah screensaver, typed his new number into the contacts, and passed it off to me. "I'm under *your new boyfriend*," he told me in altered tones. That forced a jittery smile out of me. I slid it into my pocket.

"Thanh's still alive," Byron reported under his breath. "Hölle has her hidden away somewhere." He leaned against the table, kneading the back of his neck while concentrating on the conversation. The length of his lashes hid the worried expression in his eyes until he glanced up at the door. They clouded with resignation. "A hostile's at your six o'clock. He's blocking the exit." This time I refrained from looking behind me. Byron took a steadying breath. "He's the same guy who grabbed you an hour ago. We need a distraction to get you past him." Loud laughter interrupted us from Cameron's booth. Byron's eyes gravitated to them.

PRANK WARS

"No!" Even I had my limits. "How am I supposed to...?"

"Pull a honeypot. Use your feminine wiles."

"You know I don't have any of those."

He looked distracted, listening in on Sandra's conversation. "C'mon, Mad. It's just an operational cover. You got any toilet paper on you?"

This was beginning to sound suspiciously like a Muppet scheme. "Toilet paper?"

"Call your ex and threaten his car with it. Anything to get him running out of here. Then sneak out with him and get the cops for me." Byron was still caught up with the hostile's negotiations on the other line. "Thanh's not talking," he reported. "There's still a piece missing from the device. She won't tell them where it is."

I took a deep breath, trying to gather my nerves. If I didn't bring in Cameron, Thanh could die. I didn't even want to think about what might happen to Byron. How could I get Cameron's cooperation? I knew him better than anyone else. He was lazy, selfish, thoughtless, and wouldn't hesitate to leave a female in danger. I didn't really have much to work with. He used other people's money, had no independent thought, he liked to eat...he really liked to eat. How was I going to get him out of here?

Byron still watched me expectantly. "Tell him it was a wager."

I straightened in shock, but it gave me the glimmer of an idea. "I can't be with you," I said to Byron in a louder voice. "My heart belongs to someone else. It will always be Cameron. *Cameron Hornberger*. I'm sorry...Jeremy."

Byron adjusted the phone on his ear. "He doesn't know you exist," he growled a reminder.

Ah yes. I was still Suzy Q Miller. "Well, he's still a great guy, cool and...and...hot. I just can't stop thinking about...Cameron. This will never work between us, Jeremy. I'm sorry."

The table next to us went silent. Byron bit his lip. "But he doesn't want you, and I want you." He slipped me his keys. Too bad we couldn't switch wigs too. Cameron always liked the blondes better, but I had the advantage of being female, breathing and hopelessly in love. Maybe like last time, Cameron wouldn't recognize me.

"It isn't fair to you," I told Byron. "Just…forget about me." I stood up. I saw Cameron's stiff shadow on the screen that separated us. He didn't move. The giggly girl let out another nervous giggle across the wall. After a moment of melodramatic waiting, Cameron stretched to his feet. He tried to loudly signal his friends back, but they followed behind him, nice and tacky just like I hoped they would.

Byron blew me his signature kiss with two fingers as I passed. It gave me courage, and I turned from him, edging behind the wall away from Eric. His monster of an assassin still waited by the door. The face paint was mostly rubbed off—especially around his red eyes where I got him with the perfume. Stepping closer, I knew where I had seen him before. *Dune Guy.* He had been leaving my apartment with Eric a few weeks ago, just before I found that threatening note on Thanh's door. I must've caught the two after plotting with Sandra to steal her control box. It was ironic that I had been right about them from the beginning. They were dirty spies—playing much deeper than I thought.

Cameron approached me, towering over me. He was possibly the same height as this assassin, just not as bulky. His leather wristband dangled fashionably from his wrist. He cleared his throat, but before he could talk, I stepped away from him. He took another step. I took another one, closer to the assassin and the exit. My skin tingled with fear. It had been a long time since I had appreciated Cameron this much. He had always been tall and strong, even though I couldn't imagine him fighting *anyone* unless he was backed into a corner. Maybe I could find one.

"You coming from a costume party?"

I swiveled to him and played nervously with my fingers. Cameron was always good at introductions. Getting him to stay was the hard part. "I couldn't really enjoy it." I tried to make my voice sound unlike mine, but natural. It was harder than I imagined. He had no problem with the act, and it was easy enough to lead him to the door with me. I wondered what seething girl he was leaving behind to foot the bill.

PRANK WARS

"Who are you supposed to be?" he asked.

I beamed at him, wondering why he couldn't figure out it was me—maybe because I looked too happy to see him. "Who do you want me to be?"

"You."

Did he recognize me? A chill ran through me, and I willed him not to give away my cover. We were past Eric's strange sidekick and I nudged the door open to escape. Cameron pushed his shoulder against it, stopping me from going outside. "I've wanted to talk to you for a long time now."

The blood drained from my face. *Dune Guy* would catch on any second. The smell of old lady perfume was strong on him. "Outside," I managed to whisper.

Cameron's muscular arm brushed against my bare one and he shoved the door open, letting me through. "Outside it is." His eyes backed up his words. Cameron sounded like a man caught up in the moment. Byron was going to pay for this. We reached freedom in the parking lot, and I rested my hands on my cargo pockets, taking quick breaths. One glance behind Cameron told me that *Dune Guy* wasn't after us.

"I was talking about a different Cameron Hornberger," I hurriedly told him.

He grinned. "Uh huh. So, that was you at *Battle of the Bands*, wasn't it?"

"Look." I readjusted Byron's keys in my hands, not sure how to talk myself out of this one. Despite my tough words, I wasn't cruel enough to give him the wager line. Something inside me still cared for Cameron. Maybe I could just run away. "Um," I managed to get out. "I don't really want to go out again."

"Whoa, whoa." He held his big hands up. "Who said anything about going out?"

I laughed in embarrassment. "Well, good. I guess that's settled then."

For once he looked subdued. "You do know what today is, don't you?"

Everything lurched uncomfortably in my stomach. Of course I knew. June 6th. I had dreaded this day the moment we broke up, though now the actual day threatened to erase its significance from my memory. "Yeah, weird, huh?" I muttered almost to myself. I turned from him, making my way to Byron's Suburban.

The girls piled out the door after Cameron as he watched me slip away. He looked a little confused. "Where are you going?"

"To save the world." I ripped my red wig off, blowing out my cheeks to release the tension. "Thanks Cameron. I couldn't have done it without you." I unlocked the door on Byron's Suburban, my heartbeat out of control. The girls talked loudly now, casting me looks of amusement, pity, jealousy. One of them brushed against a silver BMW and screamed.

She scrambled into Cameron's arms. Despite the awkwardness, he laughed, looking pleased in his role of protector—especially in front of me. She was a pretty little blonde and judging by the sound of her high-pitched scream, she was the giggler. "I thought I heard something from that car," she cried. "It sounded like a cat."

A cat? Instead of getting in, I closed Byron's door and peered through the windows of the silver BMW. There was nothing, except—I heard it again. It was in the trunk. This car was Eric's. "Thanh!" I whispered. The muffled sound got louder. It had to be her. I picked up a rock.

"What are you doin—?" Before Cameron could stop me, I smashed the window in on the driver's side and pulled off one of my layers of shirts, wrapping it protectively around my arm. "Stop!" he shouted.

I ignored him, thrusting my hand into the car to find the trunk release. The trunk popped and I rushed around the BMW. Thanh lay motionless inside, looking like a page ripped out of time. She wore the same skinny jeans and rumpled baby doll top from the night she was taken. Her eyes were big and her mouth was covered with duct tape. The ends of it had rolled up and she made a sad little moan. I pulled it off gingerly, knowing it would hurt. She gasped for air. Tears streamed down her face and I hugged her small body close. "Thanh, are you okay?"

Cameron looked more confused than ever. The girls huddled around us, most of them at a loss for words. "Should we call the police?" one of them asked.

I peeled off the duct tape from Thanh's wrists. She caught her breath in fear, her eyes darting to something behind my shoulder. I turned in time to see Eric running for us in a full sprint. I shrunk back, pulling Thanh behind me. "Get away from her," I shouted. There had to be something to fight him with, but what if he had a gun? I couldn't let him take her again.

I forced myself not to close my eyes at the coming impact just as Cameron stepped in front of us, shielding us with his body. "Get back," he told Eric in a commanding voice. It even impressed me. I heard a shout and then a scuffle. I peered around Cameron's broad shoulder, seeing Byron—the hick—tackle Eric to the hard pavement. Eric hit his head hard. I pulled out my old lady perfume from my pocket.

"Wait!" Thanh's fingers were free and they scraped over me.

I patted her arm, trying to ease her painful grip. "Don't worry. We've got this."

Eric tried to scramble free, but Byron had him. Cameron and his girls watched in shock. Byron wrestled Eric to the ground, and dragged out cuffs from his jeans. I jumped next to the two with my weapon in hand. Byron shot me a look that tried to pin me down too. "Oh no, you don't. Not the perfume again!"

"Stop!" Thanh rushed past me and threw herself over Eric, almost tackling me in the process. "Don't hurt him." Byron squinted up at her, confused, his blonde wig askew. She let out a wracked sob when she recognized him. "You've got the wrong guy, Byron! It's Eric!"

"He...he kidnapped you," I tried to explain. It came out lame.

"No! No! He was helping me." She hugged Eric desperately.

Eric tried to reassure her by squeezing her hand. It was the only part of him free. "Thanh. Don't worry about me."

Byron scrambled to his knees, allowing Thanh to free Eric, but he still looked like he might tackle him again. "He's my boyfriend," Thanh explained. "He saved my life."

Our eyes went to Eric and he licked his dry lips. "They said they'd kill her if I didn't give them the control box. I had to do it. I'm sorry. I did everything I could, but I made a deal…for her."

Thanh wouldn't let him go. Byron's eyes went to me. "That might explain why Eric didn't kill you, Madeleine."

"Yeah, but…" *Two timer!* Why did Eric have to flirt with me to get what he wanted? Had his feelings for me gotten the best of him? No. Probably not. My cheeks burned at the betrayal. Maybe it was my natural distrust, but I couldn't let it go. "Okay Eric, why was she in your trunk?"

"They stole my car." He ran his hands down Thanh's black hair. "Are you okay?"

"You seemed mighty close to *Dune Guy!*" I pressed.

"Who?"

I tried to point out the wannabe assassin, but he was gone. Where were the rest of our Denny's friends? Byron noticed the same time I did. He sprang to his feet. "We lost them."

"As soon as they heard the screams outside, they ran," Eric informed us with a solemn voice. "They got what they wanted. They don't need us anymore."

Byron abandoned us and rushed for his car, pulling off his sagging wig at the same time. "They said they were gonna test this thing out. Where'd they go, Eric?"

This would prove whose side Eric was on—at least to me. Eric's eyes were wary. "I can only guess some place high."

"Somewhere where they could set up wireless antennas," Byron surmised.

"You don't think they would test it here?" Thanh freed Eric from her clinging fingers, fear filling her face. "They can't! They'll kill us all!"

"What?" That diverted me from trying to find Eric guilty. "What will kill us all?"

Eric scrambled to his feet, bringing Thanh up with him. "The device locates targets and assassinates. It's lethal."

"But they don't have the capability," Byron argued. "They haven't set up any receptors or anything. It could take days."

"Unless they already have it set up?" Thanh rubbed her raw fingers against her face. She knew what she was talking about. "Everything's in place. The control box is the last piece of the puzzle…almost, but not quite."

"They said there was a missing piece," Byron said. "Can you confirm that?"

She nodded. "Yes, to the frequency remote. Did you look in your backpack?"

He shook his head, looking grim. I stepped forward, giving a halfhearted wave. "They stole it before I could get it out of there." It hurt to admit, especially when Thanh's face drained of all color like that.

"Then they have it all," she said in a hopeless voice.

"No." Byron shook his head. "They might not. We might have a chance."

I was as much out of the loop as Cameron and friends. "I don't understand."

"The missing piece will enable them to lock onto a frequency," Byron explained, "A target. And then that target will be assassinated."

"All they'd need to do is lock into a cell phone," Thanh said through quivering lips. "They'll target its frequency and kill whoever has it. The victim doesn't have to pick up the phone even. It's as simple as getting one call and you're dead."

Byron took a deep breath. "They're going to reach out and touch someone."

"Really Byron? Was that really necessary?" I cried. "Thanh! Why did you invent something like this? What were you thinking?"

"I wasn't trying to! I wanted to invent free energy…like Tesla. I…I…" she glanced at my blank face, "in layman's terms, I wanted to send energy through frequencies by priming the air. One push of a button and it powers a dead car on the road by locking onto its frequency, another zap and it powers a whole city. No need for generators or batteries or gas."

"But they'll only use it against us." Byron pushed from us to pace the parking lot. I knew he was trying to formulate a plan. It was almost impossible when we didn't know what direction Sandra and Hölle had gone. "As soon as the government recognized the project's destructive capabilities as a potential weapon," he said, "our team was sent on a PSD to keep an eye on Thanh and shut down the project if necessary. Only they sent the wrong people."

Thanh let out a low moan. "We've got to do something before it's too late!"

Eric wrapped an arm around her. "I won't see you in danger again. They'll kill anyone who's a threat."

That was all of us.

Thanh's shoulders lowered. "A lot of people will die if we don't do something. The device won't just kill its target, but anyone standing in its path. It isn't fully functional yet. The test run will be a disaster."

"I've got to warn headquarters," Byron said. He was a mess. Black paint blemished the whiteness of his once pristine tee. His jeans were ripped down the knee, his dark hair mashed down like a cat licked it. He looked very un-Byron-like—more so because I never saw him look so much like a soldier. "I'll make them listen," he growled, bringing his iPhone to his ear then turning pale, he lowered it. "The device is on."

My heart dropped. "How do you know?"

"It's wiping out all communication. They're priming the air." Testing out Byron's theory, I picked up his old iPhone. The screensaver glowed through my hand. The reception was dead. We were stuck in the current of a nightmare. Byron met my eyes. "It's interfering with the frequencies."

PRANK WARS

Cameron and his girlfriends messed with their cell phones with no luck. Eric cradled Thanh's head against his shoulder to comfort her, but his eyes were on me. What was his problem? He claimed his girl, now leave me alone. I lowered my borrowed phone. Byron climbed onto the roof of his car, the veins on his arms standing out. His Suburban groaned in complaint as he scanned the distance. "Where's the tallest building around here?"

Obviously. It covered the moon with its long and mournful shadow. "The Provocity towers," I breathed. *How ironic.*

Byron dropped his hands. "It's going to need all that electricity to make this thing work for its test run. Just tap into the cabling and wires that already exist. One generator would be more than enough. Once they figure out how to prime the air, they'll test it. They've got their dish, their antennas. All they needed was that missing piece to target the frequency."

"And thanks to us, they've got it." I met Eric's eyes over Thanh's head. He looked down.

Byron scooted off the black Suburban, grabbing my arm in a strong grip. "Head to the police department. They're the closest thing we've got for help around here."

"Not Madeleine," Eric reminded him. "They won't listen to her."

I cast him an angry look. Byron stared at him then nodded. "You're right, not Mad." I glared at Byron as he circled to Cameron.

Cameron threw his hands up. "I don't even know where the police station is!"

Did anybody? The girls studied their painted toes with renewed interest. "Center Street," Byron intoned slowly. "You might be able to find a signal to call them once you're far enough away from here." He still held tightly to my arm. "You're not coming with me, Madeleine." He dragged me from his car. Byron had always seemed so composed before turning agent. Before I could argue, he tried to give me back to Cameron. "Take Mad and Thanh out of here."

"No." I peeled my fingers free from Byron's. "You need my help."

"Stop being such a martyr." Eric gripped my elbow and shoved me headfirst into the leather bench seat in Byron's black Suburban. I wasn't sure whether to thank him or not. "You need our help," he told Byron. "I'm going too. Someone has to cover you."

"No!" Thanh wouldn't have any of it. "Eric. Please, stay with me!"

Eric's fingers found her hair and he stroked the long strands away from her face. "I'm responsible for this. Now that you're safe, I have to help these guys. It's the least I can do. Get the police. Explain everything to them. Please, Thanh. I don't want anything to happen to you, not after all I've done to keep you safe."

Thanh's lip trembled and she nodded. Her fragile eyes tearing up. I was touched…in an odd sort of way. He *still* had been flirting with me to get the device. Dirty player. Byron climbed into his car and gave me an exasperated look when he saw me on the bench next to him. "What are you still doing here?"

"Don't ask stupid questions."

Luckily he didn't. He just groaned. "Don't be too happy about this. You're not going to like it." Byron turned the keys in his ignition. The radio spat out fuzz—another side-effect of the stolen device. It was too distracting and he flipped it off, throwing his arm around me to back out of Denny's parking lot. We sped down Bulldog Avenue. The night was black ahead of us, the towers bathed in a blanket of velvety ink.

"Tell me exactly what we're doing," I said.

"It's like Thanh said," Byron said through tight lips. "She wanted to be like Tesla—you remember the crazy guy, right? He wanted free energy. Well, he's not so crazy. He had a theory on how to do it and if Thanh is right, those terrorists will have set everything up exactly as he proposed on top of the Provocity towers. It'll transmit energy from the generators straight into the upper atmosphere and prime the air like a pump. Then it will pluck the energy from the air to cause a huge chain reaction with the lower atmosphere that will eventually reach the dish antenna these terrorists set up. There it can focus and reflect this beam anywhere. If they focus it on something about the size of a human head, it's guaranteed to kill."

PRANK WARS

It was the closest I'd ever paid attention to any scientific explanation. "This is just the test run, so anything can happen," Byron said. "I'm sure they'll point it at someone important and famous and in the media frenzied aftermath, every terrorist will be scrambling to get their hands on it. It's in its crude stages now. But once they work out the kinks, it will change the nature of assassination. Find the frequency of a target and key enemies are gone. No one will be safe."

"With a cell phone."

"More than that. They're working on identifying people in more sophisticated ways, though for now, anything with a frequency signal can be targeted. Webcams, GPS, internet users, you name it."

"Why didn't the government shut down the project?"

"The potential of the experiment was too overwhelming. According to Tesla, energy can be pulled from the air and transmitted anywhere. It would've meant free energy to all with minimal cost and nonexistent prices at the pumps, but then…well, anything can be made into a weapon. They'll sell it to the highest bidder."

Eric sat silently in the back. I moved around to face him. "How did *you* get involved…lover boy?" —Okay, so I should have laid off the sneer.

The leather seat groaned when he shifted. "Thanh and I have been dating for a few years now. She started getting threats and didn't know who to trust. I transferred from the U to get closer to her. It just got worse from there."

It was a romantic story; that's why I was having a hard time swallowing it. "What about the first time I saw you? You were with that guy who attacked me."

"Walter?"

That was not the name I imagined for him. "Uh, *Dune Guy*?"

Eric nodded with a grimace. "They told me they'd hurt Thanh if I didn't help them. I had to do what they said."

"But Thanh switched her backpack with Byron, and you stole it back. Wait. Did you have it when I jumped into your car with you?"

"She was dead without it. They weren't even supposed to know the backpack was hers, but the information leaked. I don't know how."

That one was my fault. I let Sandra know. I remembered country station night when Eric broke into our apartment. Soon after, our keys to our complex came up missing. I stared at the road ahead of me. The white lines sped past in the darkness. "Did you steal our keys too?"

"I just wanted them to leave Thanh alone." He sounded testy. "I thought maybe those were the keys everyone was looking for."

That made sense, but still there were a few holes. I decided to poke at them. "Why did you say you kidnapped Thanh when you talked to me on her cell phone?"

"I never said I kidnap...why would I say that? What? You don't believe me?"

I leaned back in my seat, not answering. I supposed it was Hölle who had threatened me over the phone then. That made sense, since he called Byron immediately afterward to debrief him on Thanh. Hölle had left the threatening note too. Eric really was some stupid boyfriend trying to protect his girlfriend...and he flirted with me to do it.

I turned to Byron to see if he was buying this. One look at him and I doubted he heard a word. His brow furrowed in concentration, his whole body taut as he raced us closer to danger. The lights faded out down the street. I swiveled, seeing the lights flicker off behind us like blown out candles. "Did you see that?"

"It's like turning on a hair dryer," Byron said. I was surprised he had heard me. "The lights are going to dim."

The Suburban stalled and came to a full stop. We waited a moment, smothered in silence. The only light came from the full moon above the Provocity towers. It covered a huge part of the sky. Eric clasped the back of my seat, pulling my hair with it. "It affects cars too?"

"Their electrical systems." Byron shoved his door open, fishing through his emergency kit in the back. He pocketed some light sticks. "The air's polluted with electro smog. They've started the test run. Let's go. We don't have much time." Under the light of the moon, we slammed the Suburban doors behind us. Our shoes slapped against the pavement as we ran full speed for the Provocity towers...and whatever else waited for us there.

CHAPTER EIGHT

Day 114
0134 hours

"People are getting hurt. I'm not talking broken hearts or Jell-O packets in the shower heads; I'm talking real scary stuff. Things like this happen in New York, Chicago, Ogden even, but here in Provo? Something strange is going on here...and it's not just the students.

No one is what they seem. The player? A terrorist. The heart-breaker? A no good spy. My neighbor? They've taken her. The jerk? A pretty decent guy. My roommate? An utter sneak—but then again I always knew that.

Grades? Dates? Pranks? They're nothing to the danger that stares us in the face. You've got to believe me. If I could go back before everything—before the world went terribly wrong—would I change what I've done or have these meaningless pranks made me better able to fight this?"

—*Madeleine's War Journal Entry (Wednesday, June 6th)*

Well, that's what I would've written if I had my war journal handy. Later I would...*if I survived*. For now my war journal sat in my cargo pockets waiting to tell a tale that might not be told. I sprinted after Byron and Eric. It was obvious who was trained by the CIA, KGB, SIS, whatever it was.

PRANK WARS

I still could barely take everything in. Eric was good then bad then good, though in my opinion, still a double-crossing cheat, who was afraid of commitment. Didn't he say he was dating Thanh for years? Byron was an undercover agent. I had been right about Thanh all along. Cameron was actually a decent individual. To top that off, Sandra was even meaner than I thought, which I had no idea was possible. Oh, and terrorists had taken over Provo. All in all, it had been a pretty eventful morning.

Tall chain-link fencing surrounded the Provocity towers on all sides. They were spiked on the top. As we veered closer, it seemed impossible to get in, but I was wrong. Byron took the fence in a couple of leaps and scrambled over to the other side, almost losing the side of his shirt on the barbed ends. Eric did likewise. I wasn't about to be outdone. Taking a deep breath, I jumped and scaled to the top. Metal jutted out from it and caught my capris. I wrestled free, trying to figure out a way to get past this mess.

"Mad!" Byron called out. "Just go back."

That was the clincher. I used the main pole as a handhold and jumped, ignoring the pain that seared through my hand. I hit the ground and winced, holding my scraped palm up to the light of the moon. The metal had poked it deep. I wiped the blood off on my black shirt.

"Let me see." Byron was at my side. He unwrapped the bandage from his hand and wrapped it over mine instead. I made a face. We were officially blood brothers now. "The camera's been disabled." Byron gave it an assessing glance. "Sandra's team took out the security system." *Weird. Sandra had a team?*

"Where's the device?" I asked.

He searched the surrounding area. The Provocity tower was essentially a utility building made of brick with about twelve stories to it. Its three roofs were flat and tiered like a fortress. A blackened tower on the highest roof looked suspiciously like Rapunzel's. The second tower was taller and rose up from the ground next to the building with only a catwalk between it. It said *Provocity* on the side in big bold letters. A ladder molded to the side went straight to the top. I had to avert my face; it made me too dizzy to look up at it.

"The device is on the top of the Provocity towers." Byron pointed. "Someone's been giving the towers a paint job. See the scaffold. The hostiles went in under the cover of painters to get the wiring in."

Keeping my eyes carefully averted from the high ladder, I stared at the plank where the terrorists had worked. Ropes were rigged to the side of the cage. That's where we'd have to disable the device. I tried to mentally connect my way up the side of the building with the catwalks and ladders. No matter what, going up would be scary. One false move would prove fatal.

I tried to find an alternate entry through the building. My eyes—trained by months of prank wars—picked out broken windows in the corner of the basement. No one suspected foul play in the relatively quiet little town of Provo...*well, quiet where criminals were concerned.* There was also a coal shack to the side that could connect us to the building through a basement, and a tall metal door to the warehouse that looked like it led inside to a loading dock of sorts. Getting in would be cake, but I was afraid of what we'd find inside.

Byron firmly pulled me aside. "Mad Dog, you don't have the training to do this. I need you out here." I wanted to agree with him, but I couldn't let Byron go into this by himself, especially with *lover boy* at his heels.

Eric stopped scanning the length of the towers to give me a considering look. "We can't leave Mad out here by herself," he said after a moment.

"We need her as our lookout," Byron argued impatiently.

"How? Our cell phones don't work."

Byron's eyes were hard on Eric. "Let's fix that then. If one of us turns off the generators, it'll lessen the frequency interference so we can use our cell phones. Either way, we'll stop these guys." He gave me a measuring look. "If we don't get through, we'll need someone to take out the control box from the top of the tower."

PRANK WARS

"And who would that be? Mad?" Eric's face screwed up in anger. "You expect her to scale up the top of that tower on that ladder? That's suicide."

Byron licked dry lips, sparing me a glance. "You don't think she can hack it?"

"I can hack it," I cut in; pretty sure I was playing into Byron's trick—but we were wasting valuable time. We had to stop these guys from testing out the device. Already I could hear the creaking and the high-pitched sounds of buzzing from the generators inside.

Byron pressed his hand over mine. For once, his touch didn't stem from being undercover. My hand tingled slightly, but the look in his eyes did more. There was a tenderness in them that looked familiar; he always looked at me like that. "Thanks cuz," he said in an undertone. "I need you to be here."

It was a big sacrifice. I would be standing out here, shivering in the dark, wondering if Byron was okay. Sure, no one made me angrier; no one else felt as close to me either. I *did* like him. It was a very inconvenient thing to realize now that I might lose him, now that I didn't know if anything between us had ever been real. For the first time in a long while, I felt like someone who could love—even if that love wasn't returned, though judging by how Byron looked at me now, he felt the same way I did. I surprised us both by throwing my arms around him in a tight hug.

He grinned tensely and gently tilted my face up to his. He brought his mouth close to my ear. "There's something you should know…" he whispered. Then he kissed me fully on the lips, making me miss a breath. "Eric's a June 6th." I heard him say as he pulled away.

I took a shaky step backwards. Eric didn't look pleased; it wasn't what Byron had said, since I had barely heard him. Eric was a June 6th? Like completely? I avoided looking at Eric. He had shoved me into the Suburban to get me in the way, a lowering thought, but terribly true. Byron wasn't fighting him now, so that had to be it. When had Byron figured it out? Since he had brought Eric along, it had to be during the car ride.

Byron watched me closely until I acknowledged his words with a slight nod. "Let's split up," he said immediately after. "Eric, you take plan A. I'm on plan B."

"Plan A?" Eric asked.

Byron's eyes were on mine, and I knew these were my orders. I tried to pay attention, but my stomach felt sick. Byron had just kissed me to give me valuable information. Was it *that* or the bad news that I had a more dangerous role to play that made me want to cry? "Disable the device from the bottom," Byron said. "Go through the basement windows and find the stairs. The generators will be on the ground floor. If you turn them off in time, it'll cut off the power and stop the chain reaction. Then the hostiles won't have enough energy to get this device working. If that doesn't work—the device has already secured the energy it needs."

Eric's lips were white with tension. "Then they can target us?"

"Only if they have the missing piece." Byron kept his face devoid of anything that might betray his suspicions.

"Well, if nothing, turning off the generators will give us back our cell phones." Eric flexed his muscular arms, his athletic frame nothing short of threatening. He gave me a hard look. "You still have Byron's iPhone, right?"

Eric knew I had Byron's cell? He was a complete June 6th! He had been the one I had talked to on Byron's phone. That's how he knew I had it. I refused to give away I was onto him, and nodded instead. Did he think I was a complete moron for not catching on? Eric extended his hand out to Byron. "Give me one of your light sticks."

Byron gave one up to him and threw me the other for good measure. I slid it into the waistband of my khakis, trying not to think about going through the dark basement with some bright light making me the target for every bad guy down there. Byron's hand found my back. "Find a good place to hide, cuz." He pushed me away.

PRANK WARS

I sprinted behind the Provocity tower, almost bumping into a trailer with the figurehead of an iron pig that some insane engineer made out of spare parts. "What are *you* going to do?" I heard Eric ask Byron behind me.

"The control room." Byron meant the information for me. He headed for the ladders that made a zigzagged line between the building and the smoke stack. "They'll try to control the device from there with a laptop of sorts. I'll take out whoever mans it. Whoever meets their target first, well, we both win, right?"

I took a deep breath, resting my face against the iron pig. Whoever made it first *would* win. Eric couldn't warn his men up there with this frequency interference, and Byron couldn't let Eric know he was onto him when I was stuck in the middle. There was no time to waste on punching out our differences down here.

Eric took a step closer to the basement window. "And if we fail, you'll really send Mad up the tower for plan C?"

"Why not?" Byron's hand landed on the top rung of the metal ladder. "Don't do anything crazy, Mad. Wait for radio contact." It was a warning not to do it, but how long would I have to wait for Eric to go in before I could turn off the generators myself? Stepping behind the shadows, I watched to make sure we really got rid of Eric.

Eric smashed the rest of a broken basement window nearest him and crawled inside. As soon as his feet hit the ground, his head popped up like a meerkat and he watched me intently, his face ghostly under the light stick. Byron didn't move from the ground, staying in the shadows. After a moment of being creepy, Eric left us, disappearing hurriedly into the darkness beyond.

That was Byron's signal to scramble up the ladders. He shot up, his every movement screaming of prior training. Would it be enough to stop whatever force was inside? He crawled through the catwalk between the smokestack and the main building, morphing into shadow. He reached the top, landing onto the gravel over the lower roof then trailed out of sight. He was in. I let out my breath. Was it my turn already?

Sneaking past Eric seemed impossible. What if I just went directly to plan C? I studied the Provocity tower high above me. It cut me off from the moonlight and made my head swim. The swinging scaffold loomed threateningly near the top. The control box was attached somewhere up there. I tried to mentally work a way up the towers that didn't take me straight up the steep ladders. I could take the shorter ladders Byron took to the smokestack then catch the catwalk between it to get to the highest roof on the main building, but even after all that, I'd only be halfway to the antennas. There was still a long stretch where I'd have to climb that freakishly sheer ladder up the side of the Provocity towers—without a harness. All to take out the control box.

I forced myself to think clearly. Eric had a race to win. He wouldn't still be waiting for me down in the basement. If Byron failed to stop whoever was manning the frequency remote on the top floor, it was up to me to turn off those generators. I stared at the convenient hole Eric put in the basement window for me. I hoped he'd see the irony after I showed him how much I could get in the way. *The weasel.*

I ducked under the ladders, and vaulted through the window. Swinging my legs, I landed into an empty room on a hard cement floor. My hands met a cold wall. I could see the dim outline of the shelves against the walls. The light of the moon drifted through the cracked windows. Anything could be waiting for me down here. I listened intently for breathing. No whispers. No gentle fall of feet. Tory trained me well.

I had the whole basement to myself. Maybe that's why Byron had let me come this way? He had been the distraction; I was the action for once. Eric would've grabbed whatever back-up he could on his way upstairs to take out Byron. It left the basement unguarded, leaving me free to roam. So, where were the generators? Byron said to take the stairs to find them. I didn't know where those were either. I cracked open the light stick, and it flooded the room with light. It trailed over the door that led from the workroom. The door was still closed. I tried not to think about what waited behind it. Just pushed it open.

PRANK WARS

The air from the hallway buzzed against my ears. The generators made a loud whirring noise somewhere above this floor. I tried to follow it, picking my way through the halls. Junk piled around me in organized chaos, all sorts of chains and tubes and pulleys. Waving my light stick to glean whatever light I could, I found pocked metal stairs and stared into the darkness of the spiraling stairway above me. It trailed through twelve stories until it met the empty dome of the roof.

Anyone would see me coming up the stairs. I squeezed the yellow railing in a firm grip to keep myself from tripping, and tucked the light stick into the heel of my converses. It plunged everything into darkness. The stairs groaned under my feet and I tried to figure out how to lighten my steps, feeling my way up. I made out a faint glow of light on the floor above me. It flickered unnaturally in the distance. Flares. The foreign agents were using them as their back-up lighting, though thankfully, it allowed me to see that I was alone down here. Cords and wires flowed from open pipes like fish ladders on either side of me. I kept my distance, not sure if they were live and would take me out with a touch.

The noise from the generators rang loudly through the air the closer I came. I reached the first floor, following the sound to the loudest part of the building, and swept a careful glance behind me. No one. Again. My heart beat loudly against my chest, and I fought the urge to run. The hallway ahead would put me in the open. I sucked in my breath and dashed forward. No alarm sounded. Hope filled me as soon as I spotted the two generators near the side entrance. They were side by side with a catwalk between them. No one stood guard. I groaned, feeling sick and heavy. No instruction manual told me how to turn them off either.

I lunged up the steps, taking three at a time, feeling for buttons or handles or gauges. A switch in front read *on/off*. Feeling sheepish, I secured my feet and threw all my strength against it, stumbling out of balance. It was as easy as flipping off a light switch. The generator gave a low whine and shut down. I tripped to the other one and shut that one off too. It felt like someone stuck cotton balls in my ears, swathing the building with blessed silence. The problem was that the energy coursing through the air still felt thick like honey. It was palpable, like being caught in the quiet of a storm. I knew the device already had all the power it needed, and now Sandra's team would be onto me. I hurtled down the steps to get away from what I had done.

As soon as I found the shadows, I powered up Byron's iPhone. The screensaver flickered on. Byron answered on the first ring, the reception full of static. "I see you got my message," he said.

"Where are you?" I was breathless. "Did you find the control room? Was the remote frequency in there?"

He gave a low laugh. "I never stood a chance. We're both too late." The static ate up his words and I was afraid I was losing him.

"What did you say?" I asked.

"They're guarding the control room right now," he repeated. "I'm outnumbered. I can't get in."

"What about going up the Provocity tower and taking out the control box from there? You said—"

"That's suicide." The static got heavier. "I'll need you to be my distraction first."

"What? How?"

"Run. They're coming after you."

I heard someone rush down the stairs from a long way up and I scurried the rest of the way back down to the basement, cringing with every loud step I made. I hated the dark and I hated basements and I hated guys with guns chasing me.

"Stop!" Eric shouted. He was the one above me—maybe a few other guys judging by the heavy footsteps. "Madeleine! I need to talk to you. I know that's you!" Typical of Eric to think he could talk me into falling into his hands again. He could lie his way through anything.

"Byron," I whispered harshly into his phone. "Why are they after me?"

"Not sure." The reception was terrible down here. These were worse than walkie talkies. "Just keep them busy, okay."

PRANK WARS

"How?"

"Whatever you're doing, it's working. I'm calling back-up. Make sure they don't find you, Mad Dog." And then Byron was gone.

I stashed the iPhone back into my pocket and scurried through the machinery left over from engineers of time's past. Hiding here was out of the question. I'd be a goner once the terrorists found the light switch. Their feet pounded down the stairs. How many flights until they got to me? Maybe they'd check the ground level first and give me more time to escape. Using Byron's screensaver as my only light, I left the staircase far behind, speeding through the basement halls, feeling the lifeless cement walls under my fingertips. My path broke into three possible hallways, more like alleyways. It was impossible to decide which one to take.

Water dripped aimlessly in the darkness ahead and I half expected something to crawl out from the shadows and take me. Murmuring a quiet prayer, I took a chance on the right and tripped over a hard metal chair. It echoed through the basement. Holding to my stinging shin, I listened closely for an answer. For the moment I could only hear my breath. I swallowed it and listened again.

I heard footsteps. Someone was down here with me. Near enough to give me only moments to hide. I couldn't think of where. I flipped Byron's phone on again, using its light to see. I limped into a run, ignoring the pain. The darkness would be my best friend if only I could stay safely ensconced in it. The light from the phone flickered off and I pressed down on it again.

That was it. The light illuminated a long metal tube jutting out of the cement. The tube went through the wall and over the entryway above me. Once it had been attached to a pipe, but now it was open and exposed, ready for me to climb through and hide out of sight. The perfect hiding place.

I clambered over a table and climbed over a metal cabinet, stepping hard onto a cardboard box to reach it. I heard them coming for me. Punching my feet downward, I found purchase and propelled myself into the metal tube just in time to hide the light from Byron's phone into my back pocket. The sound of feet scurried like mice under the doorway beneath me. I tensed, feeling a jolt of warning spread through my entire body. They brought a light with them that flooded the whole room. I squeezed my eyes shut and sank as silently as I could into the tube, resting my cheek against the cold iron. My dark hair my only camouflage.

"Madeleine!" Eric called. "I know you're in here!"

Yeah? So what? I wasn't going to give myself up any sooner than they could find me. The longer it took Eric, the more of a chance Byron's back-up could get here to save me. I listened to the crashing and breaking. Their search for me was brutal, destroying everything around us. They would be just as brutal with me. My body trembled with fear.

"Hey, Mad Dog!" Eric whistled for me. "Come on out!" His voice held stark cruelty that he had masked before. I heard a click and knew it was a gun. "I'm not fooling around here." After a moment of waiting to see if I would respond, Eric growled low under his breath. "Alright, we don't get you, we get your friends. How about we surprise your little redheaded buddy? We target her phone? One call from us. Poof. She's gone. No more terrorizing the neighborhood."

I bit my lip hard to keep from crying out. Eric didn't know Tory's name. They didn't have her number. Sandra didn't even. The two despised each other. I couldn't give myself away at a meaningless threat—it was like dealing with the twins. "Either way you won't be alive to see it happen," his voice echoed eerily. "This place is going to blow. If you don't get out fast, you'll go with it." I was silent. He could be right, but I doubted I would survive if I tried to slip past him either. The goal was to survive as long as I could. "One last chance, Mad Dog. Then we lock the doors and there's no way you're getting out." There were no doors over here. I hunkered down further.

It was quiet and I listened to the shifting feet. Soon they faded away, splitting different directions. Water dripped somewhere behind us. Would this place really blow? Panic filled me at the thought of getting buried alive down here. How long did I have? The minutes ticked past.

PRANK WARS

Maybe it was too late to get away. Maybe it was a trick to smoke the rat out. I didn't know if it was safe to leave. Was Eric still below or had he left? I couldn't sniff out his Hollister. I took a deep breath and dug into my back pocket with shaky fingers, forcing myself to be silent about it. Once I had a hold of Byron's phone, I hid its light under my bandaged hand. Finding a call from two nights ago, I pushed speed dial.

A phone rang and I jumped in fear. Eric was right below me. He chuckled. "Very clever, my dear." My teeth clenched at the term of endearment. It never failed, the girl could be smashing the guy into the ground and the guy would still patronize her with dear or darling. "You were always so resourceful. That's what I like about you. Yes, *I like you*. There's something about you that's so...interesting. I think we could deal very nicely together. I really don't want you to die, Madeleine."

The place wasn't going down in flames or he wouldn't be here. Why did Eric want me so bad? He could just target my phone and assassinate me already. I *knew* he didn't like me. I glanced up at the rafters. If I could just get up there, I could find another way down and get out. My eyes followed each possible step from there to the ground. If I inched my way down like a spider, I'd have a chance, but I didn't know how to keep it quiet.

"You're not like other girls, so easy to manipulate. Thanh thought I was a bad boy. She was trying to protect me from myself, always trying to change me, but you? You never believed in me. So jaded. Still, you had a little crush on me, didn't you?"

My eyes bulged. Eric almost got me to give myself away with that dig, but instead I texted Byron. I was the slowest texter in the world and had to work by touch. Eric tirelessly monologued below me. I hoped it didn't push me over the edge. I sent Byron the text and inched forward, fighting to keep my ragged breath quiet.

"We never got that kiss," Eric said. "Such a shame you've been burnt. We could've been perfect for each other. I would've taken you out—not in the usual BYU fashion, of course." Eric laughed and I rolled my eyes. Really? A death pun? Before he pushed me beyond my capacity to endure, my phone rang. It echoed loudly in the tube. Eric lost no time. He tucked his light stick into his armpit and sprang over the metal cabinet, clutching both sides of the tube. His broad shoulders covered the opening. "Hello!"

I pulled into the shadows, watching Eric's confused face from above me. I let out a shaky breath, knowing I barely made it through the rafters in time. I had given Byron three minutes to call me back before I hit the ground. It would be the perfect distraction. Before I could rush the other direction, Eric reached for the phone that I had abandoned in the tube. A slow smile curved over his lips. My stomach fell to my toes in direct response. Eric didn't want me. He wanted Byron's iPhone.

"Got it!" Eric called to the others. His flunkies abandoned their search and ran back to join him. I slunk behind some fallen shelves, not sure I wanted to see the damage I had done. "It's where Thanh hid the missing piece." Eric jumped down from the cabinet with Byron's cell in hand.

"That was stopping the frequency remote from working?" one of the guys asked.

"I told you *she* was onto you. Thanh put it in after she switched backpacks with the operative." He couldn't be serious? Now people would die because of me. I crouched behind the shelf, wondering how to get it back.

"Now what?" I recognized *Dune Guy's* voice. "That government stiff is still unaccounted for."

Eric laughed. "New Zealand's done for once we get this in place." He shook his head. The glow from the light stick played eerily with the shadows on his face. What did he mean New Zealand was done for? Would they make him the target now? "Sandra." Eric called her on his android. He pulled the battery out of Byron's iPhone, and picked out something that looked like an SD card. He grinned broadly and took off on a run. "We're good to go," he crowed. His men followed him down the hallway. I dragged myself up and tried to keep to the shadows. I couldn't let Eric get away with that missing piece.

PRANK WARS

Eric kept the phone to his ear and grumbled out a laugh. "Let's hope New Zealand makes the call a good one. Maybe to headquarters, right." Another cruel chuckle. Why would Byron's call be dangerous? That made no sense. In two seconds, I put the pieces together. Hölle had given Byron a new phone. Of course, he had tampered with it. "He's going to reach out and touch someone," Eric told Sandra. I glared at him. He stole that line from Byron, but his men laughed anyway. And why shouldn't they? It was a foolproof plan. Once the piece was in place, Byron's phone would be the control that would point out the target. I sucked in my breath at the implications. Headquarters would trace the call to Byron and assume he was the mole. Hölle, Eric, and Sandra would be in the clear.

"Either way," Eric said through his android, "he's only got five minutes before he's a hole in the ground. Don't stand anywhere near him. Too much power with no release." He snickered again. Eric just needed a fat white cat to pet. My stomach hurt. Whether Byron used his cell or not, he would die. How long would it take Eric to put in the missing piece? Just five minutes after that and Byron would be dead. Sandra took a shower a hundred times longer. "Yeah, another kink to iron out," Eric told her. "Thanh's a tool. It'll be easy to take her. We'll put her brain on it. Make her figure it out."

There had to be a way to warn Byron—or stop Eric from reattaching the missing piece to the frequency remote. He was surrounded by three men and—I groaned—I was not some kid defending the house from burglars at Christmas. The terrorists easily outran me on the noisy stairs. I could only run so quietly and so fast when I was two flights below them.

"Find Mad Dog," Eric told Sandra. "I'm on my way to the control room." He clicked off his android, and rushed faster up the stairs. Where was the control room? The top floor? I was dying here. If these monkeys couldn't find Byron, I didn't know how I could, but maybe—Byron could find me?

"Hey, Eric! I've got Byron's new phone!" I shouted up to him. My voice echoed in the dark. "In five minutes, the next call I'll make will be to you!"

Eric hesitated on the stairs. I ran off the stairs onto the second floor. The men switched directions above me to head me off. I had a two flight running start. I hoped the noise would alert Byron to where we were. I ran past dusty cabinets and machinery, feeling like I was stuck in a haunted house—catwalks and shadows everywhere, places to hide, but I had to be found to make a commotion. So far, no Byron. I hoped Eric hadn't sent his men to head me off while he did his dirty work upstairs.

The dark sky outside beckoned through a crack in a door that was slightly ajar. Where could it possibly lead to, but to a ledge outside the building? I took my chances and jerked it open, seeing a flat roof below me and a catwalk attached to a smokestack beyond that. I was on the lowest roof where Byron had broken into the building.

A noise behind me sent me sprawling all the way outside. I landed onto the gravel and skidded to my hands and knees. I couldn't slow down. The catwalk shook beneath my running feet and I headed blindly for the ladders leading to the next roof. My bandaged hand landed on the first rung. I hoped I'd make enough noise to alert Byron before I actually made it up to the Provocity Towers. I reached the second roof, seeing another door leading back into the building. Eric's men rushed up the ladders behind me. *Dune Guy* was at the lead. His face screwed into a mask of rage. His fists human mallets. There was no sign of Eric. My body shook with cold and fear. I climbed up the ladder propped under the door.

"Byron!" I shouted, wrenching it open. I found myself on the top floor of the utility building, warning signs plastered over what could only be the control room. A gaping hole covered half of the floor. It dropped twelve stories to the basement below. My knees buckled, and I clutched at the railing. A chain hung from the ceiling and dangled through the hole dropping into the darkness. There was not a good guardrail around that thing.

PRANK WARS

The sounds of fighting drifted to where I stood. A crash and a shout. That was Byron. And Eric? I sidled around the edge of the hole, listening closely for my pursuers. I picked out the click-clack of stiletto heels and turned to see Sandra's gorgeous, spiteful face. Her hand rested lightly on the hip of her skinny jeans. She blocked my way. My fingers clenched over the railing. "I always knew you were mean, Sandra, but do you really want Byron to die?" I asked her.

Her beautiful hair splashed over her shoulder when she shrugged. "It's business, psycho. He got in the way." She pulled out a gun from her side holster, her red fingernails wrapping expertly around the handle. She raised it to my head. Byron jerked me roughly back.

"Byron!" The shot rang out over us after we landed behind a long metal cabinet full of wires. I tried to get enough air to talk. "Byron!"

Before I could get anything out, Eric smashed into us from behind, jamming my wrist behind me hard. Byron cuffed him in the face and shoved him far from me. Sandra still had her gun. I rolled behind another cabinet moments before it went off. I tried to work out how many shots she'd have. The door flew open behind us and Eric's team of hostiles shoved their way in. *Dune Guy* pushed past them, far too eager to find me. A smile tipped Sandra's lips. She had as many shots as she wanted.

I scrambled behind a wooden box, knowing it wouldn't provide enough shelter, except to hide from Eric's men. Dark shadows loomed behind me over a narrow walkway. Leftover tools hung on the wall—a wrench, a hammer—they were the most logical choices, but I didn't want to hurt anybody. I glanced over at the fire extinguisher. A loud shot echoed into the darkness and something splintered near my side. I bit down a scream, not wanting to give my position away.

"Poor Mad dog, so socially backward," Sandra called. "You can't even text." I took a deep steadying breath. "*Poor dear*. I wasn't even a real co-ed and I got more dates than you."

I pulled the tag out of the fire extinguisher and shot a steady stream of white foam at her. She screamed and landed on her back. Her gun skidded across the wooden floor and toppled down the pit of despair in the middle of the room. Our eyes met. I made a moue with my lips. "Oh, you don't have a gun, Sandra. What *will* you do now?"

She took off one of her red stiletto heels and sprang at me. *I guess she could do that.* I lifted the fire extinguisher to block it. The stiletto made a poing sound against the metal and I pushed her back. She swung again. This time the stiletto sunk into my leg. I sucked in my breath at the pain and knocked her away. "Do you really want to do this?" I was just trying to distract her with a stupid question and, for a moment, it worked. I listened to the sounds of fighting near the control room. Another crash then some buzzing. More shouts. It was driving me crazy that I couldn't get to Byron to tell him about his phone. I had been so close. I glared at Sandra. "Don't you care about him at all?"

She tilted her head at the suggestion. "*Lord Byron*…as you call him…is a self-righteous prig. You two deserve each other."

Well, rude, but… "Thanks."

"How about you die with him!" That sounded like a warning to me. I ducked behind a machine. She threw a hammer at my head. It crashed against the paned glass windows covering half the wall behind me. The windows vomited all over me in a shower of glass. I tried to cover myself from the shards as they instantly cut up my arms and hands. I stumbled to the other side of the machine to get away from her.

Byron and Eric wrestled near the edge of the gaping hole, their muscles straining. Eric kicked him in the side and Byron twisted, punching him in the face. Eric staggered to his feet and stumbled backwards just to have Byron viciously jerk his legs out from under him, making him crash against a metal cabinet. Sparks flew behind Eric and he arched in pain, rolling to the side. The cabinet toppled down on Byron. He rolled out of the way, but the cabinet caught his shoulder. He cried out in pain and pushed off the ground. I didn't know that Byron had so much fight in him.

Where did Eric's men go? *Dune Guy* was noticeably absent. If Eric had put the missing piece in place, they could very well be on the run to avoid becoming the first hole in the ground. I sprinted forward. "Byron! Your iPhone!"

PRANK WARS

"Behind you!" Byron shoved Eric away and threw all his weight against another metal cabinet, shoving it down on me. I scurried out of the way as that too groaned and fell. I turned and saw *Dune Guy*. His fingers scraped over my arm. I tripped backwards, seeing the cabinet pin him and two other pursuers neatly to the cement. They screamed in pain. I scrambled backwards, putting some distance between me and *Dune Guy's* murderous eyes. Already he was pulling free.

"Eric!" I heard Sandra's disembodied voice shout. "Tell me the device is engaged?"

"Hölle is on it," his voice echoed back.

Where was the mysterious Hölle? I searched the darkness desperately, seeing no one. Not Hölle, not Byron, not Sandra, not Eric. The back of my neck began to tingle uncomfortably and I felt my way through the debris, my converses crunching over the shattered glass. I listened to the slams and groans of pain in the distance and knew who it came from. I ran, tripping through the machinery, running towards the light. It was coming from the control room. The closer I came, the louder the fighting escalated. I gasped out as soon as it illuminated the fight before me. Byron was bleeding and fierce; he faced Eric like they were in an arena. Neither of them were giving up, their weapons long gone.

The loud roar of machinery made my ears ache. Did that mean Hölle had connected the trigger? It didn't seem like it—the device would run like a sleek piece of machinery. Still, there was definitely something wrong with the air. I took a deep breath, knowing I had to go back into the fray. "Byron!" I tried to shout over the noise.

Byron shook his head at me and waved furiously for me to go. I couldn't or he was dead. Eric was on him like glue. Byron punched him back so hard, it made my own eyes swim. Eric retaliated, his body swinging into an arc, kicking Byron's bleeding side. How had I ever believed they were mere college students?

I tried to get closer just as Byron grabbed Eric. The muscles stood out like tree roots on Eric's neck. His eyes rotated until they found me...then locked onto something next to me. Sandra stepped out of the shadows, a sultry smile smoking her lips. I jerked in surprise. She dangled a wrench between two fingers. Byron loosed Eric's fingers over his neck and punched him back into the control room. No doubt to disable the device from there, but he didn't understand. Once Hölle attached the missing piece to the frequency remote, Byron would be the trigger. The control room had nothing to do with it.

I took an uneasy step toward the control room just as Sandra stepped between us. She tightened her grip on her weapon and swung. I stumbled back, my back smashing against a ladder that led through the vaulted ceiling. I twisted to stare up at it, knowing it would take me to the highest roof and the Provocity tower. And then what? I'd risk my life by scaling to the top? I couldn't get to Byron to warn him in time. I really had no choice but to carry out plan C: Go to the roof and disable the control box from the top.

My stomach rebelled at the idea even as Sandra came closer. I lunged for the ladder and she kicked off her other stiletto. I climbed higher, hearing the heel clatter to the ground. Her bare feet padded behind me. There was no going back. She was out to kill me. I reached the ceiling and shoved on the trapdoor with all my might. I felt it scrape open the same time Sandra's fingers ripped into my ankle. I kicked back and felt the sickening impact against her face as I wriggled through the opening like a rat under a door. Once I was through, I kicked the trapdoor shut. She let out an angry shout. Her fingers retreated back inside.

I didn't have much time. I rushed across the gravel on the roof, past weird stacks and formations. The Provocity Tower cut a deep slash into the night sky. The moon shone silently over it all. My body shook uncontrollably, only now realizing the enormity of what I was about to do. Byron's life depended on my inadequate struggles against fate. A catwalk connected from the roof to the tower and I rushed over it like one possessed. The trapdoor opened behind me and Sandra staggered through the hole with a shriek, "Don't take another step, Mad Dog!"

PRANK WARS

I didn't want to. The catwalk shook under my feet. The ground stretched far below it. Already I was too far up, but I couldn't turn back now. The antenna was braced on the Provocity tower next to the painter's scaffold—the control box was attached to the bottom of it, and it all seemed impossibly high to me. I reached the end of the catwalk and measured the gap between it and the ladder—it was wider than I had expected. Sandra was gaining on me. I had no time to think about it. I took a deep breath and lunged for the ladder, and hit it hard with my bandaged hand. My fingers wrapped convulsively around the first rung and, shaking, I pulled myself upright. I took another breath, trying to gather my courage to pull myself to the next rung.

"What do you think you're doing?" she screamed.

Climbing...unfortunately. My breath wouldn't come out naturally. I forced a hand loose from the first rung on the ladder. It was moist. I wiped it against my shaking legs and found the next rung then the next and the next, forcing myself into a steady rhythm. Sandra's people had mounted some harnesses to the side, probably to help them get the device up here safely. *Please let me reach them.* My fingers wouldn't quite obey me, but I managed to brush against the first harness and drag it closer to me one-handed. There were too many buckles on it, and I gave up and wrapped the strap around my waist a couple of times. It should be enough to hold me if I slipped.

"Get away from there." Sandra was steps below me. The reminder was enough to send me scrambling higher up the ladder while she shrilled out more orders. I spotted the first row of antennas above. A catwalk curled around the tower beneath them with the painter's scaffold to the side. It was so high up there. My eyes went blurry. I took another deep breath, telling myself I didn't have much further to go before I reached the dish.

I felt a cold grip on my ankle. Sandra's fingernails dug into my flesh. Tying on the harness had slowed me down, and she was too good for one. Sandra tugged viciously and I kicked back at her, just enough to dislodge her hold on me. There was no way I wanted to send my former roommate plummeting to her death. Sandra easily dodged the kick and tugged on my ankle again, screaming loudly. I wrapped my arms around the rungs of the ladder, not really trusting that the harness tied around my stomach would really hold me if I fell. Desperately, I kicked Sandra back again—this time harder. She let go, just enough to let me inch my way up higher.

She caught me while I was mid-climb and one-handed. It ripped me from my grip. I lost my balance and my breath caught in my throat as I fell through the darkness. I screamed, the air rushing through my hair until I jerked to a stop, dangling at the same spot where I had attached my harness. Would it hold? I screamed again when something slipped from my back pocket and fluttered though the air. My *war journal.* It hit the ground far below me. The pages splayed out against the gravel. It could've been me. I tried to catch my breath, but it came out ragged.

"Mad Dog!" I peered through the darkness. The world swung below me. Byron hurried through the gravel, the ripped ends of his shirt flying behind him. He was on the roof. "Is that you?"

Hope filled me. I wouldn't have to climb the tower after all. I cupped my hands over my mouth. "Get rid of your phone!"

"Get down!" His words were lost.

"Your phone!" I repeated.

Eric tackled him from behind By now; they both were bruised and bleeding. I leaned my head back in a groan, feeling the sweat on my forehead. There was no way I could get to Byron in time. How long did Eric plan to stick around for the fireworks?

A tug on my harness made my head jerk up. Sandra was messing with the cords attached to the painter's scaffold. I shrieked, diving to the side to get away from her. I felt strangely like a worm caught on a hook, and reached for the ladder. It was too far away. Once again, Sandra was between me and what I wanted, looking just as fierce as she did when she guarded a batch of chocolate chip cookies. Even from down here, I saw her smirk. She was actually happy to see me die.

PRANK WARS

My hands balled into fists. I held my breath and swung myself back to the ladder, bringing the cords of my harness back into her reach again. She stole them...predictably, and I clasped the ladder in a killing grip, quickly undoing the cords around me before she could send me plummeting to my death. No way was some high-maintenance girl going to outdo me. "Don't be stupid," she snarled.

Why not? According to her, it's what I did best. I climbed back up the ladder without a harness this time, half aware of the sirens blaring in the streets below us. They were too late to stop any of this from happening. The static gathering from the energy around me made the hair rise on my head, my arms...my legs. It was a weird sensation, and I knew the device was fully functional. Hölle had come through for Eric. Sandra waited at the catwalk above me like an angry sentinel. I forced myself forward. She wasn't throwing anything at me. It meant she was out of ammunition—or she had a plan. I had nothing to use against her. No. Actually. I might have *something*.

I studied the flat roof to the side of the tower, not finding Byron or Eric. The dish antenna above me was lowering. Sandra ducked skittishly out of its way and I felt my hands go weak on the rungs. It was the perfect distraction from me at the worst possible moment. It had to be aiming at Byron. I struggled over the edge of the catwalk, my stomach scraping over the side. I didn't know how to stop any of this in time.

Sandra swung at me and I ducked, seeing the wrench inches from my arm. I landed flat against the catwalk, feeling the jagged metal dig into my back. I rolled out of Sandra's way, pulling out my old lady perfume. She snickered and came for me again. I sprayed it straight into her eyes. She gagged, falling back. The stench was her downfall. I yanked the wrench from her hands, rushing for the antenna. She clawed at me. I elbowed her back, never before realizing how strong she was. The antenna pointed downward, focusing on its target. I tried to jam its descent with the wrench. It kept going. I hit it a couple of times. Why wasn't it working?

I spotted the control box and lunged at it a moment before feeling a huge explosion tear through the air. Fire shot through the roof below us. I gasped, catching onto the rails of the shaking catwalk. Smoke billowed up into my face, burning my lungs. I coughed and fell to my knees, staring below at the roof, searching for any sign of life. "Byron!" I shouted. "Please, don't be hurt. Byron!" I was so shocked, I couldn't even cry. "Don't be dead."

"You think he can hear you?"

My head lifted at Sandra's nasty voice, barely able to take in the hurt, the loss, the sudden anger. Her face was smug. Black make-up streamed down her cheeks, and I felt all of my emotions erupt inside me. Nothing else mattered. "What did you do?" I whispered hoarsely. After one look at my face, she stepped back. I stood up and felt everything snap, all my self-control, all my numbness evaporated into rage. I swung the wrench and Sandra shrieked in dismay. It hit the control box behind her and I smashed it harder and harder, throwing my anguish against it.

"What are you doing?" she screamed. I swung one last time and ripped the control box from its hinges. It spun through the air and twisted until it disappeared into the darkness. A hollow clatter signaled it hit the ground below. Sparks flew up at us. Sandra screamed even louder.

"What? Why are you screaming?" I cried. "It can't *hear* you!" The tears that wouldn't come before now ran freely down my cheeks. I wanted to roll up in a ball and forget everything, but I was stuck on the top of a tower with an evil witch and my heart was dead. Byron was dead, and there was no way to bring him back. I covered my face.

"Hey, it's okay." I recognized the voice and felt his warm arms wrap around me. My face was in his chest and my hands were kind of stuck between us, so I really couldn't see, but his heart beat rapidly, strong. Freeing my hands, I lifted my face up to Byron's. He watched me tenderly.

I cried even harder, grabbing at him. "You're alive." Just barely. His hair stuck out worse than before. His white shirt was dingy and torn. His face and knuckles were swollen and bloody.

PRANK WARS

"C'mon," He smoothed down my wild hair, wrapping a hand over my elbow. "This place is going to blow." Sandra was already escaping down the ladder. Her beautiful chestnut curls floated over her face as she slid all the way down the rungs to the catwalk between the tower and the highest roof. She lunged onto the roof, her bare feet spinning against the gravel.

"She won't get out fast enough," Byron said into my hair. He pulled me to the edge of the catwalk, and I looked down the tower to the ground far below us. I could feel the energy snapping and sizzling through the air. Something was very wrong. Byron grasped the painter's scaffold the foreign agents had set up, and heaved the cage closer. I didn't have time to argue. He pushed me inside and threw himself next to me, his arm finding me.

The cage tottered dangerously beneath us. I tried not to look at the ground until I saw it come at us in a blur of color. The wind rushed through my hair. Byron had let go of the ropes, lowering us as fast as his hands could move as if he could beat the catastrophe overtaking us. Every sense inside me felt it coming. The air wasn't right. It felt prickly and heavy. It was an unexplainable fear that made it feel like we were wading through a nightmare.

We had escaped only halfway down the tower when the night sky lit up with a brilliant flash of lightning. It struck the tower from the cloudless sky. Loud resounding thunder echoed in and out of the towers. I covered my ears. A pillar of fire burned though the atmosphere above us. One glance up told me that the antennas were obliterated. I sank to the bottom of the cage, trying to escape the fire. An answering explosion sent a ripple of power trailing through the tower next to us. Jerking back with a shriek, I watched the brace holding up one side of the cage disintegrate completely. The rope fell heavily over our heads and we toppled through the air with it.

My converses dug into the scaffold's guardrail. I held on, twisting my arms through the railing as if that would stop me from falling. The cage came to a crashing halt a few feet later and my whole body flipped up, bouncing through the air—my arm the only thing holding me down. I screamed in pain, hearing Byron shout out at the same time. He threw his arm around me, holding me between him and the railing. His arms bulged against the strain. I couldn't hear what he was saying. I twisted my head up, seeing only one side of the scaffold held up by a rope. It tipped at a crazy angle. I didn't know how long we could stay upright before it broke. The arm on the other side was down. The rope from it lay tangled at our feet. I grimaced at the ground below us. It was too far away. We'd be dead if we fell. The entire cage groaned. My hands slipped against the rope. My arm wouldn't work properly.

"Hold on!" I felt Byron's arm leave my back. His long fingers edged closer to the rope. He caught it. "It's long enough," he muttered brokenly. "We can do this." He was rigging a makeshift harness, but I couldn't keep my grip. I shouted out something unintelligible. His free arm found me and he jerked me up. My chest hit the railing and it knocked the breath out of me. "C'mon!" he shouted. "Work with me, Mad Dog!" His strange endearment renewed a spark of determination through me. "Don't let go!" he said. "I can't do this by myself!" I gasped for air and reached for him, winding my arms around him as he half dragged me onto his back. "Hold onto me!"

I tried. My whole body shook. He clipped into the rope, tying us into the painter's scaffold. I gasped in pure fright. Was he seriously going to rappel down the side of the Provocity tower with me on his back? My grip tightened involuntarily around his neck and shoulders. Anything was better than waiting to die. Pain coursed through my right arm. He tensed and pulled upright. At least we would go together. I took a deep breath and he shoved off the side. Cold air whistled past us. I felt his legs pound fiercely against the tower's side, and I forced my eyes open.

The ground came up fast, but not fast enough. Fire licked over the tower. Another deafening explosion sounded above us. I twisted to stare up at the five-hundred pound cage. It swayed over us and fell with a loud crack. Almost simultaneously, we hit the gravel against the ground and rolled, trying to kick free from the scaffold before it flattened us. I tripped on the rope. My knees scraped into the ground. Byron had me, rolling us through the gravel to escape. I heard the crash behind us. Debris sprayed into me. I covered my face, feeling Byron's arms and waited for it all to be over.

I took a hoarse breath, hearing his breaths carry with mine in the sudden silence. Were we still alive? I lifted my head to see the damage. The scaffold and some of the catwalk had crushed into the ground where we had landed moments before. I turned to stare at Byron. He had me by the shirt. His head was down and his shoulders heaved while he tried to catch his breath. I could hear the sirens somewhere in front of us.

"Your iPhone?" I managed. Why was Byron still alive? "It exploded."

He swallowed another breath. "I slipped it onto Eric at the ledge." He met my eyes with a searching look. "No way I'd keep a cell phone on me. Sorry...I saw you and...I really don't know what happened to him."

I had a few ideas. Before I could say anything, I heard steps in the gravel behind us and sniffed the foul smell of old lady perfume. "I swear Mad Dog, you have nine lives. How did that *not* kill you?" I twisted to see Sandra hobble closer. She limped on bare feet. Her cheeks flushed scarlet with fury. Black mascara ran down her cheeks. "No worries," she said. "I think I can finish the job this time."

Byron tried to stand, but just toppled to his side with a groan. I noticed he was bleeding, his jeans unrecognizable. I tried to get up, but it didn't work either. My ankle had rolled weird and my arm wasn't responding. I couldn't believe it. After all this, we would die? "Sandra," Byron kept his eyes steady on hers. "Killing her won't do any good. It's over."

"Shut up!" Sandra wiped at her bleeding mascara. "You think it was a picnic pretending my life was as pathetic as these desperate coeds? The only thing keeping me sane was knowing I'd see both of you smeared all over the ground! Oh." She made a face at Byron. "You care about the brat, don't you? Well, you didn't have to live with her! You never will!"

My eyes searched Sandra for a weapon, any weapon. She held her iPhone like a gun, but even if she wanted to kill us with that, Thanh's assassination device was a little out of commission. It lay in pieces next to the remnants of the scaffold and my war journal. The sound of choppers sounded above us. Sandra smiled up at the sky. I could only guess it was Hölle. He would take us all out. Her phone rang, and she answered it with trembling fingers. "Hello?"

Tory jumped out from the shadows in usual Tory fashion. She had on a sleek gray jacket over her *Cookie Monster needs professional help* t-shirt, looking as normal as any girl in the middle of a prank war, like none of this was happening. "Hello, Sandra." She clicked off her phone with a smirk. I groaned, but before I could warn Tory to get back, she ordered Sandra back in a very un-Tory-like voice, "Put your hands up where I can see them, Agent Vincent."

Sandra froze just as shocked as I was. "W—why should I?"

Tory shrugged confidently, her red hair a blaze of fire behind her. She looked like she could back up her words. "You prefer to talk it out with control or with me?"

Sandra stepped back. None of us had seen this coming at all. Byron closed his eyes, grimacing in pain. "Looks like we found our sleeper agent. They must have activated her to find the mole."

Tory confiscated the CIA regulation iPhone from Sandra's numb fingers. Sandra tried to fight, but Tory shoved her arm behind her, pinning her easily. Tory's nose wrinkled. "Ooh. Someone needs a bath."

"Old lady perfume," I explained in a numb voice. Tory nodded with a smile. Of course she knew. I remembered all the times Tory had come at just the right time—usually when Eric was involved. I glanced over at Byron. "I think I'd be dead without her."

Byron rested his cheek back against the hard gravel. "Yeah. Probably."

"Wait? Did you know?"

"No, they probably thought I was the mole."

Tory smiled. "My suspicions leaned more toward Sandra. Then when Eric came into the picture, I knew for sure. But you know how girls are. Thanh couldn't see the guy for a jerk. Fortunately, she still had her doubts about him…until someone *else* kidnapped her." She gave Sandra a hard look. "That's how Byron ended up with the keys to the device and not Eric—good old-fashioned female intuition. At least Thanh knew *you* could be trusted, Byron."

Sandra snorted.

"Well, Tory, congratulations," Byron said. He smiled through the pain. "I've never seen a cover like that. I had no idea."

"Are you kidding?" I muttered. "I did."

She laughed. The darkness came alive behind us. Flashing lights from patrol cars flooded out the shadows. Officers in all sorts of uniforms swept in. They led Sandra away, followed by the landing helicopter that held our paramedics. A group of them worked on us. My whole body hurt, and there were parts of me that couldn't move without pain, but I was alive. It would be interesting to see Lizzie's face when she found out I had been right all along. Of course, I'd be kidding myself to think I wouldn't get slapped with a gag order, not that anyone would believe me anyway.

Tory knelt down beside me. The gravel crunched under her feet as she supervised the wrapping of my ankle. She sighed and I glanced up at her freckled face. She watched me somberly. "Well, it's been fun."

I laughed then grimaced when the paramedics found another sore spot on my right arm. "You're not leaving me, are you?"

"Nah, we have a few things to wrap up. I imagine I'll be seeing you soon, *Captain*." Her hazel eyes danced. "You'd be an invaluable asset to the field. You know you belong to us, right?" I smiled through the pain, tears welling in my eyes. Tory was in character again. She had been—and would always be—my best soldier. "We're recruiting you whether you like it or not," she said.

Byron hid a smirk and I caught it. "Oh, I couldn't do that to Byron," I said. "How could he possibly put up with me on another mission?"

"Easily." His eyes found my watering ones. "It's not a bad idea, cuz. I'll pull a few strings and put you on my team. If Hölle's still alive, we'll sic you on him."

Tory shot him a stern look. "I think everyone would be better off if *you* went rogue, New Zealand." She handed me my war journal then stretched to her feet, spreading her arms out like wings. "Watch your back, Mad Dog. You never know when I might spring out at you." She reserved a wink for me, and I grinned sadly. There was still a little Tory in there, which made me feel better. I couldn't lose her completely. She laughed, and I watched her leave with a decided *spring* to her step.

"Hey, *Suzy Q*..." Byron glanced over at me, using my most shameful cover. The paramedics worked on his leg, making it impossible to move. It wouldn't be long before they took him away and he left me too. He found my hand and squeezed it. "Where did we leave off?"

I felt myself go red. I couldn't quite take in all the things that I had done to a government official. "You're not going to rub that in my face, are you?"

"Of course not. I promise to be a perfect gentleman from now on."

That wouldn't last long...unless they transferred him. I bit my lip, but mostly to keep the pain back because my arm really hurt. "Byron..." I hesitated. "Speaking of covers, what's your real nam—?"

"Yeah, you got it, right. Lord Byron."

I laughed. He licked his bruised lips, but before he could tell me, I stopped him. "You know what? I don't care." He looked surprised, but to be honest, I wouldn't be able to take it if his name really was *Joe-Joe Rocky Joe Jr*. "Nothing else fits," I said. "I'm going with Byron. Lord Byron."

A dangerous smile curved his lips. "Fair enough." The paramedics finished working on his leg and lifted him onto a stretcher. His blue eyes didn't leave mine. And that's when I realized he still had my hand, the one without the bandage. He hadn't let me go yet. "So," he said, "I guess this is—"

"—goodbye." I felt the pain of it keenly. It hurt to lose Tory, but this one felt even worse. I wasn't sure when I would ever see him again. I would miss tormenting him. No. I'd miss more than that. We might never see each other again and I had to be honest with myself. I liked him. More than that. I loved everything about him. It had just been another cover for him, but it had been real to me. I studied his face, trying to memorize every detail before they took him away and erased his identity. That's when I saw he was laughing. I jerked in indignation.

"I wasn't going to say that," he said. He lost his American accent altogether and went completely New Zealand on me, "—*this is going somewhere good, I believe.*"

I felt myself melt. With that accent, there was no way a thousand paramedics could stand between us. My hand tightened over his. "You shouldn't talk like that. It's dangerous."

"Good. I'll use whatever unfair advantage I can get."

The paramedics piled me onto a stretcher and our hands broke apart. They felt empty without his. What a June 6th. A year ago, I thought I was getting married to Cameron. A half a year ago, I thought I'd spend it with a box of tissues. A month ago, I assumed I would be terrorizing the men in my life with meaningless pranks. Yesterday, I thought for sure I'd be dead. And now? Well, now I just wondered if I would ever see Byron again...and if the way he looked at me had ever been real. I stared up at the sky, seeing the blackened towers cover it—they were just a little charred—nothing that couldn't be explained away. Would that be Byron's fate? I'd have to explain away his whole existence to everyone we knew?

Byron and I reunited in the helicopter moments later. "By the way," he said as if we hadn't been interrupted. "I saw that bumper sticker you put on my car."

"I don't know what you're talking about?"

"Of course you don't. You know the one that said *I do what I want to do*. It's pretty suspicious, but now it says *I do what Mad Dog wants me to do*."

I stifled a laugh, but it kind of hurt. I hoped they'd give me some painkillers pretty soon, though nothing could stop this sudden loss that ached in my throat. I felt it choking me. I wiped at my eyes. "Think of the bumper sticker as a parting gift, okay?"

He sat up, much to the EMT's irritation. They were trying to get fluids into him. "Well, don't be surprised if I burn it in front of your apartment with the rest of your gifts," he said a bit too rudely for my taste.

I frowned. "Excuse me?" I met his angry eyes and got angry myself. "You don't like my gifts?" I asked. His eyes narrowed, and I felt my heart speed up at his assessing look. "What about this?" I handed him a sterilized needle that I filched from the technician at my side. "Take it. That comes straight from my heart, you player!" The EMT stole it back with an efficient move.

"Nope." The look Byron gave me spoke volumes. "I don't want that."

"Stop moving around," the EMT told him sternly. "Or I'll strap you down, sir."

Now I had a goal. I'd get him strapped down in no time. I'd at least give him something to remember me by. I realized it was a bad habit. I had always hoped to give him so much of me that he'd never forget me, though now, none of it seemed enough. Now I wanted something real. "What about this?" I handed Byron a rolled up bandage. "It'll mean a lot if you take it."

That was promptly confiscated from me too. Before I could steal something else, Byron took my good hand with a proprietary air. "Give me this, cuz. That's all I want. Is this alright with you?"

My fingers wrapped reflexively around his. "I'm not sure." The tears I had been fighting threatened to take a hold of me again. Now that I could tell him what was on my mind, it almost hurt too much to say. I took a deep breath and tried anyway. "You told me what you felt for me wasn't fake." Embarrassment filled me. I was about to completely let go. There wasn't enough trust in the world that could shield me from his possible rejection, but it didn't matter anymore. "What did you feel, Byron? Before, I mean?" I searched his eyes, trying to find something that would give me the truth. "What's real, New Zealand?"

PRANK WARS

Byron knew I had trust issues, but this was a legitimate concern. Would he think so too? If he didn't, then all of this had been his cover. I couldn't shield myself from that anymore. "What's real?" he asked. He let go of my hand, his eyes trailing around the ambulance; they found my broken arm. "Does that feel real?"

"Yeah?"

"Then it's real. Believe me, *this* is real. You don't want me to prove it, do you?" I smiled in response. Byron must have taken that as an affirmative because he leaned towards me like he was going to kiss me then jerked to a sudden halt. I beamed when I realized that he couldn't get any closer. The paramedic held him down. "Can you free my hand, ma'am?" he asked the EMT. She twisted her lips in irritation, but she was possibly a romantic because I saw the amusement behind the stern face.

She unstrapped Byron and he grinned before his lips met mine.

EPILOGUE

Day 216
1025 hours

"War. It almost did me in. Though it seems to me that the biggest war is the one waged inside your heart. I mean, it might rank pretty high up there with the war waged inside your head—you know the one where you want to tell Lizzie what happened to your crazy idea that bad guys wanted you dead, and especially when she wonders why your roommate Sandra abandoned the apartment in a rage in the middle of the night, or why you came home the next day with a broken arm, a bandaged hand, and a sprained ankle. And then when she sees you exchanging secret glances whenever you talk to Tory, and why you and Lord Byron spend so much time at the study lab with Thanh or why you actually agreed to do the boyfriend-for-a-week program with him and it's going on a lot longer than anyone ever expected. And even most mysteriously of all, why you're taking world affairs and humanitarian classes because now you know what you want to be when you grow up and it isn't what you ever imagined it would be. So yeah, I guess that would be a pretty big battle to fight...and win. Oh, and if you're reading this right now, Lizzie, don't worry about it. Just chalk it up to my vivid imagination"

—Madeleine's War Journal Entry (Monday, September 15th)

ACKNOWLEDGEMENTS

As always, I have a HUGE list of friends who have helped me in the making of this book. I'm sure many of you on this list don't even remember helping me because it's been so long since this book transformed from that twinkle in my eye to the book it now is (you grew up so fast, little "Prank Wars"). But, if you read your name and it's a complete surprise to you, just know; yes, you DID help me. Therefore, thanks to my fantastic and splendidly fanatic editors: Nancy Wakefield and Lucinda Fowers. You made my tedious ramblings sound somewhat educated.

Many thanks to my intrepid readers of my first, second, and third drafts, who helped me rip out the boring parts and smooth out *most* of the confusion: Ashley Fowers Elliott, Danyelle Ferguson, Daryl Gessel, Debbie Gessel, Hilary Hornberger, Melanie Jacobsen, Rachel Burt Fowers, Rebecca Jorgenson, Samantha Scogin, Sandra Barton, Tina Dean and Tricia Smith (if I missed anyone, feel free to give me a swift kick in the pants).

To my Science Consultants: Brent Young, Dan Yates, David Young, Eric Sweden, Jason Young, Phil Brown, Robert Palmer, and Rob Wells. Please know that your contributions were the backbone of my story. I never could have any moments of suspense without you.

Much appreciation goes to Alex Nitz and Hilary Hornberger for being my legs on this book cover; Kristi Linton for your photography; Jacqueline Fowers for your graphic design; and Heather Justesen for your interior layout expertise. Thank you for your talents and making this book look exactly how I dreamed it would be (for I don't know how many years). I truly appreciate the sacrifice and time you spent on this.

And of course, a special round of applause goes to all you pranksters out there who have touched my life: Andrea Goates

Thomson, Andy Mott, Bart Seeley, Breanne White, Brian Hansen, Cassie Burgi, Eric Russell, Erica Fowers Okere, Erika Childs, Justin Fowers and the V for Vendettas, Katie Hansen, Larissa Villers, LeAnn Bowan Wach, Lisa Hess Keillor, Lucinda Fowers Lahn, Marcus Green, Marie Young, Quinn Peterson and the rest of B5, Rachel Fowers and the Unicorns, Stacy Young Larson, Spencer Matsuura, Vanessa Swenson and the rest of the Pinegar rascals, and to the many many more who *blessed* my life with their pranks.

Also, where would I be without the good actors who helped bring "Prank Wars" to life in the book trailer? A special thank you to Lucie MacNair, Josh Miller, Annie Pulsipher, Tinesha Zandamela, Julia Sachs, Amanda Rose, Jeremy Henrie, Greg Webb, Colin Rivera, Skip Warner, Estée Arts, Gabriel Nicholas, Jon Madsen, Junyi Wang, Kim Chamberlain, Lauren Wilkins, Madison Heil, Nicole Froerer, Phil Nelson, Sheridan Bronson, Skipper Plowman, Weston Childers, and Jenica Schulz.

And to Ashley Fowers Elliott, my sister (and a talented photographer). Thank you for all your photographs that I put on my blog page and for my bio page in this book. Your artistic ability never ceases to amaze me.

Of course, I need to give a nod to my Young Women, who have shared so much of my life for these past few years: Britney, Carrie, Lindsey, Lacey, Jenny, Kelly, Stacey, (and do you notice all our names end with [ee]?). Yeah, cool.

Finally, my deep gratitude goes to my WesTech Engineering crew, who swapped stories with me to help wile away the time while spinning pounds and pounds of straw into gold: Amy Beaver, Brady Ririe, Brian Martin, Carol Williams, Cheryl Anderson, Christine Vincent, David (all of 'em—Hardin, Scott, and Snyder), Debbie Gessel, Erika Schipaanboord, Holly Gentry, Ian Anthony, Kali Wall, Jeremy Lawrence, Jodee Bielstein, Johanna Loeza, Kristi Linton, Mickaela Hawkley, Rachel Barrett, the evil twins (meaning Blake and Adam), Saul Oliveria. Deep breath—did I miss anyone? Thank you all for your stories, friendship, and name suggestions. I appreciate the great times we spent together.

All of you have touched my life for the better. Without the experience and time that we now claim as our memories, I doubt this book would ever have been possible. Thank you again.

ABOUT THE AUTHOR

Stephanie Fowers loves bringing stories to life, and depending on her latest madcap ideas will do it through written word, song, and/ or film. She absolutely adores Bollywood and bonnet movies; i.e., BBC (which she supposes includes non-bonnet movies *Sherlock* and *Dr. Who*). Presently, she lives in Salt Lake where she's living the life of the starving artist. This summer, she plans to do a reading of her musical *The Raven* with the talented composer, Hilary Hornberger. Stephanie's also excited to film some big time shorts (and possibly some features) in the near future with her talented cousin and friend, Sandra Barton, and with her brilliant sister, Jacqueline Fowers. Feel free to check out the Triad's film misadventures on YouTube. And of course, since discovering the exciting world of online books, Stephanie plans to bring more of her novels out to greet the light of day. Be sure to watch for her upcoming books, including YA fantasy, science fiction, mysteries, a compilation of short twisted fairy tales, and more—much more—romantic comedies. May the adventures begin.

Made in the USA
Lexington, KY
17 August 2012